THE Slow Lane WALKERS CLUB

Also by Rosa Temple:

Playing by the Rules

Playing Her Cards Right

Playing for Keeps

Rosa Temple began her career writing romantic comedy and chick lit novellas, short stories and books because of her passion for what she calls the 'early chick lit films', like: *Sabrina, Barefoot in the Park* and *Breakfast at Tiffany's*. She honed her skills as a ghost writer, gaining experience writing romance novellas and book series, with sweet themes as well as steamy novels for adult readers. She now specialises in contemporary romance and romantic comedies. Rosa Temple is a Londoner who recently moved to the beautiful countryside of Ross-on-Wye in Herefordshire. She is married to a musician and has two sons.

Rosa Temple

THE Slow Lane WALKERS CLUB

SIMON & SCHUSTER

London · New York · Sydney · Toronto · New Delhi

First published in Great Britain by Simon & Schuster UK Ltd, 2022

Copyright © Rosa Temple, 2022

The right of Rosa Temple to be identified as author
of this work has been asserted in accordance with
the Copyright, Designs and Patents Act, 1988.

1 3 5 7 9 10 8 6 4 2

Simon & Schuster UK Ltd
1st Floor
222 Gray's Inn Road
London WC1X 8HB

Simon & Schuster Australia,
Sydney

Simon & Schuster India,
New Delhi

www.simonandschuster.co.uk
www.simonandschuster.com.au
www.simonandschuster.co.in

A CIP catalogue record for this book is available from the British Library

Paperback ISBN: 978-1-39850-906-1
eBook ISBN: 978-1-39850-907-8
Audio ISBN: 978-1-39851-654-0

Typeset
Printed and bou
Group (UK) Ltd, Croydon, CR0 4YY

1

The train came to a stop at the station. As the doors hissed open, Daniel felt his shoulders sag. He peeled his body from the seat and gathered up his luggage. He had everything he owned with him crammed into an oversized rucksack and two large holdalls. Then there was the long case carrying his walking poles which bashed and banged until he could free everything from the train and dump it onto the platform. With all of his possessions on the ground at his feet, he looked up at the sign: Bodmin Parkway Station. Though it had never been his plan, Daniel was well and truly back in Cornwall. The other passengers for this station had dodged around him and his baggage. Places to go, people to see. But Daniel was in no hurry. When the guard at the gate looked at him curiously, Daniel decided to heap his rucksack onto his back, pull his case of walking poles over his shoulder and then stoop to pick up the two bulging holdalls. As he lifted himself to standing, his mobile buzzed with a notification. It was probably his sister, Annabelle, saying she was waiting in the car, so he ignored it and exited the station.

Daniel had slept for most of the train journey from Gatwick Airport to Bodmin. The team of tour guides he'd worked with for the last five years had given him the biggest and noisiest send-off of his life the night before his flight. He was sure he'd enjoyed himself at Bar Casa Mia, though most of the evening's events were hazy. The following morning his tour guide friends, dressed in their walking clothes, hiking boots and backpacks, had waved him off as his taxi sped away to Catania Fontanarossa Airport. From there, the journey to Cornwall had gone by in a blur.

Outside Bodmin Parkway, Daniel watched as people hopped into taxis at the rank, or were picked up by friends or relatives. He hoped his sister would have realized he was bringing home all of his worldly goods and would arrive in her four-by-four. But there was no sign of her, or a Range Rover come to that, so he dropped all the baggage he'd so carefully loaded onto his person and pulled out his phone. There was a message from Annabelle:

So sorry D. Rasmus has bucket stuck on head. On way to A&E. Key under the blue flower pot. See you later. A x

A careful negotiation of Daniel's luggage into the boot of a taxi followed until, finally, he was on his way to his child-hood village.

Daniel sat in the back seat of the taxi and rolled the window down. Fields and farmland swept past him along the Bodmin Bypass; vast verdant fields bordered by dark green hedges and brown furrowed land lay on either side of the A30. He sipped in the familiar Cornish breeze, which went some way to soothing the effects of his last night in Sicily.

'Holiday, is it?' The taxi driver was male, dumpy, with a thick neck. He glanced at Daniel through his rear view mirror.

'Er, no. Family reasons.'

'Must be a long stay.' Daniel furrowed his brow at the driver's reflection. 'All the luggage?'

'Oh, yes, of course. Yes, I'll be here a while.'

Daniel twitched in his seat. A sinking feeling rose from the pit of his stomach as it always did when the word 'family' came up in conversation. He thought back to a strained family meal, ten years ago. Daniel sat across from his father at the dining table, their faces aimed at each other like pistols at dawn. A heavy brandy glass sat nervously close to the edge of the pine table when the confrontation began. Daniel had shouted that he didn't want to follow in his father's footsteps and should never have allowed himself to be forced into taking the engineering degree. His father, fist thumping the table, had called his son a complete failure. Daniel hated university. He hated his father and their provincial life and once he'd taken his exams he would leave Cornwall and never return. His father had swung his hand and said good riddance. The brandy glass had smashed on the stone floor and Daniel's mother had rushed to gather the shards of glass. The family had shattered that evening and though she was able to collect together each piece of the broken brandy glass, Daniel's mother had never tried to bring the family back together.

The taxi driver drove past the nature reserve, a small village with a close-knit infrastructure and past signposts to place names that sounded odd to Daniel now. He was drawing nearer to the town of Padstow where his sister Annabelle had moved to when she'd married Scott. Annabelle, unlike Daniel, had only moved a ten-minute drive away from their home village of Trevone.

Since his departure Daniel and Annabelle had remained in constant contact. Annabelle was the one who had reported to Daniel the cracks as they'd begun to appear in their parents' marriage. So he wasn't surprised, years later, when the divorce was announced or when his father remarried. On his rare and fleeting visits home after the divorce, Daniel had sensed some worrying changes in his mother. She'd become distant, disengaged. But he hadn't anticipated her locking up the house and leaving the village on what seemed like a constant quest to 'find herself'. She'd sent messages to the siblings, though they'd become fewer and further between, saying she was meditating in Tibet or kayaking in Canadian lakes.

Annabelle's calls to Daniel had intensified over recent years as if his mobile was the Bat Phone and Metropolis needed his help to save them from peril. According to his sister, Daniel should be thinking about his future and not throwing away a good education on a dead-end job. She'd sent photographs of her children, the sea, the countryside, all in a bid to make her brother see what he was missing and come home. In return, he'd sent pictures of rocky grey and black mountain trails, and of ash clouds above the active Mount Etna, burning amber into a black sky. He'd sent a picture of the first time his best friend, Doc, threw up because of altitude sickness. It was clear to Daniel that Annabelle missed him, possibly more than she missed their parents, but he had made excuse after excuse for not visiting home. He was loving life in Sicily; he felt independent and free.

The driver turned onto a single track lane. The traditional hedges of Cornish stone and overhanging shrubs closed in on him, and the knot in Daniel's stomach tightened. He was close to his destination: his grandmother's house. His grandmother, who had been the last member of the family to remain in Trevone, had passed away quietly in her sleep. Daniel had made a brief visit to the village for her funeral, but just days after he'd arrived back in Sicily, Annabelle called to say that their grandmother had left her house to them both. It had come as a huge surprise to Daniel and Annabelle. Since she was their maternal grandmother, neither could understand why they had inherited the house instead of their mother. His mother acted as if she were just as confused as they were and clearly didn't want to discuss it further. She had left the country very quickly after the will had been read and hadn't been in touch again with either him or Annabelle.

Annabelle, even more desperate for Daniel to return to Cornwall, needed him to help her sort the house out and decide what they should do with it. The timing was awful. Daniel had managed to arrange a few days off work for the funeral but coming home indefinitely to help Annabelle was a sure way of being fired. The busy season for tours was fast approaching. The company he worked for had a waiting list of guides who could take his place in an instant, and though he'd been there five years, experience had shown him there was no loyalty to staff. To say he was dispensable was an understatement. The walking guide jobs were popular for young people from all around the world. In fact, it was a go-to job for people wanting to see the world, just as Daniel had in his early twenties. Age had been Annabelle's trump card for getting Daniel to commit to coming home.

'Daniel,' she had said, 'you're well over the average age of walking guides in that company. You're thirty years old. You'll wake up one morning and wonder why you ever took a degree and how walking up and down a volcano every day is going to secure you a decent future.'

It was true. The people he'd started out with had moved on eventually. Daniel was one of the 'old ones' and he found it more difficult to relate to some of the newer guides who seemed to get younger with every new intake. He didn't want to tell Annabelle she was right and that he knew how insecure the job and his future were. He resented the fact that he couldn't leave on his own terms, that Annabelle was calling the shots.

Closer to the village, the houses were dotted along the network of roads off the main road through Trevone, their white walls gleaming on this bright but crisp spring morning. So peaceful, his childhood home, so quiet, not another soul in sight and no other cars around. Daniel had liked the tranquillity at one time but he wasn't so sure he could survive a small village now.

'It's a beautiful place, Trevone,' said the taxi driver. 'You have it all. Countryside, beaches, fresh air.'

Daniel gave him a thin smile. He could hear gulls overhead and he could smell the sea. He remembered chilly autumn afternoons cycling home from school along the very road he was on and the lazy summer days on the beach with his school friends. But immediately he recollected the volatile relationship with his father as a young adult and shuddered. Not once in the ten years he'd been away did he envisage coming back indefinitely to a little village of white houses and grey slate roofs.

Daniel tried to blink away the past, block out the bad feeling and focus on the good times he'd had in Sicily. The great friends he'd made there, not to mention his job; five years of guiding tourists and adventuring around Mount Etna, one of the most thrilling landscapes he'd known. But before he could call to mind one of the many mountain walks, climbs, Jeep tours, or the way the cold weather sneaked up on you when you'd set off on a tour in just a T-shirt and sunglasses, the taxi pulled up outside his grandmother's house.

Tall and sturdy, very much like his grandmother, the house stood on a hill looking down to a crossroads where two tiny white houses bowed to the imposing Cornish stonework of Gran's house. Daniel helped the driver empty the boot of his luggage, and glanced down the hill. In the front garden of one of the houses, whose front door was painted bright red, was an elderly woman. She leaned on her walking stick while she watered her roses. She wore a coral-coloured tracksuit. Daniel couldn't help but notice the vibrancy of her clothing and her smiling face. Her afro hair was clipped short and speckled with a generous helping of silver fractal curls.

'Someone you know?' asked the driver as Daniel paid him.

'What? No. I don't think so.'

'Well, she's waving in this direction and she's not waving to me.' The driver, back in his seat, nodded to Daniel. 'Have a good one.'

As the taxi pulled away, Daniel paused to see the woman in her garden, waving her stick towards him as if she were trying to flag down a jet coming in for landing. Daniel, tired and irritable, gave her a quick nod and a half wave before going in search of the keys to his grandmother's house. Correction. His and Annabelle's house.

The blue plant pot Annabelle had mentioned in her text was filled with a large gardenia shrub and sat behind two terracotta pots with leafy geranium plants waiting to bloom later that spring in pink and scarlet. The leaves from the plant pots by the front door shrugged off the assault made on them by the walking poles Daniel clumsily shoved into the hallway. Next came his rucksack and holdalls, which he dumped by the mat just inside the door. As he did so he heard a cat mew and felt it whiz past his legs. He looked down but all he saw of it was a black fluffy tail disappearing into the kitchen. Great. Not only was he on house clearing duty, he also had a cat to look after.

Daniel looked around the hallway and spotted a picture on the wall of him and Annabelle as children. He was sat on his grandmother's lap with a big grin on his face, Annabelle standing beside them in a short yellow dress. His grandmother had placed a hand across Daniel's abdomen and he looked poised to wriggle off. As he stared at the old photograph, Daniel was gripped by a pang of guilt – he'd inherited her house but he knew so little about his grandmother. Annabelle had stayed in touch with her and he wished now that he had too. Maybe he'd have better memories of her to call upon; most of his were confused and unreliable.

His mother had taken Daniel and Annabelle on visits to see his grandparents quite regularly when they were very young. He had the impression that his mother had been overly keen to please Gran. She'd scrubbed Daniel's round face and dirty hands in case Gran complained about how she was bringing up her children, as he recalled. An impending visit to Gran had filled him with a sense of foreboding, not only because it meant having to be clean, it also meant having to be quiet, not speaking until he got a nod from his mother. His grandfather, or Gramps, was different, though. He'd grab Daniel and Annabelle's little hands and take them to have adventures in the garden. Sometimes they'd be at sea, fighting off sea monsters, other times he'd have them help with the gardening. Gramps had always made sure they kept away from Gran's vegetable patch and they had to steer clear of the herb garden, too. He recalled the quiet lunches spent in his grandmother's dining room and he couldn't remember ever seeing her happy.

Daniel looked closer at the photograph of him and his

sister with Gran and noticed how brightly he and Annabelle smiled and how serious Gran looked. If Gran had ever given him sweets or cuddles, the sort of thing you'd expect from your grandmother, he couldn't remember them. He stared hard at the photo, at his grandmother's hands around his podgy middle. In his mind her hands had felt cool and quite rough as though she'd laboured hard her whole life, but as far as he knew Gran and Gramps had always lived in this house. Their small garden couldn't have caused the calluses and bumps on her palms. The guilty feeling tightened around him. Maybe he should have talked to Gran more, visited more often as he got older. He wished he'd known about the inheritance before she passed because he would have loved to have thanked her for his share.

In the kitchen was a basket of Annabelle's famous choc-olate cookies. He grabbed one and took a big bite out of it. The cat looked up at him and mewed loudly.

'Forget it, mate, this lot is for me. Perks of having to come back to the UK under duress.' And indefinitely, he thought, again. Daniel sighed and demolished another cookie in two bites.

Having second thoughts about being so stingy to Gran's cat, he poured some milk into a saucer and left the cat lapping it up while he walked around the downstairs rooms. The house had seemed huge as a child but now he was six foot three the ceilings weren't nearly as high and the rooms not as spacious as he remembered. He noted the only two family photos on the wall in the living room, another of him and Annabelle in primary school uniform and a black and white wedding photo, presumably of his grandparents. There were none at all of his parents anywhere. Tiny, dusty figurines lined the shelves and the few house plants on the window sills and side tables hadn't been kept up.

Back in the kitchen he made a mug of tea and launched an attack on the chocolate cookies which had looked like an Instagram post, stacked in neat rows on a checked tea towel. Thank goodness Annabelle cooked as if she were expecting a coach tour to drop by. As he looked around the kitchen he remembered Gran telling him not to run through it, his grandfather winking at him and his mother not saying an awful lot. Without realizing it he had devoured the whole basket of cookies and after sloshing them down with a second mug of tea his energy reserves began to fail him. He yawned deeply as the damage of the farewell party from the night before took its toll. In the living room, he sank into his grandmother's floral sofa and drifted into a deep sleep.

Hours later, Daniel woke to the sound of something clattering onto the wooden floor in the hallway and a child zooming past the living room door making the engine sound of an aeroplane. In his sleep he'd been listening to the booming bass from the speakers in Bar Casa Mia and the unleashed laughter of his friends as they danced and drank. He stood on a wooden table telling everyone, at the top of his voice, how much he loved them and that they could come to Cornwall to stay any time.

His sister's voice calling his name shattered any chance he had of returning to the dream.

'Daniel! What the hell? Why would you leave your bags by the door? I nearly killed myself.'

He rubbed his eyes and ran his fingers through his hair. In front of him was the small child with the pounding feet and aeroplane sound effects for a voice. He stared at Daniel with big green eyes, his face stained with vanilla ice cream.

'Hey, Rasmus.' Daniel attempted to ruffle his nephew's hair

but the child darted out of reach and went to stand behind his mother.

'So you made it,' Annabelle said, hobbling towards him with open arms and a child clinging to her right thigh. 'It's lovely to see you. You look so tanned.'

Daniel got up from the sofa to hug his sister. She was shorter than he was, had been since he turned eleven and Annabelle was fourteen. They had been mistaken for twins up until that point, both with their mother's dark hair and green eyes. Now that he'd shot past her in height and developed an athletic build the question was never asked of them. Especially since Annabelle had inherited her mother's short and cuddly stature, the cuddliness enhanced by the birth of two children, Mia, now six, and Rasmus, aged four.

'Hey, sis, it's good to see you.' Daniel kissed his sister's cheek. He attempted to greet Rasmus again but he swerved a pat on the head by ducking down and entwining his mother's other thigh with his arms.

'Don't mind Rasmus. He's actually glad you're here. I told him all about his uncle Daniel coming home and he's been excited to meet you.'

Daniel looked down at his nephew.

'Good to see you got rid of that bucket.' There was not a peep from Rasmus. 'Looks like I'm going to have to charm him. I don't suppose he remembers me.'

'You haven't seen him since he was a baby, so it's hardly surprising.' Annabelle arched an eyebrow.

'I know, I know,' said Daniel. 'But I'm here now. Ready to get stuck in. I'll probably lose my tan while we're both indoors clearing this house out.' Daniel stretched and looked around the living room. 'Judging by the collection in here it's going to take us a lifetime.'

'About that,' said Annabelle. 'I'm going to have to leave most of the clearing out to you.'

'Annabelle.' Daniel's voice went up a tone on the last syllable of his sister's name, the way it had in his youth when Annabelle had said or done something to annoy him.

'I've got a husband and two small people to worry about, Daniel. Then there's the house, the garden and my vlog.'

'Your vlog?'

'I knew you didn't watch my vlog. I sent you the link. I've got loads of followers. Not to mention I'm practically an Instagram influencer now. *The Cornish Mamma Chronicles.* Haven't you seen a single video?'

He shook his head.

'Come on, Annie. You know what my life in Sicily is like. Always working. Every hour.'

'Apart from when you're in the pub.'

'I resent the inference. I'm up before sunrise and I don't get to bed until gone midnight some nights. It's a responsible job, you know? I've got the safety of up to ten people on my shoulders on some tours. Or, at least,' he said, pushing his fists into his pockets, 'I did have.'

'Look, Daniel, this is no time to start whingeing. You know how much I need you. You're not under any pressure to get the house cleared and sorted by any particular time and I'll pop in whenever I can. Right now I have to go and pick Mia up from school so I'll probably swing by tomorrow if I can.'

In the hallway, Annabelle's voice began to trail off. 'I stocked the fridge but I wasn't sure what you liked.' And then she was gone. She unlatched Rasmus from her thigh, strapped him into the booster seat in the car and drove off with a wave of her hand.

Daniel stood at the front door rustling his hair back and forth, wondering whether that whirlwind had all been part of his dream. Just before closing the front door, the woman he'd seen earlier in her front garden waved her walking stick at him again. She had a huge smile on her face. She looked as if she was about to leave her front gate, perhaps to come over and introduce herself, but Daniel felt in need of a shower before meeting the neighbours. He smiled and gave her a brief wave before he closed the door, promptly tripping backwards over his luggage and landing on his bottom.

2

Out of habit Daniel woke early and decided to go for a run. His baggage was still in a heap in the front hallway. He rooted around in one of the holdalls to try to find his trainers. Crouched on his knees, he tossed items of clothing and equipment over his shoulder onto the floor. The cat sat in the kitchen doorway, whiskers twitching, head to one side, eyes following the trajectory of Daniel's socks, pants and cargo shorts across the corridor. A pair of his diving goggles collided with the hall table.

'What you staring at?' asked Daniel. 'Haven't you seen an athlete at work?'

Finally finding the elusive trainers he went to put them on over odd socks. They felt damp and smelled weird but there wasn't much he could do about that. The cat followed Daniel into the kitchen, purring loudly and working figures of eight around his legs as Daniel opened a tin of tuna and scooped some of it into a saucer and placed it on the floor.

'Don't make a mess,' he said over his shoulder as he left the cat to it.

It was early spring and Daniel hoped the tide would be low enough for him to do a good circuit of Trevone Beach. If there weren't too many people around, he could get in a decent run, get home, tank up on some breakfast and then make a start on the house. He sprinted down the hill in the direction of the house with the red front door. The old woman who had waved to him the day before was out in her front garden. This time she had her back to Daniel and was shaking her walking stick at the trellis above her front door. He mouthed the word 'weird' and sped up. He'd catch up with her eventually but wanted a serious workout first.

Before interviewing for the job as a tour guide on Mount Etna, Daniel had qualified as a personal trainer in London. Just one in a list of jobs and career moves he'd pursued since obtaining his degree. He never quite got the hang of making it into a business. Instead he'd hung out at the local gym chatting to girls and being chased up by the staff to pay his studio time rental.

Daniel ran a short distance and got as far as the village square before a pain shot up the back of his thigh. His hamstrings tightened and he stumbled hands first onto the paving stones. Rolling over, he grimaced and clutched his thigh. An old man in a flat cap, who was walking a sullen grey whippet, stopped to shake his head at Daniel.

'You want to slow down a bit, young man.'

Daniel put up a hand to signify he was okay, not that the old man was asking. He sat on the ground, out of breath, the whippet sniffing at his trainers.

'Maybe I'm a bit out of practice,' said Daniel. He may as well have spoken to himself. The grey whippet and the old man continued on their walk and left the square without looking back. Daniel hobbled to standing and limped back towards home. Nearer the house he stopped to stretch his injured leg.

'Back already?' The old woman with the walking stick made Daniel jump and do a half turn.

'Oh, hi! Yes,' he said, 'I wasn't really feeling it today.'

'You were limping. Did you do a proper warm up before you started running?' she said. 'If you don't do a proper warm up, you'll end up with all kinds of problems.'

'Um, I suppose you're right,' said Daniel. He began to inch away, so red in the face from fatigue and embarrassment he couldn't look at her.

'Well, okay then,' she called as Daniel headed on up the hill. At his grandmother's house he turned back to see the old woman waving her stick at the trellis again. Daniel had images of her never actually entering her house but camping out in the front garden performing tricks with her walking stick. He shook his head and whispered 'weird' to himself again. When he pushed open the front door the cat shot outside with a frustrated mew. Daniel wondered why his grandmother hadn't thought of putting a cat flap on the door.

The hallway floor looked like the aftermath of Black Friday at a sports equipment and clothes sale. He blew heavily through his lips at the mess he'd made. He should really get his junk in order. But first a shower and no doubt he'd need to rest his leg, too. He limped carefully over his mound of luggage and spotted a bath towel in a holdall. Pulling it free from a tangle of items, Daniel headed up to the bathroom.

Nothing had moved or magically neatened itself away in the hallway after he'd showered and trotted back downstairs. The pain in his hamstring was barely noticeable but some refreshments wouldn't go amiss. He took an almost over-flowing mug of coffee into the living room where he sat with his feet on the sofa, mug in one hand while scrolling

16

messages on his phone. He was already missing his friends in Sicily, particularly his best friend Doc who'd been at the tour company for as long as he had and was still there. Doc's messages made Daniel homesick for his job on Mount Etna.

Daniel hadn't taken the decision to come home to Trevone lightly. He'd had to put his dramatic exit from Cornwall to the back of his mind, so far back, the bitter stings of his and his father's words wouldn't affect him. He'd hoped the lack of support he'd got from his mother might also just disappear. Having Annabelle act as go-between for Daniel and his father had made life easier for him. His sister had always looked out for Daniel. She'd stepped into the role of his parents but somehow managed to be an annoying big sister at the same time. He knew he'd upset her when he eventually left Trevone. He had no job there and he didn't think he was likely to find one. He had lived quite cheaply in Sicily and managed to save some money, and though Annabelle had promised to take care of him financially until things were settled, his money would run out and he didn't want to have to rely on her until the house was sold, if that's what they decided to do with it. At some point he might go to London to find work or take his share of the house sale to travel abroad again. He was feeling unsettled and irritated by having to go through the motions of trying to find a new job. That meant more upheaval and decision making to take into account. He longed for the easy life he'd had up until this point. Maybe the thing to do would be to hurry up and sell the house so he could leave quickly, making it a flying visit, a ripping off of a plaster. It was strange to think that this small village had once seemed enough for him.

He looked again at the old-fashioned furniture in the living room. Varnished wood tables and shelves. Edges that were dented and scratched. His grandparents must have had this furniture forever. He could get WiFi on his phone but his grandmother, more than likely, didn't have broadband. Again he wondered how he had come to be the co-owner of his grandmother's house. What was behind her decision? Why had his mother left, unwilling to say anything about it? Daniel imagined his mother must have bad feelings about them inheriting the house instead of her. Maybe between him and Annabelle they could puzzle it out.

He switched on the television. It was old, bulky, not flat screen and he couldn't find the remote. Daniel left it on one channel, allowing show after show to start and finish before his eyes, breaking away only to make himself more coffee and a sandwich or two. He felt out of place in the outdated old-fashioned kitchen, a stranger in his grandparents' house, to the whole village actually. The drone of talk shows, a shampoo advert that repeated itself in each commercial break and a glittery quiz show lulled him into a stupor and just like that a day of not sorting out anything in the house passed him by.

Daniel woke the next morning in the early hours. He'd crashed out on the sofa after a late evening call from Annabelle, apologizing for not having popped round. A quick trip to the loo told him that his leg was completely fine, but the crick in his neck from sleeping on a sofa not built for a man of six foot three inches made house clearing a non-starter. He needed a good stretch and decided on an early morning walk to the beach, no running this time. Maybe the sea air would blow some energy into him and get him motivated at last.

Nearing the beach complex car park, he saw a figure walking in from the shoreline. It was a young woman wearing a baseball cap. She held something in her hands, a camera

Daniel realized. She bent to pull a silver bicycle, which had been lying on the soft yellow sand close to the coast path, to standing. After putting her camera into the front basket of the bike, she rode away on the path, her gaze towards the sea, her face turned up to the sky. He wondered if she lived in Trevone or was there on holiday, or like him, just passing through en route to something or somewhere new – whatever that would be.

He walked towards the sea, stepping into the footprints the girl had made, and sat on the sand, his arms hanging lazily over his bent knees, hands lightly clasped. The beach was empty save for a couple walking their dog. He tried to quieten a mind filled with questions and very few answers. What would he do after the house was sorted? Where could he go? Could he take up one of the offers he'd had to visit the homes of his tour guide friends from around the world? He'd had several invitations. He thought about the friends he'd once had in Cornwall and wondered what they might be doing now. After several minutes of watching the hypnotic flow of waves gliding onto and away from the sand, the image of his junk piled up by the door in the hallway and the gurgling sound of his stomach reminded him he should get back to the house.

Daniel finally managed to get his gear back into the holdalls and take his luggage upstairs to the back bedroom. After breakfast he began to walk from room to room assessing the damage and wondering where to start. He decided to begin at the top and work his way downstairs. Three bedrooms, a living room, one dining room, a conservatory, a bathroom and a kitchen, how hard could it be? The majority of Gran's stuff was probably just junk he could throw into boxes and dump at the charity shop. On opening his grandmother's wardrobe, he wondered if a museum might not be the better option. To one side there were a couple of suits hanging on the rail. His grandfather's, he imagined. Daniel couldn't imagine why they were still there since Gramps had died over ten years ago.

He threw the suits onto the bed. Dust had collected on the shoulders and collars and he went in search of some black bin bags to shove everything into.

He felt his phone buzz in his back pocket again. Apart from messages and pictures from Doc, his other friends in Sicily had continued to message him. As usual, life for them was one long party. It wasn't going to be easy to forget them. Daniel tossed his mobile onto his grandmother's bed and put his grandfather's old suits into the bin bags. Worn clothes from a distant time, stuffed away like the problems he'd had with his father. They had been hard to compartmentalize.

Daniel flopped onto the floor and sat with his back against the bed. He swivelled one of his grandmother's berets around on his forefinger as he spun the many disagreements he'd had with his parents out of his mind. He couldn't keep dwelling on the past, it would make him crazy. He needed something to get him out of the house.

He continued to spin Gran's hat until it spun off his finger and landed on the floor beside him. His day of house clearing had amounted to his grandmother's bedroom floor being covered in half-full black bin bags and a stack of dusty books piled up in front of the rickety shelf unit in the corner. On his grandmother's bed, her old clothes and a couple of military uniforms lay across the floral quilt and all he could think was that it must be time for lunch. Daniel had eaten practically everything Annabelle had left in the cupboard and fridge, the cat had made light of the tins of tuna and the four-pint bottle of milk so he'd have to go and do a top-up shop. He went to the back bedroom to find his credit cards. In the small room his packed rucksack leaned against the wall beside his walking poles. Flashbacks of his walking tours on Mount Etna came happily to mind when the shrillness of his mobile brought him back from a reverie.

It was Annabelle. He walked along the landing and in and out of the bedrooms as he spoke to her.

'How's it going?' she asked in a cheery voice.

'So far so good,' said Daniel.

'How far have you got?'

Daniel looked around the room he was in, the back bedroom he'd taken over as his. His holdalls were spewing crumpled T-shirts and unwashed socks. He had knocked over a cold cup of coffee the day before and there was a brown stain on the beige carpet which he wasn't sure how to shift. The bed was unmade and in his mind's eye he could see the mountain of chaos he'd created in his grandmother's bedroom.

'It's going well,' he said. 'Don't worry about it.'

'I can spare you a few hours later. Scott is home early and Mia has ballet.'

'No, no. I've got a system going.'

'You sure? Because I do have a couple of vlogs I can record while Scott takes care of the kids. I like to keep at least three vlogs in advance, that way I can always upload something in good time. It pays to be organized.'

'Yeah, I get that.' He looked around the room again. 'Anyway, you just caught me on my way out to the shops. Need to stock up on a few things. Cat food for one.'

'Cat food?'

'Yes, for Gran's cat.'

'Gran never had a cat.'

'Are you sure?'

'Of course I'm sure. What does it look like?'

'Well, mostly black, cute, I suppose. Likes milk and tuna.'

'Daniel, you can't give cats cow's milk or tuna. Most are lactose intolerant and then there's the mercury in tuna.'

'How was I supposed to know? And anyway the cat seems fine. I'll try to find its owner, get it safely back home. In the meantime, both the cat and I are starving.'

'You know you can always come round for dinner. I bet it's been ages since you had a proper cooked meal.'

'Tell me about it. And thanks, I'll do that.'

The last time he ate out was with his friends in Sicily, not something that would happen here. He had lost contact with his old friends from Trevone, hadn't seen them in ten years, or been in touch, not even on social media. He looked at his walking poles and wondered how many people in Trevone shared the same sense of adventure as he did. Maybe he could find a way to hook up with them. Another look at his walking poles gave Daniel an idea.

He ran around the house searching for some paper and pens. His idea, seeming like a brilliant one in his head, would not only give him a break from clearing the house but could also help him meet new people in and around the village. Finding a writing pad and a felt pen, Daniel went about making up some signs. After several attempts at sounding fun, friendly, relatively sporty and not like a profile for a dating app, he came up with a sign that read:

Join the Saturday Walkers Club
First walk: Saturday 4th April
The South West Coast Path
Meet at 12 noon outside the café at Trevone Beach car park
See you there!

He would put his signs up in the community centre, the village hall, the church notice board and the farm shop. It was Wednesday, he was sure that enough people would see them by Saturday for at least ten people to show up. He'd get to meet some like-minded outdoor types, go out with them of an evening, have some fun again. After all, his friendship circle so far included an unnamed cat who came to mooch milk and use his house as a squat.

He made his way down to the square and successfully managed to put up three of the signs for his walking club. The last place to try was the farm shop. The woman behind the counter held his handwritten notice at arm's length and squinted at it.

'Walking?' she said after a ten-minute inspection of Daniel's handy work.

'That's right,' he said. 'It's for the health conscious. Fresh air. Good vibes. That kind of thing.'

She grunted and handed the sign back to Daniel.

'There might be a spare drawing pin in the notice board.' She shook her head and went back to dusting the shelves.

Daniel found a single drawing pin and looked around the board for a place that would give his sign maximum impact. Placing it dead centre on the board he stepped back and into something soft. He spun around and saw a young woman with short hair dyed white blonde. She had a very pretty face and a silver bar in her ear. She wore a baggy, loose knit sweater, and had the local newspaper under her arm. It was the girl he'd seen with her camera and her silver bicycle on the beach.

'I'm sorry,' he said. 'I didn't see you there.'

'I hope you're not planning to walk backwards on Saturday,' she said pointing at his sign. 'I don't think it's particularly safe to do that on the coast path.'

He gave a nervous laugh and stared at the girl for several seconds before they both began to speak at the same time.

'You first,' she said.

'I was just going to say that anyone can come. It'll be an hour-long walk. Nothing heavy.'

'Well, I know the path very well in each direction. I cycle from Crugmeer through to Harlyn Beach practically every day.' She sounded like the sporty type so he dared to ask her to consider coming along.

'But you'd be surprised how different the path can be if you walk it.' It was his best attempt at a sales pitch.

'Well, it sounds like a nice idea.' She gave him a wide smile and went over to the woman at the counter and paid for the newspaper before leaving the shop. Daniel watched her put the paper into the front basket of her bike and hop onto the saddle. With the briefest look back at the farm shop window, she cycled towards the coast path and out of sight.

'Will there be anything else?' the shopkeeper called to him.

'Um, yes,' said Daniel, looking back at his sign and checking for typos. He picked up a wire basket and aimlessly filled it with anything that needed little or no cooking. Dumping the basket onto the counter he gave the shopkeeper a bright smile, feeling pleased that he'd taken a step towards doing something with his time other than house clearing. He looked forward to Saturday.

3

On Saturday, with very little house clearing done and after several phone calls to his sister to establish how to use the washing machine, Daniel set off to the coast path in cargo shorts, hiking boots, a sweat top, and with his set of walking poles. He'd spent the morning studying the path and plotting a walk on Google Maps. It would last at least an hour in total and have the walkers back at the car park by 1pm. He was excited for the walking club, imagining the blonde girl he'd met at the farm shop, and people like her, wanting to join.

Memories of gathering the walkers setting off on a hike to Mount Etna with Daniel as their guide came to him as he made his way to the café by the sea. Before leading a walk to the volcano he'd have to go through health and safety checks, making sure everyone was equipped with the right clothing and boots and that they'd packed enough food and a good supply of water. It crossed his mind that he'd have to give a talk on safety to the walkers. Perhaps he should have had a First Aid kit with him instead of a bottle of water for himself and a Snickers.

As he entered the car park at just minutes to twelve he was disappointed to see that there was no one waiting outside the café. Someone had just locked their car but they'd headed off in the direction of Crugmeer and obviously had no intention of joining his walking club. Daniel slowed down. He looked over his shoulder to see if any potential walkers might be coming up behind him. But no, not one soul had shown up. He looked at his phone; there was still time, he supposed. It was only just twelve, he could wait fifteen minutes at least before giving up on the whole village of Trevone as a dead loss.

A little closer to the beach complex he saw the café door open and a familiar figure emerge. Carrying a large beige handbag and dressed in baby pink sweat pants was the woman from down the hill. Emblazoned across her blue sweat top was a flag with a bright red background and a white-edged black stripe running diagonally across it. The words 'Trinidad & Tobago' were printed in large letters above it. She had her walking stick with her, a sun visor around her brow and a pair of brilliant white Crocs on her feet. She looked up and, for a moment, Daniel considered ducking behind a car or marching off in the opposite direction and pretending he hadn't noticed her. It was no good, of course, because she began to wave her stick up and down, a huge grin on her face and a call of 'Coo-ee! Are you here for the Walkers Club?'

He couldn't fake not having heard her and, with a walking pole in each hand, what else could he be there for?

'Oh, hello,' he said, doing his best to mask his disappointment. 'Yes, I am here for the walk. Actually, I'm the organizer. Daniel.'

'Daniel! Pleased to meet you properly, at last. I'm Hazel.' She put out her hand, small and shaky with protruding veins. How fragile and soft it was to shake. Hazel's eyes were squeezed almost shut as she beamed up at him.

'Nice to meet you, Hazel.' Daniel couldn't help but look

down at her footwear. 'Are you sure you'll be all right walking in those? It might be a bit rough in places along the path.'

'Well, I wasn't sure what to put on and these are so comfortable. I thought that comfort should come first.'

Comfort over speed, Daniel thought to himself. Well, there went his hour long walk idea. If he stuck to the route he'd planned the Crocs alone would delay them by a day at least. He fidgeted around, looked at his phone and did several sweeps around the car park and surrounding roads. Maybe some people had already walked down to the path. Maybe the blonde girl was there chatting with the other walkers.

'Hazel, if you'd excuse me, I'm just going to do a quick recce to see if anyone else is going to join me – I mean *us*.' He handed his walking poles to her.

Daniel shot off towards the path and to the edge of the beach. There was no one in sight apart from an elderly couple holding hands as they walked close to the sea. The tide was low and the waves rippled into shore. They were slow and calm, the opposite to Daniel's anxious heart rate. He stepped from hiking boot to hiking boot, puffing and panting and willing someone else to show up for the walk. He scooted around the side of the café, trotted up and down the car park and by quarter past twelve it was blatant that no one but Hazel was going to accompany him on this walk. His only recourse was to cancel. Maybe get proper flyers printed next time and circulate them a bit further afield. He jogged back to Hazel who was busy inspecting his walking poles.

'Do you think I should get a pair of these?' she asked him. She was grinning at him again, teeth completely straight and dazzling white, dark pink lipstick neatly applied to what was a genuinely cute smile. He didn't have the heart to cancel the walk.

'And maybe you could advise me on some walking shoes,' continued Hazel. 'I think I have a new pair of trainers in a box somewhere but they might be on top of the wardrobe. I haven't been able to reach up very high and find anything in my house for nearly a year now. Anyway, Daniel, we can discuss it on the way. I think it might just be us, don't you?'

'I think you might be right. We don't have to go too far.'

'Don't worry about me, I might have a walking stick but I'm as fit as a fiddle. Shall we?' Hazel handed Daniel's walking poles back to him, hooked the handle of her handbag into the crook of her arm and placed her walking stick down with purpose. Daniel shook his head and led the way.

Once on the path and only minutes into the walk, Daniel turned back to find Hazel a good twenty metres or so behind him. She was taking it extremely slowly and shuffled her Croc'ed feet on the stony path. Daniel ran back to meet her.

'Really, Hazel, if this is too much for you, we could always turn back.' He pointed a walking pole in the direction of the car park.

'Nonsense,' Hazel said. She hooked her walking stick over Daniel's outstretched arm and unclasped her enormous handbag. 'I told you, I'm physically fit but I do have a slight touch of diabetes, the doctor told me, so I will need to stop for a snack. I've brought lots. In case I needed to share.' Looking inside her handbag and not up at a bewildered Daniel, she pulled out an egg sandwich, a tuna sandwich, a protein bar, some diabetic chocolate and a malt drink. All of these she shoved at Daniel, who gathered the food into his arms while trying to balance her walking stick and his walking poles.

'Hazel, I don't think this is very—'

'If you don't like any of these, I think I've got a sausage roll.' She looked up at him blinking, waiting for an answer.

28

What do you tell a little old woman in a sun visor, when there is no sun, that you don't want a sandwich, you want to go home and eat a Snickers and wallow in self-pity because none of the people you'd hoped for had bothered to turn up for your well-organized walk?

'Actually, I have some water,' Daniel said. 'That'll do me. You go ahead and eat something. I'll wait.'

'You sure you don't mind? You look a bit flushed, Daniel. Do you think you should have done some warm-up stretches before you started? In fact, maybe we should make that a condition, that we don't start the walk until everyone has had a good stretch.'

'I'm not sure we can call just two people "everyone".' Daniel couldn't keep his mood at bay. He had really had enough. 'Here, let me help you put some of this food back into that bag of yours. We can sit here so you can eat but you might get your tracksuit dusty.'

'I don't mind.'

They sat on a weather-worn bench, its feet rooted in the scant grass just to the side of the path, a vast field to their backs and the clifftop metres away in front of them. A couple of fast runners, clad in expensive running gear, sped past them in the direction of the village. Daniel looked up at them wistfully as he pulled out his Snickers.

'Don't worry, Daniel,' said Hazel, holding one half of an egg sandwich. 'I'm sure more people will come next week.'

'I don't know, Hazel. I'm not sure it's worth it.' He bit off a good third of the chocolate bar and chewed slowly.

'I don't mean to pry,' said Hazel. 'But you are Molly's grandson, aren't you?'

'You knew Gran?' Daniel swallowed his mouthful. Hazel smiled and nodded at him.

'I suspected you were the grandson when I saw you arrive,' she said. 'You know, I miss your grandmother terribly. In fact, Molly will be greatly missed by a lot of people in the community.' Hazel looked off into the distance as if she were reliving a memory, a happy one, Daniel thought.

'So you two were friends?' He hadn't exactly been friendly to Hazel when he'd first arrived but she seemed not to have noticed.

'Yes, we were,' she said. 'We became acquainted a little while after I moved down the hill from her. My husband and I moved to Cornwall from London when he retired years back but we've only lived in Trevone for the last two. I used to pop round to Molly's if I'd done some baking. We'd sit and have a cup of tea in her living room. She couldn't leave the house much towards the end. Up until then she was practically running around the whole village. She would have been a good candidate for the Walkers Club.'

An image of all the little old women in the village turning up to join his walking group flashed through Daniel's mind. It was definitely not the sort of group he'd planned but if they were all as charming and bubbly as Hazel, how could he let them down?

'She told me all about you, your grandmother.' Hazel nibbled off a piece of her sandwich. 'She said you lived abroad?'

'I did, up until recently. I lived in Sicily for five years and now I'm here, sorting out the house.'

'You don't sound happy to be back,' said Hazel.

'I'll get used to it.' He shrugged. 'It'll be an adjustment. This place is so quiet, it's not what I'm used to.'

'What did you do before?'

'I was a walking guide. I led tours up Mount Etna in Sicily. I used to take people on amazing journeys every day.'

'And you miss it.'

Daniel nodded and looked down.

'You could always go back,' said Hazel.

He looked at her now, really studied her face. It was a kind face, caring; he felt as if he could tell her anything and not be judged.

'In all honesty,' said Daniel, 'I would have had to move on from that job eventually. Great adventures but not much of a future. Annabelle was right, though I hate to admit it. Annabelle is my sister.'

'Yes, I know. We've met. Annabelle would visit your grandmother once in a while, but I gathered she had a bit of a hectic lifestyle so neither Molly nor I saw an awful lot of her. Molly used to talk about you both. It was kind of her to leave the house to you and your sister.'

'Gran told you about that, did she?'

'We did have very long chats over those cups of tea.' Hazel chuckled. 'We must have talked about everything under the sun. Molly said that if anyone deserved the house it would be her lovely grandchildren.'

'Lovely?' said Daniel, a sideways smirk on his face. 'I can't imagine Gran calling us lovely. My sister perhaps.'

'I don't know why you think that,' said Hazel. 'Your grandmother was a good judge of character and she meant what she said.' She looked at Daniel, taking a sharp inhale as if to say more but, with a brief shake of her head, she fell silent. Daniel wondered what it was Hazel was holding back. She cleared her throat and continued.

'Molly was ever so proud of you both. She said you went to university in London and that you were the most like her in the family. The adventurous type.'

Daniel sat around to face Hazel. He knew she was old but

could Hazel be mistaking his gran with someone else? In what way was Gran the adventurous type?

'I know an awful lot about your grandmother,' said Hazel, possibly reading the doubt in Daniel's eyes. 'A remarkable woman she was.'

Daniel shoved the last of the chocolate into his mouth, a crease in his brow. He had never thought of his grandmother as remarkable or adventurous. If she went on any adventures, no one had told him about them. He remembered her as strict, perhaps becoming eccentric in her old age, judging by the collection of scarves he'd found in her bedroom. He was curious, though. What was it about Gran that made her remarkable?

'Should we get going again?' Hazel closed her bag and attempted to push herself up from the bench.

'I was just wondering,' said Daniel, halting her progress with the palm of his hand, 'as you knew Gran so well, if you could tell me about her adventures and how am I like her?'

'Oh, Molly was definitely up for an adventure or two. Her first probably being the time she left home. It caused an uproar. She was only eighteen and had to go against her parents' wishes. Something I understand very well.'

Daniel remembered the feeling of going against his father when he'd eventually left home. Had both Gran and Hazel clashed with their parents in the exact same way as he had? Had they felt as let down by their parents as he still did?

'It wasn't all doom and gloom, Daniel,' Hazel said. Maybe his bad memories of leaving Cornwall showed on his face. 'We used to sit and compare stories. I thought I'd got up to all sorts but your gran was quite a woman. She helped a lot of people in her time, brought them happiness. As I say, I do miss her a lot.'

'Mum never told us anything about Gran. This is all news to me,' said Daniel.

Hazel lowered her eyes to the large beige handbag and began fiddling with the clasp.

'Well, we sometimes don't get the opportunity to tell our whole story to our children.' Hazel kept her eyes down.

'But she obviously passed on a lot to you.' Daniel looked intently at Hazel, keen for her to continue. He only had a few flimsy memories of his grandparents, they could almost be dreams.

'She did, Daniel, but I can't pack everything into just one walk.' Hazel went to rise from her seat again.

'Here, let me.' Daniel put an arm around her, hooking her underarms and pulling her to standing. He handed Hazel her stick and steadied her as she pushed her foot back into the Croc that had fallen off during the process. He smiled to himself as he watched her straighten up, hook that big handbag into the crook of her arm and look towards the path.

'So what about you, Hazel?' She looked up at him through her sun visor. 'You said you had to go against your parents' wishes, too.'

'Oh my goodness,' said Hazel with a timid laugh. 'Mine and Molly's circumstances were very different, yet we both found ways to get around our parents so that we could make our lives our own. I miss us exchanging our wild stories.'

Daniel couldn't imagine someone as small and as frail as Hazel having wild stories to tell. He wondered how these women had both had conflicts with their parents but had managed to make them come around, whereas he was still in a bad place with his father. He would love to find out what these two women talked about over those cups of tea. Hazel was whetting his appetite with bite-sized chunks, headlines.

He wanted to know more. He was positive Hazel must also know why he and Annabelle had inherited Gran's house. He turned to ask her another question but Hazel leaned down to massage her leg.

'Old age,' she said with a smile.

'We won't go very much further,' said Daniel. 'Best to take it easy at first.'

They set off once again. A hint of sun peeked through the smoky clouds. Rain hadn't been forecast, though Daniel had visions of Hazel's Crocs becoming waterlogged if it did rain.

'Look, Hazel,' he said, 'I could always swing by yours and get that box with the trainers down for you if you or your husband can't reach it.'

Looking out towards the cumulus sky, she said, 'That would be very kind of you. But it's just me now. Henry died a year ago, otherwise he would have fetched it down for me.'

'Hazel, I'm sorry, I didn't mean…' Daniel brought the walk to a stop.

'It's all right. I probably spoke about him in the present tense again. My daughter has been telling me, whenever she phones, that I have to stop doing that. But it's not easy.'

'Come on,' said Daniel. 'Let's turn back.'

They walked quietly along the path. Daniel was at Hazel's side slow and steady. The walk itself had been a far cry from the exciting and sometimes dangerous ones he used to lead, but it had gone some way to him discovering something, if not much, of Gran's past. Hazel had hinted at the woman she really was, which promised to be far more interesting than the impression he had of her. He looked forward to delving a little deeper into Gran's history. He was intrigued, not only by her but by Hazel, too. Judging by her sweat top she was probably from Trinidad, a part of the globe he hadn't been able to visit yet but would dearly love to one day. Was it there she'd had the adventures she'd talked to Gran about?

'I'm going to call on my best pal for lunch,' said Hazel once they'd stopped outside the café. 'So I'll see you here next Saturday?'

'Yes,' said Daniel. 'You will. And I'll come and knock on your door before then so I can help you find those trainers. I might have a small backpack you could borrow, then you'll have a free hand if you want to leave your handbag at home.'

Hazel burst out laughing.

'I know, ridiculous, isn't it? I'm pretty sure I've got a backpack, too. Again, high up somewhere and I can't reach it. Thank you, Daniel.'

'You're welcome. Enjoy your lunch.'

He watched Hazel's slow amble across the car park and waited until she disappeared down a path between a row of white houses before setting off. He realized his walking pace had slowed down considerably as he left the car park. Hazel's sweet and calm demeanour might be rubbing off on him.

4

When Daniel got back to the house he saw Annabelle's Range Rover parked outside. He slowed down and took a deep breath at the door. By now Annabelle would know that in the few days he'd been there, he'd not achieved much in the way of house clearing and she was bound to create a scene. He let himself in. Rasmus came zooming out of the kitchen and into the living room without acknowledging him. Just behind Rasmus was a little girl with mousey-coloured plaits and small round glasses. She was wearing a pink tutu, yellow tights and red wellies. She walked straight up to Daniel.

'I suppose you must be my uncle Daniel,' she said.

'I suppose I must. And you're Mia. You've grown since I last saw you.' He patted her on the head.

'Children do that, you know?' she sniffed. 'Grow.'

Annabelle shouted his name from the living room. Mia looked up at him, pulled in her lips and shook her head. As he thought, he was in serious trouble. He would have liked a little time to muster up an excuse for his more relaxed approach to house clearing but Mia grabbed hold of his hand and dragged him into the living room to face the music. Annabelle was in a khaki jumpsuit, her long hair covered by a bandanna. Rasmus had curled himself around her thigh again. There were two large cardboard boxes on the floor, one half filled with Gran's bits and bobs from the wall units, wrapped in sheets of newspaper, the other piled with books.

'I see you've made a start on this lot,' Daniel said, cheerily. 'I can take them to the recycling centre for you if you'd like.' He looked down at Mia who was staring up at him, shaking her head in despair again.

'Actually, that box is full of useful bric-a-brac and I can find a home for it,' snapped Annabelle. 'A second-hand shop in Padstow will be interested. This box has books on farming and gardening. Some of them are in very good condition so there's no way I'm binning these.'

'No way,' said Mia.

'Haven't you got to get to ballet?' Daniel asked her, trying to unstick his hand from hers, but she wasn't having any of it. She stood facing him.

'Ballet is after school on Wednesday with Miss Gomez. I do drama class on Saturday morning.'

'Oh yeah?' said Daniel, signalling to her outfit. 'And what were you dressed up as today? Clowns?'

Annabelle pursed her lips. Mia unclamped Daniel's hand and folded her arms.

'These are *my* clothes, not clowns' clothes.'

'Oh,' said Daniel. He cleared his throat. 'Sorry. I hear the colourful look is back in.'

'Whatever,' said Mia before marching back to the kitchen. Rasmus ran after her making the sound of a plane, not looking at Daniel once.

He turned to see Annabelle with a brow raised achingly high and a ballerina figurine in her hand.

'I'm sorry,' said Daniel, sliding into the sofa. 'I haven't done an awful lot. I was getting to it, though. I've just been a bit distracted and I've been feeling a bit lost. A bit out of it.'

'But why?' Annabelle exclaimed, obviously hurt by her brother's confession. She placed the figurine on the coffee table separating them. 'You're home now. This is your home. And I've missed having you here.'

'You can't have missed me that much. I'm lazy and I'm unreliable. You've said so yourself. Several times.'

'But that doesn't mean I don't want you around.' She sat on an armchair and crossed one leg over the other. 'Daniel, look, I know it was hard for you to come back. I know how badly you took the falling out with Dad and everything.'

Daniel adjusted his position and stared hard at the china ballerina.

'If it helps,' said Annabelle, 'I know he's sorry about how things ended up between you. But his life turned out fine, he's happy. In the long run that's all I want for you to be. Seriously, Dan, you've got to start taking control of your life. This could be a good base for you. A chance for you to get your act together.'

'Get my act together? I thought I had done. Coming back is the thing that's got me off whack.'

Annabelle scooched forward in her chair. 'You remember your friend James? James Lowe and that lanky one, Mike?'

'Smelly Mikey and James! I was going to ask you about the old gang. What about them?' asked Daniel.

'Well, they're both married now. James and his wife have eighteen-month-old twins and Smelly Mikey's wife just had a baby. He's on paternity leave.'

'Ah, I get it now,' said Daniel. He got up from the sofa before spinning around to face Annabelle again. 'Getting my act together means getting married and having kids, am I right?'

'Well, what's wrong with that?'

'Nothing. It's just . . . it's just not for me. And once we've sold this place I'll probably go back to London again, see if I can find a job.'

Annabelle uncrossed her legs and looked pleadingly at Daniel.

'You can't just go off again like that.' Her voice softened. 'Can't you just consider staying after the house is done? For me? Just give it some time and see how things pan out. I know you're not in contact with any of your old friends but James and Mike both seem happy. Perhaps you could take a leaf out of their book and meet someone nice yourself.'

As Annabelle talked about the possibility of his meeting 'someone nice', Daniel's mind travelled back to Sicily. The fun times he'd had, the incredible sunsets and the clear morning skies. The one and only time he'd considered settling down had been under those skies, his arms around the one woman he'd ever fallen in love with. He still missed her, even after she'd run from his embrace and he'd lost her completely. He could never tell Annabelle about Aria. He would be happy to never have to mention her name again.

'You just want me here so you can boss me around.' He tried to keep a lightness to his voice.

'I just want you here because you look lost and you need to find a direction so you don't wake up one morning, middle-aged, and decide to go rushing off to God knows where, to find yourself.'

'You mean like Mum?' Daniel sat on the arm of Annabelle's chair. 'Don't worry, I'm not going to run off without warning. I'll be here for as long as I can handle it. But I'll need a job. My savings will run out and how would your husband feel about you giving me handouts?'

'Let me worry about that. You'll find a job. I know you will. You can live here in this house, we don't have to sell it. Not ever. You can decorate it the way you'd like. I could help. I cover interior design on my vlog.'

'That's useful.'

'Don't laugh at me. And watch my channel. You might learn a thing or two about house clearing.'

'Do your videos have anything on making lunch for hungry brothers? I've not had anything since this morning.'

Annabelle stood and shook her head at him. 'Well, I forgot to kill the fatted calf but I can see what I can rustle up for you. Coming?' She gestured to the door.

'I'm right behind you, Annie.'

Daniel slumped down into the armchair. Thoughts of Aria hadn't left his mind no matter how hard he tried to shake them loose. He ran his hands through his hair, heaved himself up from the armchair and marched to the kitchen. The children had gone out to the garden. Mia was digging something up with her hands and Rasmus was chasing a butterfly with his arms flapping at his sides.

Daniel stared at them out there having fun. He looked at Annabelle in her jumpsuit, sleeves rolled up, heaping butter onto one of the many crusty rolls she'd brought and loading it with so much ham and sliced tomato it might just explode. He definitely couldn't tell her about Aria. She'd want chapter and verse and he couldn't go through all of that with his sister. All he knew was that for one beautiful year Aria was in his life and then she wasn't. No. Falling in love and settling down wasn't as easy as Annabelle suggested; he had the wounds to prove it.

'That garden needs attending,' he said. 'I can do that. I can get the house sorted, too. Leave it to me, Annabelle.' He walked to the kitchen window and bit into the ham and tomato roll. Pieces of tomato slipped out onto the floor. 'Don't worry, the cat will have that.'

'We've not seen the cat anywhere.'

'Then I guess I'm cleaning this up.' He picked up the tomato and dropped it into the bin, leaving a slithery mess of tomato seeds on the floor. He wiped his hand on the back of his cargo shorts. Annabelle pulled a face. 'I'll make a better job of the house clearing than I did of the tomato.' Another slice fell on the floor. 'In a week you won't know the place,' he said.

5

Daniel knocked on Hazel's door the next day. She was wearing another brightly coloured pair of sweat pants, sea blue with a matching long-sleeved T-shirt, and, for the first time since he'd seen her, a pair of glasses. Her lower arms were drowning in a pair of pink washing up gloves.

'Oh, Daniel, come in, come in.' She stepped to one side holding the door wide open.

'I haven't come at a bad time, have I? You doing a bit of spring cleaning?'

'No, no. I'm washing up after lunch. My daughter had a dishwasher fitted but I can't see the point in using it unless I throw a dinner party.'

'I suppose. But I'm all for labour saving devices, especially round the house. Oh, here, I found that backpack I was telling you about.' It was small and navy, perhaps a little conservative for Hazel's tastes but he imagined she'd be able to pack a fair-sized picnic inside it.

Daniel edged his way along the wall of Hazel's over-ambitious corridor. Who puts an armchair in a narrow space? Why the side table and a footstool? On either side of him, framed photographs of all sizes patterned the walls from floor to ceiling. Some were so high up Hazel would have to crane her neck to see them. Maybe that's why there was a footstool. He managed to knock one photograph askew.

'Oh sorry,' he said. 'I'll straighten this up.' He began adjusting a head to shoulder, black and white photo of three young women all dressed alike. 'Who are these gorgeous young girls?'

Hazel laughed. 'It's been many years since the words "gorgeous" and "young" have been used to describe me.'

'One of these girls is you?' Daniel's eyes bulged as he stared at the picture.

'That's me in the middle and on either side are my sisters, Pearl and Gracie.'

'You look like an all-girl pop group. Diana Ross and the Supremes.'

'Well, this was taken before they started out. It was in the early fifties and Mum took us to the studio on Brixton Hill. She made those dresses. They were satin, dusky pink. They were supposed to be for church but because they were sleeveless we wore a cardigan over our shoulders. Before we had those pictures taken we'd had our hair straightened and I wore lipstick for the first time. We giggled all the way to the studio but Mum wanted us to look sophisticated and it took an hour before we all looked sophisticated at the same time. I wore Mum's shoes because I'd broken the heel off one of mine.'

Daniel invited her to continue.

'I fell off my push bike,' she said with a shake of the head. 'I got chased by some boys when I was doing my paper round. I cycled so fast down the road, by the time I got to the park gate, I panicked and lost control. I fell off my bike but I got to my feet, one broken heel, my fists up ready, and in my broadest Trinidadian accent I asked which of them wanted to be knocked down first.'

Daniel spat out a laugh of disbelief. 'You were fighting with boys?'

'Actually, they all ran away from me. I was so upset I'd broken my shoe I must have looked like a wild thing, so they ran off.'

Daniel shook his head several times.

'Hold on. Wait,' he said. 'First of all, who does a paper round in heels?'

'I only wore them because I knew Dennis Bateson would be sorting out the papers in the shop and I wanted to make him think I was more grown up than I was.'

Daniel shook his head again.

'And, secondly,' he said, 'I can't imagine you on a bike.'

'Actually, I used to cycle everywhere. I didn't always have a walking stick, you know?'

'I know.' He blushed. 'It's just that—'

'You can't see past this little old lady? Daniel, you have no idea.' Hazel swatted his comments away like an irksome fly. She was without her stick and Daniel noticed how she had her arms out towards the walls for balance as she headed to the kitchen. Hazel was right, he couldn't connect the woman in front of him with the good-looking chick in the picture, the young girl who'd cycled like the wind in high heels or wore a satin dress in place of sweatpants.

He sat at the kitchen table. There was a salt and pepper cellar in the middle of it and one place mat opposite where he sat. The tablecloth was cream coloured with tiny posies printed on it here and there. Now this is how he saw Hazel, small and dainty and hardly likely to offer out a gang of boys with her bare fists. She slipped the washing up gloves off.

'If you'd come earlier, you could have joined me for lunch but what about a cup of tea?' she said.

'I don't want to keep you,' said Daniel.

'I'd enjoy the company.' Hazel was already filling the kettle. She moved a red teapot into place on the counter and heaped a tablespoon with loose tea, eyeing it closely. Then she tipped some of the leaves back into the packet before emptying the remainder into the red teapot. She let out a satisfied hum and repeated this action. As Hazel watched the kettle boiling she appeared to go into a state of alert. Daniel remained quiet. Hazel's nose was so close to the boiling kettle, the rising steam fogged up her glasses. She grabbed the handle within a split second of it coming to the boil and the switch flicking off. Like a magician whose hands move so fast you can't see the card disappear up a sleeve, Hazel filled the teapot and slapped the lid on with a bang. Daniel sat to attention. Hazel went over to her mug tree, looked at the mugs on display and selected the two closest to the bottom. All the time her lips were moving but she made no sound. Daniel was curious. He wondered what she was whispering to herself but dared not ask in case it was a prayer or she was reminding herself to serve the biscuits. He knew his grandmother had become forgetful, Annabelle had commented on it before. Maybe this was Hazel's way of remembering things, repeating them over and over, and a biscuit wouldn't go amiss. As Hazel stood with one hand on the kitchen counter, looking down at the teapot, the other hand cradling the fleshy top of her hip, Daniel dared to ask her if there was anything he could do to help. He went as far as opening his mouth and inhaling but Hazel, without turning to face him, stopped him short with the flick of a hand. He snapped his jaw shut.

'You have to get the timing right,' she said, eventually. 'Okay, there. Now I can pour. It'll be the perfect strength.' She lifted the teapot and steadily filled each mug through a strainer before turning to Daniel. 'You can carry these to the table. Do you take milk?'

'Please.'

'That's in the fridge. Sugar's on the counter, bring it over.' She shuffled to the table and sank into a chair. 'If you'd like a biscuit with it, you'll find a packet in the bread bin.' She pointed.

'What was all that mumbling to yourself?' Daniel asked as he sat down to open a packet of Bourbon Creams. 'Some sort of tea brewing incantation?'

'Well, I'm not a witch, Daniel, if that's what you're thinking. It's just that I don't have a timer so I have to count the brewing time. I mastered the art of making the perfect cup of tea thanks to Molly. Your grandmother.'

Daniel took a sip. 'She never taught me how to make a cup of tea.'

'Did you ever offer to make the tea?'

Daniel looked down at the red tiles on the floor. The floor was spotlessly clean. Everything in Hazel's kitchen was neat and in place. From the matching light green kitchen units with surfaces that shone to the cat-themed calendar on the wall, Hazel's kitchen had all the warmth and homeliness Daniel would expect from a cute little old lady.

'I suppose, when I was ever in Cornwall I didn't really see much of Gran,' he admitted. 'I'm sure I must have had tea with her, but you're right, I probably didn't offer to make it.'

'If you had, you would have learned her secret.' Hazel took a sip and smacked her lips together. 'Wonderful.'

Daniel silently concurred and smacked his lips together out of politeness.

'So, how is all the sorting out going at Molly's?' asked Hazel, replacing her mug.

'Okay, I suppose. It's a bit of a drag but I think I could get it done in a week. What day does the rubbish get collected? There are some old clothes and uniforms I can ditch. I won't bother taking them to a charity shop.'

Hazel sat upright.

'Uniforms?' she exclaimed.

'Yes, I'm guessing Gramps was a soldier?'

'He was a sergeant in one of the armoured divisions in the Normandy campaign. And Molly . . .'

'I'm guessing she was back here looking after their house?'

'She was here, yes, but she and your grandfather hadn't met yet. They married after the war. Make no mistake, though, Molly did her part.'

'What do you mean?'

'You really were serious when you said you didn't know a thing about her life.'

He was about to reach for another Bourbon Cream but stopped.

'I didn't think there was anything to know,' he said with a shrug. 'Not until you called her remarkable. I wish I knew what you meant by that. All I remember was that if anyone was a sergeant in that house, it was Gran. She used to order Mum around and she didn't stand for any nonsense from me and Annabelle.'

'Oh yes, she was strict all right but I'm sure that had a lot to do with where she came from and how her life was once she came to Cornwall.'

'*Came* to Cornwall? Wasn't she born here?'

'No, she wasn't. Your grandmother arrived in Cornwall when she was eighteen years old. One of those uniforms you're about to throw out belonged to her. She was a member of the Women's Land Army in World War Two.'

'You're kidding me. Mum never said anything about that, neither did Gran.'

'Did you ever ask about her life?'

Daniel quickly looked down to the handle of his mug, fiddling with it for a second or two before answering. 'I suppose not.'

'You see, Molly came from a well-to-do family from up north. Lancashire. Her father owned a factory up there and she used to be a nanny for a rich relative. She learned to play piano and she was all set to go to a music academy in London when she heard about the WLA. Signed up there and then. Caused a major upset at home, especially when she got her papers and they told her where she was going to be stationed. I suppose a lot of that tough exterior comes from those days. It couldn't have been easy going up against her parents as a young girl and then having to move miles away from home for the war years.'

'Can you tell me what it was like in the war?'

'For crying out loud, Daniel.' A chuckle burst from Hazel's lips. 'I was only little during wartime and I was still back home in Trinidad then. My father was here, though, he joined the Royal Air Force. He never talked about the war to us, sadly. My family and I came to live in London after the war. 1948.' Hazel let out a long yawn.

'Am I asking too many questions?'

'Not at all. It's just that I have a nap after lunch.' A smile slowly swept up her face.

'I'll go then,' said Daniel. 'Thank you for the tea. But I do want to hear more. I mean, I'm intrigued by Gran's background as well as yours.'

'And there's a lot to talk about, but I need to get some rest.'

'Let me help you upstairs,' said Daniel, standing.

'I'm fine on my armchair.'

'The one in the hall?'

Hazel giggled. 'No, those things are going to be collected. Someone from the council will come with a van for them. My daughter ordered me a chair that helps me stand, and there was no space for it in the living room unless I got rid of one from the three-piece suite. It took me ages to work out how to use the new chair. Too many gadgets for me. I didn't want it but she says I'm old and I need looking after.'

'Will I get to meet her, your daughter?'

'I don't think you'll meet any of my children.' Hazel sighed. 'They're all married with children of their own. They've got busy lives in London so they look after me by way of the internet. They order things for me to make my life easier. Jennifer, my oldest, bought a laptop so we could Skype. But she's always too busy to call and now I can't remember for the life of me how to get online.'

'I can help you with that.'

Daniel offered an arm for Hazel to take. He walked her to the living room. The orthopaedic chair Hazel's daughter had ordered, discernible by its light cream colour and size, was placed by the window. All the other furniture was dark brown and matched the chair in the corridor. The cream chair swallowed Hazel in and she yawned again. Daniel knelt at her side.

'Before I go, Hazel, I should find your trainers. For our walk on Saturday.'

'I'm so glad you want to walk next Saturday.' Hazel's speech had slowed. She wasn't as alert as she had been on answering the door. 'I thought you looked a bit fed up because it was just us two.'

He put his head down and fidgeted on his knee.

'It was a bit of a letdown at first,' he admitted. 'But I got to know you better, and I know a bit more about Gran now, too. In the end, I did enjoy it, really.'

'Me too, Daniel.' Hazel's eyes squeezed together as she grinned. 'My trainers are in a box on top of the wardrobe in the front bedroom.'

'I'll get them down.'

Daniel bounded up the stairs. In the front bedroom, the double bed took up a large portion of the space. The duvet cover was colourful and the bed very neatly made. Hazel's pink slippers were on the floor on one side of the bed. As he approached the wardrobe Daniel saw that there was a pair of brown, fur-lined slippers on the other side of the bed. Henry's slippers, he supposed, still sitting there after all this time. He gulped and then stretched his arm up to feel around on the top of the wardrobe. He found the box with Hazel's trainers. They were brand new. Perhaps an online gift from Hazel's daughter. They were fashionable, high end trainers which Daniel wouldn't mind owning a pair of himself.

By the time he'd got back to the living room with them, Hazel was asleep. Her lips were slightly parted and she snored, very deeply. Daniel laughed to himself and left the box just by the orthopaedic chair. Letting himself out of Hazel's house he thought about how lonely she must be. Her husband had died a year ago. She and his grandmother were friends and now Gran was gone, too. No wonder Hazel jumped at the chance of joining the walking club. Thank goodness he hadn't bailed on her on the first walk.

When he walked back into his grandmother's house, the cat rushed through Daniel's legs and scooted straight to the kitchen where it sat up next to the fridge, purring loudly.

As if the cat knew that Daniel had had the good sense to buy proper cat food and milk, he was back, looking longingly at Daniel who presented him with a saucer of milk. Daniel made a mental note to find the owner of this cheeky cat. The cat stopped slurping and looked up at Daniel, who grinned.

'Just don't get too comfortable. Your squatting days are numbered, cat.'

6

'The thing to remember is, don't maintain eye contact until he's used to your essence.'

'My essence?'

'Yes, it's important to let him know the inner you before he comes into contact with the person you project.'

Annabelle's house stood in a sleepy cul-de-sac of five detached houses in Padstow. Hedges of yellow gorse outside the double-fronted houses gave them a uniform look. Each house had a driveway up to a wide garage. With a couple of shiny and impressive parked cars, the cul-de-sac looked like a page out of a dream homes magazine. Annabelle's enormous kitchen, the hub of the house, looked onto a garden recently planted with vegetables with the assistance of her children, while shooting her most recent vlog.

Daniel nodded his head slowly as he listened to his sister's commentary on the best way to deal with Rasmus's reluctance to communicate with him. He forced himself not to look at Rasmus to allow his nephew time to get used to his essence. Rasmus had been coaxed back to the kitchen with vanilla ice cream after Daniel arrived shouting, 'Wassup, dude,' to his nephew and plonking himself at the large oak table where Rasmus had been happily colouring in his book.

Annabelle served the home-made ice cream in her son's favourite bowl and placed it on the table as close to Daniel as she dared. Daniel could feel his nephew boring holes into the side of his face with his big round eyes. Rasmus looked like a cartoon character, a cute little kid with wavy hair and not some complex being who couldn't conduct a conversation with anyone unless the moon was in Saturn or any of the new age rubbish his sister was spouting. Rasmus is just shy, Daniel thought to himself, either that or he hadn't grasped the need for manners. Gran would have had him saying a polite hello, in seconds. Daniel knew this for a fact. He didn't mention his thoughts to Annabelle. It would only upset her. She sat at the opposite end of the table to Daniel, her laptop open, helping her brother plan a poster for finding the owner of his squatter cat.

Daniel had managed to get the cat to sit still for five seconds so he could take a photo and, between him and his sister, they had designed a poster with the word 'Found' in bold letters above the cat's photograph and Daniel's mobile number at the bottom. She added the finer points to the poster before printing some out.

'Thanks for doing this, Annabelle,' he said. He glanced very quickly at Rasmus who he found staring at him but who promptly closed his eyes when he was spotted.

'That's no problem at all,' said Annabelle. 'I hope you find the owner.'

'I'm just glad you believe there's an actual cat in the house. I was beginning to wonder if I was just making him up.'

'It isn't unheard of,' his sister said, resting her chin on her elbow. 'Imaginary friends for company.' Daniel looked at her in disbelief. 'I wouldn't blame you. Your old friends have moved on and the ones in Sicily are miles away.'

'Seriously?'

'Have you thought about getting onto one of those dating apps?' She stared at him without expression as if he were in therapy.

'How did we get from lost cats to dating apps?' Daniel spluttered. 'Look, I'm not desperate for company. And don't get me started on the whole married with kids bit.' Another quick glance at Rasmus who had both hands over his eyes now. 'I should be on my way. The quicker I find the owner, the quicker I can get the house sorted.'

Annabelle raised an eyebrow as the printer continued to whir and churn out posters.

'So you're saying this little cat in the photograph is stopping you from clearing the house?'

'That and my new club.'

'What new club?'

'I started a walking club. The first meeting was on Saturday. We'll be doing a walk every Saturday.'

'Why didn't you tell me you started a club? And how many members are there?'

'A few.'

'How many?' She looked sceptical

'Look, the club exists, okay? Just like the cat. And so there's only one other person in it right now, but it'll be like *Field of Dreams*. I've built it and so they're bound to come.'

'And this one other *person*,' Annabelle said with finger quotes, 'doesn't happen to have whiskers and a tail by any chance?'

'I'm not losing the plot, honestly. It's a real person,' said Daniel. 'You know that friend of Gran's? Hazel?'

'Ah, yes, she's so sweet. Not going to get very far with her and her walking frame, though, are you?'

'Hazel's cool. Besides, it's a walking stick not a frame. And if it all gets a bit much for her then she might have to stop coming. We'll have to see. Anyway, there'll be other walkers joining. They're just taking their time to get with the programme, that's all.'

'You'd know all about that, wouldn't you?'

'Trust me.' Daniel laughed and raised his hands. 'I'll get the house sorted, just chill.'

Annabelle shuffled the 'Found' posters into a neat pile. She handed them to Daniel who sprang up from the chair, keen to get away from another nagging session from his sister.

'Before I go,' Daniel said. 'I was wondering if I could borrow some wheels. I need to be able to get around. Circulate this lot for a start.'

'I don't have the hatchback anymore,' said Annabelle. 'But I do have a bike.'

'I guess that'll do for now.'

Inside the garage Annabelle's pink bicycle leaned up against a shelving unit filled with boxes, tools and tins of paint. The bike had long handlebars and a wicker basket on the front.

'Pink!' Daniel exclaimed. 'Isn't it a bit girlie?'

They both turned around when they heard Rasmus chuckle.

'It isn't girlie and that's not the sort of thing a feminist should say,' Annabelle said.

Daniel couldn't ever remember telling Annabelle he was a feminist. With a nod to Rasmus and a 'Thanks, sis' to Annabelle, he set off on the bike, thinking he could spray paint it black. He cycled round the area near Gran's house taping posters to trees and poles. He then took one to pin up at all the places he'd put up his Walkers Club flyers. They did look a bit lame, being handmade, but at least they were still up.

On the notice board in the farm shop, just as he was about to pin up his poster Daniel noticed one advertising a surf school in Harlyn. His old surfboard was locked up in the family home and probably long past replacing by now. It had been a good while since he'd surfed but he was sure he could get the hang of it again. Strange that he had taken living in a place world famous for surfing for granted. Whenever he told anyone in Sicily where he was from, they all commented on the great surfing and assumed that Daniel must be an expert. Maybe if he went along to the club he could become one.

'Ah, a missing cat mystery,' a familiar voice said over his shoulder.

Daniel grinned to himself before turning around. Behind him, in a white sweat top and skinny jeans, was the girl with the white blonde hair.

'It is a bit of a mystery, but yes, I found a cat,' said Daniel. 'Or at least it found me.'

'It's really considerate of you to do this.' She moved closer to the notice board. 'Looks like a cute cat.'

'He's a hungry cat.'

'They're not very faithful creatures. He probably has several homes and places where he gets fed.' Daniel realized he'd given in to the cat's demands, but he had thought it had belonged to his gran. 'Still, it's good of you to help him find his way home.'

'Are you cycling through to Harlyn now?' he asked.

'Yep,' she said with a smile that lingered on her lips. She didn't seem to be in a hurry to get going this time.

'And what do you do when you're not cycling? Ever surf?' Daniel tilted his head to the poster in the centre of the board.

'I do my fair share,' she said. 'I know this school very well.'

'You do? Oh, I was thinking of going along. It's been a while since I surfed so I might need a brushing up session.'

'You should go there, then. It's one of the best.'

'Cool. It'll be great to get out on a board again.'

'Well, watch the weather reports if you want to catch the waves. I know there's a good forecast for Harlyn in a few days.' She turned and headed for the counter where she paid for the fresh pies she had in her basket. Before leaving the farm shop she turned to Daniel.

'Bye then,' she said.

'I was just on my way out, too,' he said and hurried to the door.

Her bike was leaning up against the same rail as Daniel's. She looked at the bright pink bike and then back at Daniel.

'I've only just got back to Trevone,' he said. 'I had to borrow this old thing to get around with before I get a car.'

'I thought you walked everywhere.' She pulled her bike free and got up onto the saddle, one foot on the ground for balance.

Daniel's brow creased as he stared at her.

'I'm talking about your walking club flyer,' she said pointing a thumb towards the farm shop. 'The arty one in felt pen?'

Daniel blushed. 'Oh yes, that. The Walkers Club is experimental. I'm not sure how well it will do.'

'Give it time.' She was about to pedal off.

'I'm Daniel,' he said.

'Nice to meet you, Daniel.' She rode away without another word, the wheels of her bike creaking with every second push of the pedals. The sound amused him as he watched her cycle off. At least the idea of the walking club was planted a little further into her mind.

7

As Daniel entered the car park for the second Saturday walk, he saw what looked like a full-on argument between a middle-aged man and woman outside the beach café. He slowed down when he saw Hazel there, gesturing with her hand for the couple to stop. Hazel looked relieved when she saw Daniel approaching.

'Hello, Daniel. No walking poles today?' she said loudly enough to interrupt the arguing couple who fell silent and looked at Daniel. He acknowledged them with a tentative smile before turning to Hazel.

'I thought they were a bit overkill, so I left them at home. Nice to see you in your new trainers and the backpack.'

Hazel had added her own bling to the backpack with colourful brooches and badges pinned to the front pocket and she had threaded red and gold laces around the shoulder straps.

The couple edged closer to Daniel, the woman elbowing the man aside so that she could stand in front of him. She wore a brightly coloured sweater below a dark green gilet. Her bust, generous and unapologetic, fixed itself centimetres from Daniel's sternum. Her hair was dyed auburn and was pulled up into a high ponytail. Her face, ladled with make-up, opened with a joyful smile and revealed a pattern of lines and wrinkles around her eyes, jaw and forehead.

'Hi, I'm Daniel,' he said. He looked down at her red leggings, walking boots and up to her fingers which were hooked into the straps of her backpack. 'I see you're all kitted out for the walk today.'

'I certainly am, Daniel. I'm Amanda,' she said with an American accent. She extended a well-manicured hand for Daniel to shake. 'And what a beautiful spring morning we have for our walk today.' She looked around, taking in the beach café and complex and the sea view before glancing up at an overcast sky.

The man she'd been arguing with had hovered eagerly behind her but began to edge his way into the frame, though Amanda refused to stop shaking Daniel's hand. The man was tall. The collar of his pink polo shirt was upturned and his casual sweater stretched around a solid beach ball of a stomach. His cream golfing trousers matched his sweater, but his trainers were not a match for anything he had on. As Daniel began to create a space between his hand and Amanda's, the man filled it with a large one of his own. He gave Daniel's hand a brisk shake.

'And I'm Keith Hunter. Ex-husband of Amanda here. Forgive the dramatics. We didn't know the other was joining the walk, so we were debating which one of us should stay. We seem to have carved the whole of Cornwall up into sections of who can go where and when. I can't think why Amanda hasn't gone back across the pond. It would make life a whole lot easier.' He snorted and shook his head. His hair, thick and dark, was streaked with white on either side and held firm in the salty breeze. He had a tremendous overbite and his haughty baritone reverberated above the sound of the ocean and the cry of seabirds.

'I have no intention of going anywhere.' Amanda's shoulders were up at her ears. 'And I'm sure Daniel could do without a buck-toothed, know-it-all oaf on the walk.'

'Wait a minute,' said Daniel, hands up, looking at Hazel for assistance. 'I'm sure if . . . that is . . . It's really not worth—'

'What Daniel means,' Hazel cut in, 'is that this is supposed to be a fun club. We take some exercise, we take in the healthy sea air and the beautiful sights. We don't even have to speak. Do we, Daniel?'

'Exactly,' he said. He looked at his phone. 'It's gone twelve, I guess we should head out. Does anyone have any injuries or health issues I should know about?'

'How about mental health?' said Amanda. 'Mine has definitely been tested after being followed everywhere by my ex-husband. It's causing a lot of upset, as you can probably tell.' She rapidly fanned her face with her hand. A brief hint of sadness swept across her face before she shot a vicious look at her ex-husband.

'Maybe that's something you should discuss in therapy,' said Hazel. 'Should we go now, Daniel?'

Daniel nodded, his lips tight together. As he started off, Amanda pushed her way to his side and began to inhale loudly and exhale with force through her lips. Daniel looked at her.

'Everything all right, Amanda?'

'Just calming my nervous system.' She cast another glare in her ex-husband's direction. 'I'm looking forward to this, though. I wasn't expecting a good-looking young man to be taking charge. I like that very much. I mean, you look as if you know what you're doing. Taking control.' Her smile was wide, a line of red lipstick on her teeth. Daniel didn't know where to put his eyes, especially when she began to swing her arms back and forth. Her upper body looked as if she were power walking but her lower half minced as if she were in a fashion show. He looked back at Hazel who was biting her bottom lip and then at Keith Hunter who rolled his eyes and stared daggers at his ex-wife's back.

'Hazel, please let us know when we're stopping for snacks,' Daniel said.

She gave him the thumbs up and the four continued slowly along the coast path.

The clouds whirled around in the sky. Waves rolled in high onto Trevone Beach and Daniel saw two surfers making good use of the water. He walked a few steps facing backwards, checking that his group were keeping up with him. They looked reasonably content and walked in silence. That is, apart from Amanda's deep breathing and Keith Hunter's tutting and muttering. Okay, so Amanda and Keith were not exactly the type of people he'd hoped to meet when he'd started the Walkers Club, but the same could be said about Hazel. And after one walk together he'd found her fascinating. The Hunters might surprise him.

Daniel was aware that having two new walkers might lessen his chance of discovering more about his grandmother or Hazel. Perhaps he'd pop over to her house one day and Hazel could continue where she'd left off in her stories. If anyone had told him a month ago that he'd be making friends with a woman in her eighties, he would have laughed at the idea.

As the walkers inched their way along the path, they formed a single line. Daniel led with Amanda directly behind him. She continued to puff loudly and exclaim, 'Isn't this wonderful?' every now and again. Keith walked behind her, staring daggers at her gilet and twisting his face. Hazel trailed slowly and steadily at the back of the line.

'How about stopping here?' Hazel called after some time had passed. Beside her was a grassy mound that backed onto the fields and would be easy for her to sit on.

'Good idea,' said Daniel. He sat on the opposite side of the path on a pile of rocks a little way in from the cliffside. The Hunters joined Hazel.

Gulls cried and flew overhead but the shrill and consistent whistle of skylarks conversing caused their sound to fade away into the vast sky. From below, ocean waves beat against the rocks directly below where Daniel sat. He had slowed his pace considerably to allow Hazel to keep up so they had only walked a short distance from Trevone Beach. He looked at the surfers back there, sitting meditatively on their boards, waiting for the big wave. He wondered if the girl on the bike was out surfing in Harlyn. Since their second meeting, her face came to mind often, pushing pictures of his dates with Aria into the background. He was glad about this. He was fed up of seeing Aria's face and the ring with the tiny red gem in the black jewellery box. He'd tossed it over a bridge when he knew he'd never see Aria again. Had he given her the ring and they had married, as he once hoped they would, there was every chance they could have ended up like the Hunters. He remembered Aria's fiery temper, yelling at him in Italian and him not understanding much of what she was saying, except for one word in particular: *Imbecille.*

'What do you mean, your feet hurt?' Keith's haughty exclamation brought Daniel back down to earth.

'What's this?' Daniel asked.

'My ex-wife. Her feet hurt. Typical,' said Keith.

'I'm wearing brand new boots, Daniel,' Amanda purred as she sidled up next to him on his rock. Her bosom swelled and contracted with her breath, just millimetres from Daniel's arm. He tried to edge away inconspicuously but the bosom followed closely. 'Maybe you could recommend a pair.'

He looked down at her feet.

'Well, for a start I'd invest in some good walking socks if I were you. Are those tights you've got on under your leggings?' he asked.

'Oh, I never go anywhere without my pantyhose.' She leaned closer to Daniel and took a sideways look at her ex-husband.

'The thing is,' said Daniel, clearing his throat, 'new shoes will rub and you might get blisters the first time of wearing them so good walking socks are better than a pair of tights. And make sure your walking shoes are fitted by an expert.'

'Could you accompany me to the shoe shop?' she said in a mist of perfume that made him want to cough hard. Like a ninja, Amanda had managed to get even closer to him on the low rocks. Any closer and she'd be sitting on his knee.

'I say, Daniel,' Keith said, 'who else will be joining us on the walk? Anyone under thirty?'

'He means young tottie,' said Amanda. 'That's not my term, it's his. As if he could get lucky in those golfing trousers.'

'They're a perfectly good pair of trousers,' Keith said.

'They're at least two sizes too small,' Amanda bellowed. 'And if we lifted that tight sweater up past his middle we'd see they're being held together by a large safety pin.'

Hazel spluttered out a laugh that sent tiny traces of a sausage roll across the path. She put her fragile hand to her lips.

'I'm sorry,' she said. 'Eating too fast.'

Daniel knew full well that Hazel couldn't eat fast if she tried. His face grew crimson. He took a sip from his water bottle but managed to choke.

'Hazel,' he said, finally.

'Yes, Daniel?'

'Do you think we're ready to proceed?'

Everyone looked at Hazel.

'I believe so. I might need a hand standing.'

Daniel rushed over to her and Amanda toppled towards the space he'd vacated on the rock.

'Onwards then,' said Daniel. 'Hazel and I will lead the way.'

As they continued for a further fifteen minutes along the path, managing to walk a good four hundred metres further than the last walk, Daniel could hear the Hunters bickering in the background. He leaned down to Hazel.

'I hope they're not ruining it for you,' he said.

'No, it's fine. Rather entertaining.' She let out a coy giggle. A loud bark from Keith Hunter brought the group to a standstill.

'How dare you?' Amanda yelled.

The Hunters had fallen behind and were standing too close to the cliff edge for Daniel's liking.

'Let's turn back,' said Hazel.

'Yes. I think you could be right.'

Once back at the car park the ex Mr and Mrs Hunter thanked Daniel and stormed away in opposite directions. Daniel didn't expect to see either of them on the walk again, unless of course they could come to some agreement about which part of the South West Coast Path belonged to whom.

'We didn't get much time to talk,' Daniel said, turning to Hazel.

'Of course, you wanted to hear about your grandmother. There's a whole history there you should know about, Daniel. Your gran didn't have many photos up but I believe you'll find a few more packed away somewhere, along with her journals.'

'She kept journals?' asked Daniel.

'Yes. She kept them during her time in the war. You'll find them as you sort through the house, I'd expect.'

'Great, I'll look out for them. Thanks, Hazel.'

'You're very welcome, but you will drop by so I can tell you more about her, won't you?' she said.

Daniel nodded enthusiastically.

'Right, I'm off to have lunch with my best pal,' said Hazel. 'Thank you, Daniel, for another lovely day. That was fun. See you soon.'

'Yes, see you soon,' said Daniel. He watched Hazel making her way out of the car park and became curious about her lunch date. She hadn't talked about this pal of hers and Daniel wondered if he or she would come walking with them one day. Maybe Hazel's friend was less mobile than she was. There were already questions about her past he would like to ask her.

Before he set off for home, Daniel made a stop at the small surf shop in Trevone and purchased a wetsuit and surf-board. He then called Annabelle to ask if he could borrow her car. He planned on paying an early morning visit to Harlyn Beach the next day. The girl on the silver bicycle had said the surf school he'd seen advertised was a good one. He wanted to see how much of a surfer he still was and maybe join the surf school on her recommendation.

8

Light was only just breaking through the clouds as Daniel drove along the country roads. Undulating fields of brown and green stretched for miles on either side. Hedges of wild flowers in purple, white and yellow lined the way, waving and bowing to the roadside. Sheep stood still as statues across the farmland as Daniel sped by in Annabelle's four-by-four. He rolled the window down; the cool breeze on his face kept him alert, though his mind lingered on the comfort of his bed and thoughts of throwing his phone out of the window when the alarm went off at 5.30am. The cat had slept curled in a ball by the kitchen doorway and opened a lazy eye when Daniel walked in, desperate for a strong coffee and for someone to make it for him. The cat had gone back to sleep.

Daniel turned off the car radio when he approached the beach car park at Harlyn. As he'd expected, the place was deserted, the golden sand still smooth and free of footprints. Daniel's surfboard was in the back of the car. He'd worn his wetsuit up to his waist on the short drive but slipped his arms through now, zipping the suit up as far as he could. He carried his board, as well as his new neoprene boots and gloves, out onto the beach and ran towards the sea. He stopped when something white and billowy fluttered into view by the rocks just to his left.

The girl with the white blonde hair was standing with her back to him holding a camera to her face, the lens pointed upwards at the rock face. Daniel looked up to see what had captured her interest. The herring gull pecking at a patch of moss? The grey and white fulmar with its stiff wing beats following the updraught to the top of the cliff? Daniel quietly drew nearer to the girl and cleared his throat. She snapped her shot before turning around.

'You,' she exclaimed happily. 'You're up early.'

'Yes, I wanted to catch the early waves.'

'Cool.' She walked towards him in a white, loose-fitting shirt that fluttered upwards in the breeze. She shivered and put her camera down before pulling on a baggy sweater which was lying on the sand next to her metal camera case. 'I love the early morning air on my skin and to feel the wind, even if that means goosebumps.'

'It is a chilly one,' said Daniel, shivering in the same way she had. 'I saw you taking pictures at Trevone Beach the other week. Is it just seascapes you're in to?'

'Not especially. But I do love the sea. I used to take pictures, all kinds, for a living once.' She looked down at the expensive film camera sitting on top of the case. 'But it didn't work out for me. Like a lot of things in my life. I guess you could say I'm a bit of a drifter.' She smiled up at Daniel. 'Nice suit. Looks new.'

'Got it yesterday.'

'You live in Trevone, right?' she asked casually while she packed her camera away.

'I do.'

'You know the surf would be just as good there as it is here this morning.'

'I know, but I think I remember it being better here for some reason. A distant memory from my youth, I suppose.' He stood the surfboard up beside him. 'And I got to run into you again.'

He liked her smile. Quick to appear on her face. Her eyes, a light shade of grey, sparkled like gems.

'I'm Jess,' she said. 'Nice to meet you. Again.' She quickly raised and lowered her hand.

'Nice to meet you, Jess.' Daniel gave a slight bow. 'I wasn't sure I'd get to know your name, you come and go so quickly.'

'I have been told that I should slow down a bit.'

'Well,' he said, suddenly feeling self-conscious, 'before you vanish again, I wonder if . . . well I was thinking that maybe you'd like to have a drink some time?'

'Sure.' She spoke as if they were old friends. 'How about coffee and some breakfast? After your surf.'

'Sounds good to me. Great. I mean, good.' He looked down at his board. 'Like I said to you before, I'm a little out of practice. I've been away from Cornwall a long time.'

'Well, it's lucky we ran into each other today. I'm a surfing instructor.' She turned back to the surf shop and school behind them. The one that had been advertised on the farm shop notice board. 'The school doesn't open until half past nine so I could give you the benefit of my knowledge until then.'

'You just said you were a photographer,' said Daniel.

'Long story.' She hooked the strap of the camera box over her shoulder. 'Come on.'

He followed her along the soft sand, his feet sinking into the coolness of it as he looked at the blonde feathered hair at the nape of her neck. Her loose sweater fell off her shoulder so that the fine blue lines of a tattoo showed on her milky skin.

'Okay, I'll go through the very basics,' said Jess, kneeling on the sand. Daniel sat with his legs crossed. Jess collected some sand in one hand and let it slip through her fingers.

'Is that part of the training?' he asked.

'No, I just like the feel of it. I can sit here in the mornings – when the sand is this cool it feels like water – and just let it pass through my fingers over and over again. My family think I waste too much time doing things like this. They think I'm a waste of time full stop.' She lifted a hand full of sand and let the grains fall from it like a waterfall.

'That seems a bit harsh, calling you a waste of time,' said Daniel. 'At least you have a job.'

'The problem they have is that I've had several. Photography is only one of the things I've trained to do in my life.'

'But still, teaching at the surf school is pretty cool.'

'What is it you do?'

'Me? I'm between jobs at the moment. I'm clearing out my gran's house, now that she's passed away.'

'Oh, I'm sorry to hear that,' said Jess, looking deep into Daniel's eyes.

'Thanks. Gran went peacefully.' He looked at the sand, tempted to grab a handful and let it fall through his fingers, too. What could he say about his grandmother? One of those inane responses people have if an elderly person dies? *She had a good innings. She had a full life, we should celebrate it.* He had yet to learn about his grandmother's life because all he had was the sketch that Hazel had drawn of it.

'You inherited her house?' Jess said softly.

'My sister and I did.'

'So now you have a home here. Since I've been back I've been dossing at my brother's house. It's a converted barn in Crugmeer. It'll be beautiful when it's finished but he's taking his time. Right now I wake up coughing with all the dust flying around.' She giggled.

'Since you've been back? Where were you before?'

'Travelling. Taking pictures. When the work dried up, I couldn't make my family understand how competitive a business it is. When I couldn't make ends meet, I had to give it all up. I was living in Spain until a year ago. Now I'm back and everyone wonders how long I'll be around.' She used both fingers to point at herself. 'Professional waste of space, that's me.'

'For years my sister has been telling me I need to do something with my life and my dad never stopped telling me I should be more like him when I was younger. So I know how that feels. But at least you're working now.'

'My brother owns the surf shop and school. He employed me to keep my parents off my case. I did make a go at something else before this but the funding I had vanished and that's when my brother threw me a lifeline.'

'I think you landed on your feet,' said Daniel, looking from Jess's grey eyes to the blue flowing lines of what could be seen of her tattoo.

'It's true and I couldn't be more grateful to him. What about you?' Jess asked. 'What did you do before you came here?'

'Well, up until a few weeks ago I was living in Sicily. I was a walking guide on Mount Etna.'

'Ah, hence the walking club.' Jess raised a finger.

'Something like that. I just started the club so I could meet people.'

'You mean girls?'

Daniel laughed. 'It's not like that. Only three people have shown up for the walk so far. And none of them are girls.

So if I was trying to get with someone . . . well, let's just say the walking club is hardly Tinder.'

'You can meet a lot of people at a place like this.' She gestured to the beach and the surf school.

'So, have you met anyone since you've worked here?'

'Ooh, Daniel. Sounds like you're fishing into my personal life.' She glanced at him with a sly grin.

'No,' he said, shrugging timidly. 'Just curious. I mean, lots of people hang out here, as you said, and someone like you . . . I mean, surely you're with someone.'

'No, I'm happily single.'

A moment of quiet slipped between them.

'So, are we going through these surf school basics or what?' asked Daniel. 'I see some pretty decent waves coming in.'

As they spoke a few more people entered the beach. Locals coming to get a surf in before breakfast.

'You remember the pop up?' asked Jess. She went through the key ways Daniel could get to his feet on his board, showing him a good surfing position and running through the things he should and shouldn't do. 'Now, let's see you in action.'

Daniel put on his gloves and boots. The temperature was still nippy and he knew the cold water would be a shock to his system. The sky was lighter now, pink clouds drifting through a faded blue. The waves were not consistent, the wind without direction, but the swell came in at between three and five feet, good enough for Jess to see what he could do. Swimming out on his board reminded him of the times he'd wanted to swim and just keep going, far from home and his uncertain future. He sat and waited for the swell, remembering how he'd convinced himself that the only way to be happy would be to set off, travel, explore new places. Jess stood on the beach photographing him as he surfed. In a little while he jumped off his board and ran towards her.

'You haven't lost your touch, Daniel, even though you have been away a while,' said Jess as she packed her camera away again. 'I think all you need is more practice. No need to pay surf school fees. But don't tell my brother I said that.' They both grinned. Daniel made a lock and key sign by his lips.

'Breakfast is on me,' said Jess.

Daniel changed into some dry clothes by the car and met Jess inside the beach café. The smell of bacon sizzling on the grill hit him from the car park. Jess had bought a pot of coffee and was looking at a menu when Daniel joined her at the table.

'You have earned everything on the menu,' she said with a smile.

'Be careful,' he said, 'I've worked up quite an appetite. I might just take you up on that.'

Daniel looked at Jess rather than at the menu.

'We have to order at the till,' said Jess. 'So let me know what you want.'

'I'll have whatever you're having.'

Daniel liked the easy way Jess had with the staff. She must be a regular as the café was just metres from her brother's surf shop. She stood up on tiptoes, hands leaning on the stainless steel counter as she ordered their breakfast. The waitress allowed Jess to skip round to the service side to pick out some pastries. She put four large ones into a basket with a checked serviette and placed it in the middle of their table before she sat down.

Jess pulled off her sweater; the short layers of her hair

spiked upwards. She teased it into tousled disorder, her baggy shirt slipping down her shoulder.

'I see you're fascinated by my tattoo,' she said as she began to pour out two mugs of coffee.

'Sorry, was I staring?'

'Oh, just a lot. But don't worry, lots of people are fascinated by it. It's a little hard to make out at first.' She revealed a little more of the blue markings. Daniel turned his head from side to side; the tattoo spanned the width of her deltoid muscle but not all of it could be seen.

'It's a lotus flower,' she said when he continued to look baffled.

Daniel studied Jess's silken skin, the knot of her shoulder bone and the two shades of blue that went to make up the tattoo. The thin lines of the design swirled and formed little points which were surrounded by tiny dashes of a lighter blue, depicting rays of light.

'I can't really see a flower if I'm honest,' Daniel said. Jess straightened her shirt.

'Don't worry about it. I gave the tattooist artistic licence to interpret the flower as she saw fit.' Jess sipped her coffee.

'Does it mean anything?'

'The flower? It does, depending on whether you're into Egyptology, or if you're a Buddhist or Hindu. For Yogis, it's a symbol of spiritual awakening.'

'Oh,' said Daniel. 'You're into yoga and all that meditation stuff.'

'I am. In a big way, actually. My work paid for the expensive courses I went on around the world. Loved every second of them.'

Daniel saw the joy in Jess's eyes as she talked about her passion for yoga; happy memories made her lips dance into a smile. Before he could ask her more about it, the waitress served breakfast; two bacon sandwiches, hot and greasy, were piled so high Daniel doubted he could get his mouth around his.

'Don't tell me you have this every day,' he said.

'Not every day. But their double-decker bacon butties have to be tasted to be believed.'

She chatted and took large bites and didn't care in the slightest when grease dripped on the side of her mouth. She simply rubbed it away with a paper napkin and carried on talking. She made big gestures with her arms, and Daniel, though he tried not to, couldn't help comparing Jess to Aria. His ex-girlfriend had lived on salad, was always looking at herself in a mirror and complained if he ate anything fried.

'And you're really going to eat these massive pastries after that sandwich?' he teased. Having matched Jess by finishing his sandwich, Daniel leaned back in the seat, his arm hooked over the back of the chair.

Jess nodded. 'I don't do this every day. But what can I say? I like food and I like to eat. I love to cook, too. I find it very relaxing.'

'I can't cook. Or at least I'm not very good.'

'I can teach you.' The words slipped very easily from her lips. 'I mean, I can let you have a couple of recipes. If you'd like.'

'I would like that. I rely on my sister for a cooked meal and that's not good enough,' Daniel said. 'I should learn how to rustle up something more substantial than beans on toast.'

They were quiet for a while until Jess looked up at the large clock on the café wall.

'The shop is opening soon,' she said. 'I should go.'

'Do you enjoy working there?' asked Daniel, sensing a shift in Jess's mood.

'It can be really good fun. It's just that my brother, well, he wants me to take it over from him one day. It's not like I could buy him out or anything but he wants to go away. He'd be a silent partner and I'd run the business.'

'Sounds intense.'

'I know. It's a lot to think about. But my brother, Noah, he fell in love with the beautiful Marisol when she came from Argentina to learn how to surf one day, and ever since then, all he talks about is going to live in Buenos Aires. Don't get me wrong, it's as romantic as hell. And probably the reason he never finishes the barn conversion is because his mind is on the South American beauty who stole his heart. She is absolutely amazing. I can't blame him. But can you really see me running a business?'

'Well, why not?'

'Let's just say it's given me a lot to think about.'

'You've got time, though, right?' asked Daniel.

'Well, a limited amount. Noah wants to have moved by this time next year.' She messed her hair again, and Daniel found himself mirroring her. 'So, what about you, Daniel? Will you stay in Cornwall or leave eventually?'

'I guess we're in the same boat,' he said, not committing to anything either way. 'My sister is pressuring me to stay but I don't know if I can. So I have a lot to think about, too.'

'Well, let's not think about it now.' She picked up one of the pastries, heavily layered with white icing sugar, and pushed it into Daniel's mouth so that he was forced to take a huge bite. 'This will ease all that worry about the future away.'

Daniel chewed on an enormous mouthful of pastry, smiling as Jess bit off an equally large helping. She suppressed a laugh as she chewed, the back of her hand over her mouth.

Daniel had made no solid plans for his future but with Jess there he was in no hurry to leave Cornwall straight away. He took another bite of the pastry and wondered what Jess would eventually do. Would the idea of managing her brother's business be enough to keep her here or would she up and leave one day? If she did, he really hoped it wouldn't be soon.

9

When Daniel dropped Annabelle's Range Rover back to her later that morning he caught a quick glimpse of his brother-in-law, Scott, whom he hadn't seen since Gran's funeral. Before he could ask Scott how he was, Annabelle hurried Daniel back out to the drive so that she could inspect her returned vehicle. Daniel watched the hawk-like way Annabelle looked for prangs or scratches in the bodywork. He wondered how his sister found the energy to be this intense when she had a family, a large house, a vlog, and now Daniel himself, to manage. Annabelle seemed happy with her life, settled, which was probably why she was so keen for Daniel to emulate it.

Rasmus and Mia came outside. Mia walked up to her uncle to say a happy but formal hello while Rasmus hovered by the front door. Daniel lugged the pink bicycle out from the boot of the Range Rover and after slamming the boot shut he found that, instead of taking refuge behind his mother's thigh, Rasmus was standing very close by. His face was turned up towards Daniel but his eyes were closed. Daniel didn't dare say a word to Rasmus or attempt to pat him on the head, allowing him to take in as much of Daniel's essence as needed.

'I think he likes you,' said Mia, blinking through the small spheres of her glasses. They made her blue eyes look larger than they were; her long lashes swept against the high-index plastic as she blinked.

'I'm glad about that,' said Daniel. 'Maybe when he gets more used to me you guys can come round and help me do some planting in the garden.'

Rasmus opened his eyes. Mia crossed her arms and contemplated the idea.

'We'll let you know.' She turned on her heel and Rasmus followed close behind her as they returned to the house.

'Another good male role model in their lives is going to do wonders for them,' Annabelle said.

'Me a role model?' Daniel scoffed at the idea. 'I think we should leave that to Scott, don't you?'

Annabelle sighed.

'It isn't as hard as all that, you know?' she said. 'Rasmus is already feeling your essence. The longer you stay the easier it will be for him to warm to you.'

Her little dig about Daniel sticking around didn't go unnoticed.

'I'll see what I can do but right now I'd better get off.' Daniel climbed onto the pink bike as quickly as he could and sped back to the village.

Close to Gran's, Daniel saw that Hazel was out in her front garden so he jumped off the bike to say hello.

'You're looking very bright and cheery,' Hazel said as he leaned his bike on the front gate. 'Had a good morning?'

'Very good, actually. I managed a bit of a surf earlier.'

'That's nice. And I see you have a new bike,' said Hazel, peering over the gate.

'Borrowed. You're the cycling expert, though – maybe you could show me a few tricks, a few wheelies.'

Hazel's eyes squeezed closed as she laughed at the suggestion. The sound was soft and bouncy, like a song, as it tripped from her mouth. She wiped a loose tear and sniffed.

'I don't think I can ride one of these again,' she said.

'They say you never forget.'

'True, but you can't get very far with a dodgy leg.'

'How did you hurt your leg, if you don't mind my asking?' said Daniel.

'Long story,' said Hazel. 'I'm about to have lunch. Care to join?'

He thought back to the staggering breakfast he'd had with Jess earlier. Not wishing to offend her and hopeful that Hazel's lunch might not be as calorific and stodgy, he accepted.

'What are we having?' he asked, wheeling the bike to the front trellis and leaning it close to Hazel's front door.

'Just some soup,' she said as she wiped her feet on the mat and held the door open.

'I can do soup.'

Daniel expected a bowlful of some tinned variety from the supermarket. He hadn't anticipated Hazel's traditional Trinidadian corn soup, made with creamed corn, lots of vegetables and an ample helping of oversized dumplings. The pot on the stove held enough to feed an army. Hazel poured three large ladles of the thick, heavy mixture into a deep bowl for Daniel and would have poured a fourth had he not held up a hand to stop her. For herself she poured a half ladle and sat down at the kitchen table opposite Daniel.

'This smells divine,' he said.

'I hope you like it and I hope you don't mind spicy.'

'I can handle spicy, just don't be offended if I can't eat all of it.'

'Not at all and I insist you take some away with you. I

always make too much. I never got out of the habit of cooking for a family of five, even when it was just for me and Henry.'

Daniel managed to polish off the entire bowl of soup. So intrigued by the story that led to Hazel hurting her leg, he kept piling the soup into his mouth as he listened.

In the summer before Hazel was due to start university, she decided to buy a motorbike and ride around Europe. Her father was very keen for his three daughters not to settle into any of the stereotypical roles for a black woman in fifties London, nurse, secretary or wife, if it didn't suit them. He made sure they studied hard and kept an open mind about their future. For Hazel's twelfth birthday her father had bought her a book about famous women explorers. Her favourite had been Nellie Bly until Hazel read about Annie Londonderry who had cycled around the world in a year, setting out in 1894, and she imagined herself doing the same one day.

'I was used to cycling so I wasn't afraid to ride off on a bike,' said Hazel. 'I'd finished my A levels and I was due to take up my place at the University of Leeds later that year. I couldn't do what Annie Londonderry did, I only had one summer for my cycling adventure, not a whole year. There was no way my parents would let me miss the start of university and I was determined to do something with my summer, even if I couldn't cycle the globe. So I lowered my sights. I decided on Europe only and that a motorbike could get me around quicker. My only problem was, not only did I not have a motorbike, I didn't have a clue how to ride one. I reasoned that it couldn't be much harder than cycling up and down Brixton Hill in busy traffic.'

'So you took lessons?'

'Actually . . .' She sniggered. 'I bought the bike first. I'd been saving all the money I earned on paper rounds, baby-sitting, summer and Saturday jobs at Boots, plus most of my pocket money. I'd seen an advertisement about a bike going cheap in a shop window. It read something like "BSA C11 250cc, single cylinder, rear suspension, overhead valve engine, dynamo electrics".'

'And you knew all about motorcycles?' Daniel leaned forward on his elbows.

'Not a sausage but it all sounded impressive. Plus the garage was in Streatham and that wasn't too far. I jumped on a bus and off I went to take a look at the bike. When I got there, the garage was filled with young men with greasy hands and wearing dirty overalls. Turns out it was one of the young mechanics who was selling his bike.'

'Did you take someone with you? Your dad?'

Hazel shook her head and laughed.

'My parents didn't know what I had planned exactly. All they knew was that I was thinking about taking a trip before going to Leeds. Cheekily I bought the bike before asking them first if I could, because they would only have said I couldn't.'

Daniel cleared the table and put the kettle on. He hoped he would remember how to make tea the way Hazel had, while listening to her story at the same time.

'So, the boy selling the bike,' she went on. 'He was tall. Very tall, like you, only he had the whitest skin I'd ever seen and his hair was the colour of carrots.' She put a hand over her mouth and chuckled. 'I also thought he was the hand-somest boy I'd ever seen. A red–haired version of Farley Granger.'

'I don't know what he looks like, but I take it he was buff.'

'I don't know what buff is but if that means gorgeous and sexy then yes, he was buff.'

Daniel laughed aloud. He checked the timer on his phone as the tea brewed.

'You're killing me, Hazel.'

'Well, I thought I might kill myself when this boy asked if I wanted to take the bike for a spin. I was too proud to say I didn't know how to ride, I thought I might be able to figure it out for myself. So I got up on the bike, held the handlebars, looked at the buttons and gauges in front of me and drew a blank. The whole garage had fallen silent. In fact, they'd stopped everything when I first walked in, even the radio. I looked at the boy whose bike it was and he was grinning. "It's a kickstart," he said and when I still sat there looking gormless he said, "You've not ridden one of these, have you?" I shook my head. I was so embarrassed I wanted to run off but I was determined to have this adventure of mine. Really keen. "I can learn," I told him and got off the bike again. He was very kind about it. Didn't laugh at me or smirk like the others were doing. And then when it looked as if this boy had taken a liking to me, I could feel the tension in the place mounting. But this boy,' she chuckled again. 'He didn't care at all that we were different. He offered to throw in lessons and a free helmet if I bought the bike. Who was I to refuse? I had made up my mind I was going to motor-cycle around Europe and nothing could stop me. Do you know, I was able to ride that bike in days. I made up excuses to go to Streatham every day, didn't even tell my sisters about it. Got the hang of it just like that.' Here Hazel snapped her fingers. 'But I had the best teacher.'

'And then you rode off into the sunset.' Daniel brought the mugs to the table and added his milk and sugar. Milk and sugar always comes after the pouring of the tea. That much he had learned from Hazel the week before.

'Not quite. Before I could ride off anywhere I had to decide if I wanted to do this ride across Europe solo or with a companion.'

'The carrot top from the garage?'

'The very one. He said that he didn't want me riding out of his life and could he come with me.'

'Now that's cool. I don't think I could come up with a line like that.'

'That's just it.' Hazel let out a long yawn. 'It wasn't a line. He meant it from the heart. He said he fell in love with me the minute he saw me.'

Daniel remained quiet.

'I felt the same about him,' said Hazel. 'Only it took until I learned how to go around corners and do hand signals before I realized how much I wanted him to come too. I agreed to him coming with me and said that we'd start with the UK first to make sure we got on.'

'And your parents were all right with their daughter zooming off down the highway with some mechanic from Streatham?'

'Honestly? We were up against it. I kept saying to Mum and Dad it's only around the UK to start. They said even that was too much and had I even passed a driving test.'

'Had you?'

'I only needed a provisional licence for the UK. Driving in Europe was a whole other story but I didn't want to get into that with Mum and Dad. You should have heard me pleading my case. Dad was so worried about me. It was bad enough me going on my own but with a *boy*. I told him everything would be above board, separate rooms, nothing to worry about. Then Dad worried that he was white and how would we cope with the discrimination? I told him that he'd raised us to know our worth and I wasn't afraid. Days, this went on for. Then, finally, Dad relented and said I could go as long as he met the boy first. My mum sobbed her eyes out for a whole week. They were scared to let me go but they both liked him after he'd come for tea.' Hazel's eyes began to droop and she tried to suppress another yawn. '*His* family hated me on sight, however, and they disowned him.'

'That's terrible, Hazel. I'm sorry you had to go through that.'

'I told you we were up against it.' She looked down and placed one hand on top of the other on the table. 'And, you know, I never got to go to university that year because once we made it to Europe we decided to stay on the road for as long as we could.'

'You got a full licence?'

'Not at first, but I'll tell you all about what came next another time. I did manage to take my degree when we finally returned home.'

'What about the boy? What happened after you came back?'

'We got married. Stayed married until he died last year.'

'That was Henry?'

Hazel nodded slowly and stretched her upper back.

'You need your nap,' Daniel said. He helped Hazel to her chair in the living room and placed the throw from the sofa over her knees.

'You're a good boy, Daniel. And I still haven't told you how I hurt my leg, have I?'

'That's all right. I'll catch up with you in the week. Maybe you can tell me on the next walk.'

Hazel's eyes closed as she sighed and then she was asleep.

Daniel let himself out and wheeled the bike up the hill to the house. The cat, who was sleeping on the outside doormat, raised a head when he heard Daniel come closer.

'You still here?' he asked the cat. Before opening the door he checked his phone for messages. It only occurred to him then, after days of feeding the cat, that no one had called to claim it. Maybe the owner had moved away and no longer wanted it. Maybe this mysterious cat had travelled a long distance and couldn't find its way back home. Either way it sped into the house and sat by the fridge looking anxiously up at Daniel.

Buying actual cat food for his squatter was a sure way to encourage it to stay. But with no calls since he'd put the posters up it looked as if he was stuck with the cat for now.

'Here,' said Daniel as he placed a saucer of food on the floor for the purring moggy. 'It can't beat bacon sandwiches or Trinidadian corn soup but it's the best I can do.'

Daniel realized as he sat with his feet up in the living room, resting after a heart-attack-worthy breakfast and a feast of a soup, all within the space of a few hours, that he hadn't exchanged numbers with Jess.

The cat slunk into the room and sprung up onto the arm of the sofa. He made himself as comfortable as Daniel and they both fell asleep.

10

The hallway was clear of Daniel's luggage. In fact, he'd completely unpacked everything and had managed to find a home for most of his possessions in the small back bedroom that he and the cat were camped out in. The bed, usually unmade, was where the cat curled up for most of the afternoon, allowing Daniel to get on with the serious task of organizing the house. Daniel had been on a mission since the start of the week. With an early morning warm up and stretch, he did the run he'd intended to take around the village in his first week. This time, he ran a lot further, without injury, and happened to see the grumpy man in the flat cap with the equally grumpy grey whippet. The dog had followed Daniel for a few metres of his run before letting out a defeated bark which echoed around the deserted square. The old man had nodded to Daniel and seemed to approve of the fact that Daniel remained on his feet.

He whizzed past the cat poster in the square but saw that his Walkers Club flyer had been removed. It seemed the people of Trevone were more concerned about lost cats than they were with getting fit. Strange, though, that no one had called about his squatter yet.

After breakfast and a shower, Daniel searched online for

someone to remove the antiquated furniture from the house. The local charity interested in second-hand furniture in good condition was due to come and make a collection that week of a few tables, chairs, mirrors and a shelving unit. All the large items like the sofas and armchairs that the charity couldn't use would be collected by the council as large waste. All he needed to do was pay the fee and settle on a date for collection. He was finally getting things in motion. He looked up the local recycling centre and a van hire company so that he could take other unwanted items away. His plan was to strip the house bare and redecorate from top to bottom. The house was, for the most part, in good repair. It could prob-ably use new windows, though, as the frames were rotting in places and he could update them with double glazing. He had looked at online estate agencies to see what he and Annabelle could get for the house. His share could feasibly be enough for a decent deposit on a flat if he moved back to London.

On Tuesday he'd gone as far as he could with clearing the bedrooms and bathroom. The army uniforms lay on Gran's bed. He had fished them out of the bin bag and decided to hang onto them, since hearing about his grandparents' war efforts from Hazel. Downstairs he gathered the small items, soft furnishings, ornaments, books and anything that he hadn't found a home for and sorted them into three piles. One of items to keep, one to toss out and one for charity. He'd go around the whole of the ground floor putting things into their respective piles until everything was accounted for.

In the conservatory were two chairs to be collected by the council, plus a round wooden table. The plants in the conservatory, he would sort out and keep. They sat on a waist-height shelf that ran along three of the walls in the conservatory. The shelf was covered in a pink and yellow fabric, which was also used to make a curtain that was attached to the shelf by a rail and fell to the tiles on the conservatory floor. He pulled the curtain aside and found storage shelves filled with miscellanea: empty flower pots, small garden tools, old boots and a couple of large cardboard boxes. Daniel sighed at the thought of another rummage through more boxes and shelves of old junk but instantly remembered Gran's journals. He pulled the boxes out; a spider scuttled out from under one of them, and both boxes left a trail of dust along the conservatory floor.

The first box was filled with books. An assortment of recipe and gardening books, car manuals and fiction. Some were for charity and some so yellowed and worn they would have to be thrown away. He added them to the piles he'd created in the living room.

The second box was the one he'd been hoping to find upstairs when he'd gone through the cupboards, looked under beds and pulled things off shelves. His grandmother's journals were in this box. They sat in the centre of piles of sheet music, knitting patterns, drawings and paintings that he and Annabelle had made and a partially filled photo album. He flicked through the pages of the album. He found photos of his parents' wedding. His mother had a brunette version of Lady Diana Spencer's hairstyle and flowers around her veil. His father's hair had always been wiry and someone must have brushed it down with wallpaper paste because it looked more like a helmet than actual hair. The picture of Annabelle and Scott on their wedding day looked professionally staged. A slimmer and smiley Annabelle posed under a tree beside Scott who wore a cummerbund that matched the bridesmaids' dresses. On one of the pages, Daniel found his graduation day photo. He didn't know Gran had one of those. He couldn't remember wearing his hair so long and wondered whatever happened to his engineering degree certificate. He had a vivid recollection then of Gran and Gramps presenting him with a cheque after his mother encouraged him to go to their house to show them his certificate. Gran had held his hand and said he could go anywhere and do anything now. He suspected she hadn't meant picking grapes and ending up with sunstroke, which was exactly what he'd done the summer he'd graduated. He'd taken off with a friend to Portugal and never really looked back.

Daniel left everything in the box except Gran's journals, which he carried to one of the old easy chairs in the conservatory. He placed them on the low table between the chairs. There were five journals: two were old school exercise books and three were hardback notepads. They were bound together by a ribbon. On the inside cover of each journal was the name Margaret Sneldon, and a year. The earliest was 1941, the latest, 1945. He fanned through the pages of the one dated 1941 and items fell from them like autumn leaves. In his lap was a dried flower, two black and white photos and a folded piece of paper. He was annoyed at himself for not taking more care because he wouldn't know which entry in the journal the items were for. His gran had dated each entry.

The first pages of the 1941 journal seemed official. There was a name and an address in Cornwall scribbled in block capitals. Mrs Arthur Trevarthen, Trevarthen Farm, St Austell. Below this was the name Margaret Sneldon and an address in Lancashire. The next few pages were blank but further on there was a list of rules about keeping sleeping quarters tidy, keeping the uniform clean, soap rations, meal times and working hours. In places where her handwriting was untidy,

Gran had crossed it through and rewritten the instructions more neatly. She had drawn a picture of a face, a woman with curly hair, glasses and a pig snout. Daniel wondered if this was a picture of Mrs Trevarthen or some other official who was in charge of the Land Girls and who had given them the list of Dos and Don'ts.

Daniel looked up and saw that the cat had wandered in and had been watching him, blue eyes alert and questioning. Just as he hadn't thought Gran to be a cat person, he couldn't imagine her drawing comic sketches in her journal either. Maybe she'd set it down and one of the other girls drew the picture of the woman with the pig snout.

He looked at the faded photograph that had fallen onto his lap of three young women in uniform like the one in Gran's room. They wore ties, caps, knee-length breeches and large overcoats. All three women looked proud and had wide grins on their faces. He tried to make out which of them was Gran. If he was right, she looked the youngest out of the three and she didn't appear at all nervous.

Daniel put the first journal aside. If he was going to read through them all, he'd need coffee and snacks. He eased himself out of the chair. The cat had settled down for a sleep at his feet and didn't budge while Daniel went to make himself a ham and cheese sandwich and a mug of coffee. He grabbed a packet of Hobnobs for good measure and made himself comfortable in the conservatory.

In a few hours, Daniel had read through each journal. He discovered that Gran had been stationed at several farms in Cornwall during the war. Trevarthen Farm was one she would return to and stay for nearly a year. In her years in the Land Army, Gran had learned to drive a tractor and a lorry and to ride a motorbike. She moved workers from their base to the farms they were required to work at. She drove around Cornwall keeping the directions memorized because there were no signposts permitted on the roads during the war. He learned that the women worked the land all year round in cold and rain and blazing heat. His grandmother had learned how to milk cows, sow the land, harvest the grain and how to kill the rats that tried to eat it. Daniel pictured her as a young woman working long hours in the fields and he understood then why her hands had felt rough to him as a young boy.

He stared at Gran's carefree demeanour in a snapshot alongside four young women on the beach in bathing costumes and another in which she was in uniform with another girl, each with a cigarette between their fingers.

There was even a mention of prisoners of war being held in cells in Penzance. His grandmother had sneaked them extra rations of Spam, dried eggs, and whatever food she could because they had very little to live on. She believed her generosity might somehow find its way into the heart of someone like her who would help keep imprisoned British soldiers abroad alive. This account was in the last journal in early 1945. Gran had met Gramps by then and had fallen in love with him as well as with Cornwall. Daniel found himself fascinated by the love story of the soldier who had returned to Cornwall just before the end of the war and the Land Girl who had taken very little leave over the years in order to continue her work on the land. Gramps was ten years older than Gran and he'd been sent home from active duty because of a serious back injury. The injury had been so bad he couldn't dance at the VE Day celebrations. He and Gran had stood swaying, cheek to cheek, as everyone danced around them.

The cat was woken when someone knocked on the door. He looked accusingly at Daniel and arched his back into a deep stretch. Daniel put the photos down onto the table and raised an eyebrow at the cat.

'Could it be that someone has come to claim you at last, you good for nothing squatter?' The cat rushed into the garden as Daniel went to answer the door.

Hazel stood there leaning on her stick and holding a plastic bowl with a lid.

'You didn't take any soup with you on Sunday and I don't think it will keep much longer.' Hazel wore a pea green tracksuit and her trainers.

'Come in, Hazel.' Daniel took the bowl. 'I know what I'm having for dinner tonight.'

Hazel stayed for a cup of tea. They sat in the conservatory to drink it as Daniel told her everything he now knew about his grandmother.

'I suspect Annabelle won't know half of this,' said Daniel. 'I can't wait to show her. Thanks for telling me about Gran's journals.'

'Well, you would have found them eventually,' said Hazel.

'Yes, but I might easily have binned them if I didn't know they existed.'

'And that would have been a great pity.' Hazel looked around at the empty shelves. 'I see you're all organized.'

'The journals were the last things to go through. Gran was a different person from the one I knew. I can't get over seeing her smiling in photos. In a swimsuit. Being so young.'

'And it's while you're young that you make sure you live as full a life as you can. Don't get to my age and have regrets.'

'Regrets such as getting a move on and settling down? As Annabelle keeps saying.'

'If settling down would make you happy then perhaps you should.'

'And what about Gran? Do you think she had any regrets?'

Hazel hesitated before she answered. 'Maybe . . . perhaps.' She gazed anxiously around as though the dry plants in the conservatory had suddenly become of great importance.

'Anything I should know?' asked Daniel. Hazel refused to make eye contact.

'Well,' she said after some thought, 'Molly didn't regret leaving home and coming to Cornwall. And her family came round to her way of thinking in the end, even though it was hard at first. They understood she was determined to join the WLA and wanted to do her duty. She used to send them photos. I suppose that's why there aren't that many here. Her entire family came down to Cornwall when she married your grandfather.'

Daniel sensed that Hazel was being evasive but couldn't understand why. He suspected that Gran must have had at least one regret. He didn't think he could prise it out of Hazel but he tried all the same.

'What about music college?' he said. 'Do you think she ever regretted not going to London to study?'

'I don't believe she did. During the war, the powers that be used to send variety acts out every weekend to entertain the workers who stayed at the camps and hostels. But mostly everyone wanted to hear your gran play the piano. She'd rally the girls around the old stand up for a singsong. And when she was driving the lorries, transporting them from farm to farm, she used to start a sing-a-long. She was bashful to admit it but I believe she had quite a good singing voice.'

'I can imagine that,' said Daniel. 'Every time I find something else out about Gran it triggers a memory that I never knew I had.'

'Like?'

'Like, I can actually remember hearing my gran sing. Not to me particularly, but she sang when she was cooking. I'm sure of it.' He looked off into the distance and had a vivid recollection of her singing in the kitchen. The kitchen where she'd told him he wasn't allowed to run. 'I think I got Gran all wrong. She couldn't have been so stern and serious, could she?'

Hazel smiled and slowly shook her head.

'And the fact that Gran worked on farms brought back another memory,' Daniel continued. 'In my mind it was Gramps who had the green fingers. Even though he was the one who took me and Annabelle out to play in the garden, it really belonged to Gran. She was the one who had me on my knees, digging up the earth and teaching me all kinds of things about growing vegetables. I guess I was too young to appreciate it but I'm pretty sure I loved it.'

'She told me you did,' said Hazel. She nodded knowingly.

Daniel grinned to himself.

'There is another thing, though, Hazel.' Daniel leaned back in his chair.

'What's that?' asked Hazel.

'Well, I found an awful lot of scarves in the drawers upstairs. Annabelle took them all to charity, which is fine, but I just wondered why there were so many?'

Hazel chuckled, her shoulders shaking while her eyes scrunched closed.

'What's so funny?'

'Most, if not all, of those scarves were presents from your grandfather. Every year, birthday, Christmas, anniversary, you name it, a scarf would make up part of his present to your gran.'

'But why scarves?'

'You'll see in old footage and photographs that many of the Land Girls tied their hair off their faces and necks with cotton scarves while they worked. Molly had wanted to keep all of her scarves from those days for old time's sake. Your grandfather never knew that and threw them all out when they moved here shortly after getting married. Molly was livid. So he'd tried to make it up to her. You can imagine the number of scarves she owned after so many years of marriage. More than you found.'

'What happened to them all?'

'Molly would have given some away as presents or to charity. One thing is for sure, she did miss his presents when he passed away. They were ever such a romantic couple from what I can gather.'

Daniel couldn't get his head around the Gran he knew being lovey dovey and having candlelit dinners, but the girl in the photos would most certainly have gone in for a few.

'And now I'll get out of your hair and let you carry on, Daniel.' Hazel rose to her feet, leaning heavily on her walking stick.

'I'm nearly finished here,' said Daniel, rising to see Hazel out. 'Everything will be out of the house by the end of next week and then I can start decorating.'

Hazel stopped at the front door.

'So you've decided to stay?' She looked hopeful but Daniel still hadn't made a plan for his future. He had to weigh up the possibilities. His ideal job had to be as fulfilling as his last, and even if it didn't have all the excitement, it should have some security. At least that was something to have rubbed off on him from Annabelle's lectures.

'Don't worry, Daniel, I think you'll find what you're

searching for,' said Hazel. 'And when you do, I hope you find
it here.'

'That's nice of you to say, Hazel,' said Daniel.

'Well, I'm just being honest. And you know, sometimes
the thing you are looking for is staring you right in the face.'

'Does that mean I have to look harder? I obviously can't
see anything. Nothing concrete.'

'Maybe that's because you're still holding on to the past.'

Daniel looked at Hazel, at the smiley face and round
cheeks. Surely she couldn't tap into his memories of the past.
He was already reconciled to the loss of his job. Practically
everyone he knew from university had moved into a job
with security, one that at least came with a pension. There
was Aria from his past, of course. He'd never had closure
where she was concerned. Aria had left him high and dry
and he never knew what he'd done wrong and what made
her go rushing back into the arms of her ex-boyfriend.

'Who knows?' said Daniel. 'Maybe when the house business is all finished, I can sort my head out properly.'

'And move on with your life?'

'Here's hoping.'

Daniel stood in the doorway, deep in thought with his
arms folded, while Hazel made her way back down the hill
to her house.

11

At first light the waves were between four and six feet high. A lively Dalmatian ran across the sand, leaping up to catch the ball its owner threw out towards the shoreline every time the dog bounded back with the soggy ball in its mouth. Two people were out on their surfboards. The temperature was low, the breeze cool on Daniel's face as he lay on his board and paddled his arms through the water.

He was feeling relaxed, not worried or even thinking about his future. He'd organized everything in the house. The large waste items had been collected. The drivers from the charity were due to arrive in the afternoon and all he needed to do was hire a van to take boxes and bags to either the charity shop in Padstow or to the recycling centre.

The waves settled to a wild ripple, lashing against the rockface at the sides of the beach and becoming nothing but a small swell which the other surfers gave up on. They waved to Daniel before heading back to their van. He bent to pick up his board as he left the sea and saw a familiar figure near the car park pointing a camera in his direction. Jess signalled that she was coming over to him and snapped one more shot. Daniel wondered how long she had been there taking pictures.

'Didn't expect to see you here,' Daniel said as she approached.

'I saw the surfers as I was cycling. I wanted to capture their mood. I didn't realize one of them was you.'

'I can't seem to keep away from the sea. I've really missed this.' Daniel thought back to his teenage years when his surfing skills were at their best. He and his friends were quite competitive back then but now he revelled in the sheer pleasure the water brought him. He grinned at Jess. 'I'd love to see the photos when they're developed.'

'Of course.' She smiled back, sun sparkling off the water reflected in her eyes.

'We didn't swap numbers last time we ran into each other,' said Daniel.

'Here.' Jess took her phone out of the back pocket of her jeans. She unlocked it and handed the phone to Daniel. 'Put your digits in here. I like the element of surprise, but it would be nice to actually co-ordinate a meet up.'

He handed the phone back. 'You mean like a date?'

'Yes, exactly like a date.' Jess tapped her phone before putting it away. 'Now I have your number I can call you.'

'Any time,' Daniel said. His cheeks turned pink. 'That is, I have all this time on my hands now that I've practically finished clearing the house. Next I'm going to decorate it.'

'In between surfs?'

'Something like that.'

They walked back towards the surf shop where Jess had left her bike.

'What about now?' said Daniel.

'What about now, what?'

'A date,' said Daniel. 'How about breakfast? This time it's my treat.'

'Sounds good to me. I can always eat.'

'I don't live too far and I have to get my wetsuit off,' said Daniel. 'So I'll rustle something up.'

Daniel carried his board and Jess wheeled her bike back to the house. While walking, he tried to remember what was in the kitchen to eat apart from a box of Shreddies and whether he'd used the last of the milk.

Jess nodded to one of Daniel's 'Found' posters, pinned to a tree, flapping so furiously in the wind it was likely to blow away.

'You still haven't found a home for your cat?'

'Not a single person has phoned,' he said as they passed Hazel's house and walked up the hill.

'You could always keep it,' said Jess.

'I can't commit to that. I don't know how long I'm going to be around.'

Jess blushed at this and remained silent.

'I'm not going as soon as all that,' he said. 'I've still got to decorate and everything, but my future is uncertain. I'm sorry.'

'Hey, don't apologize to me. You do you. You know I get it.'

Jess leaned her bike against the side of the front door and Daniel let them into the house.

'Excuse the mess. Make yourself at home and I'll change out of this.' He tugged at his wetsuit and bounded up the stairs to his room.

The house was in a real mess. Though he had shifted some furniture out and Annabelle had taken things away, he hadn't done much in the way of cleaning. Jess could hardly make herself comfortable in a place whose surfaces were under several layers of dust. Then he remembered what she'd said about her brother's barn conversion. Maybe she wouldn't mind the state of the house so much. Someone like Aria would have complained non-stop. But why was he thinking of her now? The question of what he could put together for Jess for breakfast was far more important. He threw on a sweat top and jeans and raced back downstairs.

Jess was in the kitchen, the fridge door open as she and the cat peered into it.

'Your menu more or less sucks, Daniel.' She let the fridge door close. 'Soup, a couple of eggs and . . .' She picked up a box of Shreddies from the kitchen counter and shook it. It sounded as though there was less than a bowlful of cereal in it. 'I suppose you could whip up an omelette with the tomatoes and that sorry-looking slice of ham you've got in there.'

Daniel stared at her and at the cereal packet she continued to shake, his lips pulled in.

'You can't make an omelette, can you, Daniel?'

He shook his head. 'I think I can boil an egg.'

'You *think*?' Jess looked down at the cat who looked back up at her.

'I did tell you I wasn't much of a cook,' he whimpered. 'You knew what you were getting into when I said I'd make you breakfast.'

'Well, okay, Daniel. You do the drinks and I'll do the omelette.'

'Deal. I make a serious cup of tea. You'll see.' He pushed up his sleeves and set about brewing a pot of tea, leaving Jess shaking her head and pulling out food, past or very close to its 'Best Before' date, out of the fridge.

They sat with plates on their laps in the conservatory on two of the few remaining chairs. The dining and kitchen table had gone, which left the low table in the conservatory as the only one in the whole house. That is if you didn't count the upside-down bucket Daniel was using to balance his cereal bowl on in front of the television.

'What will you sit on when all of this has gone?' asked Jess, waving her fork around the conservatory.

'My sister has offered to put me up when the house is down to its bare walls. Then I'll just come over to decorate.'

'And then you'll sell the house and then you'll leave.'

'And you?' he asked, putting a large mouthful of omelette into his mouth. It was easier to redirect the question than to try to explain how impossible it was for him to come to any kind of decision. Maybe he could become a professional house clearer. Or a cat trainer. A beach bum. Or perhaps he'd just go with the flow for a while and see where life took him. At his feet was the box of Gran's journals. She had been able to make decisions about her life. She'd wanted to fulfil a need to help with the war effort and ended up staying in Cornwall because she'd met the love of her life.

'Let's make a pact,' said Jess, putting her plate on the low table so she could pick up her mug of tea. 'How about we never ask each other what we're going to do next? When we meet, we keep it casual, nothing heavy. Let's face it, you've got pressure from your family and I've got pressure from mine. So you and I can just be chill with each other. We see each other while we're still here and go on a few dates that don't involve stale food?'

'That sounds perfect. All I know is, I'll probably be here for the summer at least and perhaps you will, too.'

Jess raised her mug. 'Here's to no stress, no decision days.' She knocked her mug against Daniel's and they sipped their tea. 'This really is a good cup of tea, Daniel. I seriously had you down as a loser before I tasted this.' She drank some more.

'It's a bit of a family secret. I could teach you.'

'But then you'd have to kill me?' Jess turned her phone over. 'I'm late.'

'You off to Harlyn?'

'Yes, the surf shop awaits. I have to go.'

She carried her mug and plate to the kitchen, Daniel following close behind.

At the front door she stepped up on her toes to kiss Daniel on the cheek.

'No decisions. No drama,' she said and rode away. The creak of her bicycle faded into the distance.

Now that Jess had his number, and despite their no decisions pact, he really hoped she would decide to call him soon.

12

Hazel was about to enter the car park at Trevone Beach just ahead of Daniel when he arrived for the Walkers Club walk. It was set to be a sunny spring day, fresh and breezy. There were wisps of white in the blue sky.

'Hi, Hazel,' Daniel said as he got closer to her.

'Oh, Daniel, you made me jump.'

'I'm sorry.'

'I was miles away. I was wondering if the couple from last week would be nicer to each other today.'

'I doubt it,' said Daniel, looking around to see if either would show up.

The ownership of the coastal path walk had been awarded to Amanda. Keith Hunter was nowhere in sight and his ex-wife jiggled up and down with glee when she saw Daniel.

'It's going to be a lovely day, Daniel,' said Amanda. 'I can't wait to get going.' There was a vast difference in colour between her face and her neck today. The skin on her neck was pink and crepey and her face was a light shade of brown. Her cheeks had been blobbed indiscriminately with red blusher and the muscles on her forehead refused to move.

'Look,' she said. 'I have my walking socks. As recommended by our intrepid leader.'

Daniel might have described himself as intrepid when he lived in Sicily but this group of walkers had not managed to walk for more than thirty minutes. He had originally planned to have them walk to Harlyn, sit on the beach to catch their breath, and then head back to Trevone. He'd calculated the walk would take an hour to complete. Not only had his group not walked for an hour, they had never come close to the halfway point. He realized that it wasn't worth stressing over the timing of the walk, not since meeting Hazel, her Crocs and her walking stick. At some stage, if more people joined the walk, he might be able to head up a faster group while Hazel took charge of the more leisurely walkers. He realized, instantly, that he was planning ahead and he'd vowed with Jess not to make decisions.

Very soon a couple of women in tracksuits similar to Hazel's approached and waved at him.

'Hi,' said Daniel as the two women arrived. 'Have you come for the Walkers Club?'

'Yes,' said the taller of the two. 'Hazel told us all about it so here we are. I'm Mary.' Mary waved a thin hand and gestured to the woman beside her. 'And this is my sister, Eileen. We bumped into Hazel at the farm shop and she told us how much fun she has on a Saturday walking along the path with you all.'

'Have you done much in the way of exercise?' Daniel asked. Like Amanda the sisters were probably in their late sixties. Unlike Amanda they wore no make-up. Their hair was identical in style and colour, mousey grey and held up in a bun with lots of straight pins. Mary's tracksuit was lime green and Eileen's was blossom white. He looked at their feet. Sensible footwear. Walking shoes and thick walking socks. They both had backpacks and Mary had a walking cane with her.

'Any injuries I should know about?' asked Daniel.

'You sound like a fitness instructor,' Mary said.

'I am actually a qualified personal trainer,' said Daniel. He wanted to go on to explain that he had also been a walking guide but his statement had caused a stir of excitement with Amanda and the sisters.

'I've been looking to hire someone to train me for aeons,' said Amanda. 'No one around here has the right skills, or patience come to that, for my liking.'

'Really?' said Daniel, wishing he had never opened his mouth.

'Really,' said Amanda. She took out her phone. 'Could I trouble you for your number? I need to get working on this body of mine.' She pulled back her shoulders and stuck out her chest so that Daniel would be in no doubt as to which body she was referring to.

Slowly, he took her phone and entered his number.

'We're looking for a trainer, too,' said Mary. 'Would you mind?' She held her mobile out smiling to Daniel who obliged by giving her his number. 'How incredible that we should meet today.'

'Incredible,' said Daniel. 'Maybe we should get going now.'

Daniel led the charge from the car park, around the back of the café, and onto the beach to join the coastal path. 'This way,' he called. 'Hazel is in charge of breaks and water stops. Let's do this.'

A golden retriever bounded up to Daniel, circled his legs and ran back to its owner. Walk number three of the Walkers Club had begun. Amanda was at Daniel's heels breathing deeply and stretching her arms above her head every now and then. Mary was behind her, chatting to Eileen. Hazel brought up the rear and took her time to progress along the path.

After a while, Daniel let Amanda take the lead and dropped back to walk with Hazel.

'Let me take your bag, Hazel,' he said. 'It looks as if you're carrying more snacks than you need.' Daniel helped Hazel off with her backpack. As he suspected, Hazel had anticipated more walkers today, so thought it only fair to have extra supplies. She'd obviously been trying to spread the word about the Walkers Club and it seemed to be working.

'You're a good person, Daniel,' said Hazel after he'd helped her shed some of the weight. 'Very considerate.'

Daniel considered Hazel's compliments and he wondered if she would think him a 'good person' if she knew how rarely he'd come home to his family, how little contact he kept with his parents and that, had it not been for his inheritance, he would never have got to know his niece and nephew. He knew he'd been popular in his last job but how many of his colleagues, apart from Doc, had he really taken the time to get to know? He knew he'd made a great deal of effort to be good and considerate when it came to his relationship with Aria, yet she'd still left him.

'What is it, Daniel?' Hazel burst his bubble of thought. 'You've become quite pensive all of a sudden.'

'Sorry, didn't mean to.'

'You can talk to me.'

'I know. I was just thinking about what you were saying about me being good and considerate.'

'Well, you've certainly been very kind to an old woman you only recently met. Not many people would give someone like me the time of day, but you have. I stand by my decision. You're a good person, Daniel.'

'It's nice of you to say but I'm not even sure that's true.'

'Anything you want to share with an old lady?' Hazel looked up at him and stopped.

'It's a long story,' said Daniel. He laughed to alleviate the weight their conversation had gained and forced a chuckle into his voice as he continued. 'You don't want to know about my evil past but I do want to know how you hurt your leg. You never finished the story.'

'Goodness me, you're right,' she said. 'I remember what happened to my leg as if it were yesterday.' They continued along the path. 'When Henry and I first set off on our adventure we headed north. We got as far as the northernmost tip of Scotland. Not without a few mechanical stops along the way. Henry admitted to me that part of the reason he wanted to come with me was because the bike he sold me was a bit of a dud.'

'Now that's sneaky. Trying to make a fast buck off a poor unsuspecting young woman.'

Hazel giggled and the sisters dropped back to listen to her account. By now their progress was as slow as a tortoise. Even Amanda, whose efforts came more from her breathing than actual pace, was not too far ahead.

'Ah, but he did feel guilty and tried to warn me that the bike was on its last legs,' said Hazel. 'Henry had upgraded his bike so he knew if anything happened to the old one I could always get on the back of his. I was determined to ride my own bike. I'd become quite the motorbiker. I told Henry that I'd keep riding until it gave up on me. I wasn't going to quit.'

'So your accident happened in Scotland?' asked Daniel.

'Actually, no. It happened when we got down here a week or so later. One of the reasons Henry always wanted to retire to Cornwall was because of how beautiful we found it all those years ago on our bike tour. Oh, Daniel, we had some remarkable rides. Saw some breathtaking views. We were a couple of people who hadn't been outside of London, Henry for all of his life and me for the whole time since I arrived there, so we were always agog. It's a shame we neither of us had a camera. I suppose you would use a phone now. But we had to travel light and cheaply, so we saved our money for campsites and hostels. And to eat of course.

'It was near Truro the accident happened. We hadn't found a place to stay for the night. We were hungry, it was turning dark on the country road. We thought we'd find a town soon with a bed and breakfast. One that wouldn't look at us with disdain and make nasty, racist remarks. Don't look like that, Daniel. It did happen.'

Daniel turned to her. 'But you were just this young couple, having fun. Getting on with your lives. It upsets me that you had to go through that. I feel angry.'

'Not as angry as me.' Hazel shook her head. 'That kind of racism was something I'd been dealing with since we arrived here back in 1948, Daniel.'

'I'm sorry,' he said softly as Mary and Eileen nodded in agreement.

'It was a different time back then, it's not so blatant now.' Hazel stepped up the pace which had dragged to almost a standstill. 'Anyway, Henry was riding ahead of me. He passed a side road but when I got to it a car pulled out without stopping. I put the brakes on but the car was right there. I tried to turn but all I did was skid directly into the car's passenger side, my leg caught between the bike and the car and then I was down. You know they say accidents feel as if they happen in slow motion? Well, this happened fast. I had no time to think. One minute I was riding, the next I was on my side, the bike was over, I was lying on the ground and the man in the car was shouting at me for not looking where I was going.'

'That's ridiculous,' said Mary.

'I know, I know.' Hazel nodded. 'I was dazed and in a lot of pain. I thought I'd had it, I can tell you. Henry came back and took the man by his collar. He always had a temper on him. But when he saw I couldn't get up he panicked and pulled me away from the bike. My skin scraped along the ground and I think I passed out for a while. Because I saw the blood, you see?'

'What did you do?' Mary asked. 'Out in the countryside, in the middle of nowhere.'

'Henry sent the man in the car to the town to get help; he didn't dare move me. It was awful. I went off in an ambulance on my own and Henry had to get both bikes into town on foot. He got lucky when he came across a man driving a truck. He flagged him down. At the hospital they gave me a couple of stitches and a bandage and sent me off. No X-ray. Nothing. It turned out I had a fracture in my tibia that went unnoticed. I walked out limping but in a few weeks my leg felt right as rain. It was only after an X-ray, about twenty years later mind you, after I'd had a serious fall during the protest, that the doctor asked how I broke my leg. That's the first I ever knew about my fracture.'

'What protest?' asked Daniel. Hazel looked up and gave him a deep wink. 'Don't tell me, that's a story for another day, right?'

Hazel nodded.

'It's only recently, with age, that my leg has been playing up. That's why I need the stick, Daniel. I also need to take a break for a while. I've got food enough for everyone.'

The path made a giant U-shape above the rocks looking down onto Newtrain Bay. The tide was low and from their position on the clifftop the slopes and scree below were visible. Daniel called out to Amanda who hadn't noticed them stop. She came back puffing and panting.

'Anything wrong?' she asked.

'I need to stop for a quick something to eat,' said Hazel. 'I have plenty.' Daniel handed back her blinged up backpack and they settled themselves on the rocky terrain.

Amanda sat close to Daniel as if he were an oracle. She refused anything to eat and began talking about her weight and how Daniel could help her achieve her goals once he'd become her personal trainer. He hadn't agreed to anything yet but then Mary began to quiz him further about her and Eileen's health training needs. Eileen nodded an approval of Mary's summation of her fitness levels. Daniel was pretty sure he hadn't heard Eileen speak a word so far.

'How much do you charge?' asked Mary.

'£50 an hour,' said Daniel off the top of his head. He had absolutely no idea what personal trainers charged in the area but knew that after he had qualified in London, £50 had been his fee back then.

'That's reasonable,' said Amanda. 'Do you come to the house? Do we meet at the park? Or will I come to you?'

'Look.' Daniel put his hands up. Hazel nibbled her roll and peered over her glasses at him. 'I'm so rusty at the moment. I'd have to really brush up on everything I ever learned just to do one session.'

Somehow that didn't deter any of the women; in fact, Mary showed him that she could still do a plank and Amanda went one further and began a set of knee press-ups until she had to stop and hold her chest.

110

'Of course, with your training I think I could manage more than three,' she said.

Daniel had spotted at least five mistakes in their technique. With desperation he looked over at Hazel for a way out of the whole conversation but she continued to sip tea from her flask and dabbed her lips with a pink serviette.

'Are you married?' Mary asked Daniel out of the blue.

Amanda drew nearer to him.

'No. No, I'm not,' he said, again looking at Hazel who, this time, shrugged her shoulders.

'I was just thinking about a young girl who lives near here who is into health and fitness. You two could make a good pair,' Mary went on.

Eileen nodded enthusiastically.

'Very nice. Very pretty,' said Mary. 'But I don't remember her name. You remember her, don't you, Hazel? From the class at the community centre?'

'Yes, I do,' she said, packing up her food. 'I remember her being very thoughtful and kind to the older generation, but, like the rest of the older generation, I don't remember what she was called either.' She closed the zip of her backpack.

'Oh, she's a lovely girl, Daniel. Long blonde hair. You like blondes?' continued Mary but she didn't give him an opportunity to express a preference. 'Such a shame her classes had to end. Not through any fault of her own, you understand? She was adorable. I tell you what, Daniel, the next time I run into her I'll ask her along on the walk.'

'No, really. Don't go out of your way,' said Daniel. 'I mean, I'm grateful and everything but don't feel as if you need to hook me up. I'm seriously fine as I am.' The last thing he wanted was to get fixed up by Mary. They'd only just met so how would she know what sort of girl he considered lovely?

111

'I don't mind,' said Mary. 'I don't mind at all. We'll be on the lookout for her, won't we, Eileen?'

Eileen wordlessly agreed.

Daniel pulled his bottom lip in with his teeth and looked at Hazel.

'Are we carrying on or heading back, Daniel?' she asked. He rushed to help Hazel up so they could get going.

'We'll start back, I think,' said Daniel. 'Everyone ready?'

Amanda sprang to her feet and stood beside him.

'Ready,' she said and took in a deep breath which she slowly blew directly into Daniel's face.

'Um, well, let's head back then,' he said, avoiding eye contact with Amanda.

For the two and a half kilometre walk back to base Amanda continually commented about the blonde girl Mary had talked about.

'Daniel, you need to be discerning when it comes to women,' Amanda said, gravely. 'This girl might be very nice. Young, I imagine. But have you ever thought about dating someone older than twenty?'

Daniel paused for a moment. Amanda was considerably older than twenty so surely she wasn't suggesting that he ask her out.

'I'm taking Mary's idea with a pinch of salt. I'm just too busy to see anyone – and look,' he said raising his voice and facing the other walkers, 'we're back at base! Thanks for a great afternoon, everyone, and I hope to see you all again next Saturday.'

Amanda and Mary said they couldn't wait for next time and with some reluctance the three women left the car park.

'Now, I'm off to have lunch,' said Hazel.

'With your best pal?' asked Daniel.

'The very one.'

'Should I walk with you?'

'That's okay. I catch the bus.'

'Do you go to lunch every Saturday?' he asked.

'Saturday is convenient now because of the walk but I used to go on a Friday.'

'Your friend is very lucky to have such good company. Once I get my hands on a set of wheels then I can drive you. It can't be easy getting about in the village with your stick.'

'Oh, I get by. Thank you, Daniel.' She patted his arm. 'See you soon.'

Hazel left on her usual route out of the beach complex. Daniel hadn't asked her why this friend couldn't join them for the Saturday walk. He got the sense that Hazel was being evasive regarding her pal so decided not to dig deeper for now. As with all of Hazel's stories, Daniel would get another instalment when she was ready.

13

Before he knew it, Daniel finally managed to have everything organized in the house. He had found it easy, once he'd got into the swing of things, to just keep going. He'd managed to stop dwelling on the circumstances that brought him back to Trevone. The unfortunate passing of his grandmother, his realization, thanks to Annabelle's insistence, that his job held no real future or security. Even the reasons that had driven him away, the constant battle of wills with his father which led to the bad feeling he'd had for his home town, he'd put to the back of his mind to focus on the here and now.

There were positives to his being back. If he hadn't come home, his niece and nephew would remain as strangers to him. Up until his return Mia and Rasmus had merely been snapshots on his Instagram feed. They were his flesh and blood, a part of his family he would never have become close to or really got to know. He was enjoying his relationship with his sister again. He'd missed their in-person bickering and disagreements which had never been as fun via text. He'd grown very fond of Hazel. She was so easy to like. They were becoming good friends and Hazel was the one person who held the key to his finding out more about his grandparents. There was Jess, too. She had immediately softened the blow of his return to Trevone; he enjoyed being in her easy-going yet quirky company.

A few days before the next walk, Annabelle came to the house with Rasmus in the late morning. She'd helped her brother as often as she could but was amazed at how quickly Daniel had arranged the majority of the house clearing tasks.

Dents and ridges remained in the carpets where furniture had sat in the same position for decades. There were tell-tale shapes on the walls of ornaments and photographs now removed for good. Daniel's memory of the smell of his grandparents' house – tea, baking and wood polish – had vanished days after he'd arrived, and as Daniel, Annabelle and Rasmus walked around the near empty house, he had begun to feel like its co-owner.

Rasmus stuck like glue to Daniel, staring up at him with eyes as round as saucers, not blinking once. Even though Annabelle insisted that Rasmus was now used to Daniel's essence, he still had not uttered a word to his uncle. Daniel winked at him, patted his shoulder and smiled wholeheartedly as often as he could as the three of them wandered from room to room. He wanted his essence to be a good one, especially if Rasmus was going to keep such a close watch on his every move.

In the living room they sat on the floor. Rasmus was cross-legged, his elbows on his knees, chin on his tiny fists. He looked up at Daniel as Annabelle rummaged inside the suitcase of her grandparents' army uniforms. She pored over the cuttings from the *Cornwall Women's Land Army Newsletter*, which included knitting patterns for jumpers and socks and articles written by some of the Land Girls. Gran's journals were sat on top of the newsletters and other paperwork.

'You read all the journals?' Annabelle asked Daniel.

'I did. It was a revelation. I mean, did you know about Gran being part of the war effort?'

'Not a thing.' She shook her head. 'It makes me sad to think I never found out about Gran's past until now. It would have been wonderful to have known more about her but I guess I got out of the habit of visiting her when Mum stopped taking us.'

'Is that what happened?

'You probably weren't aware we'd stopped visiting. I remember asking Mum over and over when were we going to visit Gran and Gramps and every time she brushed the subject aside until one day she said we couldn't go there anymore.'

'What? But why?'

'I was too young to understand her reason why. I just accepted it but in the years leading up to Gramps dying I used to drop in to see them. After we lost Gramps I made an effort to visit Gran. I went over as often as I could but when the children came along and I got involved in Parent and Teacher meetings and God knows what else, I went less and less. She only ever wanted to talk about me and the children, not herself. And you, she always asked about you. Is it bad that I neglected Gran?' Her lip began to quiver.

'You were there for her when Mum wasn't, Annie. I was hardly here at all. I feel bad for the both of us so don't be upset. It's not your fault. It's just the way things turned out. Gran loved you. She loved us.'

Annabelle ran her hand over Gran's heavy duty overcoat before closing the suitcase.

'Is it weird to miss someone you hardly knew and never really made the time for?' she said. 'I cried so hard at the funeral but it was mostly out of guilt for not being there for her.'

Rasmus looked from his mother to Daniel, blinking at them curiously.

'If you don't mind,' said Annabelle, 'I'll keep all of their things. The uniforms and everything. Is that all right?'

'Absolutely,' said Daniel. 'And I've decided to stay here while I'm decorating rather than at yours.'

'But the place is empty.'

'I know, but I thought it would make more sense than cycling over every day. I'll need a sleeping bag and a few supplies. Once I've got everything I need I can get going on it straight away.'

'Does that also mean you want to leave us straight away?'

Their voices echoed within the bare walls of the living room. Daniel noticed that Annabelle's eyes were glassy. She blinked and turned away. Daniel looked down at Rasmus.

'Hey, mate? The cat's on his own in the kitchen. Do you think he might like someone to play with in there?'

'I'll ask him,' said Rasmus. These were the first words Daniel had heard from his nephew since he'd arrived from Italy a month ago. He looked quickly at Annabelle who gave him a tearful smile. Daniel's essence had met his nephew's approval. Rasmus left the room and flew his aeroplane to the kitchen to locate the cat.

Annabelle was drying her eyes with the sleeve of her cardigan.

'Seriously, Annie, don't beat yourself up about how many times you visited Gran. Hazel assured me that she had no hard feelings for us. She really cared about us.'

'I know,' she said, looking down. 'It's not about that.'

'So why the tears?'

Annabelle got up and made her way to the window. Daniel had taken the nets and curtains down. She stared outside.

'The tears are because I'm going to lose you, too.' She sniffed.

'I'm not going anywhere.'

'Yet.'

'I thought this was clear from the beginning.' Daniel got to his feet. He stood beside Annabelle as they looked out at Gran's potted plants in the front garden. 'If I stay, I have to find a job here and, let's face it, there isn't much chance of that.' Annabelle said nothing, only sniffed again. He turned his sister to face him, holding her upper arms. 'You've never cried about me leaving before. There's something more, isn't there? I do care, you know?' Daniel dabbed her tears with his fingertips.

'It's just that everyone leaves. First Dad, then Mum, Gran and then . . .'

'Then who? What's happened, Annabelle?' asked Daniel.

Annabelle sighed heavily.

'It's Scott.' She tilted her head upwards and tutted. 'He drives into Plymouth every day. He works long hours and comes home exhausted. I feel as if we've drifted apart.' Annabelle's voice was soft. 'What if . . . What if, he's had enough of me?'

'I don't believe that for one moment. You're amazing, Annie, and if anyone can fix what's broken between you it'll be you. You're the master fixer. You were always the one to act as a buffer between me and Dad. And to be honest, Mum is more in contact with us because of how much you do to make that happen. And don't forget who got me back here – kicking and screaming.'

'I know. But it's easier to fix other people. When it comes to yourself . . . My friend says we're just at that seven-year blip. All married couples go through it apparently. Maybe I spend too much time vlogging.'

Daniel put his arms around his sister and she disappeared into the reach of his big hug.

'Oh Annie, no one ever divorced because of excessive vlogging.' He stepped back. 'You guys need some alone time, that's all. Time to talk things through so you both know where you stand. I'll babysit the kids and you two go on a romantic getaway.'

'You mean for the weekend?'

'I mean for an evening. Your kids are sweet but I don't think I can do forty-eight hours. I'm not that good a role model.'

The door opened and Rasmus walked in with the cat in his arms. Its legs were splayed out in front and it let out a complaining groan before wriggling out of Rasmus's grasp.

'Uncle Daniel,' said the boy, 'can you play too?'

'Of course I can and I've got the perfect game.' Daniel crept playfully towards Rasmus. 'And it's called the upside-down game.' He picked his nephew up and threw him over his shoulder in a fireman hold.

'You're very good with him,' said Annabelle. 'You'll be the perfect babysitter. How about if I arrange something with Scott for this Saturday evening?'

'You're on.' Daniel bounced his nephew up and down and heard a strange hiccupping sound coming from him.

'I forgot to say,' said Annabelle, pulling a face at her brother. 'Rasmus has only just had a morning snack and I think he's just vomited it down the back of your jeans.'

'Bloody hell,' said Daniel. He turned his nephew up the right way. 'Sorry, mate. You okay?'

Rasmus nodded quietly, eyes watering, his little pink lips turned down. Annabelle wiped his mouth with a tissue from her bag.

'Perhaps don't turn them upside down after food when you're over on Saturday,' said Annabelle.

'Got it,' said Daniel. 'And don't worry. You two will sort this out. I'm sure of it.'

Annabelle and a very pale-looking Rasmus left for home.

14

Daniel was crashed out in his sleeping bag in the living room watching *Line of Duty* on iPlayer on Annabelle's old laptop. It was Friday evening, he'd ordered an extra-large pizza and had bought a six pack of beer to wash it down with. His eyelids drooped as the drama unfolded but he was determined to finish the feast he'd treated himself to after having made a start on some house cleaning in preparation for the weeks of decorating ahead. He only wished the sofa was back in the living room; he was getting a crick in his neck from leaning up to watch the screen and three quarters through the pizza he realized that lying down to eat was a sure way to get indigestion. His stomach grumbled a protest as his phone sprang to life. His friend Doc was video calling him from Sicily.

'*Ciao!*' Doc bellowed against the music and loud chatter of Bar Casa Mia. 'I was missing your ugly face.'

Daniel knelt up, shaking off the sleeping bag. 'I miss you too, mate. What's going on there?'

Doc's real name was Vincenzo. He was from Pisa and had been a medical student for three years before deciding to drop out and bum around Europe. He and Daniel had joined the same touring company as walking guides at the same time. Doc had greeted Daniel in perfect English when they'd first met. Daniel had discovered later that Doc got his American-tinged accent from watching *Seinfeld* and *NCIS*. The two had rapidly become best friends.

'It's a party. You're missing it.' The call ended as a girl Daniel didn't recognize grabbed Doc around the neck. Daniel smiled at the blank screen and picked up the last pizza slice, washing it down with the dregs of his Nastro Azzurro. His stomach felt as heavy as his eyes and he fell asleep realizing that, though he missed his friends in Italy, a part of him was glad to be in Trevone.

The phone rang loud and early the following morning. He groaned at the intrusion, felt for his phone and growled into it.

'Yes?'

'Well, that's a nice greeting.' Jess was as bubbly as ever. 'You sound as if I've roused you from your crypt.'

Daniel cleared his throat and swallowed.

'Sorry. I just woke up.' He rubbed his eyes and leaned up on one elbow. 'I'm glad you called.'

'Sorry it's taken so long, I've been really busy.'

'It's good to hear from you. Even if it is ridiculous o'clock in the morning.'

'My bad. I just wanted to catch you before you made plans. Wondered about dinner tonight?'

'Tonight?' Daniel sat up properly. 'Oh no. I promised my sister I'd babysit.'

'Not to worry. It's short notice anyway.'

'Tomorrow night? I'm free every other night for the fore-seeable. What do you say?'

'I say you're on. I'll pick you up at seven.'

'On your bike?'

Jess laughed loudly down the phone.

'I've got my hands on my brother's motor. His girlfriend Marisol is over from Argentina and I can't see them needing the car. They're not likely to leave the bedroom for the next few days. So I've been full time at the shop. He deserves some time off.'

'He's lucky to have you, Jess. I'll see you tomorrow.'

Daniel lay back. He looked up at the ceiling and smiled. A proper date with Jess, finally. Still tired, he set his alarm to be sure not to oversleep and turn up late for the Walkers Club.

Daniel was surprised when he got to the beach complex car park. The Walkers Club had grown in size and Hazel was gathering the walkers together and giving some sort of speech.

'Hey,' he called as he drew closer. He was dishevelled and unshaven and one of his laces had come undone.

'Oh, and here is Daniel,' Hazel announced with a sweeping gesture towards him.

'Morning, everyone.' Daniel nodded and balanced on one leg to tie his shoelace as he acknowledged the new faces as well as Amanda and the sisters. Amanda waved with just her fingertips and a full-on smile. Mary called, 'Hello, Daniel,' over the heads of the new walkers and Eileen repeated, 'Hello, Daniel,' with exactly the same inflections and tone of voice as her sister.

'Great,' said Daniel, swiftly turning his attention to the newcomers. 'We've got some new walking companions today. Nice to meet you. I'm Daniel. Looks like you've already met Hazel.'

One of the newbies, Daniel realized, he had met before. Twice, to be exact, in the village square. It was the old man who wore a grey flat cap and walked his grouchy grey whippet. The whippet was on a lead and bent his sloping back downwards, completely ignoring the tracksuit-clad legs around him.

'I don't suppose you remember me.' Daniel leaned towards the old man with an outstretched hand. 'I was running around the square?'

'Like a madman. I remember,' replied the old man as he shook Daniel's hand. 'This is a walk, though, isn't it? No speeding involved?'

'Absolutely none.' Daniel winked at Hazel.

'Good,' said the man, nodding his approval. 'I'm Eric Laverty and this is Benny – the dog.'

'Nice to meet you, Eric and Benny the dog.' Daniel stroked the whippet's head and it sniffed his hand.

'I bumped into Eric during the week and told him about the Walkers Club,' said Hazel. 'I know Eric through your gran. He knew her very well.'

'I knew Mrs Tremaine when she was a Land Girl back in the forties.' Eric confirmed his credentials with a puffed-out chest. 'She was Molly Sneldon then and I was but a boy.'

'Seriously?' said Daniel, smiling eagerly. The old man looked at him as if to ask why he would joke about a thing like that. Of course he was serious.

'Oh yes,' Eric said. 'Molly worked on my family farm back in those days. I taught her milking and she helped me with my reading.'

'That's so cool.'

'What's so cool is that Molly, Mrs Tremaine, kept in touch with me. Writing letters so I'd reply and that helped me with my grammar at school. Remarkable woman, that one. The farm didn't last much past the war but our friendship did.'

'Wow.' Daniel felt a lump come to his throat. 'That's an amazing story.'

'You going to move into her house?' asked Eric.

'Not sure yet,' said Daniel. 'But I'm here for now.'

He turned to the timid-looking woman in a handknitted striped sweater. She looked younger than the other walkers, perhaps in her forties.

'I'm Hannah,' she said softly. Her brown hair was styled in a thick bob which flicked from side to side as she smiled at everyone and dipped her head in acknowledgement.

'Hannah is my hairdresser,' bellowed Amanda. 'Mobile.'

Daniel gave her a quizzical look.

'As in mobile hairdresser,' said Hannah, blushing crimson. 'I come to you, you don't come to me.'

'Hannah the hairdresser. I'll remember that if I'm ever in need of a trim,' said Daniel. His hair was a mess from rushing out of the house with only minutes to spare. The alarm he'd set after speaking to Jess had woken him but hadn't kept him awake. His hair was damp and his sweat top was inside out.

'So, Eric and Hannah,' said Daniel, 'ours is a slow and leisurely walk in a north-westerly direction towards Harlyn. If you have any injuries or health concerns, let me know before we set off—'

'Daniel is a trained and professional fitness instructor,' Mary interrupted, her sister nodding in agreement.

'He's going to train me,' added Amanda, who looked as if she was getting ready to demonstrate a few more knee press-ups.

'I don't mind taking some of your business cards and handing them to clients,' said Hannah before dropping her gaze to the ground.

'That's very kind of you but I don't actually have—'

'You can have some printed in Padstow,' called Mary.

'Yes,' added Eileen. 'In Padstow.'

'I'll look into it,' said Daniel, trying to lead them towards the coast path.

Amanda took charge of Hannah, leading her in the deep breathing ritual she'd adopted and encouraging Hannah to swing her arms to burn more calories as they walked. Hannah, who had such a slight build and didn't look as if she had any weight to shed, went along with Amanda's suggestion. As the two of them puffed and panted, Hannah kept one eye on Amanda to make sure she had the right technique. The sisters followed merrily behind. Eric looked at Daniel sideways, inspecting him through an invisible magnifying glass. Daniel walked slowly, trying not to trip over or pull a muscle in case he met with Eric's disapproval. Benny skulked at Eric's side.

Eventually, Daniel hung back to walk with Hazel.

'Looks like our little club is growing,' he said.

'I knew it would. I remember how disappointed you looked when you saw it was only me the first time.'

'Not disappointed, exactly,' he said.

'But not exactly ecstatic. I'm sure that had a nice young girl turned up at the café you wouldn't have looked so glum.' She looked up at him through her sun visor and glasses. 'Be honest.'

'Well, Hazel, if I'm perfectly honest, I once knew a girl I thought was nice and we went on lots of walks together. And, well, let's just say it didn't turn out so well.'

'Oh, Daniel.' Hazel slowed even more. 'How sad you look right now. I didn't mean to bring up a bad memory.'

'It's okay. You know I loved my life in Sicily but it wasn't all happy times.'

'Because of the nice girl you once knew?'

Daniel nodded and glanced ahead at the others. They were out of earshot. He never liked to talk about his breakup with Aria but something about the way Hazel looked at him made him want to open up completely. They were happy times when Aria and he led walks together. He used to make sure they were on the same walks by bribing his supervisor with shots over at Bar Casa Mia. Aria looked like a model. She was the most unlikely person to have worked for the tour company with her manicured nails and not a strand of her long dark hair out of place. Her skin looked glowing and natural but she'd wake an hour earlier than necessary to achieve these results. If she'd said she was an actress doing research for a role as a walking guide, he would have believed it.

'Yes, it was because of a girl,' Daniel said.

'You were in love with her.'

'In a big way. I'd never seen myself as the romantic type until Aria. I fell in love, my first real romance. It was deep and intense. I liked being in a couple, thinking about a future with someone. I thought it was the same for her, but when it turned out otherwise I was put off the whole idea of commitment. I've had emotional upsets in the past, everyone has, but losing someone you think you're going to build a life with, well . . . it wasn't easy. I'm not getting into anything that deep again.'

'But Daniel—'

'I know what you're going to say. Not all relationships are the same. I know that. But I just want to forget it all. Sorry. Anyway, we should try to keep up. It is our walking club after all.'

'Ours?' Hazel smiled up at him.

'Why not? You're as much a leader of this club as I am. And by now you're just as qualified and experienced.'

'Well, come on, partner, you'd better get to the front before Amanda leads Hannah all the way to the Trevose Head Lighthouse.'

'You're right.' He began to pick up his pace. 'Don't stay too far behind, Hazel, and we'll stop at Newtrain again.'

He could have said a lot more about Aria. About the instant attraction between them. The way she pronounced his name and how her hand fitted so perfectly into his the first night they went out together. He walked quickly to the front of the group and tried to place memories of Aria where they belonged – to the back of and, one day, out of his mind.

'How are we doing?' asked Daniel when he caught up with Amanda and a red-faced Hannah.

'We're fine,' said Amanda. 'Loving all of this sea air.'

'Great,' he said. 'We'll stop at the same place as last time and grab some water and a quick breather.'

Daniel and the others waited on the clifftop over Newtrain Bay as Hazel caught them up. Eric and his dog had dropped back to accompany her and, as usual, Hazel had snacks available for everyone. They sat on the windy path and shared Pringles and fig rolls. They were a silent gathering until Mary piped up about Daniel's sweat top being inside out. Daniel stretched the neckline of his top to take a look. He tutted and went to pull it over his head. Mary waved her hands at him.

'No, don't change it,' she exclaimed. 'Our mother told us it was good luck if you accidentally put your jumper on inside out and you'd change your fortune if you turned it the right way.'

'Don't turn it the right way,' said her sister.

'I was in a bit of a hurry to get out today,' said Daniel, leaving his top on wrong. 'Slept late.'

'You'll have to do better than that, Daniel,' said Mary with a disapproving shake of the head. 'Set an alarm or something. If that young girl we were talking about last week comes and joins us on the walk, you'll have to think about your appearance.'

'Why don't you give the man a break?' said Amanda. 'After all, he may already be spoken for and he might prefer an older woman.'

Eric slipped his fingers into his flat cap to scratch his head while looking at Daniel.

'And a shave wouldn't hurt for next Saturday either, Daniel,' Mary insisted. 'It's spring. Love is in the air.' She sniffed until her lungs were fully expanded.

'I think that's just the fuel oil coming off that boat over yonder,' said Eric. 'That's what I smell.'

'No, no,' Mary insisted. 'I don't mean what I can smell, I mean a feeling, all around us, filling the air. Daniel, you must know what I mean.'

'Um . . .' Daniel began.

'Aren't you even a little curious to meet this girl I've been going on about?' Mary spluttered.

'To be honest—'

'No, of course he's not,' said Amanda. 'He's far too busy for all that. Leave him alone.'

'I wouldn't mind meeting someone,' said Hannah in such a little voice the breeze almost blew it out to sea. Everyone turned to look at her. 'I mean, it must be nice to have a significant other out there somewhere and have the forces of nature bring you together.' She clasped a Pringle to her chest.

'Yes, but nature won't have anything to do with this,' Amanda said hotly. 'It'll be Mary interfering where she's not wanted.' The group fell silent.

Eric walked closer to the cliff edge and looked down to the bay.

'Now there's a rare site,' he said. 'Pretty sure that's a curlew down there.' He pointed down to the speckled plumage of the spindly-legged bird that hopped across the rocks very close to the sea. 'They say that seeing a curlew can mean a new beginning.'

'There you go,' said Mary with a clap of her hands. 'A new beginning. That has to be fate.'

Eric sat back down and shrugged an apology to Daniel.

'I didn't actually see the curlew,' said Daniel. 'So it won't affect me, will it? Now, who's ready to get going again?'

They all shouted an enthusiastic 'Me!'

Hazel and Daniel started off together but very quickly they fell behind the others.

'Don't mind Mary,' said Hazel. 'She means well. And be prepared, because she won't drop the subject and she won't stop trying to fix you up with that young girl.'

'I wish she wouldn't keep going on about her. I don't want anything heavy.' Daniel shook his head.

'You say that because you had your heart broken,' said Hazel, carefully placing her feet. 'But one day you will meet the right one.'

'I did that once. Remember? Aria and I went out for a year before she decided she didn't love me anymore. If she ever did.' He felt his cheeks turn hot.

'I'm sure she did, Daniel, but maybe she never loved you in the right way. One day you'll find the woman who will. One day. You're still young.'

'Try saying that to Mary.'

The other walkers arrived back at Trevone Beach well before Daniel and Hazel. He decided to stay at the back with her to avoid Mary's matchmaking and general interfering. Eric and his dog came to thank Daniel and Hazel.

'I wasn't sure I'd enjoy that but it's nice to share a walk with you all,' he said.

It was probably the first time Daniel had seen the old man smile. Deep lines appeared down the side of his face and Daniel thought he saw the boy his grandmother had helped with his homework behind Eric's friendly but brief smile.

'So we'll see you next week?' he asked.

'Most likely,' said Eric and turned to leave. He gave the dog's lead a little tug and he and Benny ambled away.

Daniel and Hazel waved goodbye to the others, who said how much they were looking forward to next Saturday.

'You off on your lunch date with your pal?' Daniel asked Hazel when the others had dispersed.

Hazel nodded.

'Any chance we'll see this mysterious pal on one of our walks?'

'Sadly, no, but I do talk about the walk and all the progress the Walkers Club is making when I go. That's seven of us now. Eight if you count Benny.'

'We'll be the hottest ticket in Trevone before we know it.'

'Imagine that. Well, I'd better get going, don't want to miss the bus. See you soon, Daniel.'

Daniel wondered if any of the others knew who Hazel's friend was and what she was hiding.

15

When Daniel arrived for babysitting duty, Annabelle answered the door to him dressed in a close-fitting black dress. Her hair was loose and blow-dried bone straight so that it fell past her shoulders. She fidgeted in front of the hall mirror, pulling at her dress and complaining it made her look the size of a house.

'You look amazing, Annie,' Daniel told her. 'Doesn't she, kids?'

The family were all in the hallway. Scott wore a suit and Mia held his hand.

'You look like a glittery princess, Mummy,' she said. Wearing pink and purple striped pyjamas and puppy face slippers, she had a serious expression on her face. Rasmus stood halfway up the stairs, his bottom lip trembling.

'We're only going to have a meal, darling,' Annabelle reassured him. 'Uncle Daniel can't wait to spend some time with you and Mia.'

'That's very true,' said Daniel, bounding up the stairs to grab Rasmus. He picked him up under his arms and carried him downstairs. 'We are going to have so much fun and Mummy and Daddy can tell you all about their meal at breakfast tomorrow.'

Rasmus sat on Daniel's hip and blinked a large blob of a tear onto his round cheek and sniffed. Annabelle kissed his damp face, squeezed Mia to her chest and hurried to the open door where she and Scott blew kisses into the hallway. They left quickly; the click of the car's remote control and Annabelle's heels on the paved path outside caused another tear to roll down Rasmus's cheek.

'Right,' said Daniel. 'What do we do first?'

'Mummy said we can watch a film before bed,' said Mia.

'And what time is bed?' asked Daniel.

Mia looked at Rasmus and smiled. 'Ten-thirty.'

'That seems a bit late for people your age,' Daniel said.

'It's Saturday,' said Mia, heading for the living room. 'Chill.'

Rasmus wriggled out of Daniel's arms and trotted after Mia.

Daniel sat on the sofa with his feet up scrolling messages on his phone. The children pulled out their entire DVD and Blu-ray collection from the shelf. The discs ended up in a pile in front of the television and Rasmus made it his business to either try to spin them on the carpet or throw them around the room like a Frisbee.

'Easy, kids,' said Daniel, not looking up once. One of his messages was from Jess wishing him luck with the babysitting. He messaged back saying he was a natural and looked forward to their date the following evening. From what he could tell babysitting was easy. The kids would soon wear themselves out and fall asleep hours before ten-thirty.

He read the string of messages that had been buzzing through from the group chat with his walking guide friends. As usual Doc sent the majority of the messages. He claimed the job was so boring without Daniel that he might just take him up on his offer to come to Cornwall. Daniel told him he was welcome and to bring it on. *Fai come fossi a casa tua.* Just then Daniel heard a scream and sat up to see what his niece and nephew had been up to. They were kneeling down by the television. Rasmus's cheeks were flushed. Mia's lips were pulled in, her eyes bulging up at Daniel.

'What is it? What happened?' Daniel knelt in front of them. Slowly Mia pointed at Rasmus.

'He just ate something he shouldn't, Uncle Daniel.'

'What? What did you eat, Rasmus?' Daniel placed a thumb on his nephew's now very dimpled chin, hoping to open his downturned mouth, but Rasmus squirmed away and raced up the stairs. Daniel chased after him and Mia followed behind saying, 'I'm telling Mummy.'

'No one has to tell Mummy anything,' said Daniel, scrambling on all fours up the stairs. He followed Rasmus into the children's bedroom and caught him by the ankle just before it vanished under the bed with the rest of his tiny body. He pulled him back out and rolled him onto his back.

'Okay, open up.' Daniel's voice was shaky. 'What did you swallow?'

Rasmus looked at Mia and then up at Daniel who had him pinned to the floor.

'What did Rasmus swallow, Mia?' Daniel, now very panicked, wished he'd just kept his eyes on them both until bedtime.

'Something crawling on the carpet,' said Mia. 'He ate a horrible creepy thing.'

'You mean like a spider?' asked Daniel, trying to prise Rasmus's lips apart as gently as he could.

'It *was* a spider. Mummy said he mustn't do that.'

'You mean he's eaten spiders before?'

Mia nodded. As did Rasmus.

'In that case,' said Daniel, getting up off the floor, 'we have nothing to worry about. I've eaten the odd insect in my time and, look, I grew up to be big and tall. Still alive and kicking.'

'For now,' said Mia under her breath.

Rasmus stretched his arms up to Daniel who picked him up and let him climb onto his shoulders.

'Right, let's head back downstairs and find a film.' Daniel began to lead the way but stopped suddenly when he heard a loud 'Ow' and realized he'd walked Rasmus into the door frame.

'Definitely don't mention this to Mummy,' said Daniel, glaring at Mia while setting Rasmus on his feet. 'And Rasmus, you can walk down the stairs. Slowly.'

In the living room, after he'd inspected Rasmus's forehead for bumps, Daniel, with Mia's help, cleared away the discs that Rasmus had used for target practice. Content that most of the films were back in their respective sleeves, Daniel decided that a game before bed might be a good idea. Half an hour later, neither child could agree on what to play. Rasmus crinkled his nose at everything Mia suggested and Mia thought Rasmus's choices were for babies. Daniel said they could find something to play on his phone and went to the kitchen to make himself a coffee. It was obviously going to be a long night.

Daniel returned to the living room with a mug of black coffee. The room was silent – he'd finally found a way to keep the children amused. They sat quietly on a shared armchair, Rasmus cross-legged with a finger inside his right nostril and Mia's slippered feet stretched out in front of her onto the footstool so that she was in a reclined position. Daniel sat with his legs stretched along the sofa, hot coffee in hand as he looked over at the children who were focusing hard on their game. He smiled to himself. Not bad for his first time of babysitting.

It was after he'd finished his coffee and browsing through *Woman and Home* that he heard Mia exclaim, 'Eugh! That's disgusting!' Daniel looked over and saw Mia turning the phone sideways and upside down.

'What are you doing?' he said, leaping from the sofa towards the armchair. 'What are you playing?'

'We're playing with Doc,' said Mia in a matter of fact way. 'Here.' She handed Daniel his phone. Doc had sent a picture of Daniel kissing Aria at a party. He quickly scrolled up the trail of messages and found that not only had the children been messaging Doc, they had also been in conversation with Jess.

'What did you do?' asked Daniel, running his fingers through his hair. 'I said you could play a game, not message my friends.' He kept scrolling to see what else Doc had sent. Jess, at least, had realized that someone other than Daniel had use of his phone. She'd asked Mia if Uncle Daniel was okay and Mia had said, *He eats spiders and now he's drinking.* Doc, on the other hand, hadn't noticed he was messaging a six-year-old child. Neither the misspellings nor the questions about which one was better, *Tangled* or *Frozen*, had alerted him. He preferred *Frozen*. Daniel worried about Doc after Mia told him she has the dress-up clothes for all the princesses and he had answered, *Cool.*

He quickly sent a message to Doc saying his six-year-old niece had hijacked his phone and why was he sending pictures of Aria? Doc didn't reply.

'Right,' said Daniel. 'You guys better brush your teeth ready for bed.'

'We have a bedtime snack first,' said Mia.

'Is this a real bedtime snack or an imaginary one?' asked Daniel. 'Like the imaginary ten-thirty bedtime on Saturdays. No way I fell for that by the way.'

Mia slowly moved her head from right to left and eased herself out of the armchair. Rasmus got up too and held Daniel's hand as they all went to the kitchen. He felt selfish for having left them to their own devices. The affectionate way Rasmus took his hand made his heart flutter. They were reliant on him as the adult and he felt protective all of a sudden, more like the good role model Annabelle had hoped he could be for them.

'Okay, you can have a slice of toast and some milk,' said Daniel.

'You don't have to sound bossy,' said Mia. 'Mummy already told us that Uncle Daniel was in charge of the bedtime snack.'

'Good,' said Daniel. 'At last we can agree on something.'

The children sat opposite each other at the oval kitchen table, their feet dangling from their chairs, and like mirror images they propped their chins onto their hands. They watched their uncle opening every cupboard in search of the bread. Then, when he'd found it, they watched him trying to lower the slices into the toaster several times before realizing it wasn't plugged in at the wall. The search for the glasses and the fridge was a great source of amusement for Rasmus when Daniel couldn't work out that the door to the fridge was an integrated one. He ended up in the utility room and the larder before realizing his mistake. Mia pushed her glasses up her nose saying, 'Embarrassing,' under her breath.

'Okay,' said Daniel. 'Bedtime snacks are served.'

'I thought I'd die of starvation,' said Mia.

'Are you sure you're only six?' Daniel asked.

Daniel didn't dare leave them alone for a second as they

began to eat their buttery toast. He worried about choking hazards, children falling from kitchen tables, drowning by milk. The children ate slowly and when they finally finished, Daniel shepherded them up to the bedroom.

'We need the toilet first,' said Mia. 'You'll have to help Rasmus so it doesn't go everywhere.'

'Doesn't he have a potty or something?' Daniel asked her.

Mia shook her head and raised her eyes to the ceiling. Daniel helped Rasmus onto the toilet and told him to go for it while Mia stood with her arms crossed looking up at Daniel.

'You don't have children, do you, Uncle Daniel?' she asked him.

'What gave it away?' he said. 'Okay, teeth and bed.'

'Bedtime story,' said Rasmus.

'And then bed,' said Daniel.

Once he'd helped Rasmus into his pyjamas and tucked them both into beds on opposite sides of the room Daniel looked at the enormous number of books they had on the shelves. He knew by now that asking which one he should read was only going to invite trouble so he pulled out the first book he found and sat on the floor in the middle of the room to read it.

Mia leaned on her elbow.

'That's not how you do it, Uncle Daniel. First Mummy reads to me and then she reads to Rasmus.' She signalled to the book on her bedside table.

'The whole thing?' Daniel whined.

'Just a chapter,' she sighed.

When he'd finished the chapter he took Mia's glasses off and folded them onto her bedside table. He switched off her lamp and kissed the top of her head.

'How did I do?' he asked.

'Well . . . Mummy says we get better with practice.' She then rolled over and hugged her teddy.

'You next, little man,' said Daniel as he knelt on the floor by Rasmus's bed. 'This your book?'

Rasmus's book was a story about a tiger cub who didn't want to go to bed. There were no chapters in this book but Rasmus, unlike Mia, looked quite sleepy once he'd come to the end of the story. Daniel leaned over to kiss his forehead and Rasmus grabbed him around the neck.

'Good night, Uncle Daniel. You're my best friend.'

Daniel looked at the little child who rubbed his eyes and unleashed a Colgate yawn into his face.

'You guys are both amazing,' whispered Daniel. 'Get some sleep and I'll see you soon.'

'Will you be here in the morning?' asked Mia.

'No, but Mummy and Daddy will be home soon.'

He tiptoed to the door and left it slightly ajar. Downstairs he checked his phone for any messages from Jess. There was nothing from her but a message from Doc answering Daniel's last text about Aria with the words: *The one that got away!* Up until then Daniel had considered Aria to be the one who ran away. He threw the phone aside and searched for a film on the television. He lay on the sofa and waited a while before starting it; he expected to have several interruptions by the children but they stayed in their beds. Daniel, relieved that they could at least get sleeping right without a fuss, pressed the OK button to watch his film.

Hours later he was shaken awake by Annabelle.

'You can stay there if you'd like or go up to the spare room,' she said. Her breath smelled of white wine and she seemed a bit unsteady on her feet.

'Good night?' Daniel asked.

'Not too bad,' said Annabelle, squeezing onto the edge of the sofa beside Daniel. 'Scott's already gone up. We talked and talked over dinner. We both know we need to do that more often. I think sometimes we take each other for granted.'

'Well, that's a start.' Through her food and drink glare, Daniel thought he could see traces of sadness in Annabelle's eyes.

'We might need your babysitting services again. We used to go on some great dates. Since the children . . .'

Daniel sat up. 'I'm here for you.'

'As in, you've decided to stay and put down some roots?'

'As in babysitting and doing whatever I can to help you guys out while I'm here.'

'Thanks, Daniel. And I really hope our relationship problems don't put you off finding someone yourself. You might find someone here, if you stick around.'

'Unbelievable.' Daniel shook his head. 'Even drunk you're still able to lecture me about finding a girlfriend.'

Annabelle wobbled to standing.

'I know you think I'm drunk,' she slurred. 'But I know what I'm saying. Married life can be wonderful.'

'Still not sold,' said Daniel.

'Honestly, Daniel, I'm this close to vlogging about you and seeing if I can't find you a date through my followers.' She signified how close with her finger and thumb and looked through the tiny gap with her face screwed up.

'Right, I'm off,' he said, rising to his feet. 'Before you get your video recorder going.'

'How were the children?' asked Annabelle.

'Perfect angels,' said Daniel.

'See? Aren't they a joy?'

'Okay, bye, Annie. See you soon.'

'All right, I've stopped.' She put a finger to her lips. 'But, honestly, you should stay the night. I know the children would love it if you did.'

Annabelle was right. The children were excited to see he was still at the house in the morning. Rasmus jumped onto Daniel's bed, shoving his mop of matted hair into Daniel's face. Mia leaned across his pillow, hands propping up her pointed chin as she peered at him through her little round glasses.

'Do you guys always wake up this early?' Daniel asked them.

'Yes,' said Mia. 'Why?'

'Because this is way too early for me,' said Daniel. 'Why don't you two go off and do what you usually do at the crack of dawn? I need more sleep.'

Daniel trotted into the kitchen with messy hair and a chin dark with stubble when he finally surfaced. He yawned his 'Good morning' to everyone. Annabelle was preparing scrambled eggs and Scott was brewing a pot of coffee. Rasmus ran from the kitchen table and leapt up into Daniel's arms. He hugged Daniel tightly around the neck.

'I hear you two shared insect swallowing stories last night.' Annabelle looked at him with a faux scowl.

Daniel stared at Mia.

'What happens in babysitting stays in babysitting,' he said to her. 'You weren't supposed to mention the spiders.'

'Don't worry,' said Mia. 'I didn't tell Mummy how you bashed Rasmus's head into the wall.'

'What?' Annabelle stopped whisking. Scott turned around.

'It was nothing,' said Daniel, carrying Rasmus to the table. 'See, not a scratch on him.' He pulled a face at Mia who merely shrugged her shoulders and moved to sit beside him at the table.

'It's okay, Mummy doesn't look too cross,' Mia whispered.

'A narrow escape,' Daniel whispered back. 'Okay, I'll do the toast. I'm an expert now.' He jumped up from his chair, closely followed by Rasmus.

Later, as he cycled back to the empty house in Trevone, Daniel thought about Annabelle's insistence that he settle down there. She seemed pretty sure that she and Scott could resolve their problems, and while he hoped that would be the case, the only relationship he was interested in was the casual one he had with Jess. His parents' marriage hadn't survived the kind of problems Annabelle and Scott were going through. In fact, their problems had gone from bad to worse resulting in an acrimonious divorce. The cracks had widened and he and Annabelle always felt as if they had to pick sides. In his early twenties he'd made a pledge to stay single and to never settle into a serious commitment with anyone. Aria, with her sexy eyes, her sultry voice and the undeniable devotion she'd shown him, caused him to let his guard down and fall deeply in love. He remembered thinking that a lifetime with Aria could be possible if this was how it would be. He'd gone as far as believing he could teach his own parents how it was done. How ridiculous, he thought now, as he remembered the catalogue of misunderstandings he'd had with Aria in the end. They'd resulted in lots of shouting and angry silences. Marriage, settling down, that worked for some people but not for others. Before reaching home Daniel had made his case for never wanting to get serious about anyone ever again.

16

Daniel wheeled his pink bicycle up to the front door when he got home. Turning, he noticed Hazel in her garden and decided to pop over for a quick chat.

'I'm not bothering you, am I?' he asked as he approached her gate.

'Not in the slightest. Planning a cycling trip?'

'Not today. I just came back from Annabelle's. I was babysitting.'

'How did that go?'

'Better than I thought. There were two children in the house to start with and when I left there were still two.'

'Well, thank goodness for that.' Hazel grinned at him. 'Do you fancy some tea?'

'Love some.'

In the tight squeeze of her corridor, Daniel stopped to inspect the photographs on the walls more closely. He had learned a lot about his grandmother from journals and photographs. Hazel's hallway was a gallery of memories and there was a vast amount he could learn about her life from her pictures.

'Which of these are of your children, Hazel?'

The clothes and hairstyles, the cars and the quality of some of the pictures showed that they spanned decades.

'Just up there is a studio picture of all my three.' Hazel balanced on her walking stick and pointed upwards. 'They took that one as part of the present they gave us for our fiftieth wedding anniversary.'

'Part of the present?'

'Yes, it was lovely. They paid for a cruise for Henry and me. We'd sailed in boats and swam in oceans but we'd never gone on a cruise. Very luxurious it was. A week on the Amalfi Coast. One of the most wonderful holidays I've had.'

'Have you got pictures of you two on the cruise ship?'

'In an album somewhere, I'd have to dig them out,' said Hazel.

'Just imagine if you had photos going back to your motor-cycle holiday. That would have been something for the gallery.' Daniel smiled and looked back up at the pictures.

'Especially the European leg of it,' said Hazel.

'Even after the motorbike accident in Cornwall you made it to Europe. Impressive.' He pulled in his lips and nodded as he stared up at the photographs.

'The accident was only a temporary hitch.' Hazel beckoned with a crooked finger. 'Come on, I'll make that tea.'

Daniel stood at the kitchen counter as Hazel made tea. The cat calendar on her notice board had a birthday penned in on it, plus a doctor's appointment. Hazel pushed her glasses up her nose as she squinted at the heap of tea leaves on the spoon, making sure it was the appropriate amount. She encouraged Daniel to find the biscuits as she continued the account of her motorcycling accident.

'My bike had pretty much had it,' said Hazel as steam rose from the kettle. 'But Henry and I didn't want to quit. At the start of the ride we said we'd do the UK first and see how we got on. Well, we got on very well indeed.' Hazel stopped to giggle before pouring boiled water into the teapot.

'I'll time it with my phone,' said Daniel. 'I have to know more.'

'Okay then. So, where was I?'

'UK first and Europe next,' said Daniel, studying the timer on his phone.

'Well, in the end we ditched my bike and took off on Henry's Royal Enfield. The speed of that thing.' She threw up her hands. 'So much faster and heavier than mine. Thank goodness I didn't go over on a bike that big! Imagine, Daniel, your gran rode a bike as big as Henry's when she was a Land Girl.'

'Seriously? She never mentioned the actual make and model in her journal.'

'Oh yes. Took it to ride errands in and around Truro and rode like the wind. No helmets in those days. Just a headscarf tied under her chin and off she'd have gone in her muddy dungarees.'

'Go Gran.' Daniel stopped to imagine a young Molly on her motorbike. 'And what about you and Henry? Where did you go after you got rid of your bike?'

'We sold my bike, didn't get much for it of course, but our first European stop was Italy. We worked in a vineyard then went on to find jobs in a restaurant. I was in the back washing dishes and Henry cleaned. But we made the money to keep going. We travelled around western Europe, got to see parts of Germany, Austria and the Netherlands and then we ran out of money.'

'And how was it, you know, you two being so different?'

'To be honest, we were a bit of a novelty, a rarity and being as we were both just foreigners wherever we went we were asked lots of questions, but we had an easier time of it compared to being together in the UK.'

Daniel brought the mugs of tea to the table and sat in quiet acknowledgement of the problems the couple would have faced. Hazel continued.

'We would have loved to have ridden into Scandinavia and to this day it's a part of the world we never got to see. Henry said it was just as well as it would probably be too cold for him. He always loved our holidays in Trinidad. We went most years. We wanted the children to know where I came from.'

'What did you and Henry do for a living?'

'Well, Henry worked as a mechanic as you know but eventually owned his own garage. In fact, he had two in the end. None of the children wanted to keep them going. It wasn't for them, you see? Grease and oil under your fingernails every day. But Henry kept the business for as long as he could before selling it.'

'And you?' said Daniel. 'After you finally took your degree?'

'I became a humanities lecturer. It was the most sensible and grown-up job I did in my life. I loved being a lecturer but I had to settle down and stop travelling so much after Jennifer was born.'

'You don't have any regrets about settling down then?'

'Why would I? I've had a very fulfilling life. Absolutely amazing so far. If I were to change anything it would be to have my children call me more often. But they're living their lives now and as long as they're happy so am I.'

Daniel ran a finger down the side of his mug.

'What is it, Daniel?' said Hazel.

'I'm not very good at keeping in touch with my folks. Can't remember the last time I called my mum.'

'If that's the case, there's nothing stopping you calling her right now, is there?' Hazel raised an eyebrow.

'You're right. I'll do it. I'll go and call her. Thanks for the tea, Hazel.'

Daniel glanced up at the photographs in the hallway on his way out.

'By any chance,' he asked, 'is there a picture of you on that march?'

'Oh,' said Hazel with a chuckle. 'You remembered I mentioned hurting my leg for a second time. I did go on my fair share of those from the sixties to the seventies.'

'What did you march against?' Daniel looked to the upper-most pictures right down to the bottom, expecting to see a picture of Hazel in a beret, shouting through a megaphone.

'My first was in Bristol. Around the time of the Bristol Bus Boycott in 1963. I was always in support of Race Relations and so was Henry. We were keen to see the laws amended, especially so that our children wouldn't have to suffer discrimination.'

'Did your children know about the marches you went on?'

'We told them, and I'm sure they appreciate it in their way. The marches and rallies I went on were to give them an easier life than I had. I'm thankful that they went on to do well for themselves. They had their own struggles, mind you, so I'm very proud of how far they've all come.'

Hazel had a faraway look as she gazed at the photographs. Daniel could sense the grief that she must feel, standing in a corridor of memories with no one but him to share them with.

'You get yourself off now, Daniel,' she said, giving him a gentle nudge towards the front door. 'You don't want to listen to an old woman blathering on about the past.'

'I find it really interesting, actually. I'd like to hear the story behind all of these photographs one day.'

'It was Henry who chose to cover the wall with our past. I didn't like the idea at first but I enjoy it now. It was a good idea.'

'Annabelle is keeping hold of all Gran's stuff. It's important to remember the past.'

Hazel nodded and Daniel let himself out.

'Enjoy the rest of your day, Hazel, and I'll see you on Saturday if I don't run into you sooner.'

'Take care, Daniel. Off you go and write yourself some wonderful memories.'

He would have liked to have told Hazel that he had a date with Jess to look forward to. He wondered what sort of memories he and Jess would write together. Uncomplicated and casual ones, he hoped.

17

Jess arrived as arranged at seven in the evening. She wore a long jacket over a dark blue dress. Her hair was neatly combed, so unlike the messy crop whose layers landed in whichever way the wind took them. She wore a hint of make-up: a slight shimmer of gloss on her lips and liquid eye liner ticks above her light grey eyes.

'You look beautiful,' said Daniel as he opened the door.

'Why, thank you. You don't look so bad yourself.'

Daniel looked down at his dark jeans and light blue shirt. Apart from walking boots and trainers the only other footwear he owned was a pair of classic black Oxfords that he'd had to polish with Mr Sheen and an old rag. He pulled a sweater over his head and managed to disrupt the smoothness of his hair, which had grown to his collar and was in need of a trim or, according to Annabelle, a decent cut.

Jess drove her brother's car. She had chosen the restaurant and taken care of the booking.

'Where are we going?' asked Daniel as she started the car.

'A little Mediterranean restaurant not far from here. I hope that's okay.'

'Sounds perfect.'

'We could walk but I figured you get enough of that

on a Saturday afternoon.' She shot a cheeky grin in his direction.

'Don't knock the Walkers Club,' said Daniel. 'It's growing in number. Granted we don't actually walk a great distance and it's mostly strolling along and a bit of sitting down. But what we lack in mileage we gain in animation.'

'So a lively bunch then?' Jess, taking her eyes briefly off the narrow road, smiled at Daniel.

Her perfume was a mix of gentle lavender and neroli that filled the chill air of the evening with a warm and feminine aroma. He wanted to make a comment about liking the scent but he had already told her she looked beautiful, which was probably a bit heavy on the compliments scale and he didn't want to scare Jess off or come across as eager.

'Each of them is so different,' said Daniel. 'Some lively, some chatty, some a bit reserved.'

Jess was quiet for a while and then asked, 'How many are you now?'

'Including me we're seven strong. Eight if you count Benny the dog.'

'Goodness me, you must take up the whole of the path. Remind me not to try to cycle that way on Saturday after twelve, I'll never get through the crowd.'

'Think quality not quantity,' said Daniel, wagging a finger at her. 'I didn't know what to expect when I started it but I've met some great characters and made a very good friend.'

'That sounds intriguing,' said Jess, slowing the car down. 'I would come but I work on Saturday.'

'That's a shame,' said Daniel as lightly as he could. 'Originally our walk was supposed to take us as far as your surf school, but it might take several weeks to get up the speed and stamina to make it.'

'Well, if your walkers ever get to Harlyn, the drinks are on me.'

'That's a deal.'

Jess laughed and parked close to a small restaurant painted white with a dark green sign. Outside was a large flower trough and a potted plant at the front door. The interior was tiny: a couple of tables by the door and banquette seating along one wall. They were welcomed by a friendly-looking woman with a cheery grin.

'Are you Jess?' she asked.

'That's right. I did book.'

'Well, you have a choice of tables, Jess. It's a quiet time of year and Sunday isn't busy.'

Only two other couples were dining. Jess and Daniel chose a table near the window and sat opposite each other on high-backed banquette sofas. They were served a bottle of wine very quickly and looked on as the waitress poured. Jess slipped off her jacket. Her dress was sleeveless and Daniel could see the complete lotus flower tattoo at the top of her arm.

'Is there a story of drunken regret surrounding that tattoo?' he asked.

Jess looked at her shoulder.

'No way. I love my lotus flower,' she said. 'Although I should have had a few before she started. They don't tell you how much it hurts. I really don't understand the people who get a whole sleeve done. I can tell you're not really into them.'

'I don't have a problem with tattoos, especially if they have a meaning. Yours does, so that's okay.'

'I was in Goa when I had it done. I was on my last training course before becoming a fully qualified yoga teacher.'

'I didn't know you were a yoga teacher, too.'

Jess laughed and put the menu down.

'I don't want people to think I'm a total flake so when I first meet someone I tend to just drop the various jobs I've had into the conversation bit by bit. Hopefully they lose count and don't realize I've had two thousand jobs and I'm still in my twenties.'

Daniel laughed.

'Well, I can't say I've had that many jobs,' he said. 'But a couple of the walkers want me to brush up on my personal trainer qualification so I can give them sessions.'

'Whoa, wait a minute. I thought you were a walking guide. So whereabouts does personal trainer come on your résumé?'

He shrugged. 'On a whim I trained and qualified as a PT. I used to go to the gym a lot at uni. I was doing engineering but I always knew it wasn't for me. I never really knew what I wanted to do but I did enjoy training people. That is for the six or so months it lasted. After that I worked as a waiter in a bar in Soho and it was through someone I met there that I found out about the walking guide jobs on Mount Etna.'

Jess raised her glass of wine.

'Here's to being a couple of flakes.' She took a sip then put her glass down. 'But seriously, you could get a lot of business as a personal trainer if you wanted to.'

'That's just it, I don't know what I want.'

'Some gem of an idea will come to you.' Jess smiled at him.

'What about you? You've had lots of jobs. Surfing instructor, photographer, yoga teacher. You still haven't decided.'

Jess played with the shiny cutlery before looking up at Daniel, traces of a lingering fantasy shining through her eyes.

'I did make a decision,' she said. 'But it's become more of a dream now and I don't know if it will ever come true.'

'What is it? What's your dream job?'

'I've always wanted to own my own yoga studio. In a place I could call home. Designed to my tastes. Maybe I'd rent space to other yoga teachers. Plan yoga breaks, yoga weekends and week-long meditation events.' She sniffed out a laugh. 'Sounds silly, right? How could I ever afford it?'

'It's not silly at all. It's a wonderful thing to aspire to. I believe you can do it.'

Candlelight sparkled in her light eyes. 'Thank you, Daniel. It's good to know someone believes in me.'

Daniel felt his heartbeat quicken as Jess blushed and looked down. The waitress stood silently a short distance from their table. She lightly tapped her notepad.

'We should decide on something to eat,' said Jess. 'Don't know about you but I'm starving.'

Daniel stole several glances at Jess as they ate. He hoped it wouldn't seem like ogling but he was finding it hard not to look at her. He imagined the good times they could have if they both stuck around for the summer. Surfing, eating out; she might actually teach him how to cook and he might finally learn.

'Can I pour you another glass?' he asked her, the bottle hovering above her first glass.

'No, no, I'm driving, remember. You go ahead, though.'

When they left the restaurant, they decided to walk off the large meal before heading home. It had turned cooler and dark. They ambled around the quiet streets, walking in the direction of the sea for a while before circling back to the restaurant. Jess shivered and Daniel had to hold back the urge to put his arm around her. She was just the right amount of small for his arm to reach around her shoulders and pull her close to him. In the end he had to create a wide gap between them because the need to hold her hand as it swung so close to his side was overwhelming.

'It's a beautiful night,' he said.

'It is. Didn't expect it to turn out to be so chilly, though.' Jess folded her arms around her body.

'Let's go then,' said Daniel.

'Sick of my company already, are you?' Jess looked up at him, mock annoyance on her face.

'No, I didn't mean that. I mean, if I had a jacket I'd offer it to you. Here.' He pulled off his sweater before he thought his actions through. 'You can put this on over your dress if you like.'

Jess giggled.

'Now *you'll* be cold,' she said. 'It's okay. I'll be all right in my jacket. Put your jumper back on, no need to be so chivalrous, Daniel.'

'Sorry, I wasn't trying to be pushy.'

'You're allowed to be pushy,' she said.

'It's just . . . what we said, you know? About keeping it casual.' He put his sweater on again.

'I know,' said Jess, placing her hand in his. 'But you can afford to let yourself go once in a while.'

Daniel laughed inwardly at himself for acting like a jerk, and yet he did wonder if Jess saw him as more than a casual date. There was an energy passing between them that he couldn't ignore. He wondered if she sensed it, too. They'd barely taken their eyes off each other on their slow walk back to the car.

'Please don't tell me that this is how you walk on Saturdays,' said Jess, breaking the spell. 'It's no wonder you can't make it as far as Harlyn.'

'We'll make it there one day, you'll see.'

'Can I drive you home?' she asked. Daniel found it hard to let go of her hand and they stood facing each other for the longest of beats before they somehow pulled apart.

Sitting in the car outside his house, Daniel looked towards the front door and back at Jess.

'I won't come in,' she said. 'I've got to get up early. While big brother is entertaining Marisol, I'm going to be up to my eyes at the surf school with his assistant going through books and paperwork so I can learn more about the day to day business side.'

'That sounds like you're considering staying,' said Daniel.

'It does, doesn't it?' Jess looked upwards, off into the distance. The white paint of the nearby houses was luminous in the moonlight. Stars dotted the indigo sky and Daniel looked up, too.

'Want to discuss it over coffee?' he said.

'I don't know if there is anything to discuss. I do love it here. I'm even happy at the surf school. I get to take photographs, lots of them, and I've got a studio at my brother's house for developing.'

'But?'

'But I don't quite feel complete.'

'I know exactly what you mean.'

'You do?' She turned sideways on to face him.

'I'm not unhappy here,' he said. 'But there's a missing piece of the jigsaw and I can't seem to find it. I don't know if I will.' He looked intently at her.

'Noah has an empty space on the top floor of the school.' Jess looked very serious now. 'I've thought about starting the yoga school there.'

'You should talk to him.'

'Perhaps.' Daniel could see her mind travelling as she gazed just past him at nothing in particular. A smile returned to her face.

'If we're not careful,' she said, 'we'll find ourselves making decisions.'

'We can't avoid them completely, though, can we?'

'I think it's called growing up. Do you think it's time?' She pulled a face.

'It could be. Sad but true.' He considered the idea of being a responsible grown up, whatever that meant, for a split second.

Jess touched his cheek. 'I've had a great evening, Daniel. See you soon?'

'Definitely.' He leaned towards her and kissed her lips. 'That's me letting myself go.'

She kissed him lightly and smiled. Daniel took his time stepping out of the car. He stood at the roadside as Jess drove away and saw her wave to him at the crossroads by Hazel's house. The lights of Jess's car vanished and the sound of the engine faded. Daniel shivered in the cold and let himself into the empty house. It seemed cavernous, the walls so bare. He wished Jess had decided to come in.

18

Hazel waved to Daniel from her front garden early on Tuesday morning as he wheeled his bike out of the house. Just earlier he had got off the phone to Annabelle who had called to say she would hire a car for Daniel to run around in while he went about the business of decorating the house.

'Are you sure about this?' he had asked. 'I mean, I could get quite a large tin of paint into the girlie basket on the front of your pink bike.'

'I call it practical, not girlie. But with all the work you're doing, going backwards and forwards for materials at the DIY store, it would be easier if you had a car. And I wanted to repay you for babysitting on Saturday.'

'It's my pleasure, Annie. I'm happy to look after Mia and Rasmus whenever you need me.'

'That's kind. Maybe Rasmus could wear a crash helmet next time.'

'I can't believe Mia grassed on me. I thought we had a connection.'

'Well, you're the talk of the town in this house. They both want to come to see you and hang out with you and they both keep asking when you're coming over next.'

Daniel waved back to Hazel and wheeled the pink bike over to her front garden. He leaned it on the low wooden gate.

'I do like your bike,' she said, smiling. 'It reminds me of the one I had as a girl.'

'Do you fancy hopping on and taking it for a spin?'

'You have got to be joking.' Hazel gave a downward flick of her hand.

'Not in the slightest. You might find it more practical than walking with a stick. Faster, for one thing. Tell you what, I'll dig out a helmet from somewhere, maybe Annabelle has one, and I'll help you get back in the saddle.'

'You have no idea how tempting that sounds. I get so frustrated with this stick.'

'Is that why I see you waving it in the air sometimes?' Daniel thought back to his second day in Trevone when he'd watched Hazel shaking her stick at some imaginary object.

'Waving my stick?' said Hazel. 'When?'

'I've seen you do it a couple of times, here in the garden.' He gestured with his head. 'You were shaking it up at the trellis. I did think it a little strange, but if the stick gets you down sometimes, I get that.'

Hazel leaned against the gate, the sparkle in her eyes dimming.

'You're right,' she said. 'It is a strange thing to do. But I wasn't angry with the stick; I was angry with Henry.'

'Really?' Daniel frowned.

'When I'm out here trying to keep up the garden, I'm doing it for Henry. It was his garden, you see? Both the front and the back. I never did have a knack for gardening. Any plant I was ever given died on me. Henry was the one who kept them up.'

'So why are you angry with Henry? He left you a beautiful garden.'

'Ah, now you've hit the nail on the head, son.' She pursed her lips before continuing. 'That's what he did. He left me. Henry left me.' Hazel looked around at the roses in the front garden. 'We were supposed to be together forever. Neither of us was supposed to go anywhere this soon. No one lives forever, I know that, but I miss him terribly and I get so lonely. I shake my stick up at the heavens because that's where I believe he is, looking down on me, telling me not to overdo it on the plant food. I shake my stick and tell him he should be here doing the garden himself.'

'I'm sorry, Hazel, I wish I'd kept my big mouth shut.'

He was annoyed at himself for having made Hazel think about losing Henry right at a point when she'd looked so happy. After falling deeply in love with Aria, her leaving had ripped a chunk from his heart after just one year together. He couldn't imagine the depth of sorrow Hazel must have in her heart.

'Oh, Daniel, don't say that. Your grandfather passed away ten years before Molly did and she learned to live with her loss eventually. It'll just take time. I have some wonderful friends and now I have the Walkers Club.'

'It really means a lot to you, doesn't it?'

'You have no idea.'

'Look, Hazel, I can help you with your garden, you know? If it becomes too much. I'd really like to.'

'Well, I'm going to have to learn to cope somehow. I won't have you around forever, will I?'

'I'm here now,' he said. 'And I really want to help.'

'You can help by giving me some lessons on your bike.' Hazel straightened up. A smile brightened her eyes.

'So you're up for it then?'

Hazel nodded. 'I am if you really think I can do it?'

'I don't see why not? It's low impact so it could be good exercise for your leg. Better check with your doctor first, though.'

'I certainly will. Thank you, Daniel.' Hazel cast an eye over the pink bicycle. 'Weren't you planning to go somewhere on it just now?' she asked.

'Only a quick ride along the coast path, maybe to Harlyn. I have to get back in time for when Annabelle comes. She's getting me a hire car.'

'Well, lucky you. Anything special in Harlyn?'

Daniel hopped onto the bike.

'I was hoping to see a friend. Just for a catch up. Oh, and when I get my car the bike's all yours, Hazel.'

He cycled away and waved as he sped off.

19

•

It seemed strange to be taking the coast path at such speed. Daniel had got used to the slow pace of his walking club and accepted that the walk was all about the people, not the pace or the distance. The fast cycle along the path on his own was a different experience completely. The wind blew in from the sea. He could feel the freshness of it and hear the hiss and splash of waves against the rocks. There was no one else on the coast path. Daniel cycled faster, a sense of ocean spray on his face, though the sea was far below him now. His cheeks were chilly and red. Eric wasn't there to identify them and Jess wasn't there to photograph them but he listened to the music of the seabirds and the harmonies they made with each other and the rushing sea.

Once in Harlyn, Daniel jumped off his bike and locked it up close to the surf shop. Jess had been on his mind when he'd woken that morning and though he had nothing in particular to say to her, and it had only been two days since they'd had dinner together, he'd felt like seeing her. But, as he approached the shop, he was suddenly aware that this was her place of work and perhaps he should have called first.

Surfboards and wetsuits of all sizes were stacked on rails

on the walkway outside the surf school and shop. Various other surfing essentials like swimsuits and shortboards hung in the window. The shop door was open. Inside, Daniel saw Jess right away but she was leaning across the counter, head down, poring over some books and papers and an open laptop. She was alongside a tall man with fair hair who suddenly looked up.

'Can I help you?' he asked.

'Daniel!' said Jess. 'What are you doing here?'

'Sorry, I was just passing and thought I'd pop in.' Daniel held up a hand. 'I'm interrupting. I can go.'

Both Jess and the man she had been talking to insisted that Daniel stay.

'We were just finishing up for now,' said the man.

'Daniel, this is my brother, Noah,' Jess said. 'Noah, meet Daniel.'

The two shook hands while Jess slipped on a hooded jacket and wrapped her arms around her body.

'Noah and I have been talking business plans all morning and my mind is fried.' She turned to her brother. 'I'll be back soon, then you can get off.'

'No worries,' he said. 'Catch you later.'

Daniel and Jess began to walk towards the beach. A light rain had begun. Daniel, still flushed from his cycle, could feel the chill through his long-sleeved T-shirt. The air grew cooler the closer they got to the water. The waves were at about two feet; a lone surfer was taking advantage of them to improve her skills. A couple plodded along the beach in padded jackets, the woman trying to shelter her face from the rain as it became heavier.

'I think you're a bit underdressed,' said Jess. 'I'd offer you my jacket but you'd only stretch it out.' She laughed lightly.

'It's fine,' said Daniel. 'I can't stay anyway. I just wanted to say hi.'

'You could have called.'

'I know but I wanted to come and see you.' A strange wave ran up his stomach as his brain told him that he should dial back the intensity of their conversation.

'Well, I'm glad you did.' Jess smiled.

'Because I saved you from your business meeting?'

'Because I wanted to see you.' Her cheeks reddened very quickly and she turned her face away. It seemed as if Jess wanted to dial back her enthusiasm to see him, too.

'I was thinking about our date,' said Daniel. 'Maybe we could do it again soon?'

Jess nodded and Daniel beamed a smile at her.

They walked to the dark rocks to the right of the beach and sat on the damp stones. The rain began to flatten Daniel's hair to his forehead. Jess blew into her hands and put them into her pockets.

'You'll never guess what?' she said.

Daniel turned to face her.

'Noah has decided not to leave the country after all. Can you believe he proposed to Marisol and she said yes? And she really wants to stay here in Cornwall. He's done a complete about turn with his plans and he wants to stay and grow the business. He's thinking about a snack bar or café out the back. He's got bookings for the whole of the summer and he thinks it's crazy to stop now. And something else happened.'

'Tell me.' He brushed rain from his brow.

'Noah thought my idea about running a yoga studio above the shop was genius. But when I told him it'd take me forever to afford the renovations he got straight onto our parents.

They're ecstatic about me settling down to something and have offered to invest some money into the studio.'

'That's brilliant, Jess. Your dream is about to come true.' He resisted the urge to hug her in celebration. 'So that means you'll be staying.'

She nodded slowly.

'I know we made a no decisions pact but it seemed like a logical step. I get to do what I want to do and I help Noah when I can. It's a no brainer really.'

'Some decisions are worth making.'

'I know. And now that everything is decided, it just feels amazing.'

They sat quietly on the rocks, just a whisper of wind between them. The rain came down more heavily.

'Daniel, you'll be soaked. I'm sure I can find you something waterproof to put on. Come with me.'

They ran back to the shop, the raindrops splattering their clothes. The sand was dark and sluggish as they hurried along.

'Come on,' said Jess. She grabbed a T-shirt with the surf school logo on it from one of the rails and pushed it into Daniel's arms. Under the counter was a waterproof jacket that had been folded away. 'You don't mind if Daniel borrows this, do you, Noah?'

Noah had been tidying shelves and gave Daniel a thumbs up.

'Come upstairs,' Jess breathed.

On the upper floor was a messy open space filled with boxes of stock and supplies.

'Put these on.' Jess gestured to the clothes she'd handed him. 'I'll dry your T-shirt and return it next time I see you.'

Daniel peeled off his layer of wet clothing and handed it

to Jess. He slipped on the new T-shirt which revealed each contour of his muscular torso.

'So this is where you'll do the yoga?' asked Daniel, looking around the musty room. The windows were dirty. Some were covered in paper but the view outside was of the sea.

'Yes,' said Jess. 'Pretty cool, don't you think? It'll take a bit of work to get it organized. Building plans, health and safety, you name it. But when it's done it'll be a great space.'

'I'm happy for you, Jess.'

She clapped her hands together at her chest. 'I can tell. One day, when you know what you'll do next, I know I'll be just as happy for you.'

He loved her smile. He wanted to say as much, but spilling his feelings to someone he'd known for only a short time hadn't worked out for him in the past. For now he would just be content to know that Jess wasn't leaving. He bent to kiss her but in that moment Noah called up to Jess.

'I should go and let you get on,' said Daniel. His lips were a breath away from Jess's.

Noah's waterproof jacket was a much better fit than the snug T-shirt Jess had given him.

'I'll return this,' Daniel called to Noah, who gave him the peace sign from behind the counter. 'See you soon?' he said to Jess.

'You will.'

He kissed her cheek before leaving and jogged over to the pink bicycle. He pedalled home fast along the path. Jess's decision to stay in Cornwall might just make him rethink leaving Trevone so soon.

20

Oliver Bishop joined the Walkers Club the following Saturday. He was a short and stout man who wore long shorts and a baseball cap on his first walk. He had stubby calves and his arms were curiously short for his body. He told Daniel that he'd had a heart attack a year ago and his doctor had insisted that he take more exercise. He'd bought a stationary bike that he hadn't unpacked yet. His son had put a step counter app on his phone but he couldn't work out how to use it. His newly acquired gym membership expired long before he'd got the hang of the rowing machine.

'Well,' said Daniel, 'if you want to make a start on getting your fitness levels up, then walking is the thing to do.'

'Great,' said Oliver. His cheeks were round, and his smile was contagious. 'It was lucky that I heard about you. Apparently you had notices up but I didn't see a single one.'

'How did you hear about us, then?' asked Daniel.

'It was Hazel,' said Oliver, turning to her. 'Once upon a time I fixed a leaky tap in Hazel's kitchen and she made me a marvellous cup of tea.'

'Well, Oliver did a marvellous job,' said Hazel. 'He used to have an electronics shop in Padstow but has since retired. Luckily I kept his card and it had his mobile number on it.'

'Amanda,' said Hazel, 'do you think Oliver can walk at the front with you?'

Amanda was absolutely delighted to take charge of Oliver and Oliver seemed very happy to make Amanda's acquaintance. He was the height of her bosom and standing beside it would obscure half of his peripheral vision.

The group set off slowly. As usual Amanda, with her cacophonous breath support system, was at the front of the group. The new walker, Oliver, was right beside her. Amanda advised him that vigorous arm movement would get his heart rate up and his calories down. He swung his arms across the front of his round body from side to side, puffy hands partially clenched, elbows bent. His eyes pointed sideways on to Amanda's buoyant chest. Daniel wished Oliver would look where he was going and really didn't want their leisurely walk to turn into an abseiling adventure with no ropes. That said, he was grateful to Hazel for getting Amanda off his back and had graciously returned the wink she had given him when it was clear that Amanda and Oliver had made an instant connection.

Daniel walked in the middle of the group, surrounded by the sisters and Hannah the hairdresser. Eric Laverty and his dog walked alongside Hazel at the back.

'By the way, Daniel,' said Mary, turning to face him, 'I did catch a glimpse of the young girl I was talking to you about.'

The group was less than five minutes out from their starting point on the South West Coast Path and already Mary was on his case about the mysterious lovely girl she wanted to fix Daniel up with. Just then, a stonechat, perched on a branch along the path, chirped its characteristic light clicking sound and accompanying whistle.

'Look at that,' said Daniel, with more enthusiasm than an

ornithologist at a birdwatching convention. 'That's an interesting bird. I wonder if any of us know what it's called.' He
pointed at the bird, but his voice was so loud it quickly flew
away before anyone could see what he was talking about.

'Never mind that,' said Mary, pulling at his arm. 'I said, I
caught a glimpse of her riding by but I didn't get to speak
to her. I thought I might ask at the village hall where she
did that stint of stretching classes. They might have her details.
I'll be so happy when I can get you two lonely hearts together.'

'Are you a lonely heart, Daniel?' asked Hannah.

'He most certainly is,' said Mary, her shoulders gathering
at her ears. 'I said to Eileen that a good-looking young man
like Daniel oughtn't to be on his own. Not when there are
good-looking single women around.' Eileen nodded in agreement.

'You ought to get cracking,' said Hannah in her soft voice.
'If she's a nice girl, she won't stay single long.'

'I will try to stop her,' said Mary. 'Flag her down when I
next see her.'

'Flag her down,' parroted Eileen.

'Of course it's all dating apps these days, Daniel,' Hannah
said to him in no more than a whisper.

'I know someone who's tried one or two of those,' declared
Mary. 'Dating apps. Apparently all the men *my* age want
women who are half *their* age. Can you imagine? If I ever
wrote a profile of my own saying that I want a tall and
handsome younger man to go out with, I'd probably get
deleted.'

'Because you're a cougar?' asked Eileen.

'No, because men get away with absolutely everything,'
said Mary.

'Would you try an app, Daniel?' asked Hannah.

'I really do think we're getting off the point,' insisted Mary. 'We're supposed to be fixing Daniel up with an actual person, not having him swipe left and right on pictures that are at least ten years out of date.'

Everyone stared at her.

'Well, at least that's what my friend says about it,' said Mary.

'Er, I'm happy on my own,' said Daniel who had positioned himself behind Hazel and Eric for protection. 'I wish you'd believe me.'

'We're just concerned about you, Daniel,' said Mary. 'We're all friends by now and friends look out for each other.'

'Thanks,' said Daniel, but it seemed to him that the friendly thing to do would be for everyone to just give him a break. He wished Jess didn't have to work on Saturday so she could come on the walk and stop all the chat about his love life.

Just then a loud voice behind him called, 'Step aside, coming through!'

Daniel turned around and saw a group of people coming up fast behind his walkers. They all wore black tracksuit bottoms and white T-shirts with a logo that read 'The Padstow Pace Masters'.

'What on earth?' said Mary.

All the members of Daniel's Walkers Club stopped and stood at either side of the path while the Pace Masters jetted through the middle of them and bolted ahead. They didn't utter a word, just power-walked their way along the path. Very soon they were around a bend in the path and out of sight.

Amanda came back to Daniel, her mouth dropped open. 'Did you see that?'

'I certainly did,' said Daniel.

'Well, what are we going to do about it?'

'What do you suggest?'

'I suggest we train. Hard. Probably get some tactics for faster speeds. They can't just come along and outwalk us like that.'

'It is a public footpath,' said Hazel. 'They have every right to come along and walk as fast or as slowly as they like.'

'We could get matching T-shirts, though, couldn't we, Daniel?' Amanda pleaded. 'It might make us look more like a club.'

'We already look like a club,' said Daniel. 'We do it our way. Let them do it theirs.'

They continued to walk. Admittedly, Daniel would have loved a fast-paced walking group. But seeing the determination and focus of the Padstow Pace Masters he preferred the signature chilled-out walk of his club. It wasn't that he'd lost his sense of excitement and adventure, but at a leisurely pace he was able to take in the sights and sounds of his childhood home. As a boy he had taken for granted just how beautiful the surroundings were. Like Jess with her camera, walking slowly, he had been able to absorb the vibrancy of colour of the land, the wildlife and the ever-changing sea and sky. He'd begun to appreciate the lush fields, felt the invitation of the waves and often found himself deeply inhaling the fresh sea air. He had been missing his friends from Sicily less and less.

Back on Mount Etna he never got to see any of the tourists again once their walking and touring holidays were over. But here he was learning about the lives of the walkers and getting to know his neighbours. Hazel was a real friend to him now; he was sure she felt the same of him.

'You're doing a grand job, son,' said Eric. 'Don't get derailed by the likes of them fast walkers.'

'Thanks, Eric, I won't.'

The walkers stopped just a little way on for some refreshments.

'Do you think those fast walkers will overtake us on the way home?' Amanda asked.

'So what if they do?' said Daniel. 'We'll always be the walking club that came first. I'd never heard of the Padstow Pace Masters or whatever it is they call themselves before.'

'I'd never heard of them, either,' said Hannah. 'They did seem a bit stuffy. I like our casual club better.'

'It wouldn't do us any harm to have a name for our club, though, would it?' said Amanda.

'Well, let's do that,' said Daniel. 'We'll see if anyone can come up with a name for next week and we'll take a vote to see which one we like the best.'

'Wonderful,' said Amanda.

'And I'll give you a call about starting those personal training sessions, Amanda,' Daniel said. She immediately perked up. 'You too, Mary and Eileen.'

'Oh, thank you, Daniel,' said Mary. 'I'm looking forward to it. And how about the idea of meeting with the girl I was telling you about?'

'Easy now, Mary,' said Daniel. 'If I'm going to be busy training you three, I won't have much time for a date.'

Daniel was able to get them up and on their feet again before anyone could say 'blind date'.

Back at base the walkers stopped for little chats before going their separate ways. Daniel noticed that Amanda and Oliver were particularly talkative and walked away together.

'By the way, Hazel,' Daniel said when they were the last two walkers in the car park, 'I've got my hire car now. Shall I nip back for it so I can drive you to your lunch date with your best pal?'

Hazel remained quiet for a long time. She looked at her stick, her eyes trailing down to the rubber stopper at the end of it and then to the ground.

'I'll be quick,' said Daniel, getting ready to rush off. 'What is it, Hazel?'

'Well,' said Hazel, meeting his gaze, 'my best pal was always Henry.'

'Of course he was. So who is it now?'

'Still Henry.'

'Still Henry? So?'

'So that's where I go every Saturday. To the cemetery, to sit with Henry and eat my lunch and talk to him about my week.'

'I see. But why didn't you just say?'

'My children kept telling me it was excessive, making a weekly trip, and that I'm not getting any younger and I should be taking it easy. They don't understand what these chats mean to me.'

'Don't let them put you off, Hazel. How far is the cemetery from here?'

'Not far. I walk a little way and catch the 53 bus to Woodlands Country House. The receptionist there calls a taxi for me. It's a short ride up the road to the cemetery. The taxi waits for me and then drives me back home. I have the same driver mostly. They all know me.'

'Maybe your children will come around and not hassle you so much when they see how much it means to you.'

'Perhaps.' Hazel didn't look convinced. 'And now it's time for me to get going.'

'Sure,' said Daniel. 'I won't keep you, but I'd be more than happy to bring the car up on a Saturday, drive you to the cemetery and wait for you and drop you home after.'

'Because you're a good man, Daniel. I'm happy with my arrangement so far. But I'll let you know if that changes.'

He understood that Hazel going to have lunch with Henry was her own private arrangement. Though she allowed her children to manage her care remotely, Hazel had her independence and exercised it. She slowly left the car park and crossed the road. Daniel waved to her, though she was out of sight, off to have lunch with her best pal.

21

Before the next walk Daniel had given a personal training session to both Amanda and the sisters, Mary and Eileen. Their respective sessions hadn't been as daunting as he'd expected. In fact, apart from Amanda's impromptu cartwheel, which brought down a small table lamp in the living room, and Eileen hovering dangerously close to the sinkhole in Trevone, all four had come away smiling. The women congratulated him on his expertise and Daniel had cycled away from the session with the sisters smiling to himself and realizing he was a much better trainer than he'd thought.

The rest of the week he'd spent indoors, stripping wallpaper and sanding down walls in preparation for painting. Since he'd begun he realized the job of redecorating the house would take a lot longer than he'd anticipated. His hair, usually uncombed, was dusted with plaster and grit as he worked. At the end of the day he'd hold the shower head above his body in the old-fashioned bathroom and watch the sandy dirt spiral down the drain with the water.

He had managed to speak to Jess on the phone a few times but she was also very busy with the changes to the surf shop and they hadn't had an opportunity to spend time together.

On Saturday morning rain trailed down the living room windows. Daniel stood eating a bowl of Shreddies as he looked out at the dark clouds in the distance and he doubted very much that anyone would show up for the walk. He looked down the hill as he munched, the cat purring at his feet, and saw Hazel's front door open. She was headed for Trevone Beach in a canary yellow rain jacket, the hood tied tight under her chin. Hazel always arrived at the beach before Daniel. They'd walked together for five Saturdays and only once had he made it to the beach as early as Hazel. He usually arrived with seconds to spare, bounding down to the beach in minutes whereas it would have taken Hazel a good twenty. Daniel saw the little yellow figure head slowly round the corner as he drank the last of the milk from his cereal straight from the bowl. At least Hazel would be there even if the others cried off.

At the car park, Daniel found that all the walkers had shown up. Everyone wore a waterproof cape or jacket of some description. Just as they were getting ready to set off Daniel saw Annabelle's Range Rover approaching the car park. She hurriedly parked at an angle and leapt out of the car wearing a camouflage print raincoat. Another woman jumped out of the passenger seat and together they ran over to the walking group.

'Thank goodness, we made it,' said Annabelle as they panted up to Daniel. 'And I've brought a friend.' She beckoned for her friend to push through the group. 'This is my neighbour, Margot. I told her all about your walking party and she wanted to come along.'

'Hi, Margot,' said Daniel. 'You didn't choose the best weather for your first walk with us.'

'Well, this is England,' she said. Margot had an Eastern

European accent, a gappy smile and lots of energy. 'I think it's a great idea to get out and take some exercise.'

'I did tell Margot that you were very friendly and so the walking group must be, too,' said Annabelle. She squeezed Hazel's shoulder.

'Annabelle, it's lovely to see you.' Hazel smiled up at her and began asking after Mia and Rasmus whom she hadn't seen in quite some time.

'They're both wonderful,' said Annabelle. 'Scott has been reducing his hours at the office so he'll be taking Mia to drama class and looking after Rasmus and I finally get to come on the walk.'

Once Annabelle and Margot were warmly welcomed into the group, Daniel waved his arms and said, 'Okay, that's introductions taken care of. Let's head out.' The newly expanded group set off through the drizzle along the damp path.

During their customary break, the fast-paced walking group, the Padstow Pace Masters, whom the walkers had encountered last week, darted past them. Daniel's walkers, who had been busy munching biscuits and pieces of fruit while taking care not to get too wet on the soggy grass, watched them storm by.

'It's them,' said Amanda through gritted teeth.

'Who are they?' whispered Annabelle.

'They're our nemesis,' said Amanda. She scowled along the path as the walkers in their matching combos hotfooted it towards Harlyn.

'It's not a race,' said Daniel. 'Don't stress about them.'

'Didn't we say we were going to come up with a name for our club this week, Daniel?' said Mary eagerly. She whipped a sheet of paper out of her tracksuit pocket and began to reel off a list of possible names. South Coast Sizzlers. Trail Blazers. The Trevone Troupers. The Walking Wonders. And the list went on. No one was enthused by any of Mary's ideas apart from Eileen.

'They don't really describe us that well,' said Eric, reluctant to look Mary in the eye. His dog had dozed off at his feet. 'All a bit racy and street gang of New York if you ask me. We need something that sounds like us.'

Everyone fell quiet, apart from the occasional 'um' or 'ah' whenever someone shouted out an idea. Minutes went by before Hazel raised a finger.

'I thought of something,' she said. 'It might be silly.'

'What is it?' Daniel sat forward.

'I was thinking, how about "The Slow Lane"?'

Approving 'oohs' and 'ahs' rippled around the group as everyone sounded the name out to themselves, alternating the stress and emphasis on each word.

'The Slow Lane Walkers Club,' said Eric. 'I like the sound of that.' He and the others looked at Daniel.

'Oh yes,' said Daniel nodding. 'I love it, Hazel. It's perfect.'

'I know we're as slow as we are because of me,' she said. 'But if you like the name . . .'

'Sold!' said Amanda. 'Now we can get T-shirts printed?'

There were murmurs of doubt and non-committal.

'Perhaps just having a name is enough for us,' said Daniel. 'But thank you for the suggestion, Amanda.'

She shrugged and edged closer to Oliver, who patted her shoulder and nodded his appreciation for her suggestion.

'Oh!' Mary piped up. 'When I see the young lady, I can tell her that our walking group has a name now.'

Daniel put his hands over his face.

'What young lady?' asked Annabelle.

'I've been telling Daniel for weeks that I know the perfect girl for him. Someone who won't let him out of the house with messy hair and his clothes on inside out.' Mary tutted at Daniel, who checked his sweater. Eileen tutted her agreement with her sister with an added shake of the head.

'Oh, you must tell her to come along,' said Annabelle.

'I am trying,' said Mary. 'But she seems to have dropped off the face of the earth. I might have to put an advert up for her.'

Annabelle and Mary began a conversation about the best ways to track the young girl down. Daniel leapt to his feet and clapped his hands.

'Right,' he said. 'I don't know about you guys but I'm cold and soaked so I think we should head home.'

The group gathered themselves together for the short and slow walk back.

'That is a brilliant name you came up with,' Daniel said to Hazel as they drew nearer to Trevone Beach.

'I'm glad you like it.'

'The offer is still there to drive you to the cemetery,' he said. 'It's always an option.'

'When I can't get there under my own steam anymore I'll let you know. Until then I need to keep walking. Use it or lose it, right?'

Daniel nodded.

Later, before Hazel arrived back home from her lunch date with Henry, Daniel wheeled the pink bicycle down to her house. He leaned it next to the front door and locked it to the trellis. He would have liked to have tied a bow on it but all he had in the house was a scrap of paper and some string. He attached a note to the bike with the words:

For Hazel
Fast bicycle rides for the slowest walker I know.
Love, Daniel.
PS Look forward to helping you ride again x

The rain had eased off by the late afternoon. Faint rays of sun shone through the remaining grey clouds. The cat was at the doorstep when Daniel trotted back after delivering the bike. He had a feeling he'd never get rid of the cat so maybe he should name him, just as they'd named the walking club. He'd ask Hazel for help. The cat whizzed straight into the house the moment the front door was slightly ajar. Maybe Speedy or Lightning, thought Daniel. He was definitely not a slow lane cat.

Before he closed his front door, Daniel looked back down the hill towards the crossroads and saw the tall arc of a rainbow in the sky high above Hazel's house.

22

Daniel lowered the seat of the pink bicycle so that it was a good height for Hazel. It was days until the next coastal walk and they had arranged a time for Hazel to practise her cycling.

'We won't go far,' he'd said. 'You won't need to change gears or go very fast. As soon as you feel unsure just pull the brakes and I'll be right beside you to help you out of the saddle.'

With the bike all ready for her, Daniel waited in the front garden for Hazel to venture out of the house. He'd bought her a brand new helmet, bright pink with a swirling orange design around it. He'd hoped it was colourful enough. Hazel had loved it on sight, trying it on right away.

'Here I am,' said Hazel. She came out of the house with her walking stick, wearing her new helmet and a matching pink tracksuit with the ankle cuffs tucked into her socks. It was a mild May morning, ideal for a bike ride. 'I'm not so sure about this anymore, Daniel.'

'Don't worry and don't doubt yourself,' he said. 'We're just going to walk to the quiet cul-de-sac around the corner. You can practise your balance and I won't let go of you for a second.'

Hazel nodded but she looked sceptical. Around the corner,

Daniel set up the bike so that it was facing the middle house in the cul-de-sac.

'Just put your stick down, Hazel, and I'll help you up.'

Hazel was unsteady on the bike and Daniel took the strain of her weight against his chest while trying to help her balance. He had aimed the bike towards a bushy hedge in front of the middle house.

'As soon as we're upright, just pedal,' he said. 'Aim for the hedge. I'll be right at your side.'

'I can't seem to balance the way I used to,' said Hazel. 'It used to be so instinctive. I think I might be wasting your time, Daniel.'

'Don't worry, Hazel. I'm here for you.'

Daniel could feel her struggle to remain upright. She fell against him several times, tutting in disappointment at not being able to manage the first basic stage – balance. She puffed and panted occasionally as the physical strain on her small body became a challenge. Her feet slipped off the pedals and she looked at Daniel in despair.

'It's fine,' he said. 'Even if you don't manage to pedal at all, at least you got up on the saddle and that's a start. We've got plenty of time.'

Hazel wobbled on the bike a few more times but trying to stay stable enough to start pedalling was proving difficult.

'The great thing about cycling is that you have no pressure on your bones,' said Daniel. 'Just imagine being able to get around and not having to use a walking stick.'

Hazel nodded at this. Supported by Daniel's chest and his hands on the handlebar and the back of the saddle, she sat upright, both feet on the pedals. For a split second she had the bike steady.

'Now push,' said Daniel softly into her ear. All of a sudden momentum was established and in seconds Hazel had pedalled once, twice and then again.

'I can do it!' she exclaimed and quickly squeezed the brakes, stopping a good distance from the hedge.

'I told you,' said Daniel. 'Should we try again?'

It had taken almost an hour of effort, but Hazel had found her balance on the bike without Daniel's assistance. She rode a few times from the middle of the cul-de-sac to the hedge and back, with Daniel running beside her. Though the bike moved in a zigzag, Hazel managed to stop and start on her own.

'We can learn how to go around the close next,' said Daniel. 'But maybe you need a break for now? I don't want you to wear yourself out. Save it for another day.'

'I am pretty exhausted,' said Hazel.

They walked very carefully back to Hazel's house. Daniel pushed the bike and Hazel relied heavily on her walking stick to get her back around the corner.

'Imagine if I could give up my old stick for good,' she said.

'One step at a time.' Daniel grinned at her. 'I never promised you'd be able to bin it altogether.'

'I know, Daniel, but just being able to cycle again was an amazing feeling. Now, you've definitely earned a nice cup of tea and some of the oat and apple loaf I baked earlier.'

'Count me in,' said Daniel. He locked the pink bicycle up against the trellis for Hazel once they'd made it home.

Hazel sat in her orthopaedic chair in the living room, her mug of tea and a side plate of the sweet loaf on the table beside her. Daniel sat on the sofa, devouring his slice in seconds.

'You know,' said Hazel, 'just that little spin on the bike has taken me back several years.'

'To your paper round days?'

'To the time Henry and I borrowed a couple of rickety push bikes from the farm in Beaune. We'd done our morning of labour and found the bikes in the barn covered in old rags. My schoolgirl French was just good enough for the farmer to understand that we fancied a bit of a cycle. We had a great time riding down country roads. It was September. We were planting onions in one field and sowing spinach in another with a bunch of other farm labourers.'

'How long did you and Henry stay away for? You said you didn't get to go to university the year you were supposed to.'

'Oh, we were gone a year. I don't know how many times Henry proposed to me during that year.'

'And you said no each time?'

'I said yes each time but Henry wanted us to rush off and get wed then and there.' Hazel chuckled. 'But I insisted that we kept separate rooms. I had promised my mother. And even though my parents approved of Henry, Dad had given him stern warnings to treat me with respect as well as to look after me. I wouldn't get married abroad somewhere without my family being there. Mum and Dad trusted me and gave me the opportunity to travel and I had the time of my life.'

'So was it a letdown, coming back home and settling into a routine?' asked Daniel.

'I wouldn't say we settled into a routine, Daniel. I know you see settling down with someone as mundane, but if you find the right person to settle down with, life doesn't have to be boring and it doesn't have to be routine. Or lame, as you millennial youngsters call it.'

Daniel laughed.

'So when is the next lesson?' asked Hazel.

'Tomorrow if you like.'

'I don't want to get in the way of your decorating work.'

'It's nice to have a break, actually. Besides, I started working as a personal trainer last week.'

'For Amanda?'

'Yes, and I was booked by Mary and Eileen, too.'

'It's good that you can put your skills to use, Daniel. I hope you found it satisfying.'

Daniel grinned at the memory of putting Amanda through her paces in her living room and the number of times he'd had to steer Eileen to safety, away from the sinkhole, during her bear walk exercise.

'Surprisingly,' he said, 'I did find it satisfying. I had flashbacks of some good times when I was training people in London.'

'You're good with people, Daniel. You should keep it up and see where it leads you.'

Although he'd returned to personal training reluctantly, Hazel was right, he had put his training to good use. He could see himself honing his skills as a personal trainer, developing the idea of making it a business and enjoying it. Maybe Jess was right when she said that sometimes decisions are made for you and your future writes itself.

'We'll see,' he said. 'I'll call on you tomorrow around the same kind of time. Maybe we can get you doing some wheelies in the cul-de-sac.'

'I'll hold you to that.' Hazel's face lit up.

In a short space of time Daniel had become involved in several lives in the small village. For the first time since he'd been back to Trevone he hadn't once thought about escaping it.

23

The waves were quiet and slow as they glided onto the sand and rolled away again. The sky was a bluish grey, thin white clouds streaked the expanse of it. On the horizon the sea was a deep shade of blue but closer to shore were hints of aqua. Frothy white waves cascaded over the rocks jutting out of the sea and beat gently against the face of the cliffs on either side of the bay. A flock of gulls landed on the sand for a brief moment before flapping their wings and heading out in formation towards the water.

Daniel arrived at Trevone Bay at six-thirty on Friday evening for the date he'd arranged with Jess. He had with him a picnic blanket, a bottle of red wine and two plastic glasses. He laid the blanket on the verge of grass near the car park and looked out to sea.

He wore a sweater and sat cross-legged on the blanket waiting for Jess to cycle along the path on her way back from the surf school. Moments later he heard the lazy creak of the wheels of Jess's bike. He turned to see her cycling towards him, waving. She jumped off the bike and let it fall beside the blanket before bending down to kiss Daniel, slowly and deeply on his lips.

'I'm not late, am I?' she asked.

'No, you're right on time. How are you?'

'All the better for seeing you and, I have to say, that bottle of wine.'

'Left over from Christmas,' he said. 'And stolen from my sister. As with most of my food and drink, I'm ashamed to say.'

Jess was casually dressed in jeans and a black hooded top. 'A picnic blanket but no picnic?' she said.

'Oh, it's coming. I hope you like anchovies. You look like the type who likes anchovies.'

'Love them. Good call. So we're having pizza?'

'Is that okay?' He looked sheepish. He had told her he'd bring the food and drink but when she asked if he was actually preparing something he'd implied that he would be. Looking up the local takeaway menu was a kind of preparation, he'd thought. 'It should be here in the next few minutes.'

'Good, because I'm famished.' Jess settled down on the blanket beside Daniel.

'How was work?' he asked.

'Busy. Still getting to grips with the business side of things and Marisol was helping me plan the yoga studio.'

'I still can't believe that you went from not making decisions to becoming an entrepreneur.'

'Well, I'm not quite there yet. But it all seems to be falling into place. Once Marisol announced she was going to stay, things just took off from there. I'm really excited about it but at the same time I'm sorry I went back on our no decisions pact.'

'It's fine. I've had a similar experience myself.'

'Oh yeah? What happened?'

'I started training a few of the ladies from the Walkers

Club. I finally gave in to them and actually it's been okay. I would do more sessions, if I had the clients.'

'And you'll probably get them. Sometimes the thing you least expect to happen just happens.'

Very soon a young man pulled into the car park on a moped and lifted a large pizza out of the top box at the back. He carried it over to Daniel and Jess on the beach. Daniel observed the hungry way Jess devoured her first slice of pizza.

'Don't judge me,' she said. 'I told you I was famished, I've been busy all day and didn't get time to eat.'

Daniel laughed.

'No judgement here.'

His whole week had been hectic. He'd taken Hazel on a few tense cycling lessons as well as having personal training sessions with Amanda and the sisters. Then there was the vast amount of work he'd done on the house so far. He had spent long hours up a ladder, priming the hall walls, as well as removing tiles in the kitchen and tending to the garden. He could feel the soreness in his muscles from the hours of decorating, but as he watched the profile of Jess's face becoming a silhouette in the fading light, the aches melted away.

Jess had been on his mind a lot but he'd resisted reading anything into his roaming thoughts, telling himself over and over that theirs was nothing more than an easy-going relationship. But as he looked at Jess now he knew his feelings for her were becoming deeper than he'd wanted. It's okay, he thought, it's not as if he wanted to propose marriage. He just wanted to be around Jess, see more of her. After all, he might only be there until the summer.

'What are you looking at?' she asked, leaning on her elbow and mirroring his posture.

'At you,' he said. He moved closer to her and ran a finger along the contours of her face. She smiled and kissed his fingertips as they smoothed over her mouth.

'Should we be worried that this is becoming more than casual?' Jess moved closer and looked deep into Daniel's eyes.

'I don't know,' he said. 'We did make a pact.'

'And you were quick to agree to it. I wondered why.'

Daniel sensed a seriousness in her mood.

'What do you mean?' he asked.

'I mean, why are you so keen to keep things chill between us? Something to do with your last relationship?'

Daniel rolled onto his back. At some stage the question about exes was bound to come up but a reminder of Aria was not what he wanted in that moment. Jess would ask another question and then another and he'd find himself in the dark corner of his mind where he'd firmly placed thoughts about Aria. The dark corner was a place of confusion and jumbled emotions for his ex-girlfriend if he were being honest; sometimes he felt lucky to have escaped with a broken heart because that could be mended, but he still had a store of fond memories and wishes that his relationship with Aria would have worked out better. How could he tell any of this to Jess, with her kissing distance away and him hoping that they could go back seconds before when it seemed as if they were about to kiss? His thoughts caused chaos and he tried to shrug off the feeling. His expression must have betrayed him.

'It's okay,' Jess said quickly. 'We don't have to go there.'

'Let's just say my last relationship ended on bad terms and I'm glad to be out of it.'

'You don't sound glad.'

'Well, what about you?' He leaned up on his elbow again. 'Who did you last go out with?'

'A complete twit who I met here last year when he was on holiday. Thankfully he's back up north and won't be venturing round these parts again.' She laughed, lightly.

'Mine is further away. So let's not even talk about them.'

'Deal,' said Jess, bouncing up and into a cross-legged seat. She looked up and sighed. 'It's getting dark and the lights on my bike aren't all that. I should go.'

'Really?'

She nodded slowly.

'Stay a while longer,' said Daniel. 'We can walk back to mine and I can put your bike in the car and drive you home.' In the dim grey of dusk he looked pleadingly at her. He took her hand as the sun behind the clouds began to sink towards the sea.

'I would like this evening to carry on,' she said quietly. 'We said no drama and I'm worried that a drama is what we're heading for. The good kind, of course, and, if I'm honest, I'm starting to like the idea.'

'Of having a good kind of drama with me?' He grinned at her. She pushed him off balance so that he rolled backwards.

'Of course with you. But maybe we shouldn't.'

Before Daniel could say that he was on the same wavelength as Jess and that he was also worried about taking the relationship a step further, she sat up abruptly on her haunches.

'Let's clear this lot up.' Jess pointed at the empty pizza box and the wine bottle and glasses. 'There's a lot happening at the house and Noah and Marisol need my help. I really have to get going.'

Jess having to leave meant that the conversation about whether they should take their relationship a step further could be put off for another day. No decisions had to be made, kept or broken.

'I should let you go then,' he said.

They set about tidying everything away. When they had finished, Daniel held the folded picnic blanket over his arm as Jess mounted her bike and used one foot as a kick stand.

'Daniel.' Jess looked a little on the serious side and he feared that she was about to tell him that they should cool things off completely; there was a heat building between them and it was clearly worrying her as well as him. 'Tomorrow evening Noah and Marisol are throwing a party. Their engagement party, actually. I said I'd help them get the place in order. They're starting to cook tonight and the food will be great. Marisol's sister is over from Argentina and a load of Noah's friends will be coming. What do you think? Would you like to come?'

He smiled at her. 'Sounds amazing. I'd love to. Thanks.'

'Brilliant,' she said. 'I'm really glad you can make it. About eight, okay? I'll send the directions.'

Daniel waited until Jess was completely out of sight before he walked back home in the dimming light.

24

The following morning, Daniel woke from a deep sleep, feeling refreshed and ready for the walk with The Slow Lane. After his date with Jess on the beach the night before, he'd walked around with a cheesy smile on his face, thinking about her the whole time. His train of thought was only broken when his friend Doc began a long running conversation with him from Sicily throughout the evening. Doc, who was sounding more cryptic than usual, communicated with a series of texts, pictures, a video call and an actual telephone conversation. He'd made little or no sense to a very tired Daniel who realized, by about one o'clock in the morning, that he and Doc had talked circles around the same three subjects: partying, women in general and women Doc had slept with. Eventually Daniel closed his eyes while Doc was still talking and woke to the sound of the cat purring heavily at the foot of his sleeping bag.

Daniel showered and left the house, just as Hazel was leaving hers. He rushed to catch her up.

'Good morning, Daniel,' said Hazel.

'Before you say it, yes, I'm out early. I even had time to shave and comb my hair today. Mary won't be able to moan about me.'

'It is nice to see you looking smart. I wonder if today is the day Mary manages to arrange your blind date.' Hazel chuckled hard.

'Don't get me started on that. Imagine if she did bring that girl she's always going on about. She and Annabelle will have me marching up the aisle in no time.'

'I've said it before, marriage isn't a bad thing, Daniel.' Hazel gave him a sideways look.

'If it works out, then that's fine but that's not always what happens. So it's not something you want to rush into.'

'You sound awfully experienced for someone who has never been married.'

Daniel was quiet.

'Are you telling me that you have?' asked Hazel, slowing her pace a little more. 'Were you married to the girl who left you?'

Daniel snorted a laugh. 'No, not married. Not me. But she made me think seriously about it. That is, I wanted to ask her. I bought the ring but I never got to get down on one knee because she left before . . .'

Hazel stopped walking.

'I'm sorry, Daniel. To have your heart broken like that can't have been easy.'

'It wasn't easy. It was bloody hard actually. After she left I felt really lost. Confused and a little angry, to tell the truth. I had so many questions, so many things I wanted to say to her. Maybe I was an idiot even thinking about it, rushing into the whole marriage idea. I mean, we hadn't been together long, what was I thinking?'

'That you were in love and you believed she was the one.'

Daniel sighed deeply. 'I did think that. Even though I'd sworn off the idea of marriage. I'd already seen one fail miserably, no one left standing.'

'You mean your parents' marriage?' asked Hazel. Daniel nodded solemnly and they continued to walk. 'I can see how much it's affected you. Have you ever talked to Annabelle about it?'

'I can't talk to Annabelle the way I talk to you,' he said, 'as caring as she is. Besides, her own marriage is going through a bad patch.'

'Oh, bad patches are a part of marriage, Daniel. I can't imagine a single happy ever after that didn't have a wobble or two, a disagreement, a misunderstanding. Maybe that's what happened with *your* girl.'

'I'll never know, will I? All I know is, I'm not in a rush to feel like that again.' They were close to the beach now and a breeze tangled itself around them. The sea looked wild. 'You and Gran got it right, though,' Daniel said. 'You married the right people.'

Hazel stopped again.

'Daniel, would you like to meet Henry?'

'I'd love to meet him.' Daniel raised his brow in surprise, a feeling of honour sweeping over him and showing crimson in his cheeks. 'If you're sure it's okay.'

'I am, Daniel. How about today? I can wait for you while you pick up your car after the walk.'

'Thanks, Hazel. It's a plan.'

They arrived at the club's meeting point just ahead of Eric and Benny the dog, Benny stopping to sniff out the corners of the car park as well as the registration plate of a Vauxhall Astra. Eric tapped the tip of his flat cap and motioned Benny to sit. Amanda and Oliver came next. Being far shorter than Amanda, Oliver's neck was in a constant upward tilt as he listened to her speaking, something she did a lot of. The sisters turned up in bright sweat suits, their hoodies zipped up to their chins.

'Great news,' said Mary, rushing over to Daniel. 'I managed to talk to that young lady at last. Apparently, she knows all about us and she's going to do her best to come next week! Said she was busy today.' Mary winked. 'Now that you appear to have found a comb, please carry on using it.'

Daniel nodded. He spotted his sister and her friend Margot parking up. Hannah the mobile hairdresser arrived last. Amanda insisted on a few spinal flexions and a couple of squats before everyone set off for the walk.

'I was thinking, Daniel,' said Hazel, as they started on the incline from the beach. 'What about the idea of me cycling to and from the beach now that I'm improving?'

'That's a good idea,' said Daniel. 'But I'd prefer to take you out on roads with traffic beforehand. The cul-de-sac is fine but we need to get the hand signals going.'

'Well, I knew how to do them once. I'm sure it'll come back to me.'

'Of course it will. But I'll try to get hold of another bike so we can go together.'

'Perfect.'

The walkers took a short refreshment break above Newtrain Bay as usual and, as usual, Hazel opened her rucksack and handed around additional food that she insisted they needed to keep their energy up for the walk. Mary was excited and could not wait to report to the others that she had located the girl she believed would be perfect for Daniel and that she might join them on the walk next Saturday. As he'd expected, the announcement caused a stir with most of the others. Amanda didn't seem too bothered about a young girl coming along on the walk. She sat very close to Oliver, jiggling and giggling, indifferent to the whole affair. Annabelle, however, was ecstatic.

'Who is she, what's her name?' she asked Mary.

'I couldn't remember her name and I was too embarrassed to ask her. But Eileen, Hazel and I know her from when she taught fitness and stretch classes for a time at the community centre.'

'I suppose I can cancel the profile I was making for you, Daniel,' said Annabelle.

'What profile?' he asked. He had slid off to crouch behind Eric and Benny for protection but he sat upright, his interest piqued.

'Oh, I was writing your profile for a dating website,' Annabelle said. 'It's brilliant actually. It's one of those sites where someone other than the lonely heart writes about your attributes and sends in a photograph that best depicts the lonely heart.'

'I'm not a lonely heart,' said Daniel. 'Could you stop saying "lonely heart"?'

'Oh, come on, Daniel. I was only trying to prevent you from becoming a male spinster,' his sister said.

'Don't you mean a bachelor?' he asked.

'No,' said Margot. 'Bachelor doesn't have the same stigma attached to it as spinster. Bachelors have an element of cool about them. Mysterious and sought after by single women. From what Annabelle tells me, you are slowly becoming a male spinster. You live on your own and you have a cat.'

Daniel stood up. 'It's not my cat. Look, can we go, please?'

'Is it sad that I want a cat?' asked Hannah in her timid voice.

'Well, possibly,' said Amanda. 'You are single. Do you like scented candles?'

Hannah nodded.

'Don't listen to this, Hannah,' said Daniel. 'Don't let other people try to put you in a box. And if you want a cat, get a cat. In fact take my cat.'

'Thank you,' said Hannah. 'I will. If that's okay.'

'My pleasure.' Daniel winked at her.

'So no one claimed your stray?' asked Annabelle.

'Are you the one who put the posters up?' asked Mary.

'That's right,' Daniel said. He pulled a face and shrugged. 'And that was weeks ago.'

'It looked a handsome cat,' Mary added. 'I'm surprised no one has claimed it yet.'

'I'm not,' said Eric, whose dog was asleep with one paw over his eyes.

Everyone looked at Eric.

'That poster,' he said. 'The phone number on it is wrong.'

'Wrong?' said Annabelle. 'I typed that up. How could it be wrong? That's Daniel's number.'

'Can't be,' said Eric. 'I've rung it several times and get a message saying number not in use.'

'So you know whose cat I've got?' said Daniel, sitting again.

'He's my cat,' said Eric. 'Only I wouldn't say he's lost. He never stays put at my house. Always on the move, that one. Of course he comes over to your house because he's done that for years. Went over to see your gran and came home again when he was ready.'

'You're kidding me.' Daniel was stunned. 'So, all this time I thought he really liked me, he must have been wondering who the hell I was and what I was doing in Gran's house.'

'Probably,' said Eric. 'Don't go feeding him too much, mind. Always been a greedy cat.'

'Tell me about it. Thanks, Eric.' Daniel turned to Annabelle. 'So, mystery solved, then.'

'Sorry about the poster,' she said.

'All's well that ends well,' said Eric.

'Hold on,' said Hannah, in a loud and impatient voice. The other walkers looked at her. 'I suppose this means I can't have your cat now, doesn't it?'

'And good job,' said Amanda. 'You'd only stay a spinster if you did.'

Before a conversation began about what constituted a spinster, or a male spinster come to that, Daniel got the group on their feet and they set off again.

That Saturday, not only did The Slow Lane manage to increase the distance of their walk by about a kilometre, but also the Padstow Pace Masters didn't show up.

'Maybe they've changed their route,' said Mary.

'I hope so,' said Amanda.

Back at the meeting point everyone said their goodbyes. Annabelle apologized again about the poster before leaving with Margot. Mary suggested Daniel wear a tie for the following walk, Amanda and Oliver set off together and Hannah glared at Daniel before she left. Eric and Benny sauntered away last of all.

'Well, that was a dramatic walk,' said Hazel to Daniel.

'Tell me about it. Right, I'll jog home for the car,' he said.

'Yes, I'll be here.'

Daniel ran all the way, his mind on the party later at Jess's house. She'd sent the address and he was looking forward to seeing her again. Whoever it was Mary had invited to the next walk, there was no way she could compare to Jess.

25

The last time Daniel had entered the cemetery was for Gran's funeral. He remembered the sadness surrounding the day and the large number of people at the church, most, if not all, of whom he hadn't recognized. It occurred to Daniel as he and Hazel followed the paths around the headstones to Henry's resting place that Hazel would have been at his grandmother's funeral but he didn't remember seeing her. He'd noted that his father had been a no show and had wondered if he'd wanted to avoid Daniel in the same way he'd hoped to avoid his father. Daniel's mother was calm that day, sombre, and had said very little to Daniel other than to ask if he was okay. Annabelle had sniffed and dabbed her eyes for most of the morning's ceremony.

'Here we are,' said Hazel, coming to a stop. 'Hello, Henry. Look who we have here. Daniel. Molly's grandson from the walking club. Daniel, this is Henry, my husband.'

Daniel smiled at Hazel and nodded. 'Hello, Henry.'

Henry's gravestone was granite. The engraving was bold and handsome, as he'd expected, considering Hazel's descriptions of her late husband. It read: *In Memory of a Loving Husband, Proud Father and Grandfather, Henry John Taylor. Beloved and Missed Forever.*

Daniel stood beside Hazel unsure of what to do or say. A fresh flower arrangement, mostly of red roses and white freesias, sat in a black onyx vase at the base of the headstone.

'I pay someone to keep up the grave as I find it hard to manage myself,' said Hazel. 'Henry must approve of this flower arrangement – they're beautiful, aren't they?' She smiled up at Daniel and looked back at the headstone.

'Beautiful,' said Daniel.

Hazel rummaged to the bottom of her backpack.

'I have a little plastic sheet to sit on,' she said. 'I'm sure we can both fit.'

Daniel opened the small sheet and spread it on the tufts of grass separating Henry's grave from the grave of a young woman, '*Taken Too Soon*'. He attempted to help Hazel down to the sheet but she stopped him.

'I can still do this.'

Daniel watched Hazel lower herself first to one knee and into a seated position with the stick for balance and one hand on the headstone. She sighed with an 'ah' sound as she sat with most of her weight on one thigh.

'I know this will become harder but I'll buy one of those walking sticks with a seat when it does.' She gave a deep wink to Daniel, who gave a shaky smile, a worry at the back of his mind that perhaps Hazel's children could be right about their mother not making so many visits on her own to see Henry.

Hazel shared the food in her backpack with Daniel, who accepted a slice of fruit cake and some tea from her flask.

'Daniel reminded me of how lucky I was to have met you, Henry,' said Hazel. She turned to Daniel. 'You said that your grandmother and I chose the right partners. You see, I worried about whether I should marry Henry. Society was against us and his family would never have him back if he went through with it. When I asked him if he was absolutely sure, he said, *Hazel, you're the right girl for me.* And he was the right boy for me. What a marriage we had, what a life we shared.' She stared back at the headstone for a long moment. 'Just remember, Daniel, your gran and I were lucky to have fallen in love with the right one first time around. Sometimes, it can take time. Don't give up on the idea of marriage or of falling in love again.'

'I wish I had your moves, Henry.' Daniel grinned. 'And your good luck.' He touched Hazel's tiny hand. She giggled and continued to chat to Henry about how Daniel had been keeping himself busy decorating Molly's house.

'I should go and see her while I'm here,' said Daniel.

'You remember the plot? Follow the path in the middle, there. Your grandparents are by the far wall where the lavender grows.'

Daniel took a short walk to visit his grandparents and gave Hazel some time alone with Henry.

On the drive home Hazel was cheerful and bubbly.

'I wish you could have met Henry before,' she said as Daniel parked outside her house.

'Me too.'

'I told him all about the walk today and how Mary is still trying to arrange a date for you.'

'I'm sure Henry would tell me to run a mile.' Daniel jumped out of the driver's seat and came around to the passenger side to help Hazel out of the car.

'From what I remember of this girl,' said Hazel, 'she seemed nice and friendly. I only ever went to the one class, mind you. But I'm sure you can trust Mary.'

'Can I let you into a secret?' said Daniel.

'What secret?'

'I've already sort of met someone and we've been on a couple of dates.'

Hazel's eyes widened, a look of approval on her face.

'You are a dark horse, Daniel. Why didn't you just tell them earlier?'

'To be honest, I don't know what's happening between us. I like her a lot but I can't rush into anything. You know, I'm busy with the house, my future is uncertain . . .'

'Someone broke your heart.'

He nodded, lips pulled into a line.

'Don't worry, Daniel. Your secret is safe with me. But don't let your past close the door to your future.'

'I won't. See you for the next cycle, Hazel.'

'I'm very excited about it. I want to practise as much as possible. Do you think I could cycle to the cemetery one day?'

'Steady on,' said Daniel, walking Hazel to her front door. 'Let's try a few main roads first and see how we go. But honestly, as long as you have the energy and you feel strong enough, it's a pretty direct route, so why not?'

Hazel gave him a thumbs up and disappeared indoors.

Between decorating and trying to sort out a clean shirt to wear to Noah and Marisol's engagement party, Daniel received even more texts from Doc. In the end he stopped messaging back. Surely Doc was on a walking trip at Mount Etna. Saturday was always a busy day and Doc should be concentrating on his walkers, not asking him what the weather was like where he was.

In the evening, Daniel took a bath. He pulled out a clean T-shirt from the pile on his floor and inspected the legs of his best jeans and a pair of cotton drill trousers to see which had the fewer stains. His hair was still damp; he combed it and immediately made a mess of it when he pulled on a sweater. Daniel grabbed for the car keys on the bottom step in the hallway and was about to leave for the party when there was a knock on the door. He could hear male voices outside and wondered who it could be.

In the kitchen doorway the cat twitched and looked up at Daniel. There was another knock, a louder one this time. Daniel looked at the cat.

'I don't know,' said Daniel, raising his shoulders. He opened the door and had the shock of his life.

'Doc?'

'*Ciao, fratello!*' Doc's arms were open wide. He was a broad man and as tall as Daniel. His skin was bronzed and his hair was a tangle of dark waves and curls. His light blue eyes sparkled with happiness as he stepped inside and pulled Daniel into a hug. He raised Daniel up and spun him.

'What the . . .?' Daniel spluttered. 'What are you doing here?'

'What kind of greeting is that? I come all the way here to surprise you and that's how you greet me.'

'Yo, Danny boy!'

Daniel recognized the voice of another of his friends from Italy. Like Doc, Greg had a massive rucksack on his shoulders. They smelled of cigarettes and a long day of travelling. Daniel hugged Greg.

'I'm seriously glad to see you guys,' said Daniel. 'Is that why you kept asking me what the weather was like?'

'Dude,' said Doc, 'how come you didn't take the hint?'

'Because . . . I don't know, man. I never expected you to show up.'

'Well, you did invite us. I know you were drunk when you said it but I thought you'd like the surprise.'

'I do. I love it.' Daniel patted their shoulders. 'How long are you here for?'

'Indefinitely,' said Greg. 'After Doc and I had a massive bust up with the manager and Doc shouted "We quit" in his face without consulting me, we jacked it all in.'

'We're planning on finding something else, another job,' said Doc. 'But there's no rush, right?' He blasted a loud laugh into Daniel's face. 'We thought we could hang out here for a while, catch some waves with our man, Daniel.'

'Of course,' said Daniel. 'That's brilliant.'

'You must have lost the plot by now living out here in the countryside all alone,' said Doc. 'Thought you might appreciate a bit of company, right?'

'Right,' said Daniel, thinking about the company he had been keeping. He would have a hard time explaining his new companions to Doc and Greg. He couldn't imagine what they'd think if they knew he'd been hanging out with a bunch of over-sixties for the last few weeks.

'*Daniele*,' shouted Doc and hugged him for a second time before jabbing his upper arm as if it were a boxing bag. 'Why are you looking so lost? The party is here and guess what?'

'What?' said Daniel.

'We have one more little surprise for you.'

Daniel had a slight quiver in his voice. 'What is it?'

'Look,' said Doc. He shuffled his rucksack off and signalled to someone out of sight at the open door. In the next second another surprise visitor stepped inside.

'*Ciao, Daniele*,' came a familiar dark and sultry voice.

'Aria.'

Daniel stood and stared at his ex-girlfriend for a long time.

'She followed us here,' said Doc. 'Hey. You have a cat. Sweet. You got any food in here, man?'

Greg and Doc headed into the kitchen, closely followed by the cat.

'You haven't exactly invited me in,' said Aria, who stood timidly on the mat.

'No. Yes. Of course. Come in, come in.' He went to close the door and Aria grabbed him around the waist.

'Daniel,' she whispered. 'I really missed you.'

Daniel wrapped his arms around her. He bent down so that his cheek was against her soft hair, long and brown right down to her hips, smelling of fruit and flowers as always. He closed his eyes and inhaled her.

'How did you manage to hook up with these guys?' Daniel stepped away but Aria drew closer to him and hooked her arms around his neck.

'It's a long story,' she breathed. 'You let your hair grow long again. I like it.'

'I thought you liked it short.'

'I never said that.'

'You did. You told me I looked like a hippy.'

Aria laughed.

'What is it?' he said.

'Two minutes and we're already arguing. Nothing changes, huh?'

'Seems like it.'

'Well, those arguments are something I really want to change,' she said. 'And I will.'

Doc burst into the hallway.

'I found some pasta but not much else,' he said. 'We'll go to the shop. I can cook.'

Daniel was lost for words. He didn't know how to tell his friend that he already had plans. If he did, Doc would insist they all go with him. He couldn't imagine a worse way for Jess to meet Aria so he said nothing about the party.

'We'd better order pizza,' said Daniel. 'Not much in the way of shops close by.'

'Daniel?' said Aria, slipping her hand into his.

'Yes?'

'Could you bring my bags in? Show me where I'm sleeping?'

Doc raised both hands and backed up to the kitchen door.

'I'll be in here if anybody needs me,' he said, jabbing a thumb behind him. He laughed loudly and went back into the kitchen.

26

Sunlight trickled through a gap between the curtains in his bedroom window. Daniel opened his eyes and blinked. He lifted up onto his elbow, holding one hand over his face as he viewed the room. The cat was nowhere to be seen but another figure slept soundly in a sleeping bag beside his. For a second he was confused until Aria rolled over. Her long brown hair covered most of her face. She looked peaceful, her breaths coming slow and deep. On a faint exhale Aria turned away from him again. It hadn't been a dream. Doc, Greg and Aria had all appeared at his door unannounced last night. He swallowed and remembered the shock of seeing Aria. He couldn't believe it was her, after all this time, standing in the doorway. He'd spent almost a year wondering what he'd done wrong and how she could just leave without giving him a chance to put right whatever he'd done. He would have apologized for anything, guilty or not, so that she would stay.

Daniel remembered the anger he felt when he was told that Aria was back in Rome with her ex-boyfriend. The rumours were that she was happy now, that she would never return to Mount Etna and that she never wanted to see Daniel again.

There was still the mystery hanging over why she should show up at his door with Doc and Greg of all people. They were his best friends and as such were on his side when the breakup happened. They'd taken Daniel out on many a beer-filled night to help him get over her and move on. How did they run into Aria? Why did they bring her?

Doc had dominated the evening with his tales from Mount Etna and the massive falling out he'd had with the tour company manager, so there hadn't been time to discuss the finer details leading up to the surprise visit.

Doc and Greg had brought lots of alcohol with them, all of which had been consumed along with the massive takeaway feast they'd had. He imagined the empty pizza boxes, wine bottles and beer cans down in the living room and in the kitchen. They had sprawled their drunk and tired bodies across the living room. Greg had passed out on the floor, his head on his rucksack. Doc hadn't managed to make sense of his sleeping bag. He had fallen asleep in the middle of the room, still wearing his outdoor jacket. Loud and distorted music peeled from the laptop speakers. It had been quite a party.

Daniel lay back and rubbed the throbbing area just above his eyes. He remembered Aria sticking to him like glue all night. She'd obviously wanted to talk but he'd been trying to find a moment to send a message to Jess to say he couldn't make the party after all. It had proved impossible; Aria was either at his shoulder or snuggling up to him. He remembered putting his mobile down somewhere, giving up on sending a text under Aria's watchful eye.

At some stage during the evening, Daniel had found himself alone in the kitchen with Aria. His head was in the cupboard as he searched for coffee for her. She hadn't wanted any alcohol all night. Daniel had difficulty finding the jar of instant coffee, his focus somewhat blurred by the number of shots he'd knocked back with Doc and Greg.

'When are we going to talk?' Aria had said. Daniel had continued the search, not looking up. 'Forget about the coffee. Just clear your head so we can speak.'

He remembered the cat had tried to make friends with Aria, rubbing his head against her leg. Aria got angry, said something in Italian and shooed the cat away into the garden and slammed the door.

'Why would you do that?' Daniel had said, looking outside into the dark night but he couldn't make out where the cat had gone in the shadows.

'I didn't think you liked cats,' said Aria.

'He's not mine,' said Daniel. 'He just comes for a visit. I don't even know his name.'

Greg had found his way to the kitchen at that point. 'Whose name?' he'd asked.

'Oh, just the cat.' Daniel had been glad to have someone come and diffuse the atmosphere in the kitchen, someone as equally drunk and who didn't want to talk about breakups.

'Where's the cat?' Greg had slurred. 'I love the cat.'

'Just keep it away from me.' Aria had stormed away then and Daniel didn't know if he should chase after her. He used to do that a lot once.

Aria had taken herself to bed. It was only in the early hours of the morning, when an intoxicated Daniel found himself in his bedroom, did he notice the smell of Aria's hair filling the air and feel her soft body rolling closer to him. She had stroked his face but Daniel must have passed out.

He pressed his forefinger and thumb into the hollows at the top of his nose. The headache wouldn't leave him alone;

neither would the swirling memory of loud conversations that made no sense from the night before. Doc had been loud, so bloody loud, and Greg had been just as boisterous. It was clear, from what he remembered of the conversation, that his guests were going to be around for a while. Though it was great to see them again, their being there posed a few problems. He couldn't see that he'd get an awful lot done in the house. Doc and Greg loved to party. Their brain waves were constantly tuned to holiday mode. All the work he needed to do on the house would come to a standstill and set him back. As for his other plans – helping Hazel with her garden and her cycling lessons, personal training appointments – he might have to put them all on hold. He couldn't imagine the guys coming on the Saturday walk either.

He scrunched his eyes tight to see if the pain in his temples would ease. He saw Jess's face. He imagined she'd be disappointed he hadn't shown up for the party, maybe even upset. They'd both been looking forward to it. If only he'd thought of messaging her before his own party with his friends got under way. He needed to see Jess urgently, to explain. Thinking of her looking out for him and him not turning up gave him a horrible feeling in his stomach. He let out a long sigh.

'Good morning to you, too.' Aria was leaning up on her elbow, moving her long hair from her face. The bangles on her wrist jangled as her fingers laced through the long strands she tossed off her bare shoulder. 'I slept like a baby. You?'

'What? Me?' said Daniel.

'Of course you. Who else would I be speaking to? But you never could function before coffee. We should go out. Find a coffee shop.'

'What, now?'

'*Daniele.* Wake up, please. I am in desperate need of a coffee and to talk to you.'

Daniel turned his face to the ceiling. There were cobwebs he needed to dust away, cracks he needed to smooth over. He looked back at Aria.

'I'd better leave them a note if we're going out.'

'Who, those lazy idiots downstairs?' Aria tutted. 'They will sleep a day at least. Can I use your shower?'

'Of course.'

Aria emptied herself from her sleeping bag. She was completely naked. She riffled through her rucksack and pulled out a washbag and a towel which she loosely held in front of her. At the door she stopped.

'Which one?'

'Oh,' said Daniel. 'The door to the left.'

'*Grazie.*'

Daniel blew through his lips. When she'd left him, he had so wanted Aria back in his life. The feeling didn't let go of him for a very long time. Seeing her olive skin, the birth mark on her hip and her messy morning hair filled him with confusion. He didn't know what he wanted. He heard the water running in the bathroom across the hallway and felt like jumping into the car and driving all the way to Jess's house. There were probably party guests crashed out in her living room, too, sleeping off the effects of the booze and the good food he had missed out on. He could text Jess now that Aria was out of the way. Perhaps she had messaged him, even called, though he didn't remember receiving any notifications. He looked around the room for his phone while on his elbows. Normally he left it on the floor beside him when he slept but it was nowhere to be seen. The cat not being around felt odd. Then he remembered Aria tossing him out into the garden.

He unfolded himself from his sleeping bag and stretched. At the window he pulled open the curtains and pressed his forehead to the cold glass. Wherever the cat was, he wasn't in the garden. Aria had probably frightened him off, back to Eric's house.

'I see you've been staying in shape,' said Aria.

He turned around and looked down at his torso, his body nude but for his underwear. Aria leaned against him.

'Well, I've been keeping myself busy,' he said, turning his face away. 'Look, I need a shower. We'll grab that coffee as soon as we're changed.'

When they left the house, it was to the symphony of snores coming from Doc. Greg and he were still passed out but looked peaceful. Daniel searched for something to write on to tell them where they were going and to come and join him and Aria.

'Silly,' she said. 'Why don't you just text and you can send the location?'

'I would,' said Daniel. 'But I can't find my phone. Have you seen it?'

Aria shook her head and unlatched the front door.

They let themselves out softly and walked down the hill. Aria slipped her hand into Daniel's. She reached up to kiss his cheek, but the kiss landed on his chin, close to his lips.

Hazel opened her door just as Daniel and Aria walked down the hill. Aria greeted Hazel with a friendly wave. She reciprocated with a silent nod of the head. There was a question behind Hazel's eyes when they met Daniel's. All he could do was to gently shake his head and pull his lips into a line. He hoped he had sufficiently communicated to Hazel that Aria wasn't the girl he'd told her he'd met and that she was in the next village probably very annoyed and disappointed in him.

Daniel and Aria headed for the café at the beach complex. There was every chance Jess could cycle past and see them en route. He had to speak to Jess before she saw his Italian guests.

'What a beautiful ocean,' said Aria, looking out to the bay when they arrived at the café. 'You've been surfing?'

'Yes. Quite a few times since I've been back,' said Daniel.

'Can we go?'

'Now?'

'Soon, maybe.' She looked around the beach complex. 'But first, coffee.'

The terrace outside the café was deserted apart from one man and his Labrador retriever. The umbrellas over the tables flapped in the wind. The brick barbecue and outside oven lay in wait for the summer crowds, only a couple of months away now. Inside, the café was small but inviting with the smell of breakfast cooking and coffee brewing. A couple of people sat indoors to escape the cold morning.

'Do you want breakfast?' asked Daniel.

'You know I don't eat breakfast, but you go ahead.' Aria sat at a table by the window.

Daniel ordered himself a Full English and a pot of tea. For Aria he ordered a black coffee, knowing already that she would complain about its strength and would probably send it back.

'How did you hook up with Doc and Greg?' Daniel asked after he'd paid the bill and sat at their table.

Aria put her head down and laughed lightly.

'What's funny?' he asked.

'I thought you would ask me why I left Mount Etna and where did I go. Instead you've acted as if it never happened. It's been a year, Daniel.'

He shook his head, eyes closed. He didn't understand his

reaction to seeing her either. It was as if the vision of her had wiped away the months of pain, frustration and anger that followed her disappearance and her silence. Did his indifference mean he'd forgiven her? Or that he didn't love her anymore? Yet something had stirred within him on seeing Aria at the door, and until he could explain the feeling to himself he couldn't explain his reaction to her.

'Well?' said Aria. 'Did you wonder about me?'

'Of course I did. You changed your number. You didn't leave a contact address. What did you expect?'

The waiter set down a pot of tea, a large mug of coffee and some milk and sugar in a matching white jug and bowl.

'I know you must be very angry with me,' said Aria with her eyes fixed on the view outside. 'I hoped you would stop being angry by now and maybe we could talk about our mistakes.'

'Our mistakes?' Daniel shook his head. 'I know I'm not perfect, Aria, but the time to talk about mistakes is when they arise. Not to leave meaningless messages on my phone and disappear in the night. I waited for you at La Copita like an idiot that night. I messaged you, called you. I thought something had happened to you.'

She lowered her gaze.

'I'm sorry for that, Daniel. It was mean of me. Childish and stupid.'

'Plus a few more adjectives I could name.'

'I know. Just tell me what you want to say.'

'What I *wanted* to say.' He huffed out a short laugh. 'I don't think I even care now.'

'I think you do, Daniel.' Aria leaned across the table. 'I can tell we still have something between us. I can see it in the way you look at me.'

'So you're saying you still feel something for me?'

'I never stopped feeling it.'

'So why the hell did you leave?' Daniel raised his voice as the server brought over his breakfast plate and a round of toast. He lifted a hand as an apology for his behaviour.

'Daniel,' said Aria, 'are you really going to eat all that?'

'Every morsel,' he said. He began to eat, cutting the food vigorously with his knife, shovelling heaps of scrambled egg into his mouth. He piled his fork so high, the food slipped right off the sides. He carried on like this for a while.

'Daniel, if you don't chew, you are going to choke.'

'I am chewing. If I don't eat, I might say something I might regret later.' He slammed down his knife and fork. They clattered against the plate and table. Aria winced and the server looked over at them.

'I'm not hungry anymore,' he said.

Aria put her head down and remained silent. Daniel stared at the silky locks of her hair veiling her face, the odd streak of chestnut and honey gold. After a few minutes he realized she was crying.

'I think we should go,' said Daniel.

Aria sniffed and dried her eyes with her forefingers, wiping the wetness to the side of her cheeks.

'You didn't finish your breakfast,' she said.

'To hell with the breakfast.' Daniel stormed out of the café and marched to the glass rail along the terrace that looked out to the beach. Aria caught him up seconds later. She stood beside him and placed a delicate touch on his arm.

'I wish I hadn't hurt you like that,' she said. 'I hate myself for being so callous. So mean with your heart. You would never have done this to me.'

He turned to her. 'Damn right I wouldn't.' He looked back to the sea. 'Why, Aria? Why did you leave me?'

'Daniel, I was confused.' She briefly put her hands to her temples. 'I just came out of a relationship when we met. In fact, I was running away from it, that's how I ended up at Mount Etna. A friend of mine was going. I just followed her. I was so lost and pathetic. I hated the way I was then.'

'And you're not like that now?'

'No, never. I would never hurt you like that again. I've got my feet firmly planted. I want to stand by you, Daniel.' Aria looked directly into his eyes as if she were searching for something.

'You assume I'm going to give you another chance to hurt me.' His gaze twitched back and forth from her.

'I know I have to make up for what I did.'

'What if you're too late?'

'Why do you say that? You met someone?' Her eyes narrowed.

'I mean, what if I can't forgive you?' said Daniel. 'What if I don't love you anymore?'

She pushed her way to his chest, lay her head against it and held him tightly.

'I think you love me, *Daniele*,' she said. 'I am going to do everything I can to make you forgive me.'

She looked up at him; he slid his arms around her and she laid her head back on his chest.

27

Daniel searched high and low for his mobile. What could he have done in one drunken night with Doc and Greg that could result in a missing phone? He'd asked Doc to ring the number. All four of them listened carefully, walking around the house bent forward, hand cupped around an ear, anticipating a ring or vibration. Nothing.

'Let's go back out to the garden and you try it again,' said Daniel. 'It has to be here somewhere.'

Doc rang the number but there wasn't a sound from Daniel's phone. Still he searched among the vegetables, the flowers. He looked high into the apple tree and got onto his hands and knees to rummage around the hedges.

'I haven't checked the car. We went out for pizza,' said Daniel. 'I'll go out and look.'

'I'll come, too,' said Aria.

Daniel opened the glove compartment, searched the door wells and seats, the entire floor and even the boot.

'Have you lost something, Daniel?' a voice said.

He popped his head up from under the passenger side seat to see Hazel in a cerise tracksuit, leaning both hands on her walking stick.

'Oh, hello, Hazel,' he said. 'Yes, I seem to have lost my phone. I've looked everywhere.' He slammed the door shut.

'Well, you can't have looked everywhere,' Hazel replied with one eyebrow raised, 'or you would have found it. You need to retrace your steps.'

'*Ciao!*' Aria said to Hazel, putting a hand to her chest. 'I'm Aria.'

Hazel nodded and smiled.

'Aria, this is my neighbour, Hazel,' said Daniel.

'I saw you both earlier,' said Hazel, looking at Aria over her glasses. 'But you didn't stop.'

'We went for breakfast,' said Daniel, scratching his head as he stared at the car.

'If you took the car out,' said Hazel as she wagged a knowing forefinger, 'maybe your phone is at the place you drove to.'

Daniel slapped his head. 'Of course. The pizza place. I'll nip down there to see if anyone has handed it in.'

Just then Doc and Greg emerged, still bleary eyed since rising from their drunken sleep.

'Hey,' said Doc. 'Any luck?'

'Hazel,' said Daniel, gesturing to his friends, 'these are my friends from the tour guide company I used to work for at Mount Etna. This is Doc and this is Greg. Guys, this is Hazel.'

'*Piacere di conoscerla.*' Doc bowed low and kissed Hazel's hand. 'And I'm so sorry you live near to this ugly brute.' He nudged Daniel's shoulder who stumbled backwards.

'Oh, Daniel's a lovely man,' said Hazel. 'And a very good neighbour.'

'Who is lucky to know all the good-looking women around here. Am I right?' said Doc to Hazel as he rapidly raised his eyebrows.

Hazel tutted and exhaled a little laugh.

'How long will you be staying in Trevone?' she asked.

'Oh, we'll be here a while,' Doc replied.

'That's nice. And Daniel will be putting you up the whole time?'

Doc and Greg nodded.

'I suppose you've seen all the work he has done on the house and still has yet to do.'

'He's done a good job,' Greg agreed.

'I think,' said Hazel, pointing at the house with her stick, 'that Daniel could use a little help, and being as you capable-looking youngsters are here . . .'

Doc and Greg responded with a series of non-committal grunts followed by nods of agreement. Daniel knew it would take a lot of coaxing to get them both on board. As for Aria, he'd be surprised if she'd risk getting paint splashes on any of her clothes.

'Good luck finding your phone,' said Hazel, getting ready to leave. 'I suppose now that you have guests our lessons might have to wait?'

'Not necessarily,' said Daniel with a shrug. 'I'll see how things pan out.'

'But you will be leading the walk?' Hazel said.

Daniel's guests were all inquisitive to find out which walk Hazel was referring to until Daniel told them all about the Walkers Club.

'You never mentioned this before,' Doc exclaimed. 'So secretive. What else have you been keeping from us?'

'Nothing,' said Daniel quickly. He looked directly at Aria who was poised with folded arms as she waited for his answer. 'Nothing at all. Now let's go for a walk to the pizza place to see if I dropped my phone there.'

'Can't we drive?' asked Greg with a loud yawn. 'I'm knackered. Sorry,' he said, bowing to Hazel. 'I mean I'm well and truly exhausted.'

'The walk will do you good,' said Hazel. 'Might blow away some of the lager fumes floating around you.' Hazel winked at Daniel and slowly made her way back down the hill.

'You heard the lady,' said Daniel. 'Let's find that phone.'

Daniel took them on a walk around the village. Greg complained of fatigue and Doc wanted to stop at a shop for food so that he could cook later. Daniel walked with his hands in his jeans pockets and talked to them about the village, reliving memories of his youth, each tale reminding him that he was once very happy here. Aria walked close beside him and linked her arm through his.

Daniel's phone didn't materialize. It wasn't at the pizza restaurant, it wasn't anywhere. They found themselves at the seafront and Daniel had become more and more fed up and anxious about not seeing his messages. In the end he assumed he must have blacked out at some stage, so he questioned Doc and Greg about what actually happened the night before.

'Seriously, guys, if this is some sort of game you're playing then stop,' he said. 'I need to have that phone back.'

'It's nothing to do with me,' said Greg. 'I was out of it long before you guys stopped.'

Doc raised his shoulders.

'Mate, I have no idea.' Doc frowned and gestured with his fingertips pinched together. 'You think I would have been ringing you all day and searching around like an idiot if I knew where the phone was? Besides, I don't think it's very cool to do something like that.'

'You've done worse,' said Daniel.

219

'But not to you.' He playfully slapped Daniel's cheek before trotting down to the shore. He took his trainers and socks off as he ran straight for the waves. When the white foam rolled onto his feet he let out a high-pitched scream and ran straight back to Daniel and the others.

'That sea is cold!' He looked accusingly at Daniel. 'And when can we go surfing?'

'Whenever the waves are good. I'll look at the weather forecast. You can hire gear from the little shop over there.'

Daniel turned and pointed to the beach complex. As he did so he saw a young woman cycling along the coast path on a silver bicycle. He squinted at her, studying the bike and the woman's form though she wore a windcheater over her jeans. Under her red helmet, Daniel couldn't tell if she had cropped blonde hair and her face was turned away.

'What are you staring at, Daniel?' Aria stood in front of him.

'Nothing,' he said. 'Nothing. I thought I saw someone I know.'

'Who?' said Aria, her eyes following the girl on the bike.

'It's not who I thought it was, never mind,' said Daniel. 'How about we get supplies so Doc can cook?'

Doc raised his arms like a prize fighter who had just won his match.

'And for sure we must come back to the beach,' said Doc after he'd finished bobbing and weaving in front of Daniel. 'Hire some surfboards. Maybe have a beach party. Invite some girls.'

'That's all this guy ever thinks about,' said Greg, placing an arm over Doc's shoulder as they walked away from the sea.

Aria slipped her hand into Daniel's. His arm twitched and flexed, releasing her fingers as they walked.

'What's the matter?' asked Aria. 'Is something wrong?'

'Nothing,' he said, looking back at the coast path. 'Nothing at all.'

28

At the farm shop, Daniel looked out of the window, craning his neck at any blonde woman or any cyclist he saw, while Greg and Doc piled food into a couple of wire baskets. Aria stared at Daniel through the long sweep of tresses at the side of her face. He smiled at her when he noticed her observing him. He went to put his arm around her but changed his mind, reaching instead for a loaf of bread.

They walked up the hill to the house laden with bags of food and drink. Annabelle had just parked her Range Rover at the front of the house. She leapt out of the driver's seat with her mobile in her hand and ran towards Daniel.

'Where on earth have you been?' she yelled. Her cheeks were flushed as she looked at Daniel's companions.

'Have you been trying to call me?' asked Daniel.

Everyone dropped their bags and stared at the red-faced Annabelle.

'*Have* I?' she spluttered. 'I thought something was wrong, that something had happened to you. I was so worried I thought I'd better come and look for you and here you are swanning around as if everything is okay.'

'Everything *is* okay.' Daniel picked up his bags and walked to the front door. 'Hey, buddy!' he called to Rasmus who was in his booster seat, trying to make himself invisible to Daniel's friends by burying his face into the armrest.

Daniel unlocked the front door and turned to the others.

'Sorry, guys. This is my sister, Annabelle. These are my friends from Mount Etna. They dropped by yesterday evening and I managed to lose my phone so I'm sorry you were worried.'

Doc held out a hand to Annabelle.

'I can see you are the beauty of the family,' he said before kissing her hand. Annabelle blushed.

'Well,' she giggled, 'it has been said once or twice.'

Daniel rolled his eyes. 'You coming in?'

'I'll just get Rasmus out of the car.'

In the kitchen, Daniel tried to unpack the shopping with Rasmus wrapped like a vine around his thigh. Doc and Greg took a couple of cans of lager out to the garden while Aria tried to help with the shopping.

'So,' said Annabelle to Aria, 'you're a walking guide?'

'I used to be. I went back to live in Rome. Then I worked in a bar while I decided what I wanted to do with my life.'

'I thought you went back to live with your ex,' said Daniel with a box of free range eggs in his hand.

'Who told you that?' asked Aria, crossing her arms.

'That's what everyone was saying,' said Daniel, placing the eggs in the fridge.

'Well, everyone was wrong. I left to have time to think,' said Aria.

'You've been thinking for a year,' said Daniel. 'Why did it take so long to decide to come looking for me?'

'Because I was confused,' said Aria, throwing her arms up. 'Isn't that allowed? A person can become confused can't they?'

'Yes, but if a person becomes confused then surely they

should talk it through. Not move miles away so the other person doesn't know why you left. Does that make any sense to you at all?' He pointed at his temple.

Annabelle watched the exchange in silence, looking from her brother to Aria and back, open mouthed. Rasmus squinted through the thick lashes of one eye and dared to take a quick glance at Aria before squeezing his eyes shut again.

'I think you are being very unfair, Daniel,' said Aria. 'Every time I wanted to talk, you wanted to go out and party with your friends. You ignored me.'

'I didn't ignore you. I devoted all my time to you. We were never apart. If I was out anywhere, you were there, too.'

'You say that as if you resent me wanting to be with you.'

'I never said that.' Daniel's eyes bulged and he shook his head.

As the argument raged on, Rasmus clung tighter to Daniel's leg and Annabelle tried to speak in between the merest gap in their heated conversation.

'I'm sorry.' Annabelle finally butted in. 'I was just trying to say, I should go now.'

'No!' shouted Daniel and Aria at the same time.

'It's just that Mia is on a play date and I need to go and collect her.'

'Sorry, sis,' said Daniel, putting an arm around her. He walked her to the door. Annabelle called goodbye to Aria over her shoulder.

'Who is that?' she whispered when the door was open and she was on the front step.

'A long story,' said Daniel.

'A long story? Seems like the box set. Is she an ex or a current?'

'An absolute ex,' he said.

'How could you say that?' cried Aria who stood aghast in the hallway. 'I came all this way to make things right between us and you haven't given us a chance.' She stomped up the stairs. Daniel and Annabelle heard loud sobs from the bedroom and Rasmus stepped out from behind Daniel.

'I think she needs ice cream, Uncle Daniel,' he said with his hand cupped to the side of his mouth.

'I think it might take a few scoops,' said Daniel, rubbing Rasmus's mop of hair.

'Seriously,' said Annabelle. 'She obviously loves you. She's very passionate about your relationship. You should at least give it a try.'

'I don't know,' whispered Daniel. 'I just don't know.'

Daniel leaned his back against the door as Annabelle drove away. He looked up the stairs remembering the fiery discussions and the times he'd run after Aria because she was crying. Her passion exhausted him at times but he couldn't deny the wave of happiness he'd felt when she arrived the night before, looking as beautiful and as sexy as ever. His impulse had been to hold her tight, to kiss her. As if none of the ugly stuff had happened, as if he were still so in love with Aria and wanted to marry her. Had Jess and the party not been on his mind, he might have given in.

No decisions, no dramas. That was what being with Jess was all about and it suited him. But Aria was different, she'd had his heart, she'd had all of him. He never could fathom how he'd allowed himself to fall so deeply for Aria after seeing the destruction caused by his own parents' breakup. Maybe it was the thrill of first love that made Aria so alluring. His commitment to her had been full on; if he was going to be with her he'd be all in. He'd refused to have his relationship with her end as his parents' had. The divorce had split the already frail threads of his family apart, so he'd decided to throw his heart and soul into loving her. It was no wonder he hadn't wanted a serious relationship after the breakup – there was nothing left to give. Only Jess, whom he'd met a year after Aria left him, had made him think differently. He hadn't planned to get serious about Jess, mind you, but he could feel it happening. Maybe it wasn't too late to draw a halt to his feelings for Jess. He hadn't known her for very long.

He squeezed his hands against his head and tried to shut off his rambling thoughts. They made no sense to him. He felt torn and confused.

Maybe the best thing to do would be to walk away from it all. The women, that is. Carry on his life with absolutely no drama at all. Seconds later he heard Aria sniff. He ran up the stairs to make sure she was okay.

29

The next day, Daniel bought himself a new phone. He and Doc jumped in the car and headed to town while Aria was washing her hair and Greg was doing a video call to his family in Ireland.

'I still don't know how you ended up bringing Aria with you,' said Daniel on the way.

'She came looking for you. She was in Sicily and I had no idea until she caught hold of me at the bar. She was weepy, sad, said she loved you and wanted to know where you'd gone.'

'And you didn't think to give me a heads up?' Daniel glanced at him, inadvertently speeding up along the single lane road.

'Well, the way I looked at it is, you never got over her so I didn't think it would do any harm for you two to talk.' Doc threw up his large hands. 'I mean, I thought she was coming for a weekend. That's what she said when I told her we were planning to surprise you.'

'You could have just told her to call me, if she was that desperate.'

'True, but she was very persuasive. One weekend. I didn't think it would hurt. Sorry, mate, I messed up.'

'It's not your fault. She always knew how to get her way.'

'So she dumped her ex for you?'

'Aria says she was confused, never went back to him.'

'You believe her?'

'I don't know what to believe. I just know I have to get a phone and get organized again.'

During the week, Daniel saw Amanda and the sisters for their training sessions and exchanged his new number with them all. He had not had time to see Hazel for cycling lessons but had reconciled with Aria. After he'd gone upstairs to comfort her he had held her in his arms and stroked her hair. She had turned her face to kiss him.

'No, Aria, I don't think that's a good idea,' he'd sighed while removing her hand from his cheek.

She'd sniffed and nodded in agreement. 'But nothing has changed for me. I love you, Daniel, and I won't stop. I never did.'

He had looked deep into her dark brown eyes. They were soft and sad. Her pink lips no longer trembling were as tempting as always but he'd held her arms and stood back.

'We have to agree not to fight,' he'd said. Aria had smiled. She'd continued to do so, wiping away the last of the tears.

It was usual, in the past, that an argument between Daniel and Aria would shortly be followed by another. But she and Daniel were getting on the best they ever had. Aria had told him, when she first arrived, that she would prove she still loved him. Daniel was beginning to believe her. Still, his thoughts were never far from Jess and confusion set in. For every joke or walk he shared with Aria he pictured Jess on her bike or at the surf shop or planning her yoga studio. He imagined her taking photographs on the beach and letting sand slip through the spaces between her fingers, a beautiful smile on her face. He was being cowardly about contacting

Jess because he didn't know how to explain Aria or his feelings for her, neither could he be clear in his mind about how he felt for Jess. He kept putting off going to see her, knowing that she had a right to an explanation, but he let the whole week go by without having been in touch.

On Saturday morning, Daniel got ready for the coastal path walk. He was grateful that none of his friends stirred as he got ready to leave. They hadn't got to bed until three in the morning after the barbecue in the garden the night before. He slipped out of the house and quietly closed the door behind him before jogging down to the beach complex. He was already a few minutes late.

'Here he is,' said Hazel. She gave Daniel a wave as he trotted up to the group in the car park.

'Sorry about that,' he said. 'I've got house guests and I had a late night.'

'Daniel, you look awful,' said Mary, her bottom lip protruding. 'There's no sign of your date yet but it's probably better she doesn't meet you looking like a homeless person.' Mary's eyes scanned Daniel up and down in despair.

'It's okay, Mary,' said Annabelle. 'I don't think we need worry about Daniel's love life at the moment. He seems to have that taken care of.'

Daniel rolled his eyes to the sky.

'Please,' he said. 'Don't start.'

As he spoke, something caught his eye. A flash of silver and with it the sound of a bicycle's creaking wheels, even above the hiss of the ocean. Jess casually cycled by on the coast path. She looked over at Daniel, as if she were looking straight through him. Her gaze returned to the path and she continued on her way. Daniel was staggered. He went to lift his hand to wave at her but he was seconds too late. Jess was gone.

'I don't believe that,' said Mary, shaking her head.

'What?' said Amanda.

'Well, that was her,' Mary gasped. 'That was the girl I wanted Daniel to meet and she's just cycled straight past. She said she would come on the walk today. How could she have changed her mind?'

Hazel looked up at Daniel.

'You look as if you've seen a ghost,' she said softly. 'Was that the girl you told me about? The one you like?'

'It was,' he said.

Daniel scratched his head. He looked wistfully over to the coast path as if he could conjure Jess up again. If he could replay what had just happened, have Jess cycle by the way she just had, he would run towards her this time, wave his hands for her to stop. Call out her name until she had no choice but to look back. The whole group stared at Daniel in silence.

Hazel placed a palm on Daniel's arm and brought his attention back to the waiting group of walkers. He looked at Hazel, a half smile making his lips twitch.

'Well,' he said absently. 'Looks like I won't know how things might have turned out with her after all. She doesn't want to know me now.'

'But why didn't she stop? What happened, Daniel?' Hazel asked.

The rest of the group moved in closer to him.

'The most ridiculous thing,' said Daniel. 'I lost my phone and I couldn't get a message to her to tell her I couldn't make an arrangement we made last week.' A small part of the story was better than the whole truth.

'You let a week go by without apologizing?' Hazel wasn't scolding him. There was concern in her expression.

Daniel shook his head, eyes downcast, but quickly tried to shake off the growing feeling of gloom. He clapped his hands together.

'Okay, gang, we're late as it is. We'd better get a move on.'

There was a collective sigh and a mixture of disappointment and concern, as the walkers took a step back from the huddle.

'We can't go anywhere,' Mary announced. 'Not until we clear this up.' She looked quizzically at Daniel. 'So, all this time I was trying to arrange a cosy get-together for you with a nice girl, you knew her all along?'

'How was I supposed to know who you meant?' Daniel was becoming impatient. He drew a breath to calm himself down. 'For one thing you said she had long blonde hair and you never told me her name. It's Jess, by the way.' Daniel looked down at his feet. There was a quiver on his inhale as he looked around the expectant faces. He sighed. 'I wasn't playing a game with you, I just wanted to keep this to myself.'

'It's a small village,' Amanda piped up. 'Nothing escapes certain people. Especially if they make it their business to interfere.'

'I wasn't interfering,' said Mary.

'No,' Eileen agreed. 'Not interfering. What were you doing?'

'Goodness me,' said Mary, her hands on her hips as she looked around the group. 'I just thought they would make a good fit.'

'Well, they certainly aren't a good fit,' said Hannah. 'Did you notice the look she gave him?'

'What was the look?' asked Daniel, forgetting that it was late and that if they didn't start walking they'd be back at the beginning without having moved an inch.

'She snubbed you good and proper,' said Eric. 'You must have done more than not send a message. What did you do?'

'Nothing,' said Daniel. 'I did nothing. Now we really should go.'

They finally set off. It was quarter past twelve and they might have to cut what was already a short walk, even shorter.

Daniel couldn't stop thinking about Jess. He wondered if Eric was right when he said Jess had snubbed him. He wanted to believe she hadn't noticed he was there, and that maybe he was being obscured by his fellow walkers. There was every chance that when she appeared to be looking in his direction, Jess's attention was somewhere else and Hannah was wrong about the look Jess had given him.

Daniel fell to the back of the group with Hazel, Annabelle at his other side.

'You're awfully good at not keeping me up to date with your love life,' said his sister.

'Er, probably because it isn't any of your business,' replied Daniel.

'But you look upset now that this Jess girl rode off without stopping,' she continued. 'Did you two have an argument? Like the one you had with that Italian girl?'

'No,' said Daniel. 'I've made a mess of things but it doesn't matter now. It's not a big deal, so don't make it one.'

'I'm not making it a big deal, Daniel, but Jess looked really nice and it would be a shame to blow it.'

'I can't blow something that wasn't there to blow. A handful of dates, less than that. That's all it was. We're not getting married or anything. I'm still a male spinster.'

'With an ex-girlfriend living in.' Annabelle huffed and went to catch up with her neighbour, Margot, who was keeping a good pace with the sisters.

'When are your friends from Italy leaving?' asked Hazel. 'Have they said anything?'

'They're not about to rush off.'

'And that Aria girl, extremely beautiful. Is this just a holiday for her?'

'I think she wants more than that.'

'And what about the young lady on the bike?' Hazel smiled up at him.

'Jess? Well, we haven't got to know each other that well, I don't think. It's just been a nice fling before she settles into her new job.'

'Seems to me it might be a bit more than that.'

Daniel stopped.

'Please, Hazel. Don't read more into it than there is. That's just asking for trouble.'

Hazel nodded and carried on walking.

'Sorry, I didn't mean to snap at you,' he muttered.

Amanda and Oliver, who were at the front of the walking group, had already come to a stop at the usual spot for refreshments. The group, having walked together weekly for over a month, had already established routines.

Daniel was worried that the walkers had become too concerned with his love life and he hoped he could steer them away from bringing the subject of Jess up again. Like his nephew Rasmus, who closed his eyes so as not to be seen, Daniel thought if he sat a little way from the group it would discourage another dating discussion. Despite this, sisters Mary and Eileen came and sat down next to him.

'Annabelle has caught us up with the ex coming from Italy,' said Mary, shaking her head from side to side. 'You're very lucky to have two women fighting over you.'

'It really isn't like that,' said Daniel.

'Well, what is it like, Daniel, and what can we do to help?' she asked.

'Absolutely nothing, because there is nothing that can be done.'

'Might I suggest,' said Mary, gingerly, 'that perhaps you have a talk with the girl on the bike?'

'Her name is Jess.' Daniel ran out of patience completely. How could he talk to her when she had clearly snubbed him?

'I've got an idea,' Mary said, standing so that she could make a declaration to the whole group. 'We all know the way back to the beach complex. So, Daniel, why don't you go after Jess?'

'Oh silly,' said Amanda. 'She left on her bike ages ago. How would Daniel know where to find her?'

Everyone looked to Daniel, who sat with his head lowered.

'Do you know where she is?' asked Annabelle.

Daniel nodded. 'She works at Harlyn Beach.'

'That's not all that far to go,' said Eric, one thick eyebrow raised.

Daniel turned to face Hazel.

'You should at least have a chat,' said Hazel. 'I can lead the team back to base.'

Just then the Padstow Pace Masters came streaking by and caused a whirl of debris to rise off the path and create a mini-cloud in their wake.

'You could probably overtake those show-offs if you started now,' said Amanda, shielding her eyes as she watched them go.

This was it: the time to stop procrastinating, to finally give Jess the apology she deserved, had come. As the thought of seeing her played on his mind it began to tug at something in his heart, something he'd been trying to deny all week. He wanted to see Jess. He didn't know how the long-awaited apology would play out but he couldn't let their relationship come to an end because he was being a coward and a fool.

'And you won't mind if I desert you for a day?' asked Daniel.

'Go for it,' said Hazel. 'There might be a silver lining in that cloud over your head.'

Daniel got to his feet, dusted off the back of his shorts and headed to Harlyn Beach.

30

Daniel walked hard and fast against the wind on the path, his chest heaving and his breath sounding not unlike Amanda in full flow. He caught up with the Pace Masters. He didn't shout for them to move aside, the way they had the first time they'd encountered The Slow Lane; instead he tried to dodge in and around them to get ahead saying, 'Sorry. Excuse me. Do you mind if I just . . .'

Caught in a tangle of marching feet and swinging elbows he edged his way to the front of the pack. The lead walker for the Padstow Pace Masters took this as a challenge and upped the pace. The Pace Masters had no choice but to respond and began to overtake Daniel so that he was in a scrum with some of the walkers. He swung his arms vigorously and widened his step until he was shoulder to shoulder with the leader, a square-shaped man with a thin moustache who looked sideways at Daniel and not at where he was going. Veins stood out on his neck as he battled to stay ahead of Daniel for a good hundred metres. Daniel gave it one last push and broke free from the Pace Masters and was ahead of them at last. They breathed down his back with such an intensity he felt the pressure to surge on even further ahead. He thought he felt a lung collapse and he certainly heard one of the Pace Masters say, 'We can't beat that.'

Daniel was hot and out of breath as he entered the surf school.

'Can I help you?' The young man at the till was balancing on a chair with only two of its legs on the floor. His feet were up on the counter, a book in his hands.

'I was looking for Jess?' Daniel's eyes darted around the shop and to the stairs leading up to the proposed yoga studio.

'Jess?' The young man jumped to his feet. 'You missed her by a second. She's taking a bunch of people out for a paddle-boarding lesson. You in her paddleboarding group?'

'No,' said Daniel, 'I'm her . . . I'm a friend. I just wanted a chat.'

'Oh, safe. Well, she'll be about an hour. I can leave a message. She got your number?' He put his book down and looked around the counter.

'Yes. No. No, I've got a new number,' said Daniel.

'Want to leave it with me?' He found a notepad and pen.

'Actually, I think I might just hang around. Will she come back to the shop?'

'Sure, yeah. After the class.'

They both stood looking at each other. The young man looked around the shop as if he could offer Daniel something to do while he waited for Jess to return. Daniel gestured to the door.

'I'll just hang out by the beach,' he said. 'Keep an eye out for her.'

'Yeah, safe, safe. No problem.' He gave a half salute and sat back on his chair with his book. He pushed the front legs of the chair up and lifted his feet back onto the counter.

Eventually Daniel's heart rate began to calm down after his

fast walk along the path. It was cool for spring but the sun, when the clouds permitted, was warm on his skin. He wanted to look for Jess but he didn't want to interrupt her work so he sat facing the water and watched as people walked by, some with dogs chasing sticks, some in bare feet, braving the elements.

He thought back to the first time he'd gone to Harlyn and bumped into Jess there. She had been happy to see him that day and the times after. He wasn't so sure how she'd react today. It was likely after her lesson, she would see him sitting alone on the beach and walk straight by, avoiding him completely. For that reason he looked around periodically in the direction of the surf school and glanced all around the beach. If he knew where her bike was locked he could sit beside it, then Jess wouldn't be able to avoid seeing him. She could snub him again, mind you, or call the police and say he was a stalker and still not talk to him.

When the hour for the paddleboarding lesson was nearly over, Daniel began to walk up and down the beach, keeping an eye out for Jess. He had a sinking feeling in his stomach. The longer he waited the more he convinced himself he should just go home. Yes, he really liked Jess but waiting there an hour to say sorry for not showing up at the party smacked of the drama they had both been trying to avoid. The kind of drama that led to this sort of pain, this jumble of feelings and emotion that formed knots in his stomach. Besides, what was he to say to her after the apology? Where, if anywhere, was their relationship going?

'Daniel.'

He turned in the direction of the voice and there was Jess.

'I'm sorry,' he said. He walked towards her. She wore a baseball cap and a T-shirt with the surf school logo under a windcheater.

'Sorry?' she said. 'What for?'

'You know.' He sighed. 'I didn't make it to the party last week.'

'It was a great party,' said Jess, shoving her hands in her pockets. 'It's a shame you missed it.'

'I really did want to come. To see you. But something came up and I couldn't get away.'

'I understand, Daniel. Apology accepted. I should get back.' She turned to leave, kicking sand up at her heels. Daniel jogged to catch her up. He touched her arm and she stopped short.

'I know you're busy,' said Daniel. 'But can we talk? Just for a second?'

'Look, Daniel, I get it, okay?' said Jess. She took a deep breath and let her shoulders relax. 'I was worried about you last week, that's all. When you didn't come to the party, I figured something came up. But because I'd sent you messages that you didn't respond to I thought I'd drop by on my way to work the next morning. You know, make sure you hadn't fallen off a stepladder, had an accident with a monkey wrench.'

He let out a short, shaky laugh.

'And I saw you,' she continued, straight faced. 'Saw you were fine.'

'You saw me? Where?'

'I cycled into your street and saw you walking down the hill with someone.'

Daniel dipped his head down.

'I'd like to explain,' he said. 'What you saw, who that was.'

Jess, who had been making very little eye contact with Daniel, now looked directly into his eyes. 'I assumed it was the ex-girlfriend you didn't want to talk about.'

He heaved a sigh, shoulders sloping forward.

'Okay, look. She and a couple of my friends from Mount Etna just showed up that night. Just as I was leaving for the party.'

'Two things here, Daniel.' Jess pulled her windcheater around her body. 'Firstly, you could have brought them to the party. You wouldn't have needed to ask. Just shown up. Secondly, the fact that you didn't bring them makes me think you have something to hide. Something you don't want to tell me about this ex you're supposed to be over.'

'It was over. I mean, it is. I never thought I'd see her again.'

'Listen, Daniel, I think we got carried away on the beach the other week. But you obviously have things to sort out and I don't want to be strung along. Let's not complicate things and let's just forget about any pacts or promises we made to each other. It's easier that way.' She looked over in the direction of the surf school.

'Jess . . . I'm just . . . I'm just really sorry,' Daniel said. 'I didn't know what to do. How to explain. I was an idiot.'

'You know, it's one thing seeing the pair of you walking off in the morning looking so pleased with yourselves, it's another to simply answer my messages, let me know you were all right.'

'That's true but . . . I lost my phone.'

'Convenient.'

'Honestly. I looked everywhere for it. I had to get a new one in the end.' He pulled it out from a back pocket. 'I didn't have your number memorized.' He held the phone out to her.

'What am I supposed to do with that?' she asked flatly.

'Um, I just thought . . . Could I get your number again?'

'Look, you've obviously got stuff on and so do I. I think it's best if we got on with our own individual stuff and not get the two mixed up.'

'I don't want you to be angry with me.'

'But I am. I am angry with you, Daniel. But it will pass. Just like this thing we had going on. That will pass too. I thought that . . . I was hoping we . . . But in the end, it doesn't really matter.' She put up her hands and started to move backwards along the sand the second Daniel tried to speak. 'I'm needed at the shop. I really have to go.'

He called after her.

'They'll be gone soon,' he said. Jess stopped but didn't turn. 'My house guests. They'll leave and we can talk then.' She shook her head and continued walking. Daniel called after her. 'I'm sorry, Jess.'

31

Daniel let himself into the house. It was noticeably quiet without Doc's booming voice or music blaring from the laptop speakers. The cat had not been around since the party arrived from Italy the week before so it wasn't there purring in the kitchen doorway, waiting for Daniel to have the good sense to feed it.

'Daniel? Is that you?' called Aria from the living room.

He put his head around the door and found her on one of the cotton deckchairs that Doc and Greg had bought from a camping shop. Along with the scatter cushions Annabelle had already dropped off, the chairs made the sparse living room a bit more comfortable.

'Where is everyone?' Daniel asked.

'They have gone for something to eat.'

Daniel looked at his watch. It was almost four o'clock. He'd walked back slowly from Harlyn after having sat and watched Jess walk away from him on the beach and never once look back.

'A late lunch?' Daniel asked, taking a seat on one of the deckchairs and hugging a cushion to his stomach. 'Didn't you want to join them?'

'I wasn't hungry.' Aria put down the week-old local paper she had been reading.

'You've hardly eaten since you arrived,' said Daniel, a crease in his brow. 'You'll waste away.'

Aria blew through her lips.

'They sell chips with everything here,' she said with a scowl.

'No one said you had to eat chips.'

'What are you so mad about, Daniel? Where have you been?'

'I told you about my walking group. You were all crashed out so I left you to it.'

'You said it was a short walk and it wasn't worth going.'

'True.'

'Yet you left at midday and now it's nearly four in the afternoon. That is a long walk.'

'Are you keeping tabs on me?'

'I don't understand "tabs",' said Aria.

'I mean tracking my every move.'

'Like a spy?' Aria laughed. 'Oh, *Daniele*, you are so transparent, I can see right through you. That's how I can tell something is wrong.'

'Nothing's wrong.' He sat back and crossed his legs at the ankles. 'Why is everyone so hell bent on trying to sort my life out for me?'

'Like who?'

'Never mind.'

'A girl?'

'Yes, my sister,' said Daniel.

'Your sister is the only girl in your life?' Aria swept her hair off her shoulder and leaned forward in her chair.

Daniel was quiet, not quite able to meet her glare.

'You are a good-looking man, Daniel. It's only to be expected that there is a girl lurking around here, somewhere.

Crazy for you,' said Aria. 'Maybe you're mad because she doesn't want to see you now?'

'Why do you say that?' said Daniel, quickly adding, 'Not that there is a girl.'

'I say that because you have been happy all week and today you go out for a long walk on your own and you come back sad.'

'I'm not sad. I'm just hungry. I didn't have lunch.' He got to his feet and Aria bounced up from her chair.

'I will make you something,' she said.

'Really?'

She mocked the way Daniel said 'really'.

'Yes, *really*,' she said. 'I can cook, you know?'

'It's just that I never associate you with cooking.'

'Oh, Daniel, there are so many things you don't know about me.'

She took his hand and led him to the kitchen. It smelled of garlic and burnt sausage meat. The sink was overflowing with Gran's pots, pans, plates and bowls. The kitchen counters, so old the patterns had worn off them, were overloaded with cans of food, empty food packets, stirring spoons with food fixed dry to them, shopping bags, most of them empty, a couple of messy tea towels and a dirty T-shirt. Daniel couldn't blame the cat for not returning; he had probably stayed at Eric's house where the conditions were better and he wouldn't have to eat food out of a bowl Greg had managed to step into or kick across the kitchen floor at least three times so far.

Aria put her tiny hands onto her slim hips. She looked up at Daniel and frowned.

'Well,' she said, 'I wanted to cook for you but maybe we should try to find the others and have something with them. Maybe they are at the pub?'

'More than likely. Anyway, don't worry. I'll sort this lot out.' He heaved a long exhale as he surveyed the wreckage again.

'You sure?' Aria walked back to the kitchen door.

'Yes, of course. I've become a champion fixer-upper since I've been here. I might even tackle the bathroom, too.'

He turned to find Aria had already left him to it. He sighed in disbelief at how much mess they'd made in such a short time. He hadn't realized he'd kept that amount of kitchen equipment when he was clearing the house. He thought back to an earlier time in his grandmother's kitchen. He was never allowed to run in it but he was allowed to stand on a chair and watch Gran put together a fruit pie or a stew for dinner. He remembered her talking him through the recipes. She'd let him stir the pots and lick the sweet stuff out of the mixing bowls. In his flashbacks he looked an awful lot like Rasmus did now. He was as quiet as Rasmus, not because Gran said he should be, but he was interested in what she was doing. He wondered if she'd spoken to him about the war times. Maybe it was then she learned to cook. If she did talk about those days, he didn't remember, but he knew his Gran would be very upset to see her kitchen as upside down and messy as it was.

He began by throwing rubbish away and sorting out anything for recycling. He put Doc and Greg's clothes, the socks and T-shirts that landed on top of or in front of the washing machine, inside the machine. He rolled up the sleeves of his top and began to sort out the disorder of the sink. He thought of Hazel's dishwasher, unused in her lovely clean kitchen. He wished he could escape there now for one of their afternoon chats over tea. He had neglected his friend;

he hadn't made time for any more cycling lessons, despite her progress and the joy they'd given her. He expected Hazel would be keen to know if he'd managed to speak to Jess. He would have dropped round to Hazel and told her all about it, about how his stupidity had lost him Jess and how she'd said they had nothing more to talk about. Instead he had gone home to his house guests, who, if truth be told, were the real reason he'd blown it with Jess. Had they not shown up . . . He tried not to let bitterness take hold, even while trying to mitigate the degree to which the kitchen had been trashed.

From the living room, Daniel could hear Aria listening to a film on the laptop. He had cleaned the whole kitchen, including the cat's bowl, and wondered if he should make some ground rules so that the place wouldn't get into such a mess again. He didn't want to make his friends feel uncomfortable or unwelcome but he wished they would decide how long they would stay.

He stood in the kitchen, pleased with the job he'd done, when his stomach began to rumble. He'd felt hungry an hour ago when he'd returned home and was more so now. He picked up the last piece of a French stick from the day before. It was dry and crunchy and the only thing he could find to put on it was some raspberry jam. He munched on that as Aria giggled from the living room. He decided to make a start on the bathroom. He would get as far as picking up Greg's soggy bath towel and kicking Doc's boxers into a corner at least.

Most of the decorating work he had done had been in the bathroom. He looked around at his handy work. Like the kitchen, he and Annabelle would have to pay for proper fittings and fixtures. He needed to find time to discuss this with her but didn't know when that would be. As with everything else, his life was on hold while Doc, Greg and Aria were staying.

He hooked Greg's towel on the door, poured bleach down the toilet bowl and while wiping the sink he spotted Aria's necklace. One of her favourites, an aqua stone on a long silver chain. He dried his hands on his trouser legs and picked up the necklace. He briefly thought about taking it down to her but decided to just put it away. In the bedroom he found her rucksack and opened the inner section. He knew she had a small leather pouch in which she kept her valuables. Just when he thought he'd located it he came across something he thought he recognized. Sleek, black and shiny, he saw his mobile phone between one of Aria's sweaters and her washbag.

Daniel dropped the necklace on the floor by his side and sat with a bump in front of Aria's rucksack. He hadn't taken the phone out. His mind wouldn't allow him to believe that, for a week, Aria had secreted his phone away, watched him search high and low for it, saw him worry about missing messages and not said a single word. But she had. And why? He pulled the rucksack to him and opened it. He scrambled around to find the phone again, half hoping he had imagined seeing it there. Yet, there it was, just at his fingertips, just where he'd found it a second ago. This time he pulled it out. He saw the missed calls from Annabelle, her texts, messages from Amanda and, of course, the texts from Jess.

He read all of Jess's messages. They were very playful, just like Jess. She wondered if he was lost in Crugmeer and needed her to send out a search team. There was a message sent very late the night of the party:

I'm sorry you couldn't make it but I was worried in case you're not okay and something's up. Let me know x

Daniel turned the phone over in his hand and heard the hinge of the bedroom door moan open.

'What are you doing up here on your own?' asked Aria, hovering half inside and half outside of the room. '*Daniele?*'

Daniel turned around. He sat on one hip, a foot to prop him up. He brought the phone to his chest.

'What's this?' he said. The wide smile on Aria's face dropped. Daniel's eyes as he glared at her were glassy with rage.

'You looked through my things?' she said in Italian.

'Answer the bloody question.' His jaw was clenched. 'Why do you have my phone?'

She walked in, dragging her feet like a little child about to be told off for something they knew they shouldn't have done. Her eyes were on the phone as Daniel placed it on the floor and rose to his feet.

'You were drunk and you dropped it,' she said. 'I was looking after it for you.'

'Nice try, Aria. Just tell me why you did it. Why you hid it away.' He held out both hands, shoulders up to his ears.

'Because, you . . . because I . . .' she stuttered.

'What?' said Daniel.

'Look, you went out to the garden with the guys and I heard it vibrate. I was bringing it out and I saw a name. Jess. Who is Jess?'

'My friend.'

'So you lied when you said there was no girl. I knew you were lying earlier because I read her messages. She doesn't just want to be your friend, Daniel. Wake up.'

'Hold on,' said Daniel, turning around a complete 360

degrees before coming face to face with Aria again. He had a hand to his brow. 'Why do you get to be angry? *You* invaded *my* privacy. If anyone gets to be indignant here it should be me.'

'I don't understand "indignant".'

'You don't understand when it suits you.' Daniel walked to the window and sat on the sill. He heard Doc and Greg arrive and shout out to him and Aria.

'I know it was a childish thing to do, Daniel. I'm sorry,' said Aria. 'But I got jealous.'

'You don't have the right to be jealous. You left me. You were gone a year. Did you think I was just sitting and waiting for you to come back?'

'Well, no. I don't know, but you were happy to see me. You didn't turn me away.' She pointed down at the sleeping bags, spooning, like the lovers she and Daniel used to be. 'I just wanted you to hold me again like before but you never once did. It's because of her, isn't it?'

Daniel rubbed his face with both hands.

'No, Aria, it's because of you. I don't trust you.'

'With your phone?'

'With my heart. You broke it once already. I'm not letting that happen again.'

She paced quickly to the window sill, wrapped her arms around Daniel's waist and pressed her body close to his.

'I told you, I promised you,' she said. 'I would never hurt you again. I love you, Daniel, and this week you showed me how you love me too. I know it.'

'You don't know anything,' said Daniel, 'because I don't. I didn't. I was just confused. Seeing you again. But I'm not confused anymore.' He pulled away from her and walked to the other side of the room.

'It's all because of the bloody phone,' said Aria.

'It's not that, Aria. We don't work, you and I. Nothing is easy between us. I loved you, really loved you, and I would have done anything for you. To keep you. But I'm not going back to the way it was.'

'No, Daniel. It would be different this time,' she pleaded and approached him with hands in prayer position. She laid her hands on his chest. 'I can be different.'

'It's ridiculous to think that, for us to believe that,' said Daniel. 'We are who we are. Nothing changes that drastically. If anything, I've grown up. I see things a lot clearer now.'

'You see that girl, that's what you see.'

'That girl – Jess – she doesn't want to see me. So I'm not choosing her over you. I'm just choosing not to be with you.' He took her hands off his chest and walked to the door.

'You want me to go?' said Aria. 'Right now? Right this second?' Her voice modulated upwards in pitch at each question.

'Why does everything have to be a drama with you, Aria? No, not right this second, but is there any point in you staying much longer?'

She dropped to her knees and began to throw her belongings into her rucksack.

'Why did you go spying into my bag?' She swung around.

'I didn't,' snapped Daniel. 'I was just putting your necklace away for you. I was trying to be considerate.'

Aria looked down at the necklace with the aqua stone. She picked it up and hurled it across the room. With scarlet cheeks, tears welling in her eyes, she looked up at Daniel and yelled, 'Get out!'

32

Daniel found Doc and Greg sitting on the scatter cushions in the living room after pounding his way downstairs from the bedroom.

'We weren't sure if we should leave again,' said Greg.

'Everything all right?' asked Doc.

Daniel sat down with force in one of the deckchairs. It rocked on its legs before settling under his weight.

'Yes, it's all okay now,' said Daniel.

'Is she leaving?' Doc asked. He lowered his voice considerably and referred to 'she' with an upwards glance of his eyes.

'It was never going to work out. I couldn't exactly kick her out and I couldn't exactly invite her to stay.'

'Mate,' said Doc. 'You sound as confused as you were when you were together. She messes with your head.' He tapped a heavy forefinger to his temple. They all fell silent when they heard Aria on the stairs.

'I've booked a flight home,' she said simply, standing at the door with bloodshot eyes. 'I'll move my things into another room tonight. Can you call me a taxi for the morning? Eight o'clock?'

'Of course I can,' boomed Doc.

Daniel glared at him. 'I think she was talking to me. But, yes, Aria, I'll do that.' He got to his feet. 'I'm sorry it turned out like this. I'm sorry you had to come all this way.'

'Well, it was the only way to know, wasn't it?' Her voice was thick with tears.

Daniel put his head down and Aria ran out of the room.

'Man,' said Doc. 'That was intense. What are we doing for dinner?'

Just then there was a knock on the door. The men all looked at each other.

'I'll go, shall I?' said Daniel.

Hazel and Annabelle stood at the front door. Hazel leaned on her stick and Annabelle signalled him towards her with a curl of her finger.

'We need to talk,' she said.

'Guys,' called Daniel towards the hallway, 'order some food for later. I'll be back soon.'

As Daniel walked down the hill towards Hazel's house he could feel Doc and Greg's eyes boring into the back of his head from the living room window. Aria's from upstairs, too, come to that.

In her kitchen Hazel put on the kettle and told the siblings to take a seat while she brewed a pot of tea.

'Hazel and I planned this little meet up after the walk today,' said Annabelle.

'I can't believe I didn't finish our walk,' said Daniel, shaking his head before sorting out the mugs, sugar, milk and biscuits. Hazel prepared the tea in silence as Daniel leaned against the base unit on one elbow.

'Never mind that,' said Annabelle. 'Hazel and I want to know what happened with the girl.'

'Jess,' said Hazel.

Daniel eased himself up, stood in deep silence and crossed his arms.

'That bad?' asked Annabelle.

'Surely not,' said Hazel, her face twisting with concern.

Daniel carried three mugs of tea to the table.

'Come on, Daniel,' said Annabelle after he had sat down. 'Don't keep us waiting. I'm letting Scott make dinner tonight so I can be here now. You have no idea what a rotten cook he is and I'm going to have to pretend to like it.'

'Why?' said Daniel. 'Why not just tell the truth?' He blew into his mug. 'Honesty is the best policy, right?'

'That's right,' said Hazel. 'I told Henry all about Jess and that you were planning to see her, talk things through. Henry and I always managed to smooth things out somehow.'

'I always seem to make a mess of everything,' said Daniel.

'Tell us what happened,' urged Annabelle. 'Spare no details because I'm going to have to tell everyone on the WhatsApp group the results of your chat with Jess.'

'WhatsApp group?' exclaimed Daniel.

'The Slow Lane WhatsApp group,' said Annabelle. 'We all wanted to know what she'd say so I created a group chat.'

'And you guys couldn't wait until next Saturday?'

Hazel shook her head. 'We were concerned about you, Daniel. That's all.'

'That's right,' said Annabelle. 'Everyone was hoping you would make up with Jess. By the way, Eric isn't on WhatsApp.'

'So Eric has to wait until next week?' said Daniel. 'That hardly seems fair.'

'I'll pop over to his later when I get the address off Hazel. Anyway, forget that for now,' said Annabelle.

'Well, you all could have waited until next week for the

update,' said Daniel. 'Jess didn't want to know me.' He brushed imaginary lint from his sweat top.

'Really?' said Hazel. 'You did tell her you lost your phone, didn't you?'

'Oh yes, I told her that but that didn't make any difference, not after she saw me with Aria.'

'The skinny Italian girl?' said Annabelle, hand on her cheek. 'What did she see you doing?'

'Nothing,' pleaded Daniel. 'Aria held my hand and Jess cycled by and she might have seen her kiss me.'

'Bloody hell,' said Annabelle exasperated.

'It was nothing,' said Daniel, looking to Hazel for support.

'Daniel, it's very obvious that Jess didn't think it was nothing,' said Hazel with a raised brow. 'Aria is staying at your house. What is Jess to think?'

'Aria is leaving tomorrow,' said Daniel.

'That's good,' said Annabelle. 'You know, I really wasn't sure she was right for you. Very bossy.'

Daniel sighed.

'After tomorrow Aria will be well and truly in the past.'

'So you think you're well and truly over her?' asked Hazel.

'I know I am. I didn't get to say goodbye to Aria the first time. I always blamed myself for her leaving. But in this one week of having her back I realized that we just don't fit. We're over, it's over. Finally. I can say goodbye to her and I'm really relieved.'

'Thank goodness,' Hazel said.

'It might be worth mentioning to Jess that Aria's leaving,' Annabelle put in.

Daniel got up.

'Take a picture of this face,' said Daniel. 'Post it on WhatsApp. It's the look of a confirmed bachelor. A male spinster. I've had it with relationships. I'm well and truly certain of that.'

He turned to leave. Hazel got up to walk him to the door but by the time she was halfway down the hall he had already left. Annabelle whipped out her phone and sent a message to the group chat.

33

Daniel waited at the front door, his hands in the pockets of his cargo shorts, as Aria came down the stairs. Her eyes were puffy and she barely lifted her head. She filled the hallway with the scent of flowers after having spent over an hour in the bathroom getting ready. Daniel had heard her sniffing, his head against the bathroom door, willing himself not to allow her tears to affect his judgement. He'd worked hard to get over Aria after she'd left him high and dry a year ago but it was obvious to him now he hadn't been entirely successful. Having been with her for a week and knowing what she'd done only confirmed it was time. Time to let go completely and to move on. On to what, he wasn't exactly sure, but a weight had been lifted from his head and his heart and he felt free. Carrying Aria's luggage downstairs was a poignant moment for him; all that was needed was to say a final goodbye.

He had called the taxi. It was parked outside, the engine idling on the roadside. Doc and Greg were at the foot of the steps but Aria barely acknowledged them as they wished her all the best. Doc, wearing only a pair of boxers and with a cold pizza slice in one hand, wished her a good trip in Italian and waved a greasy paw at her. Greg kissed her cheek.

'Should I carry this out to the taxi?' Daniel asked, lamely, nodding to her luggage. She gave him a vague look. 'I'll carry this to the taxi,' he said. Without looking at Aria he picked up her rucksack and her large bag and took them outside. The taxi driver nodded and Daniel opened the boot.

'What time is your flight?' he asked Aria after she'd walked slowly and aimlessly towards the taxi.

'It's not until tomorrow morning, actually. I'm staying at a hotel near Heathrow for the night.'

'God, Aria, you could have stopped another night if you needed to. I thought the flight was today.'

'I'm going now because I thought you didn't want me around for another second.'

Daniel looked down and then placed her things into the boot. He slammed the door.

'So, it's true,' she said. 'You hate me.'

'I don't hate you,' said Daniel, lightly touching her arm. She looked down at his hand. 'I just wish it could have ended better, in some other way.'

'You mean you and me back together again?' Her brow creased upwards.

'I don't think that would have happened if I'm honest.'

She placed a hand on his cheek. 'Oh, *Daniele*. Of course not, because your heart is already with somebody else.'

He shook his head and stepped back.

'Goodbye, Aria.'

She climbed into the back of the taxi and closed the door. Daniel stood at the front door until the taxi was out of sight. Just as he went to close the door he felt something warm and fluffy against his bare legs and heard the familiar sound of the cat mewing before he whizzed his way to the kitchen. From the kitchen he heard Doc and Greg give a cheer because the cat was back. He only hoped they wouldn't try to feed him cold pizza.

Daniel stood at the doorstep, not sure if he felt relieved or sad or just an uncomfortable combination of both. As he looked up he saw Hazel leave her front door. She waved to him, the way she had on the very first day he arrived. Only this time Daniel waved back and he didn't try to back away when he saw she was making her way to his house.

He invited her in and led her to the living room before she could see, through the open kitchen door, that Doc and Greg were sitting on the kitchen counters eating old food and bowls of Shreddies in their underpants.

'It looks strange to see your grandmother's house like this,' said Hazel. Daniel helped her ease into one of the deckchairs. 'It can't be very comfortable for you all.'

'We make it work,' said Daniel, softly.

'So it's only the three of you now?'

'Yes, Aria just left in a taxi.'

Doc and Greg entered the living room to greet Hazel.

'Going to sunbathe?' she asked, looking at their underwear.

'Back in a sec,' said Greg and pushed Doc out of the door. They clambered up the stairs and returned seconds later wearing trousers and pulling on sweaters.

'So now that you've been here a week,' said Hazel, addressing Doc and Greg, 'do you think it might be time to start helping Daniel with the decorating?' She waved her stick around the room.

'Seriously?' said Doc.

'Very serious,' said Hazel. 'Daniel has a lot to do here. Don't worry, you'll still find time to relax and to chill.' She looked at them over her glasses. 'But I'm sure Daniel will appreciate the help. He's got personal training sessions to do and the walls won't paint themselves if he's got you two to entertain all day. Am I right, Daniel?'

'Well, I wouldn't mind a bit of help,' he said, looking apologetic. 'Could get it finished in half the time if you did give us a hand.'

'That's settled,' said Hazel, trying to get up. All three rushed to her assistance. 'And another thing, you're all invited to lunch at my house today. Trousers are not optional.'

34

The Slow Lane Walkers Club had three new members. Two of them were on a temporary membership and one was a handsome man in his forties.

Doc and Greg had been inspired by Hazel to come on the Saturday walk. She had told them over lunch the previous Sunday what a great club it was and what a wonderful leader Daniel made. They had set their alarms to ensure they'd be up in time to leave for the coast with Daniel. All three were unshaven and rather bedraggled when they left for the walk. A week of surfing, home improvements and booze had taken its toll.

Daniel knew that the other walkers were bound to bring up Jess in conversation so it was with trepidation that he stopped in front of the beach café with Doc and Greg on Saturday.

Doc put his arm around Hazel.

'*Ciao, bella*,' he said to her. Hazel chuckled and tried to nudge him away.

'We've got a couple of new walkers today,' said Daniel. 'But only for today.' Although he was disappointed that he couldn't dissuade Doc and Greg from coming along, he did his best not to let it show. They had, after all, made a great job of painting the hallway with him.

'And I have to introduce you to a new member,' said Hazel. 'Hopefully a permanent one.'

The handsome man in his forties who had been standing a few steps behind Hazel joined the group and smiled at them all. He was greeted with a warm welcome.

'This is Curtis,' said Hazel. 'We met a while ago and I've convinced him to give our little gang a go.'

Curtis chuckled nervously.

'Curtis,' Hazel continued, 'why don't you stick with Hannah? She is one of our best walkers and you and she have a lot in common.'

'Do we?' asked Hannah.

'Well, you both like cats for one thing. I'm sure on the way you might find there's more.'

Hazel gently guided Curtis towards Hannah with her stick. Heat filled Hannah's cheeks and turned them pink. Daniel could not help but give Hazel a wry smile and shake his head. She winked back at him.

Mary elbowed Daniel in the ribs.

'So I suppose your friends are up to date, are they?' said Mary, wasting no time getting to the serious business of Daniel's catastrophic love life. 'I'm sorry Jess doesn't want to have anything to do with you. I suppose by now she must be spoken for.' Mary shook her head in dismay and Eileen followed suit uttering the words 'spoken for' under her breath.

'Okay, let's go, let's go!' Daniel held both arms in the air and marshalled them towards the path.

'Wait a minute, my friend,' said Doc, also raising his arms. 'Who is this Jess and why are we only learning that there is a Jess now?'

'I'll explain later,' said Daniel. He quickly set off and the group half-heartedly followed behind. 'Come on, people,' he said. 'I thought we could beat our record today. Go just a little further.'

'Challenge accepted,' yelled Amanda, who was keen to show off the progress she was making from her training sessions with Daniel.

'I think it's only fair,' said Mary, dragging the group backwards with a walking pace slower than Hazel's, 'if we have new members that they be brought up to speed with what has happened with you and Jess, Daniel.'

'No, there's no need,' called Daniel, keeping up with Amanda.

'Yes there is!' shouted Doc.

As the walk commenced, Daniel was in a cluster group with Amanda and Oliver. The others lagged behind while Mary informed Doc and Greg of the current situation regarding Jess and Daniel. Hannah, in a timid voice, told Curtis all about the Daniel–Jess–Aria love triangle.

Daniel stood close to the cliff edge while the others stopped for a refreshment break. Even though he felt ambushed by Mary, he had tried to stay calm, looking out to sea. He tried to lose himself in the fresh feel of the air, the curls and ripples of the waves and the hypnotic effect it had on him. On the slow walks he was learning to appreciate the landscape and the way the coast path, with all its wildlife and vegetation, transformed and captivated him. He noticed how spring was gracefully transforming into a new season. The sea view was lulling him, relaxing him, until Doc came and stood beside him.

'Greg and I thought there was a reason Aria left so suddenly,' he said. 'Did she find out about the other girl?'

'She found out all right,' said Daniel. He sighed heavily. 'If I tell you what happened, will you promise to just leave it alone?'

'Promise,' said Doc, making a lacklustre attempt at the sign of the cross before kissing the tips of his fingers to his lips.

'I was supposed to meet Jess the night you guys arrived,' said Daniel. 'She'd invited me to a party.'

'You should have said. We would have come with you. We wouldn't have cramped your style.'

'Maybe not you two.'

'But Aria.'

'That's not the worst of it. You know it was Aria who had my phone? Hid it so I wouldn't see my messages from Jess.'

'So when Jess saw you kissing Aria—'

'Kissing?' Daniel spun around and stirred up some gravel from the clifftop. 'Wait, Aria kissed me. I didn't kiss her back.'

'Well, that's what the others were saying,' said Doc. 'Jess saw you kissing Aria and last Saturday she almost ran over your feet with her bike. That is so deep.'

Daniel looked over at Mary who had blown the whole situation right out of proportion and at Annabelle who must have reported the kiss to them on WhatsApp. Daniel was too fed up to put Doc straight. One day Doc would be on his way home and one day the walkers would forget all about his love life and leave him in peace. They could pester some other poor soul. Maybe the new guy, Curtis, might have a back story that could divert their attention.

'So,' said Daniel, turning to the group, 'who's up for pushing on a few metres further this week?'

Amanda immediately jumped to her feet and took in a deep breath.

'Anyone else?' asked Daniel, looking around at the relaxed group, nibbling on the banana bread slices that Annabelle had handed round.

'I'd like to go further,' Hannah said with her hand raised.

New walker Curtis was quick to smile at Hannah and also raised his hand.

'Well, let's do this,' said Daniel, clenching an encouraging fist.

At that moment the Padstow Pace Masters steamed by in their matching walking outfits. One of their number, right at the back of the group, limped after them as fast as he could while clutching his right gluteus muscle.

'Did you see who that was at the back?' asked Amanda hand over her mouth to stop herself laughing.

'Who?' asked Daniel.

'Only my ex-husband. Well, if the Padstow Pace Masters let that joker into their group, I'm not intimidated by them at all anymore. Come on, let's walk. Slowly.'

The group were not far from Harlyn Beach when Daniel declared that this was a good time to turn back. They stood on the clifftops overlooking the yellow sand.

'Doesn't Jess work at Harlyn Beach?' asked Annabelle as the rest of the walkers used the time to stop for another refreshment break.

'Yes,' said Daniel. 'Probably best if we don't keep going that way.'

'And you don't want to pop in and tell her Aria has left Cornwall for good?' his sister asked.

'It's not worth it.' Daniel shrugged.

'What about telling her that she hid your phone because she was jealous?' called Doc, who looked around the group, nodding his head, his palms turned up.

There was a great deal of unrest among The Slow Lane who exclaimed in disgust and gasped in shock at this additional piece of information. Who did this Aria person think she was?

'Well, there you are,' said Mary. 'Tell Jess about the phone and she might reconsider.'

Daniel shook his head.

'Listen, guys, I'm sorry to say,' said Daniel, glowering at Doc, 'that I decided to take control of *my* relationships, on my own, and without being goaded on – by anyone. I decided I want to remain single.'

'A male spinster?' gasped Hannah.

'A lonely heart?' Annabelle put a hand on her chest and slowly shook her head from side to side.

'Yes,' said Daniel. 'So that's it. End of discussion. Next week I'm setting a new trail. We're heading in the opposite direction from now on. There are some amazing sights on the way to Crugmeer. You've got the sinkhole, ragged rocks and islets. Amanda, you'll love the little valley. Great cardio workout. But a gentle one. So, next week, people!' He squeezed a fist. 'Nothing says we have to do the same walk every time.' He looked around the other members of the group with a very wide smile on his lips but no one, not even Amanda, looked enthused. 'Let's go, Slow Lane, let's go.' He clapped his hands and pointed in the direction of home. He adopted a high stomping movement back along the path. He was a good few metres away when he looked back and saw that not one walker had budged so much as a millimetre.

'Well, come on, you lot.' He was as cheery as could be. 'Let's get back.'

It was a very quiet walk to base. Daniel was at such a distance ahead he wasn't likely to hear any more talk of Jess. Each time he looked around the others would stop their chatter and look off to either side of the path to avoid eye contact with him. Even Doc, who had his hand over his mouth and was whispering something to Annabelle, stopped short and began to whistle while looking upwards at the sky.

Once the group had dispersed at the end of the walk, and Doc and Greg had gone to wait for him on the veranda of the café, Daniel turned to Hazel. She looked more tired than usual and leaned heavily on her stick.

'How much of an idiot was I?' he said. 'On a scale of one to ten?'

'You really want to know?' asked Hazel.

'Not really, no.' Daniel puffed and rubbed his head. 'By the way, how did you come to meet Curtis?'

'Oh, he's a widower I met a good while ago on a trip to see Henry. I don't see him too often but I did last week and got chatting again. His wife has been gone three years.'

'So you thought it was time for him to move on?'

Hazel nodded with a cheeky grin.

'You never know, things may just work out for him and Hannah,' she said. 'I thought they'd make a good match. The way I thought you and Jess might.'

Daniel cleared his throat and quickly changed the subject.

'Did you want me to drive you to the cemetery today, Hazel?'

'No, I'd like to go alone today. But thank you.'

'I haven't forgotten your cycling lessons, by the way.'

'That's absolutely fine. I can wait until you have more time.'

'No, Hazel. I managed to do some training sessions with the ladies and I've neglected you. I know how much you want to get going, how you'd like to get as far as the cemetery. This coming week I promise I'll take you out on the roads on your bike,' said Daniel.

'I must say, it'll be nice to get back on the bike again. If we leave it any longer, we may have to start again from scratch.'

'Not at all. You're a good rider. Don't underestimate yourself. I'll get hold of my brother-in-law's bike and we'll get you out there. How about Friday morning? That gives me time to organize a bike and helmet for me. Then we're all set. I'll knock on your door on Friday morning at eleven. I promise.' He saluted.

'I'll hold you to that promise,' said Hazel. She walked away slowly to her lunch engagement.

'And don't tell Henry what a jerk I was today,' Daniel called after her.

'That I can't promise you,' she said.

35

The week flew by for Daniel. Between training sessions for Amanda and the sisters, trips to the DIY store and some scenic local trails with his friends, Daniel managed a trip to Annabelle's house to borrow Scott's bike and helmet for his cycling lesson with Hazel. Scott was only too happy to oblige. He hadn't used the helmet at all and his mountain bike was, thankfully, a sensible shade of blue.

With everything in place for Hazel's lesson on Friday morning, Daniel, Doc and Greg took an evening trip to the beach the night before. By sunset, their best Cub Scout fire was ablaze, keeping them warm as they sipped their way through a crate of cold beer. The sky was an indigo backdrop to the stars sparkling against it. Doc and Greg chatted loudly and drank heartily while Daniel, who had been on the go non-stop all week, settled back on his elbows and looked across the cool sand, which appeared silver in the moonlight. In his mind, he was picturing the picnic he and Jess had shared two weeks ago, remembering what a beautiful evening it had been. They'd laughed and joked. Daniel had sat and gazed at Jess for so long, a sky full of stars would not have distracted him from her smile.

Suddenly Doc and Greg launched into a rousing song by

a nineties pop band before falling into fits of raucous laughter when Doc sang a line that made absolutely no sense in English.

'What?' he said to Greg. 'That's what they sing.'

'There isn't a line in the song that mentions "pumped up nuns and pistol gums". Mate, you're losing it.'

'Tell him,' said Doc, punching Daniel in the ribs. 'Tell him I'm right.'

Daniel knitted his brow and looked vaguely at his friends. He had no idea what he should be telling anyone. He was wrapped up in thoughts of Jess. How could their conversation on Harlyn Beach be their last when her face came into his mind when he was out surfing, working on the house, in fact in everything he did?

'Don't tell me you're missing Aria,' Doc said. 'Oh, of course, you're thinking about Jess.' He pulled a can of lager free from a plastic yoke of four and tossed it to Daniel, who pulled the ring. He drank until he'd reached the level of intoxication of his friends but in half the time. The night grew chilly and dark around him until he couldn't feel his cheeks and realized that Doc and Greg were stamping out the fire. Still carousing, they picked Daniel up off the sand by his underarms and dragged him off the beach, his arms over their shoulders, all the way home.

On Friday morning, Daniel woke with a thick head. He thought his eyes were deceiving him when he looked at his phone only to see that it was gone midday. A nagging feeling took hold of him. He was supposed to be somewhere but he wasn't sure where. It wasn't Saturday, was it? Was he late for the walk? Then it dawned on him where he was supposed to have been over an hour ago and he was instantly guilt ridden. He'd slept right past the time he should have called on Hazel for her lesson. He cursed himself as he stumbled around, trying to shower and brush his teeth at the same time. He pulled his clothes over a hot and damp body and ran halfway to Hazel's before realizing he didn't have Scott's bike or helmet with him. He knocked on Hazel's door seconds later, trying to come up with an excuse that didn't have to have the words 'drunk', 'beer' or 'overslept' in it.

Hazel didn't answer the door. He assumed she'd given up on him and gone out for a walk or shopping or anywhere where she wouldn't have to look at him. Then he remembered her after-lunch snooze so he stopped tapping at the door and tried her again an hour or so later. When Hazel didn't come to the door he thought she must be so fed up with him, she'd taken herself off for the day. What an idiot he'd been.

Saturday morning arrived bringing bright sunshine and a clear sky. Gulls and skylarks filled the air with their song and Daniel was still laden with the guilt of his unfulfilled promise to Hazel. He stood in the garden eating a bowl of Shreddies and wondered what he would say to her when the group met later for their walk. Hazel wasn't likely to chastise him but he was annoyed at himself.

Daniel put his head around his grandmother's bedroom door and asked if Doc and Greg wanted to come on the coastal walk. Maybe Doc could distract Hazel with his Italian charm. But Doc threw a trainer at him and Greg made a rude gesture with his middle finger so they wouldn't be joining him.

Daniel left the house and trotted towards the beach. Although he was embarrassed for having acted like a loser the week before, the group appeared to have forgiven him as they were out in full force, chatting and limbering up and waving when they saw him arrive. He smiled and nodded, cheeks a little flushed, and looked sheepishly around for Hazel. For the first time since the conception of the walking group, Hazel had not been the first to arrive.

'Anyone seen Hazel?' Daniel asked. He looked over shoulders, around backs, up to the café. He looked back in the direction he'd come, though he knew he hadn't passed her.

'She's usually here well before the rest of us,' said Eric.

'That's what I was just thinking,' said Daniel. He looked towards the café again. The first time he'd shown up for the walk, Hazel was just coming out of the door. He remembered her cheerful smile and the urge he'd felt to turn and run. How stupid it would have been of him if he had. As the minutes ticked by, and he watched each of them clock up on his phone, he became anxious about his friend. This was not like Hazel. He didn't have a telephone number for her either, so he couldn't call to see if she was coming. She might be too unwell to go on the walk. Maybe that's why she hadn't come to the door on Friday, in which case he'd drop by later and try her again. Yet still he worried that someone as determined as Hazel must be seriously unwell not to show up. Maybe he should run back now and check she was all right.

The others were still milling around, muttering and becoming restless. They checked their watches and looked along the adjoining roads for any signs of Hazel.

'Amanda, Oliver,' called Daniel above the chatter. 'Could you just check inside the café for her? I'll go back a little way to see if she might just be running late.'

'Of course,' they both said and marched off to the café.

'I'll check the shop,' said Mary and pulled Eileen along with her.

'I'll just have a look along the beach front,' said Annabelle. 'A long shot, but just in case.'

'Right,' said Daniel as he ran off towards home.

He thought he'd bump into Hazel at some point but he was nearing her house already and there was still no sign of her. He gave Annabelle a quick call to see if the others had had any luck finding her.

'Not so far,' she replied.

'Then I'll go back to her house.'

He was out of breath when he arrived at Hazel's door having tried to will her into view all the way along. He even had a crazy idea that the Padstow Pace Masters had abducted The Slow Lane's favourite walker because he'd outpaced them the other week.

Daniel pushed open Hazel's gate and knocked on the glass pane of her door. He waited and waited but she didn't answer. He peered in through the living room window, trying to make out her small figure sitting in the enormous orthopaedic chair, but she wasn't in it. He looked through the frosted window in the door as he knocked again, hoping she'd emerge from the kitchen to tell him she just wasn't up to it today and would he like to come in for tea. He knocked with intention and called her name through the letterbox. He stood back and looked at the upstairs windows to see if he'd glimpse her there. He tried to send out vibes the way Annabelle did so that Hazel would pick up on his racing heart rate and come to the door straight away. He envisaged Hazel lying on the floor unable to get up. She was usually very stable on her stick, slow and accurate, but still he worried. He looked along the roads, up to his house, ran to the quiet cul-de-sac round the corner where she had learned to ride a bike again, but Hazel was nowhere to be seen. Then, it occurred to him, it was a nice day, the first to really feel like summer, so if Hazel wasn't up for the walk she could be in her back garden.

Daniel returned to Hazel's house, his phone pinging with messages from the Slow Lane WhatsApp Group. He looked at them briefly. None of them said 'Hazel is here' so he slipped the phone back into his pocket as he stood on a low wall and peered over the side gate hoping to see Hazel in her garden.

'Hazel,' he called. 'Hazel? Are you out here?'

There was no reply. Daniel jumped off the wall. Checking his phone again, he stopped to read the messages properly. They were all from Annabelle.

'*Any sign? She's not here.*'

'*Checked everywhere. Will wait for you here.*'

'*Where are you now?*'

'*Did you knock on her door?*'

'*Call me.*'

'*Where is Hazel?*'

That question was etched in his own head. He called into the letterbox again and then stood at the gate gazing up and praying she'd appear at a window. Still nothing. Daniel took a deep breath and stared at the house. There was nothing unusual about it, nothing that would suggest from the outside that Hazel was inside and in some sort of trouble. And then he saw it. The dead giveaway that Hazel may not actually be home. The pink bicycle was not locked to the side trellis. It was gone. Hazel must have gone out on it without Daniel. But why on a Saturday? Why on their walk day?

Hazel had hinted she would like to cycle to the beach someday, and to the cemetery come to that. Maybe that was her plan; cycle to the path, walk with the group and go on to the cemetery afterwards. No matter how ridiculous it sounded in his head, Daniel had to see if it was true. He raced towards the beach again. He couldn't imagine Hazel taking any other route than the one he'd already travelled on. It was the safest and quickest but he hadn't seen her the first time so what would change this time? He kept hoping Hazel would be at the beach complex on his return but the bewildered walking club stared anxiously at him with their mouths and palms open. Hazel wasn't with them.

'Well?' asked Annabelle, red cheeked and looking wired.

'I can't get any answer at the door.' He was out of breath, bent over and clinging to his thighs. He straightened and looked all around the complex again and wondered about running towards the road to the cemetery. Surely Hazel wouldn't have gone on her own. He knew she loved an adventure but surely not this kind.

'I noticed that her bike was gone,' said Daniel. 'I know she wouldn't have gone for a ride on her own but I don't know what to think now. If only I—'

'What?' said Annabelle.

'Yesterday I was supposed to have shown her hand signals on the main roads but I got to hers really late. She wasn't in.' He tried to hold back the break in his voice but the walkers had noticed it, looking round at each other, muttering.

'Was the bike there yesterday?' asked Mary.

'I don't remember.'

They suggested possible scenarios that could have led to Hazel's disappearance. Maybe someone stole the bike and whoever it was might know something about Hazel's whereabouts.

'I should go and report her missing to the police,' said Daniel. 'Where is the local police station? Maybe they could break in. She's old and vulnerable and anything could have happened.'

'I'll drive,' said Annabelle.

'What can we do?' asked Hannah, tears glistening in her eyes.

'Don't worry,' said Daniel. 'Just wait for a message on the group chat. As soon as I know anything, I'll get Annabelle to contact you.'

'Will you come and let me know?' asked Eric.

'Of course,' said Daniel. He went to hurry away and then remembered why they'd all gathered there in the first place. 'You could still do the walk.'

'Not without Hazel!' Amanda exclaimed. This was followed by an overwhelming agreement.

Daniel waved to the walkers from the back seat of Annabelle's car as they, joined by Margot, set off for the police station.

36

Following Trevone Road, Wadebridge Police Station was a twenty-minute drive from the beach. Annabelle got there in less than fifteen.

'Aren't you driving a bit fast?' said Margot, head flush against the headrest, hand clutching the door handle.

'You've seen emergencies on the television, Margot.' Annabelle's knuckles were white on the steering wheel. 'They zip along the road, no time to spare.'

'Only the police and the baddies drive like this on TV,' Margot breathed.

'One of our members is missing, Margot,' said Annabelle. 'The police will understand.' She screeched on her brakes at the corner where the grey-brick police station stood. She skidded into the walled car park at the back of the building and did an emergency stop.

'I'll jump out,' said Daniel. 'You don't need to wait.'

'We'll be right here,' said Annabelle. 'I'll message the group.'

Daniel ran around to the front of the building and found the entrance. It was a lazy afternoon. There was very little movement in the entire building until a thickset female officer with frizzy white hair came to the front desk.

'I've come to report a missing person,' said Daniel.

'Ooh,' said the officer, eyes lighting up. She grabbed a pen and opened a large book with a smile on her face. 'Who is missing?'

'My friend.'

'Friend?' she said. 'Girlfriend, boyfriend?'

'Just a friend,' said Daniel, looking at the big blank page of the officer's book. 'A very good friend of mine, actually.'

'Name?'

'Hazel.'

The officer looked at Daniel. 'Hazel . . .?'

'Oh,' said Daniel. 'Her surname?' He furrowed his brow and rambled under his breath. 'It's probably the same as Henry's, I'm guessing. What did it say on his gravestone? Damn it, I don't know.'

The officer dropped the pen and rested her chin on her hand. 'A very good friend of yours and you don't her surname.'

'I know it sounds silly. But I've known her for a couple of months now and we've become close and she didn't show up for the walk today and that's why I was worried.'

'Walk?'

'Yes, we walk the South West Coast Path on a Saturday.'

'Oh,' said the police officer, picking up the pen. 'You're one of the Padstow Pace Masters. You raised money for the repairs to the community centre roof.'

'Um, no,' said Daniel. 'That's not our walking group. We're called something else.'

She dropped the pen again. 'So your walking group has a name but your friend doesn't.'

'Please,' said Daniel. 'We're wasting time. We should be out searching for Hazel. She's in her eighties and she walks with a walking stick. I went to her house and knocked. Several times. I tried to climb over the garden gate.' At this the police officer raised an eyebrow and picked up her pen. 'I was trying to see if Hazel was in her garden, not break in. I was hoping you could do that. Make sure she isn't collapsed or knocked her head or something serious like that.'

'Does this Hazel friend of yours have family who might have a key?'

'Her family is in London. So there isn't anyone nearby.'

'So, it's just you then and you don't even know her name.' The police officer sighed through her lips with puffed cheeks. 'If you're concerned about her wellbeing, try calling the hospital. There might be a social worker involved if she's an old woman on her own.'

'But she's not on her own, she's got me. And the rest of The Slow Lane. They'll all be on WhatsApp waiting to hear how I got on.'

The police officer looked at Daniel incredulously for a full minute and then pursed her lips.

'This is a missing persons case,' Daniel insisted. 'She wasn't in when I knocked for her yesterday either. You're not taking this seriously.'

The officer closed her big book. 'You go back to Hazel's house. She might have just gone for a little walk of her own. If she's not back in the late afternoon, call the hospital. If she's not back by the evening, call us. We'll see what we can do.'

'That's it? On the television, they break in and stuff. I've seen it.'

'Well, this is real life, sir, not *Broadchurch*. There is no crime here. Like I say, give us a call later and we'll take a wander over and see if we can't find some clues. You know, like on the TV?' She tutted and got up.

'Thanks a lot,' said Daniel. He stormed to the door and ran back to the car park.

Annabelle and Margot were out of the car.

'Well?' asked Annabelle. 'You were awfully quick. Are they sending a squad car?'

'Hardly,' said Daniel, pulling out his phone. 'I've got to call the hospital. Where's the nearest one?'

The hospital switchboard was slow to answer and took forever to locate an appropriate person for Daniel to speak to. Then he was told that unless he was family, no information could be given.

'Drop me home,' he said to Annabelle. 'I'll drive up there myself.'

37

When Daniel set up the Walkers Club, not once did he envisage haring around Cornwall on a Saturday afternoon, in a car, miles from the coast path. When Annabelle dropped him at the house he had rushed inside to grab the car keys. From the top stair, a wild and grizzly Doc had belted out a yawn and asked, 'What the hell, man?'

'It's an emergency situation,' Daniel had yelled back up the stairs. 'Hazel is missing and I'm worried something bad has happened.' He was at the open door. Doc took a few steps down in a crumpled T-shirt and briefs.

'You want me to come?' he'd said.

'It's okay,' Daniel had called while stepping out the door. 'I think I've got this.'

He'd slammed the door shut just as Doc was saying, 'Okay, *ciao*.'

Daniel pulled up at a space in the hospital car park. He ran to the A&E department, assuming Hazel would be there. He sensed some sort of accident must have occurred, and only hoped it wasn't as serious as the pictures in his mind. These didn't look good at all. He tried to relax and calm his breathing but he couldn't make that happen. All he could do was charge up to the desk in A&E and begin to interrogate a very bored-looking man on reception.

'I'm trying to find my friend. She might have been admitted but I'm not sure and I really need you to check for me. And please don't send me back to the police because they are the ones who sent me here.'

The man looked back over his shoulder to his colleague with a 'here we go again' expression, eyes rolling under the lids, scowling just enough for dimples to appear on his chin.

'And before you ask,' Daniel bellowed, 'I don't have her last name. She's Hazel and she's a little old woman on a pink bicycle and she might have been brought in earlier this morning.'

A nurse was walking into the department from the main door and had caught Daniel's emotive speech. She touched Daniel's arm.

'Hi, sorry,' she said. She was waist high to Daniel with a tight pigtail that pulled her brow into a look of surprise. 'I heard what you were saying. A woman was brought in after a road accident. She was elderly and came off a pink bicycle. But it wasn't today, that was yesterday morning. Could that be her?'

'It must be,' gasped Daniel. 'Where is she?' He looked around, his head snapping towards all directions.

'I can look for you,' said the nurse. 'Give me one second.' She buzzed herself into a side door and emerged in reception behind the sullen receptionist. She leaned over him and tapped something into the computer.

'That's it,' she said. 'You'll find her on Mortimer Ward. Go out of here, into the main building and up to the third floor.'

'Thank you, thank you,' said Daniel. At the door he narrowed his eyes at the receptionist and hurried out to the main building.

On Mortimer Ward there was an intercom system. The nurse on reception was reluctant to let Daniel through the door. He wasn't family and this ward was for intensive cases. He swallowed hard resisting the urge to bang his fist on the little window of the door. The nurse had already turned his back on Daniel after telling him that he had to come back the next day. The next day wasn't good enough, he needed to see Hazel now. As he stared through the glass a woman began walking towards the door. If she was on her way out, Daniel thought he'd sneak in when the door opened and go in search of Hazel himself. The woman approaching the door looked tired. There was something about her face that Daniel recognized but couldn't quite place.

The door hissed open slowly and the woman looked directly at Daniel. There was no way he could dodge around her and sneak in; she was probably well equipped to deal with that sort of thing judging by the no-nonsense look in her eye.

'Are you Daniel?' she said. She was an elegant, middle-aged woman, well dressed in dark jeans, a silk top and dark blue blazer. Her hair was light brown and wavy, pulled back into a short ponytail at the nape of her neck; her skin was a sandy brown colour with faint freckles on her cheeks.

'I– I am,' he said. 'Are you Hazel's doctor?'

'No,' she said. 'I'm Jennifer. I'm Hazel's daughter.'

Daniel took a deep inhale and nodded his head at how striking the resemblance was between Hazel and her oldest child, now that he knew who she was.

'Hazel wasn't at the club, so—' Daniel began.

'Club? What club?'

'Um, Hazel and I run a Saturday walking club and when she didn't show up I was really worried about her.' He looked over her shoulder through the window in the door. The nurse wasn't at his station; it would have been a good time to sneak in, only the door had closed and Hazel's daughter didn't look as if she would let him sneak anywhere. Her shoulders hunched as she slipped her hands into the front pockets of her jeans. She pursed her lips and took a snort of air through her nostrils, which to Daniel looked flared in anger. Why was she upset with him? Wasn't her mother permitted to join a club? He knew full well that Hazel's children managed her welfare online from their homes in London. Perhaps joining clubs was on their list of no-nos. They had already deemed that a weekly visit to the cemetery to see Henry was too much for her. Did they really believe that their mother, a woman so full of life, was going to sit all day in her orthopaedic chair and knit jumpers?

'We're a very casual walking club,' said Daniel. 'We take it very slowly and gently along the coast path.'

'My mother has a walking stick, she has no business walking up and down cliffs at her age.' She looked at Daniel as if he were incompetent.

'With respect,' said Daniel, taking a step back from Jennifer as she seemed to loom over him, gathering momentum with each word, 'Hazel is what the club is all about. As I say, we take it slow and steady and the path isn't as treacherous as you think.'

'Mum told me Daniel gave her a bike as a present.'

He wasn't sure if this was a question or a statement but Daniel affirmed with several nods of the head.

'Well, Daniel,' she said, 'Mum came off that bike yesterday and yesterday evening she had to have an emergency hip replacement.'

Daniel slapped his hand to his lips.

'So,' Jennifer went on. 'Walking up mountains and riding bikes are not suitable pursuits for frail old ladies, especially now.'

'Hazel isn't a frail old lady,' Daniel said softly while looking to the floor. Jennifer made him feel as if he were being reprimanded in the headmistress's office and only seconds away from expulsion.

'What did you say?' asked Jennifer. 'You don't know how serious this is, do you?'

'Of course I do,' said Daniel, straightening. 'Why do you think I'm here? Hazel is my friend. When she didn't turn up for the walk I rushed straight to her house. I knocked and knocked. I went to the police and now I'm here.'

Jennifer took a step back and looked Daniel up and down.

'The annoying thing is,' she said, 'since she's been coherent, all she's talked about is Daniel, Daniel, Daniel. She even asked me to go down to the coast to pass on a message this morning.'

He sensed her annoyance but hoped Jennifer wouldn't stop him seeing Hazel.

'Although we're friends,' he said, 'we haven't exchanged numbers so she couldn't call me. I mean, not that she has a mobile phone.'

'Oh, Mum has a mobile phone all right. One in a list of things I've bought for her and that she never uses.'

'Maybe she doesn't know how,' said Daniel.

'Don't you think I would have shown her?' said Jennifer with a sniff. 'Anyway, Mum assumed you'd find her somehow and she wants to see you.' Jennifer looked at him from top to toe again.

'Sorry, I'm a bit hot and all over the place,' said Daniel. He pulled at the fabric on the front of his top which clung to his skin. 'But tell me, how is Hazel? How did the operation go? And can I see her now?'

Jennifer pressed the intercom and the nurse released the lock. The doors slowly opened. There was an overwhelming scent coming from a large bouquet of fresh flowers in a vase on the desk mixed with the undeniable, antiseptic smell of hospital wards. Daniel was suddenly aware that he had nothing with him. Nothing to give to Hazel. In his pockets were his keys. His hand folded around them.

'He is family to Hazel,' said Jennifer to the nurse. 'She wants to see him.' The nurse seemed helpless to deny him entry. Jennifer meant business. She beckoned Daniel to follow her down a dim corridor. She turned back to him.

'Mum talked about you as if you were family. Another son.'

Jennifer opened the door to a private room and Daniel saw Hazel in the hospital bed nestled into a multitude of pillows. He sighed with relief at seeing her and pulled his lips tight to stop them quivering.

'Daniel.' Hazel breathed his name, emphasizing each syllable. She tried to sit herself up but only grimaced and fell back against the pillows. Jennifer rushed to her and began to punch and pummel the pillows.

'You're not supposed to move without a physiotherapist being present,' Jennifer said in her strict headmistress manner.

'I'm supposed to be up walking every few hours,' Hazel said and grinned to Daniel.

'Yes, but with help, and they said to rest now.' Jennifer tutted.

Daniel moved slowly across the room to the bed and stood behind the adjacent chair. He noticed a walking frame on the other side of the bed. It seemed so big compared to Hazel.

'Take a seat, Daniel. It's all right, I won't snap in two.' Hazel eyed her daughter as she said this. 'I bet you could do with a tea, couldn't you, Daniel? If you don't mind, Jennifer, the poor boy looks parched.'

Daniel didn't know how to respond to the series of looks the two women gave each other. The last look Jennifer threw was in Daniel's direction. He blushed and created a barrier between Jennifer and himself with the chair he'd been gripping the back of. Jennifer closed the door as she left.

'Come on, Daniel,' Hazel encouraged. 'Sit down. How was the walk today?'

'Forget the walk,' said Daniel, crashing to the seat and leaning towards Hazel. 'We didn't even do the walk. How are you? What happened? Why did you go out on the road on your own?'

'Slow down, son,' she said. 'I'm a bit woozy on drugs for the pain.' Hazel took a deep breath and tried to adjust her position before she could continue. 'I know I shouldn't have gone out on my own. I'm sorry, Daniel.'

'No, don't you apologize to me. This is all my fault because I'm a flipping idiot. I made you a promise. I was supposed to give you a lesson on Friday and I didn't. I'm so sorry this happened to you, Hazel. You have no idea. I've been so worried and when Jennifer told me that—'

'Daniel, it's fine. I should have been patient. You were busy.'

'No, that's not good enough. I'd sorted out a bike so we could go out on the road. But I slept in past our lesson time.' Daniel lowered his gaze. 'I'd been out the night before, with the guys. I shouldn't have stayed out so late. I wanted you to get your confidence back on the bike.'

'That's probably my problem,' said Hazel. 'Too much confidence. I should have stopped at riding the motorbike round Europe all those years ago when I was a young girl. My days of adventures are over.'

Daniel leaned onto Hazel's bed. He saw the brightness was gone from her eyes, the tiredness within and the dullness of her skin. Her lips were thin and cracked and her smiling cheeks appeared to have sunk.

'What have the doctors said?' he asked.

'Oh, they were wonderful, everyone has been so helpful. The consultant says I need physiotherapy. They want me up and walking, getting used to my new hip. I'll need a frame for getting around on at first, until I'm stronger and I'll be back to the stick in time. Recovery isn't easy at my age, they said, but I'll get there. But as for the Saturday walks . . .'

Daniel looked down, a lump coming to his throat.

'Don't worry, Daniel, I should get back to normal, they said. If I keep up the exercise.' Hazel sighed. 'But I won't come on Saturdays anymore, that's for certain.'

'Oh, Hazel.' Daniel shook his head. 'Without you, there is no Slow Lane. I'll have to end it all.'

'Who says anything about ending?' Hazel opened her eyes wide. 'No, the club continues. Without me you can show the Padstow pain-in-the-neck Pace Masters what's what.'

He let out a slight laugh. 'You said it wasn't a competition.'

'Daniel, you know me. You know I love a challenge. If I could have done, I would have tried to outwalk that group. I would have been right up there with Amanda, specially printed T-shirt and all.' Hazel began to chuckle quietly. Her shoulders heaved as she chuckled louder, finally bursting into a full-on laugh. Daniel couldn't help but join in, imagining Amanda puffing for all she was worth to overtake the team that had her ex-husband as a member. He imagined Hazel prodding the Padstow Pace Masters' leader with her walking stick and asking him to step to one side. The laughter dissipated and the two sat staring at each other.

'I'm sorry, Hazel. I wasn't there for you and I should have been. Will you forgive me?'

'There's nothing to forgive. I assumed you'd had a big night with the lads when you didn't knock yesterday. A bit later I wheeled the bike to the cul-de-sac and I rode it, Daniel. All on my own. It was one of the best feelings I've had since I lost Henry. It made me feel young again. Independent. And free. I couldn't stop there, so I ventured down to the road. Just one little ride for myself, just to say, "You've done it, Hazel, you're not the helpless little old lady your children think you are." And the next thing I knew I was looking up at the sky. I was in more pain than when I came off my motorbike all those years ago, I can tell you. I don't have much recollection of what actually happened yesterday. Another car coming? Or I saw a pedestrian? I still can't remember. I know no one else was hurt or property damaged because of me.'

'But *you* got hurt, Hazel. It's . . . I'm really . . . When you're out of here, I can help you, with the physio exercises. You said it yourself, you'll heal in time, and you wait, you'll be back on the coast path before you know it.'

Hazel blinked and a tear rolled down to her chin.

'My children want me back in London,' she said, dismissing the tear with a swipe of her finger. 'Probably shove me in a home, I'd imagine. They've had a meeting and decided I can't be alone here anymore.'

'You're not alone.' Daniel took Hazel's hand. 'There's me.'

'Darling boy, you don't even know how long you'll be here yourself. And the last thing you should do is attach yourself to an old lady. I've had my time, Daniel, and what a time it's been. All my memories are on the walls in the corridor. Just like your gran's are in her journal. We had amazing journeys.'

'It's not over.' Daniel's voice was small, a whimper. The whites of his eyes becoming pink.

'I can't be in the group anymore, Daniel, it's just something I have to face. I know I'll miss it. Just like I'll miss visiting Henry.'

'That's more reason to stay. I can drive you. Every Saturday.'

'Daniel, don't make promises you can't keep.'

Just then the door opened. Jennifer appeared holding a disposable cup with a lid.

'I hope you've had long enough to talk,' she said, offering the drink to Daniel.

'We have,' he said. 'Thanks for the tea. Hazel, I should go and report back to the others. They'll be desperate to know what happened. That you're okay. I'd like to come tomorrow if that's all right.' He looked at Jennifer.

'Oh, I look forward to that,' said Hazel. Her eyes squeezed together as she smiled, cheeks puffed, but Daniel sensed the loss within her.

Outside he disposed of the tea Jennifer had bought him and looked to the sky, searching the gathering clouds for a happy ending to this devastating situation. He could see how upsetting it was for Hazel to have to leave Trevone, but how could he make promises to look after her if she stayed when he had no idea if he was staying himself?

Hazel's accident had made him pause and consider his next move seriously. He had friends in Trevone now, a community. He had people who cared about his future and his happiness. He even had a means of supporting himself if he put his mind to increasing the number of clients he trained. Then he could be there for Hazel, for Annabelle, his family, his new friends.

Before he knew it he was letting his imagination flow. Jess

had said, sometimes decisions have a way of being made for you. Was a plan for his future being mapped out?

Daniel walked back to his car not knowing how he was going to recount Hazel's accident to the other walkers without breaking down and telling them how it was all his fault, how he should have been a better friend. Not only that, how on earth was he going to tell them that Hazel would be leaving The Slow Lane?

38

Doc and Greg were not able to convince Daniel to go with them for a few cans of beer on the beach once he'd arrived home. It was a mild evening, the start of summer, and they'd spent the day trying to cheer him up after he'd returned from the hospital. Daniel was in no mood for a laugh and a joke with them. He was too concerned about Hazel.

'Tell you what,' Greg said. 'You know where we are, so come and join us later if you're up for it.'

Once they'd left, Daniel switched on the laptop and looked up information about recovery after a hip replacement. He read his way through several sites looking for expert advice. He knew that Hazel would have to follow a programme of physiotherapy exercise once she was out of the hospital. Her daughter Jennifer was likely to be helping her with those after the physiotherapist had shown her how to cope with the programme at home, but he would ask if there was anything he could do to assist. He thought about how sad it would be for Hazel not to return to The Slow Lane. He'd miss her and he still wasn't convinced he should continue the club without her. He hoped Hazel wouldn't leave for London immediately. Her house would probably be sold so she might be in Trevone for a good few months, at least.

The night drew in and Doc and Greg hadn't come back to the house. Daniel took the laptop up to his room. He found a documentary about migrating birds to help him take his mind off the last few traumatic weeks. But the documentary drifted into the background and the image of Hazel, of all people, looking so helpless in the hospital bed made him sad. Maybe he'd messed things up enough for her and he should let the responsibility of Hazel's care rest on her children's shoulders.

He drifted into a restless sleep. At some stage during the night he was woken by the racket Doc and Greg made when they returned home. After a brief doze he fell in and out of shallow naps throughout the night. A jumble of scenes featuring Hazel, Jess and Aria took over his mind. His emotions raged like a storm within him. Had he been responsible for all this upset? He thought so. He spent a sleepless dawn trying to come up with ways to escape any more drama and letting anyone else down.

At dawn, Greg and Doc were still awake, laughing in the living room downstairs. He wished he could capture just some of the carefree attitude his friends had. They had no immediate plans and maybe his best option would be to tag along with them, wherever it was they took off to next. At least he'd have a laugh and not have to worry about who he was hurting. He'd attach himself to Doc and Greg, go with the flow. By sunrise, his heart was feeling battered and he'd come to accept a fact he knew to be true: running away doesn't eliminate your troubles.

Later that morning, Annabelle came to the house with a huge bouquet of vibrant flowers, a bowl of fruit, chocolates and a large Get Well Soon card.

'These are from the walkers,' she announced to an

astounded Daniel who stood in the hallway. Rasmus clung to Annabelle, on the lookout for Daniel's house guests. Annabelle made her way to the kitchen to put Hazel's presents onto the counter.

'Everyone said on the WhatsApp group they'd donate so I bought these for Hazel. You could give them to her when you go,' said Annabelle.

'The walkers are just too kind,' said Daniel. 'Thank you for organizing this.'

'Do you want me to come with you to the hospital?'

'It's okay. Best if Hazel doesn't have too many visitors at first. She'll have a lot of physiotherapy to do before she can come home.'

'When will that be?' Annabelle asked. 'And do you think you'll keep the club going while she's out of action?'

He shrugged. 'I'd feel bad keeping it going without Hazel but I know she wants me to. I don't know what I'll do when she moves back to London.'

'What?' Annabelle gasped. 'Hazel leaving The Slow Lane?'

'I know,' said Daniel. 'I think I should abandon the whole idea.'

Rasmus came out from behind his mother and looked up at Daniel with the corner of his lips turned downwards.

'Don't be sad, Uncle Daniel. More people will join your walking Saturday.'

Daniel picked his nephew up and propped him on his hip.

'I might be going to London myself one day, buddy,' said Daniel. Rasmus's eyes widened. 'But it might not be for a long time – we'll see.' He let Rasmus back down. 'But for now I should get off to the hospital to see Hazel. Visiting is after lunch.'

Hazel was sitting in a chair in her room when Daniel

arrived. She looked closer to her normal self and she gave him a broad smile when he walked in, his arms full of the goodies the walking group had sent to her.

'This is from all the walkers, Hazel,' said Daniel. He put everything down on her side table and bent to give Hazel a kiss on her cheek.

'This is too much,' she said. 'Please thank them all for me.'

'I suspect a few of them might visit you. Everyone was so worried when you didn't come on Saturday.'

Jennifer sat in the corner of the room. Daniel could feel the tension in her shoulders and a stabbing sensation in his back from her gaze.

'You have to understand, Daniel,' she said, getting up. 'Mum isn't up for all this gallivanting around, it's dangerous at her age. I'll go and see if I can find a vase or two for all these flowers.' She left the room with the bouquet and closed the door behind her.

'I've been trying to get my head around you going back to London.' Daniel pulled up a chair and sat very close to Hazel.

'I miss my children and I hardly see my grandchildren.' Hazel lowered her gaze.

'I suppose it's for the best, then?' Inside he longed to ask her to consider staying but what right did he have?

'I suppose it is.' Hazel smiled and nodded. 'Having my family around at this stage in my life makes sense.'

Daniel nodded slowly in agreement. 'You know, I was reading up on hip replacement recovery and when you come home I can help you with the exercises.'

'Thank you, Daniel.'

He puffed out a sigh and the two sat in silence for a moment until Hazel hooked her elbows onto the armrests of her chair and leaned towards him.

'What about you, Daniel?' she said. 'How are your plans coming along?'

'I don't have any to speak of for now. Still taking things day by day.'

'That's what I'm having to do with my recovery, so I understand.'

'If you're not leaving for London straight away,' said Daniel, brightening, 'you might be able to walk with us when you've recovered.'

'Jennifer has had to ask for special leave to come and look after me. She'll be staying with me until I'm up and running, as it were. I have to show that I'm grateful for everything she has sacrificed for me. I can't continue doing the walk and upsetting her. It would break her heart.'

'I had to ask.' He was silent again for a moment. 'And what about going to visit Henry? Will she allow you to go while you're still here?'

Hazel giggled.

'She's not an ogre, Daniel. She loves me, the way Annabelle loves you and wants the best for you. Jennifer does things her way. Even though that might seem stern to you, it all comes from the heart and I do appreciate it.'

Hazel returned home at the end of the week. On Friday morning, Daniel looked down the hill and saw a couple of cars outside Hazel's door. Presumably her family had come to see her and were making plans to take her back to London. The Slow Lane was due to walk the next day and he had to decide whether to cancel out of respect for Hazel or to carry on because the rest of the group were keen to keep going until she came back. He hadn't told any of them that Hazel had had her last walk with them.

On Friday evening, Daniel popped over to see Hazel.

'Oh,' said Jennifer when she answered the door, 'I wondered when you might come over.'

'I won't stay,' said Daniel. 'I just wanted to make sure Hazel has settled in okay.'

He found Hazel sat in her big chair, all the other seats taken up by familiar-looking faces, a couple of young children sitting on the floor beside her.

'Lovely to see you,' she said. 'All ready for the walk tomorrow?'

'Um, that's what I wanted to talk to you about,' said Daniel. 'I'm feeling so torn about doing the walk without you. Are you sure it's okay?'

'Of course,' exclaimed Hazel. 'The walking group lives on and I'll be there in spirit if nothing else.'

Daniel desperately wanted to suggest that Hazel come on one last walk to say farewell to the group when she was up to it, but the daggers he felt from Jennifer stopped him. Instead he leaned over Hazel and quietly whispered, 'Thank you, Hazel, and I'll see you during the week. Promise.'

She smiled up at him and waved as he said his goodbyes to Hazel's family.

39

Daniel felt obliged to arrive early for the walk. Hazel had always been there to greet the walkers as they arrived and she spent time making sure they had done some stretches before they started. Of course, Daniel hadn't realized this until Amanda and Oliver, who arrived shortly after, informed him. He'd stood there smiling at them, not knowing what else to talk about, after saying hello.

'Hazel is amazing,' said Amanda. 'She gives us little pep talks and asks about our week.'

'Does she really?' said Daniel. He shouldn't have been surprised. He realized that he'd have to make sure his alarm was set so that he could keep up the great job Hazel had obviously been doing of boosting morale. There was a very friendly and welcoming atmosphere in the group and Daniel realized this was all down to Hazel. He hoped he could live up to her standards.

Daniel made sure he led the walkers in a few stretches. He had stopped doing any health and safety checks and knew that he'd have to reinstate those. He'd been awfully slack as a leader and felt even less of one without Hazel as they set off on the very first walk without her.

The group ambled up to the coast path and strolled along

for a good few metres, walking even more slowly without Hazel. There wasn't a great deal of chatter among the group. If they'd talked about his dismal love life, Daniel wouldn't have minded. Anything was better than this woeful walk.

After they finished their break over Newtrain Bay, they slowly gathered their belongings together when the determined tread of walking shoes began to close in on them.

'Padstow Pace Masters,' Amanda said with gritted teeth. 'Right on our heels.'

The Slow Lane was ready to continue on the path but out of courtesy they thought it best to wait until the fast walkers went ahead. Daniel had other ideas.

'What are we waiting for?' he called.

The others looked at him quizzically but Daniel's cheeky smirk told them everything they needed to know. Large smiles grew on their faces, and before the Pace Masters could advance The Slow Lane crowded the path and continued their trail towards Harlyn.

'Excuse me. Pardon me. Coming by,' said the Pace Masters' lead walker, but The Slow Lane picked up their pace and refused to move aside. From behind them came the harrumphs, loud coughs and exaggerated clearing of throats of the agitated Padstow Pace Masters, but Daniel's walkers held firm.

'I think we're in the way,' called Daniel in an innocent voice. 'Better hurry it up, team.'

Amanda looked at Daniel wide eyed, glee spreading on her lips, all three coats of lipstick making her look more manic than the Joker and off she strode. Oliver, Hannah, Curtis, Eileen, Mary, Annabelle, Margot, Eric, Benny and Daniel all right there with her. The Padstow Pace Masters engaged in tactics similar to touch rugby and muscled through and around The Slow Lane.

'Okay, fall in,' Daniel shouted. His walkers had no choice but to stop. They had already begun to collapse in fits of giggles, especially since Annabelle and Margot impersonated the crazed arm movements the Pace Masters employed in their endeavour to be the fastest walkers on the South West Coast Path. Daniel laughed the loudest when visions of Hazel battling on with her walking frame to get ahead of the Pace Masters came to mind.

With the Padstow Pace Masters on their way, Amanda turned to Daniel.

'Let's keep going this time, Daniel,' she panted as she tried to stop laughing. 'All the way to Harlyn Beach. I'm up for it.'

Everyone agreed and Daniel led them off again, the gap between them and the Pace Masters widening all the time. They were completely out of sight by the time The Slow Lane entered the café at Harlyn, still buoyant from the walk, ready for a comfort stop and more refreshments. Memories of his breakfast with Jess came back all too easily as well as the feeling he had when they'd taken their long, slow stroll after their first date.

'What's up, Daniel?' asked Annabelle, who sat beside him at the table. 'Don't tell me the walk was too much for you.'

'I was thinking about Hazel,' he said without looking up. 'She and I will have a good laugh when I tell her about today.'

'You don't look like someone in the mood to laugh.'

'Don't I?' he said absently. 'Maybe I *am* a little tired after the walk.'

The group chatted among themselves, spread out at different tables at the busy seaside café, sipping tea, Amanda screeching with laughter at something Oliver was relaying to the sisters. The café door opened wide and Daniel's heart leapt upwards. The door had opened as if someone with the same bouncy flair as Jess had walked in. He looked eagerly towards the party who had entered and searched for a sign that Jess might be with them. She wasn't, of course. What were the chances? And as the newcomers made their way to the counter he remembered Jess's friendly way with the waiting staff and imagined her leaning on the counter with her toes on the foot rail as she placed an order. Her laughter the day they'd had breakfast there had caused an unexpected flutter in his chest, and if she'd been there he could have gone up to her and told her that his walking group had finally made it to Harlyn and that she'd promised that drinks would be on her if that ever happened. She would have smiled and he would have told her she didn't really have to buy them drinks.

The door opened again as a couple was about to leave. Annabelle called his name and he noticed that the walkers were getting ready to leave. He shook his meandering thoughts away and rose to join them. His coffee remained untouched on the table.

40

In the week that followed, Daniel visited Hazel every day. Her family had gone home apart from Jennifer who remained to look after her mother. Hazel had insisted that Daniel could help her work through the exercises the physiotherapist at the hospital had detailed in Hazel's at-home recovery plan. Jennifer watched with incredulity at the progress Hazel made under Daniel's strict guidance and at how well she coped with her walking frame.

'Did I tell you that Daniel is a qualified personal trainer?' Hazel said cheerily to her daughter.

'Several times,' said Jennifer, who sat with a book on her lap in the living room.

'I can get up and down the stairs now,' said Hazel.

'Mum, I know that. I've seen you do it. What are you trying to say?'

Hazel stopped and leaned on the walking frame.

'It's just that you've taken so much time off work, Jen. You really don't need to stay down here. I don't want you losing money unnecessarily. You get yourself back to London. Your family will be missing you.'

'But you're my family.' Jennifer looked sad.

'Yes, and I'm also your mother. You're not mine, remember? So believe me when I say I'll be fine, when you go back.'

'But Mum, I haven't organized a carer.'

'And I told you I can still do for myself. The bathroom adjustments are in, I can get around the place. I've got friends who will visit and have offered to shop for me. And I've got Daniel.'

The women looked at each other, long and hard. Daniel could tell they were just as determined as each other. He put his head down and said nothing. Jennifer sighed and closed her book before standing and crossing her arms.

'I'm a phone call away,' she said eventually, a little teary eyed. 'I suppose I could go home and sort out the move and everything from there. I'll have to come down if an estate agent needs access, but in the meantime we can Skype?'

'Of course we will,' said Hazel, putting one arm out to hug her daughter.

Jennifer sniffed and blinked several times. She bent down to embrace her mother, her eyes closed as they stood like this for a moment. Jennifer opened her eyes and looked at Daniel, mouthing the words 'thank you'. Daniel nodded. Jennifer made a fumbled excuse to look for something upstairs.

'Well, we still have more exercises, Daniel,' Hazel said with both hands on the walking frame.

'Yes, we do.'

Jennifer disappeared upstairs.

'She means well,' said Hazel once her daughter had left the room. 'But she can't make a decent pot of tea for toffee.'

Daniel and Hazel laughed quietly.

By the next afternoon, Jennifer was gone and Daniel found Hazel in her front garden when he called on her.

'It's good to see you out and about, Hazel,' he said as he opened the front gate.

'It's just so lovely to be out in the fresh air again.' She

turned her walker in the direction of her front door. 'Come in, Daniel.'

He noticed that each day Hazel looked brighter. She was better able to cope with the pain and her confidence with the walking frame was growing.

Once inside he made Hazel comfortable in her chair and set about making the perfect pot of tea. He brought a mug each into the living room and placed one in Hazel's waiting hands.

'You are good, Daniel. I could get used to this.' Hazel took her first sip, smacked her lips together and sighed. She set the mug down on the table beside her and rested her head against the high-backed chair.

As Daniel sipped his tea he noticed the smile leaving Hazel's face. He imagined she was thinking about going back to London. It was going to be a challenge for her. Hazel and Henry had lived in Cornwall for almost twenty years. He knew it had become home for her, even though Henry wasn't with her anymore.

'Did Jennifer or the others take you to see your best pal?' Daniel dared to ask.

Hazel shook her head. 'They went, though. To lay flowers. But Jennifer said I shouldn't be climbing into cars and putting my body through any more trauma. I tried to tell her I was fine and it wasn't as if I was walking all the way with the frame. Or trying to cycle there.'

Daniel chuckled.

'But of course,' said Hazel, 'I never let on that I'd still been going every weekend.' She giggled like a naughty schoolgirl.

'So you've missed two lunch dates,' Daniel said.

'I know.' The brightness left her eyes. 'And I feel awful for it. It's as though I've let Henry down. I've still got it in me to take a trip every week in a taxi, mind you. Maybe I could do that, at least up until the time I leave.'

Daniel had a glint in his eye.

'How about a little trip now, to make up for lost time?' he said.

Hazel leaned forward in her chair.

'Do you think we could?' she asked Daniel, her face looking even more like a naughty schoolgirl by the second.

'All I have to do is bring the car round, Hazel. You just say the word and we're there.'

'The word,' said Hazel.

Daniel sprang to his feet and darted up the hill. He folded up a deckchair from the living room and threw it into the back seat of his car. He drove the few metres back to Hazel's front door and opened the passenger door and went inside to help Hazel on with her jacket.

'I'll put your walking frame in the boot. And I've brought you a chair.'

'Well done,' said Hazel with a wide grin. He helped Hazel into the car and placed her frame into the boot before jumping into the driver's seat and giving her a conspiratorial wink.

'Just take it easy when we get there, no running because you're excited to see Henry.'

'Deal,' said Hazel and gave Daniel a thumbs up.

He drove slowly along the road. High hedges obscured the white houses along the way and views of fields in the distance. The car radio was on low and Hazel hummed to a song she recognized. He looked at her and smiled and then turned up the music. They sang along at the tops of their voices.

'Maybe you and your sisters should have formed an all-girl group after all,' said Daniel. 'Your voice isn't half bad.'

'I know,' said Hazel, cheerfully. 'I only wish I could say the same for you.'

Daniel pulled into the cemetery car park. He asked Hazel to hold on and wait for him while he trotted to Henry's grave with the deckchair. He stayed close to Hazel as she took the path with care, stopping to heave a breath every few steps. There was a large vase of flowers in front of Henry's gravestone filled with pink and yellow blooms. Daniel helped Hazel come to a seat and left her alone with Henry to pay a visit to his grandparents' graves. He told his gran, his eyes glassy with tears, that he'd got to know Hazel really well and when she goes back to London he'll be losing a very good friend.

Jennifer would have forbidden this little adventure to the cemetery, he was pretty sure of that. She had made Daniel promise her that he would not, under any circumstances, allow her mother to do anything risky, dangerous or foolish. Daniel didn't regard Hazel visiting Henry as any of these so in his mind he'd kept his promise. He wondered, as he watched Hazel lean forward and touch her hand to Henry's gravestone, how she was going to cope being so far away from the love of her life. She looked cheerful and was having an animated conversation with Henry. He wondered if she was talking about the accident. He wondered if she would tell Henry that their lunch dates would soon be coming to an end.

After a while Hazel waved to Daniel. It was time for them to go home. They barely spoke on the drive back. Hazel looked out of her window the whole time and Daniel switched off the radio. All that could be heard inside the car was Daniel's occasional sad gulp or Hazel sighing deeply enough for the passenger side window to fog up. She was going to miss visiting Henry, yet she was convinced that she should be with her family in London. The mixed emotions she had were palpable and Daniel wished there was something comforting he could say.

They arrived back at Hazel's house but Daniel didn't open the car door straight away.

'Hazel. I was thinking,' he said, 'as you seem to be coping better with the frame, that you and I could walk up to the cul-de-sac and perhaps the walkers could join us one day.'

Hazel's shoulders sank a little before she replied.

'I know it didn't sit well with you, my not wanting to come back to the walking group. But knowing I was going to have to leave eventually, I thought it best not to return at all. I knew that if I went back I'd probably end up in floods of tears when I had to say goodbye to everyone.'

'Oh, Hazel, I get it.' He rubbed her arm. 'Annabelle and I haven't told them you're planning to leave Trevone. Would it be easier if I told them for you?'

'So I wouldn't have to say goodbye?'

Daniel nodded solemnly.

'It would be terrible of me not to.' Hazel stared up the hill to Daniel's house. 'Maybe next Saturday you could drive me to the complex and I could say my goodbyes to everyone all at once. How would that be?'

Daniel pumped a fist. 'Excellent. The gang will be so happy to see you.'

'I've missed them too.' Hazel turned to Daniel, a finger over her lips. 'And seriously, you can't breathe a word of this to Jennifer.'

'What happens in The Slow Lane stays in The Slow Lane.'

41

The sky was clear and blue and the beach, now that June had arrived, was busy. The number of holiday makers would swell even more when the school holidays began. The car park was almost full and most of the outside tables at the beach café were occupied. Dogs ran off their leashes and the sea was sprinkled with surfers riding the high waves.

Daniel collected Hazel nice and early for their trip to the coast.

'Well,' Hazel said, 'wouldn't it be something if I could ditch the walking frame *and* the stick? I think my new hip has given me superhuman strength. I feel as if I could do anything.'

'That sounds like a marathon miracle story right there.'

Hazel let out a soft giggle and settled into the passenger seat. While she had made a lot of progress with her strength and agility, it could still be a matter of weeks before she could go back to her walking stick.

Daniel drove slowly to the beach feeling a sense of the excitement and anxiety emanating from Hazel. Her energy filled the car and he couldn't help but smile about what he knew was coming next.

They managed to find a parking space close to the café.

Daniel helped Hazel out of the car, supporting her weight as she climbed out of the passenger seat and helping her to lean on her walking frame.

'I don't see any of the walkers,' said Hazel. She looked around the busy beach complex.

'I think we must be early,' said Daniel.

'By my watch it's already two minutes to twelve. I would have expected one or two of the others by now.'

'I'm sure they won't be long.'

Daniel looked around the car park and out towards the beach. Just yesterday he'd been surfing with his friends. He'd been in a reflective mood since his trip to the cemetery with Hazel. He'd thought about how much she had been prepared to sacrifice and leave behind because of the impending new phase in her life. He had created his own new phase, one in which he could try to forget about Jess. So far he hadn't been successful. He found it hard to shake off the overwhelming feeling that their relationship had promised more. Three weeks of not seeing her was taking its toll but he said nothing to anyone about it, hoping that one day he'd come through the sadness and end up carefree, single and happy on the other side.

He looked at Hazel, who was becoming anxious as she scanned the view for the walkers, and he dreaded to think of the time she would actually have to say goodbye to the twenty years she'd lived here and, more importantly, saying goodbye to Henry again.

'I tell you what,' said Daniel. 'Why don't we try to walk as far as the coast path?'

'Are you sure?' said Hazel. 'What if they don't realize we're there?'

'I'll let them know on the group chat. Imagine everyone's

surprise to see you on the path. You can wave them off as they start the walk.'

'I could, couldn't I? They'll be able to walk at a better pace without me to hold them back.'

'You never held anyone back. This group is for us all.'

Daniel helped Hazel to take those first tentative steps towards the coast path. He could tell that she was unsure and with each step she would stop and look over her shoulder. With just a short distance to go before stepping a foot onto the coast path, an enormous cheer rang out. Loud, happy voices and applause stopped Hazel in her tracks and she looked up in surprise. Just in front of her were all the members of The Slow Lane Walkers Club. They had arrived early and stood waiting out of sight. They were all dressed in matching T-shirts with the club name handwritten by Amanda, across their chests. At the back of the group, held up at either side by Hannah and Mary, was a banner that read *Welcome Back, Hazel!* Hazel could not believe her eyes when she saw them all, cheering and clapping, making several heads on the beach turn.

Very soon the walkers surrounded Hazel and smothered her with hugs, pats and kisses. Everyone asking after her at the same time. She was so taken aback she was unable to utter a word. She looked over to Daniel who stood to one side with the widest of grins.

'So you knew about this all the time?' she chuckled.

'We just wanted to find a way to show you how much we missed you, Hazel. In the end I had to tell everyone that you'll be leaving us. We're all heartbroken.'

'Oh, Daniel,' said Hazel her voice breaking. 'You shouldn't have gone to all this trouble. It makes it all the harder to go. You have no idea how much I want to come at least a little part of the way with you.'

The group buzzed with excitement at the possibility. Hazel raised her hand.

'I'll come with you, just a few steps of the way. I can say my goodbyes and call this my last ever walk.'

'That would be amazing, Hazel,' said Daniel. 'We don't have to go too far.'

'I think those were the exact same words you used on our very first slow walk together.'

Daniel nodded in agreement.

'Well, if this is your last walk with us then you should lead us out.'

'Goodness me,' said Hazel. 'You realize we'll have to change our name to the Even Slower Slow Lane.'

'That's okay by us. So, if you're ready . . .' Daniel made a grand gesture with his hand in the direction of the path.

Hazel stepped onto the path for the first time in weeks. She smiled every step of the way, taking each one with care and precision. She arrived, with all members behind her, at the very first stop she and Daniel had made months ago in the springtime when he'd helped her onto the bench just metres from the beach, wearing her brand new Crocs.

As everyone sat on the grass verge and the low rocks opposite the bench, chatting, Daniel leaned close to Hazel.

'You okay?' he asked.

'I am. Very much so. I never thought I could do this again and here I am.'

'And here you are,' said Daniel.

'And each day I get better and better.'

'Well, the physiotherapist said you'd be back to your old self and you're getting there. If you keep up an exercise regime, you could end up fitter than when you started out.'

Hazel nodded and looked out to the wild waves of the

sea and up at the sky, the seabirds swooping high above them. She turned to Daniel.

'I can't leave,' she said, her face suddenly very serious.

'That's okay,' said Daniel. 'We can sit here as long as you like.'

'No. That's not what I mean. I can't leave Cornwall and go back to London. I can't give this up.' She looked around the other walkers who had stopped chatting and whose eyes were all on Hazel. 'I don't think I can say goodbye to you all. And I know for certain I can't leave Henry.'

Daniel stared at her in silence until a smile began to grow on his face, one that mirrored Hazel's exactly.

'I'm staying in Trevone,' said Hazel. 'I'll keep on walking until I can't walk anymore. Your banner said it all. *Welcome Back, Hazel!* I'm glad to be back and I intend to stay.'

The group, only minutes from their base, chatted happily, taking out refreshments to share with Hazel. A little later they made their way back to the car park to say goodbye until the following week. Hazel and Daniel stood in the car park watching them go.

'It's not going to be easy convincing my children that I've made a decision to stay,' said Hazel. 'I can just imagine their faces when I tell them. But I can't go now, Daniel. I can't ever leave.'

'You have no idea how much I hoped you'd stay.' He looked out towards the beach. 'The better weather will do you the power of good and I can drive you to the cemetery every week.'

'Now, Daniel, be careful not to overcommit.'

'It'll be my pleasure. You know that.'

Hazel took a deep breath and heaved a slow exhale. 'What I mean is, there'll come a time when you'll be the one who's leaving. You'll be saying goodbye to me when this adventure is over and you move onto your next one.'

Daniel slid his hands into the back pockets of his shorts and looked down.

'I haven't made any decisions, but Doc and Greg are talking about moving on. Greg's family is loaded and he can always go back to Ireland and work for the family business. Doc is even thinking about finishing medical school. Becoming a doctor for real. He's looking at schools in London.'

'So that just leaves you. Where will your next adventure take you?'

He shook his head.

'Who knows. For now I'm just happy you're going to stay. Just remind me to be out of the way when Jennifer turns up. She'll blame me for this, I'm sure.'

They returned to the car and set off for the cemetery. Hazel had some good news to deliver to her best pal.

42

Daniel sat at the large oval table in Annabelle's kitchen. They had spent the morning discussing fitted kitchens, modernized bathrooms and double glazing and looking at various kitchen and bathroom specialist websites. The French doors leading onto the garden were wide open on what was the warmest day of the year so far. Summer had come to stay after having peeked around clouds for the last few weeks. Daniel had been rising early to surf with his friends, coming back refreshed and relaxed and trying not to plan too far ahead.

In the garden, Rasmus ran around the flower beds in his Superman Y-fronts and Minions T-shirt to his own jet-propelled engine sound effects. This left his chin speckled with drops of spittle which Annabelle attempted to wipe away every time he ran into the kitchen for a fist bump followed by a finger explosion with Daniel.

'It's hard to imagine that after all this time of wishing you'd come home, you're actually here, sitting in my kitchen,' said Annabelle after lunging at Rasmus's face with a kitchen towel. He turned his engine louder and scooted back to the garden.

'What do you mean?' asked Daniel.

'Well, I felt as if I was dragging you away from Mount Etna, your fingernails gripping onto the igneous rocks.'

'That is what happened, though, isn't it?' He grinned up at her and winked.

'I suppose what I mean is, I have to make the most of having you around. I wish the house would take forever to sort out because I'm really not looking forward to you taking off again one day.' Annabelle reached over to her brother and briefly touched his hand. Rasmus ran back into the kitchen; he bypassed Daniel's outstretched fist to come in for a hug, pressing his damp face into Daniel's neck before dashing out again. 'As for that little guy . . . and Mia too. They're so going to miss you.'

Daniel couldn't tell his sister that she and the children weren't the only ones who'd be sad to say goodbye. It would break his heart to walk away from them. His old village was feeling more and more like home again. He'd miss the beauty of the landscape, his Cornish friends. Both Rasmus and Mia were in his heart now, their amazing characters and insight, their lovable smiles. Annabelle's eyes had become misty so he returned his to the laptop screen, wiping Rasmus's dribble off his neck.

Annabelle traced the rim of her coffee cup with her finger. 'Deep down I was kind of hoping that at your age you might be looking to put down some roots, maybe meet someone, settle down.'

'I don't know if I can get the settling down thing right. So maybe it's not for me.'

'Look, Daniel, just because Aria was such a b—' Rasmus ran back into the kitchen, his engine switched off as he hovered in front of his mother. She dabbed his lips. 'Just because Aria was a bit of a psycho—'

'What's a psycho?' asked Rasmus.

'It's someone who strings people like Uncle Daniel along

and makes him not want to get married.' Annabelle stared at her brother. Rasmus looked quizzically at Daniel.

'Don't mess with his head,' said Daniel, pulling Rasmus to sit on his lap. 'True, she wasn't a nice person but it's not the only thing that puts me off staying here, or settling down for that matter.'

'So what is it, Daniel?' Her voice softened. 'Did Jess break your heart, too?'

He clicked the open windows on the laptop, not really taking any of them in.

'I should be doing more with my life,' he said.

'More? Like what?'

'Uncle Daniel wants to go on adventures and fly a plane,' said Rasmus.

'Exactly,' said Daniel, resting a hand on Rasmus's mop of hair. 'I don't want to feel like I'm tied down.'

'Don't you get it by now, Daniel?'

'Get what?'

'If you meet the right person, it won't feel like being tied down. The right person will make your life feel like it's an adventure in itself. Oh, you know what I mean.'

Daniel pulled a face and began to scroll the page they'd been looking at for over an hour and still hadn't come to any decisions about base units.

'Don't shrug me off, Daniel. You turned thirty last year and it's your birthday very soon. It's not a bad age to think about a serious girlfriend, you know?'

'But I don't want to think about it.'

'I know you're scared. I know you took Mum and Dad's divorce badly. But that was them. It wouldn't have worked out for them, because of who they are and what they were like as a couple. And, in case you hadn't noticed, Scott and

I are in a really good place now.' She smiled and reached for Daniel's hand again, holding it this time. 'Because we worked it out and we want our relationship to work. Mum and Dad . . . well, they just didn't.'

'What if I'm like them?'

'You're not. I know you better than anyone. Better than you know yourself. Don't bury your head in the sand and let a nice girl like Jess get away all because Aria is a b—' Rasmus flicked his eyes towards Annabelle. 'A beautiful girl with no moral compass,' she said smiling merrily at her son.

Daniel sniggered and picked Rasmus up as he stood.

'I have to go. Why don't you just choose some stuff you like and I'll get the measurements sorted and arrange the fittings.'

'Okay, Daniel,' sighed Annabelle. 'I get it. I'll shut up about marriage, but you have to understand, this isn't me playing matchmaker. This is me telling you that it's all right to trust people because some of us are actually worth it. I'd hate to think that you live in fear of commitment and will never ever be settled in your life. Home is important and you should make one for yourself. One day you'll wish you listened to me.'

Daniel drove home to find Doc lying out in the garden, his shirt unbuttoned, wearing Daniel's sunglasses and sipping a tall, dark brown cocktail with lots of ice and a pink umbrella in it.

'What the hell, dude?' he said to Doc.

'Oh, we were inventing drinks. Greg might have a job in his uncle's bar in Cork when he gets back. He's upstairs on the phone to him.'

'I thought he was contemplating the family business. Didn't he fancy going into the clothing industry then?'

'I guess not. And this is Greg we're talking about. I think the bar is more his style.' Doc held up his glass. 'Help yourself to one of these. We don't know what to call it but it tastes . . .' Doc took a sip, swivelled it around in his mouth like mouthwash and swallowed. 'Well, good actually.'

Daniel watched Doc sink another gulp of his drink. 'So Greg is really leaving us?'

Just then Greg walked into the garden carrying a glass of the dark brown cocktail.

'I sure am,' he said. He sat cross-legged on the grass next to Daniel. 'My uncle has helped me out big time. He knew I didn't want to go back to work for Dad so he's offered me a job managing his bar while he takes off for a while.'

'Do you need a barman?' asked Daniel.

'You fancy a trip to Cork, do you?'

'Well, I've got to find something to do. The house will get sold and I need to work.'

'Mate,' said Doc, 'what about the personal training? I thought you were getting into that again. You like it, don't you?'

'I do . . .'

'So why would you give it up to be on your feet all day serving drinks to a bunch of drunks? No offence, Greg.'

'None taken.'

'You're right,' said Daniel, falling backwards onto his elbows and pulling at some random blades of grass. 'I do like being a personal trainer. I'm just not sure where I want to do it.'

'You've established a few clients already. You could build from that.' Doc sat up. His voice bellowed as usual but for a change his expression was solemn. 'We all have to find our place in the world, *fratello*.'

'I know that.'

'I've decided I'm going to finish medical school. Make my family proud. Be proud of myself, dude.'

'Seriously?' said Daniel, eyes bulging. 'I mean, I knew you were thinking about it but . . . You're really doing this?'

'Sure. I've been looking at applications. I won't be able to start this year but certainly next year is possible.'

'What will you do in the meantime?'

'Study. Sell my body to rich influential women and save up enough money to pay for school.'

'You two have been making plans behind my back,' said Daniel. 'I think I will have that drink after all.'

Daniel went back to the cool kitchen. The cocktail jug sat on the counter, ice cubes melting, only a small amount remaining. Judging by the number of spirit bottles beside it, the drink was likely to be lethal. The thought of Greg going back to Ireland to manage a bar and Doc getting a place at university threw him for a bit of a loop. He'd imagined himself swanning around Cornwall with them, surfing all day and drinking all night until they were completely partied out. He poured a tall glass of the dark fluid and took a sip. He didn't know what he would do with himself without his friends around. They had been the perfect distraction from thoughts of Jess. He looked at the cocktail in his hand. Could he drink himself senseless until he was able to forget her?

Back in the garden Greg was talking about the bar and the number of drunks there would actually be.

'And you know a lot of those drunks are female,' Greg was saying.

Daniel raised his glass. 'To Greg and drunk females.' Their tall glasses clashed together in the circle they formed on the grass. 'And to Doc becoming an actual doctor.' They clinked glasses and downed most of their drinks.

'And,' said Doc, 'to Daniel becoming a fitness guru and entrepreneur.'

Daniel's expression was blank but his insides raced with the possibilities of Doc's idea becoming a reality. Jess had found her niche, maybe he could find his. He sank the rest of his drink and tried to wipe images of Jess out of his mind. He tried for the rest of the day not to think about her; he tried right through to the evening but the potent cocktail did nothing to help him forget.

43

Daniel draped his arm over Hazel's shoulder as they set off on their walk.

'I reckon we're going to get an influx of walking companions,' said Daniel.

'Why do you say that?' asked Hazel.

'I think people will hear about the phenomenon you are. From walking stick to walking frame and back to a stick you hardly even need. Look at you. This is the fastest I've seen you walk.' Daniel stepped to the side to look at the improved gait Hazel had since her operation. Together they had worked hard on strength exercises for her. She was his toughest and most hard-working student. He'd expected this of Hazel. Since she'd made up her mind to stay in Trevone she'd gone all in to improve her physical strength. She reckoned it would help to convince her children to stop worrying about her welfare if they saw how mobile she was.

'I don't know where I'm getting the energy,' Hazel said, 'but I'm absolutely loving it. Besides, I think the phenomenon is you, Daniel. You've worked wonders on this little old lady.'

'I enjoyed every minute. I love training people, but since your accident I wondered about the idea of physiotherapy. I mean, becoming a physiotherapist.'

Hazel looked up at him.

'You'd retrain?'

Daniel nodded gingerly.

'It's just a thought. At least it won't have been forced on me and it's something I think I'd enjoy.'

Hazel pulled an approving expression but didn't press him on it.

Daniel looked back at the walkers on the path. As usual, they idled along, taking in the scenery and enjoying a companionable stroll along a very familiar trail. Daniel had walked, cycled and run this path a thousand times as a boy. He had always taken for granted the majestic scenery, the sounds of waves rolling in and out, the changing tides and the lively birdsong. Holiday makers were arriving daily now for their summer holidays. The campsites, caravan parks, holiday homes and rentals were filling up and so too was their trail. His team of walkers walked in a zigzag, being overtaken not only by the ever-speedy Padstow Pace Masters but by the rising number of tourists, too. Daniel might have to rethink the time of the walk. Perhaps they could set off in the early morning so that they might have the path to themselves again. Or perhaps they should abandon the idea of walks in the summer and start again in the autumn. Without realizing it Daniel was thinking about his future, making a plan that would keep him in Trevone through to the autumn. He might even find a local college if he chose to retrain.

Eric whistled as he walked Benny. Oliver tapped Amanda's arm every now and again and smiled when she giggled. Annabelle was recording the walk to use the footage for her next vlog. Ahead, Daniel saw a small group of people strolling towards him from the direction of Harlyn. Just behind them were two cyclists who rang their bells so that they could overtake

321

them. As the cyclists rode closer, Daniel could see that one of them was Jess. She pedalled slowly and with ease. He heard her creaky wheels and laughed inwardly at the fact she never oiled them. Her head was turned away from him as she cycled past, deep in conversation with the other cyclist. An athletic-looking man with long wavy hair and a tight-fitting cycling top and shorts. They laughed and joked about something and completely ignored Daniel, who had been gearing up to say something friendly and throwaway about the weather or her creaky wheels. He'd quickly thought up different ways to say 'Long time no see' without Jess reading too much into it. But she was away down the path before he could utter a word.

Annabelle rushed up to him, still filming.

'Wasn't that . . .?' she gasped.

'Yes, it was,' said Daniel. 'And don't put this on the vlog.' He held a hand in front of his face.

'Sorry,' said Annabelle. 'Forgot.' She stopped recording. 'Do you think she's got a new boyfriend?'

'Of course she has,' called Mary. 'Girls like Jess don't stay single long.'

'That's true,' said Annabelle. 'How does that make you feel?' She was about to start recording again but Daniel dared her with the narrowing of his eyes.

'Nothing,' said Daniel, turning quickly to look out to sea. 'It's nothing to me.'

As if he could feel Mary shaking her head and an exchange of looks between her and Annabelle, Daniel began to walk faster. He hadn't meant to but he knew this latest Jess incident would lead to the others interfering in his love life again and he couldn't handle it.

He'd walked a long way past their usual stopping point and caused a great confusion among the group, half of them stopping the other, half-heartedly following him but tutting and complaining as they did.

'Sorry,' he said at last as he walked back along the path. 'Forgot the refreshment point.'

They sat down, Daniel dropping his head as he listened to the group chatting amicably, taking sips of water and handing out slices of lemon drizzle cake. He waved away the slice that was offered to him. He had an uncomfortable knot in his stomach which tightened when Mary talked about Jess having moved on. What happened to his no decisions, no drama companion? They'd had a great time back when those phrases actually applied to them.

After their trip to see Henry, Hazel and Daniel drove back in silence until they were close to Hazel's door.

'The path is becoming quite congested now, don't you think?' she asked. 'I wondered if heading out early in the morning might be better than midday now.'

Daniel grunted but hadn't taken in a word.

'So,' Hazel continued, 'what do you think? Earlier start or midnight stroll?'

'Um?' said Daniel as he pulled up outside her door.

'I suppose I don't have to ask where your mind has been,' Hazel sighed. She rested a delicate palm on Daniel's hand. 'I can't tell you what to do, Daniel, but it's obvious to me, to all of us actually, that you still have feelings for Jess.'

Daniel sighed deeply.

'Mary is right. Jess has moved on.' He traced a pattern on the steering wheel.

'Well, you haven't,' Hazel said. 'Why can't you just tell her?'

'Because I've already told myself that not being in a relationship, a serious one, is better.'

'For whom?'

'Me.'

'You and I know you don't really believe that, Daniel.' Hazel arched one brow and tried to get him to look at her by leaning in closer. 'Otherwise you wouldn't feel like this.'

'With respect, Hazel, how do you, Annabelle or Mary know how I feel? Rasmus got it right when he said I needed adventure.'

'Well,' said Hazel with a slanted smile, 'my definition of an adventure is trying something you think you will enjoy but never thought was possible and could change your life in a big way. In this case, that adventure is a relationship, Daniel. And if you can't see that—'

'I think I'm too late,' Daniel blurted out.

'How would you know? You haven't even tried.' Hazel had never been annoyed with Daniel before but she obviously couldn't hold back. She must think him an out-and-out loser. They sat quietly until Hazel smiled and said warmly, 'I'll see you soon, Daniel. Again, another wonderful Saturday.'

As he let himself into the house he realized that the most wonderful thing about his Saturday had been seeing Jess. He'd heard her voice. It was full of fun and laughter. He had seen her smile. It was sunny and easy. It was a beautiful smile. He swallowed down the lump that had come to his throat.

44

Hazel had given Daniel a lot of food for thought on the ride back from the cemetery but once he was indoors, with the cat slinking his fluffy body around his legs and purring for food, Daniel had to bring his focus back to the present and push any notions of getting in contact with Jess out of his mind. Greg's farewell bash was happening later on that evening, and the last thing his friend needed was to spend his last night in Cornwall helping Daniel sort out his relationship hang ups.

Greg was traipsing up and down the stairs trying to locate, firstly, his rucksack and, secondly, all the things he'd had in his rucksack when he'd arrived. He wanted to be packed and ready for Daniel and Doc to drive him to the station the next day. Daniel couldn't understand why Greg was having such a problem finding things in a house that was all but empty. It was only when he saw Doc doubled over, clutching his stomach and trying to stifle a fit of laughter as he watched a bemused Greg trying to make sense of his missing clothes, did he realize that Doc was up to something.

'What did you do, man?' he asked Doc when Greg was out of earshot.

Unable to talk properly because he'd finally let out the

boom of laugher he'd been trying to suppress, Doc revealed that he'd hidden Greg's things in the garden shed and the boiler cupboard. Daniel shook his head. He knew they were grown men but these were just the kinds of antics they used to get up to in Sicily. Daniel longed for those times again. Those days were easy. No responsibilities and no worries.

Greg had looked up a list of the top ten cocktails from a Google search and decided that his leaving do would consist of him attempting to make them all and the three of them drinking them. They took off to the supermarket in Daniel's car where they spent a fortune on as many of the ingredients required for the drinks as they could find. Their shopping trolley contained all the necessary ingredients for the cocktails, or a suitable substitute, plus a jumbo packet of Worcestershire sauce crisps and a bunch of pre-packed sandwiches from the morning delivery.

'So what's the name of this cocktail bar in Cork you'll be working at?' asked Daniel when the party was in full swing but while he was still sober enough to think clearly.

'It's not a cocktail bar, it's a trendy pub in the city.' Greg looked at him through one eye and slurred every word.

'So why have you been practising making cocktails all night?'

'Why not?'

'Because we hate cocktails.' Daniel hiccupped. 'We don't like anyone who drinks cocktails.'

'It's true, we don't like cocktail drinkers,' said Doc, who was slouched in a deckchair, his feet up on another in front of him. 'That's why I have a supply of beer in the fridge.'

Daniel wasn't sure how many beers he had after Doc's announcement but he'd crashed out completely drunk at some unknown hour just before first light. He found himself in his room in the morning and was woken by Greg running around the house swearing and asking what that mad Italian had done with his rucksack this time. A frenzied ride to the train station followed, and after the men had said their farewells, Greg hopped on a train. Daniel had no idea when he'd see his friend again.

Just a few days later, the time finally came for Daniel to say goodbye to his good friend Doc. Doc's plans for his future had quickly fallen into place once he'd made up his mind to leave. Daniel had no idea when Doc had arranged an interview with the School of Medicine at his old university, Imperial College, but he had done. Daniel couldn't get over the transformation in his friend. In a matter of days, Doc had begun acting his grown-up age of thirty-one. He knew that once Doc was gone, it would be time for him to grow up, too. They had already taken steps towards a higher level of maturity by agreeing that Doc's send-off would be far less adventurous than Greg's. Besides which, after having drained the house of any remaining alcoholic beverages, they'd been sipping water for two days since they both had hangovers that had lasted just as long.

On Doc's last night, they walked down to one of the seafront pubs. They sat outside, in the front of the pub, saying very little at first, with a couple of barely touched beers on their table. Fairy lights were criss-crossed in the trellises above them.

'Have you made any plans for your future yet, Daniel?' Doc asked him.

'Mate, you sound like my dad.' Daniel lifted his glass and took the smallest of sips.

'I care about you and I wanted to give you the benefit of my wisdom. Actually, it's my dad's wisdom but I'm sure he won't mind me giving it to you, *fratello*.'

Doc went into a whole speech about work, saving money, having a comfortable home and finding a nice girl to settle down with.

'I was happy playing around, as you know,' said Doc. 'Different girls all the time but it becomes a bit tired. When I was at medical school I wasn't mature enough or disciplined enough to handle the academics. I just wanted to party. But deep down, being a doctor was all I ever wanted to be.'

'It's great that you have that,' said Daniel. 'A dream to follow. Plans. Good, sensible ones.' He looked around the pub. It was filling up.

'You have them, too, Daniel. But you don't want to look into them because you're at a junction in your life.'

'That's true. I am seriously thinking about upping my clients. I am enjoying being a personal trainer but I'm also thinking about the idea of training in physiotherapy.'

'Good for you, man.' Doc raised his beer glass and held it in front of Daniel. '*Salute*.' Doc had a big grin on his face but Daniel's focus had travelled and landed somewhere else entirely.

'Are you really going to leave me hanging?' Doc asked him, still holding out his glass.

'Sorry, mate,' said Daniel. 'I just noticed someone over there.'

'Who?' said Doc in his larger than life voice. He looked around, wild brown curls springing into action.

'Dude, don't make it obvious. Just be cool, okay?' said Daniel, staring from under his brow.

'Who's here?' Again Doc exclaimed loudly. He got up from his seat to look around. Daniel directed him back down with a bat of his hand.

Daniel had noticed Jess was inside the pub. A group of

people had left a table by an open window which was quickly occupied by Jess and her friends. He couldn't miss her sitting there, or the lively people she was with. He recognized Jess's brother, Noah, and assumed that the woman beside him must be Marisol. Another person he recognized was the man he'd seen Jess cycling with along the coast path. He and Jess looked very cosy together and she laughed loudly at something he was saying. He knew her laugh so well. Jess wore a white, knitted halter top and the tattoo on her arm was clearly visible. The light glinted off the silver bar in her ear if she tilted her head in the right direction. Everything and everyone blurred into the background now that Jess was in view. Daniel sat holding his glass as he stared in through the pub window.

'Have I lost you?' said Doc. He waved a large hand in front of Daniel's face. 'I know I'm not supposed to turn around but if you're going to carry on staring like that I'm going to have to see for myself.' Doc looked through the open window and then back to Daniel.

'Okay,' said Doc. 'So my first guess is Jess. Am I right?'

'Shh, not so loud,' said Daniel, but he hadn't taken his eyes off her.

'I'll take that as a yes,' said Doc. He took a sip of beer, his eyes on Daniel.

For a second Daniel thought he saw Jess look his way. He was about to nod to her but realized she hadn't noticed him at all. Instead she was looking at her friends, laughing and making hand gestures. Jess looked so happy and relaxed.

'Why don't you go and talk to her?' asked Doc.

'I . . .' This time, as he continued to stare at her, Jess did see him. She stopped mid-gesture, her smile slipping from her face but returning slowly as she held his gaze.

Daniel's lips were in the process of forming a smile but

Jess's attention was very quickly diverted away from him. Her cycling companion, the one she was so occupied with the last time he saw her that she hadn't even looked Daniel's way, put an arm around her shoulder. He pulled her into his chest and kissed her forehead. Jess blushed and giggled. Daniel clenched his teeth and looked down. The froth at the top of his beer was dissolving.

'Should we go?' asked Doc.

'No,' said Daniel. 'We were talking about being mature and that's what I'm going to be now. If I do end up staying in Trevone and starting a business here, I'll be running into her all the time. Her and her boyfriend.'

Doc whipped his head back to the window.

'She's got a boyfriend?' said Doc. He hissed an Italian expletive under his breath.

Daniel drained the rest of his beer. 'Another?' he asked Doc.

'Mate, I haven't—'

'I'll get us another,' said Daniel, rising quickly and marching into the pub. He angled his way to the bar amid the drinkers in their clusters, laughing and chatting among themselves and paying little or no attention to Daniel. He stood at the counter tapping his credit card on the shiny wooden surface but the staff were not in a hurry to serve anyone. They laughed and joked about something and Daniel exhaled with horse lips. His cheeks felt hot and his collar began to cling to his neck.

'Hey, Daniel.'

He turned around quickly when he heard Jess's voice.

'Jess.' Her name was a sigh on his lips. 'I thought that was you I saw sitting over there with that crowd of people.'

'And I thought that was you standing over here on your own. Thought I'd come up and say hi.'

'Oh, okay. Hi.'

She breathed a laugh. 'I just wanted you to know that I didn't want it to be awkward between us. The last time we saw each other we were both a little . . .'

Someone nudged Daniel in the back and brushed him away from the counter.

'Could we go outside?' Jess pointed at the beer garden. 'Is that okay?'

'Er, sure. I'm here with a friend but . . .'

'We could always leave it,' said Jess.

'No, no. I want to go outside with you. Have a quick chat.'

They stood fidgeting in front of each other for a few uncomfortable seconds until Jess said, 'Shall we?'

He followed Jess to the garden where it was just as noisy as the front and the inside of the pub. But at least Daniel didn't feel so hot, so claustrophobic, standing at a bar when he knew Jess was just metres away from him.

'So,' she said, 'I was just saying that, you know, last time we spoke, we were both pretty upset.'

'It's not surprising you were upset with me,' said Daniel, inspecting the paving stones with the tip of his trainer. 'I could have come straight over to the surf shop the next day to let you know I was sorry for not showing up.'

'And that you had me worried.' She smiled, but not the wide smile that usually shone through her eyes.

'I'm sorry about that, too,' he said.

'And you're still doing the coast path walk?'

'Oh, yes, I am. We are. Got some new members now.'

'Oh, cool, cool.'

'Yes,' said Daniel. He looked around at the characters in the garden standing beneath more fairy lights hung from tree branches. They were absorbed in their own conversations as

Daniel and Jess, who stood beside a fence covered in clematis, remained quiet. The trailing vines of the clematis spiralled the trellis with an abundance of dark green leaves, pink flowers and buds about to bloom. Jess played with the leaves, running her fingers through them before returning her focus to Daniel.

'So, that was it, really. That was all I wanted to say.' She gave a little shrug. 'I don't know how long you're going to be in Cornwall for but I just thought it would be silly to ignore each other or have bad feelings just because you had your hands full with house guests.'

'About that,' Daniel said.

'There's no need to explain.' She gently lifted a hand. 'Everyone has a past. I know the beautiful girl I saw you with was a part of yours.'

'Yes, a big part actually.'

'And that's fine because you and I only had a brief fling, Daniel. It was nothing. It hardly meant a thing. Well, it meant nothing at all in the end because it's obvious now that you hadn't let go of your relationship from before.'

'That's true, I suppose,' he said lamely and realized he should say something about Aria being out of his life for good.

'Oh, and the yoga studio plans are coming together. Really keeping me busy.' She swept fake sweat from her brow and puffed.

'Wow,' said Daniel with a broad smile. 'It's all happening, Jess. I'm really happy for you.'

'Thanks, Daniel. I know you genuinely mean that.'

'And, um . . .' he began. He realized he still had his credit card in his hand and was tapping it against his fingers. He clumsily put it into his wallet and with equally jerky movements he tried to shove the wallet into his back pocket but kept missing it.

'You all right?' asked Jess, looking around the back of him.

'Yes,' he said, finally tucking his wallet away.

'You were saying?' said Jess.

'I was just saying that like you, I've got things happening in my life. Or I will do.'

'Oh yeah?'

'Yes. I've got a plan to get my personal trainer business set up properly. I was even thinking about some training once I've got the work done on the house. Things are beginning to happen.' He had nothing finalized but he didn't want Jess to think he was as lost as he felt. She, like Doc and Greg, was soaring ahead with her plans.

Jess pulled her lips into a smile and looked as if she were staring into his soul. Her eyes gleamed under the fairy lights. They were bright enough for Daniel to see the unique shade of grey that fascinated him every time he looked into her eyes.

'I'm glad about that, Daniel,' she said. 'And if you're planning to continue your business here, we don't have to be awkward around each other.'

'Exactly,' he said.

'From no decision days to planning our respective empires.' She grinned and pulled a look of feigned worry.

'Here's to your obviously bright future,' said Daniel, wishing so much that his genuine good wishes could transform into the hug he so wanted to give her.

'I'll drink to that.' Jess raised an imaginary glass which Daniel clinked his imaginary glass against. He felt a tingle in his hand when their fingers touched.

Just then someone called Jess's name. Daniel turned to see her boyfriend approaching.

'We're heading back to Noah's in a bit,' he said, lacing his arm around her waist. 'But we're getting one last round. The usual?'

'Oh, yes please,' said Jess, leaning her body into his. 'Be back in a second.' She brushed something from the front of his tight top and he squeezed her into what was a very intimate clench. Daniel almost backed away from them.

Her boyfriend nodded at Daniel, looking at him from top to toe, before taking his leave. Both Jess and Daniel followed him with their eyes and watched him vanish once he re-entered the pub.

Their conversation was at an end but it had told Daniel a lot. Jess wanted them to be friends again, but only friends this time. It was obvious by the way she looked at her boyfriend that there was a strong connection there. He wondered if she had ever felt the same about him. He wanted to ask about him but wasn't sure he wanted to know anything about this good-looking bloke with enormous biceps. He might be a surfer. Jess might have been his teacher and he'd wasted no time asking her out and becoming close to her. The way they chatted along the coast path on their bikes, excluding everyone and forcing pedestrians, including Daniel, to step aside spoke volumes. Jess had found someone who seemed considerate, asking after her and he even knew Jess's usual drink. Daniel had no idea what it was. He took a deep breath.

'I'm sorry,' said Jess. 'I shouldn't keep you out here chatting. Did you come with your girlfriend?'

'Who?' said Daniel, rousing himself from a trance. 'You mean Aria?'

'If that was her name.'

'Um, yes. But no, I'm with my mate, Doc. We were just out having a drink. Um, obviously, as we're in a pub.' His laugh was one of embarrassment. He was aware that Jess had people waiting for her and that she'd told her boyfriend she'd be back in a sec. A sec. That was all she needed to tell Daniel that it was nice while it lasted and that she'd moved on.

'Well, I'd better go,' said Daniel, pulling away and turning to leave.

'Sure, Daniel. I'll see you around.'

Daniel left first; Jess, he assumed was walking right behind him. He hoped his body language didn't reveal that he felt as if he'd been whacked in the guts, full force with a sledge hammer. He had difficulty breathing as he walked through the garden. He could sense Jess at his heels as they entered the pub. He turned his head briefly to nod to her but she was already waving to her table of friends and they were shouting her name across the busy pub. Everyone inside the pub turned in her direction. Jess was blushing, her hands over her face. She rushed over to join her friends. Daniel stood at the door. He and Jess caught each other's eye for a fleeting moment before her boyfriend grabbed her and started tickling her. She collapsed into him in fits of laughter and Daniel left with his head down.

'And the drinks?' asked Doc when Daniel sat opposite him at their table staring into space.

'Oh no!' Daniel smacked his palm to his head.

'No worries,' said Doc. 'I already took the liberty.'

On the table were four shot glasses.

'I was hoping these would be shots of congratulations because you got the girl.' He raised a questioning brow.

Daniel said nothing but stared at the glasses, the contents reflecting the pink and yellow of the fairy lights above.

'So,' said Doc, 'if you didn't get the girl, Plan B was to salute our future. Yours, mine and Greg's. In exactly one year from now we will report back to each other. Maybe on a video call, who knows. We'll see if we're achieving everything we set out to do.'

Daniel looked into the pub and saw that Jess's table was now occupied by another group of people. She had walked away from him again and he realized that he'd feel as empty as he did in that moment, every time he watched her come and go.

Daniel picked up a shot glass and raised it high.

'I'll drink to Plan B,' he said and knocked back the shot. He winced and picked up a second glass.

'Wait,' said Doc. 'What happened in there? You were gone ages, man.'

'I know, but now I know I was right to want to move on. She already has. She's happy. She's met someone and it's time for me to get these women out of my head once and for all. So here's to Plan B. Our future. Our plans. Our dreams.' Daniel's eyes drooped for a split second before he looked Doc in the eye and said, '*Salute!*'

In a little while the two walked back home in silence until Doc put his arm over Daniel's shoulder.

'Mate,' he said. 'Tell me you haven't hidden my luggage in the garden shed.'

'Don't worry,' said Daniel. 'You're all set to go. I'm going to miss having you around.'

'You, too, mate.'

45

Doc had obviously picked up on Daniel's mood after his conversation with Jess. Not that it was hard to miss. Daniel had walked home from the pub in silent mode. Doc with his thunderous voice filled the empty spaces with small talk, odd quips and comical gestures apropos of nothing. Daniel faked smiles in response to his attempts to lighten the mood but they only reminded him that he'd soon have no friends his age to spend time with, surf with, drink with or just to be downright stupid with.

At the station, rather than making a grand speech about Doc's future and wishing him the best, it was Doc who held Daniel's shoulders, looked him square in the eyes and tried to give him a pep talk. As with most of Doc's speeches, the subject of sex and women featured highly.

'My friend, you don't have to worry about a thing. You have your future sewn up. Once you start to advertise yourself, and I'm talking a massive poster of you flexing those muscles of yours, you'll have millions of clients. A queue of women waiting for you to give them the personal touch.' He shook Daniel by the shoulders and looked at him sagely. 'You know what I mean?' Another shake of the shoulders. 'You get what I mean, right, dude? I mean women. Lots of women.'

Daniel waved to Doc as the train pulled out. He hadn't wanted to disappoint his friend by saying that if he were to have women flocking around him, where he lived, they were most likely to be over sixty-five.

As he'd expected, the house was a big and lonely place when he returned home. The cat was in the hallway sitting up curiously, whiskers twitching as he regarded Daniel. Daniel followed him to the kitchen where he promptly sat in front of his bowl before looking up at Daniel several times, expecting to be fed. Daniel looked around the kitchen, hands on his head. The fridge and the cupboards were bare. They had been living on takeaways for the last week and had done no shopping.

'Looks like you're out of luck, cat.' Daniel's mouth slanted up one cheek in an attempt to apologize to the ever-hungry creature who now ran to the front door. He mewed a protest at having been left alone in the house with no food in his bowl and rushed out as soon as Daniel opened the door. The cat would inevitably end up back with Eric and Benny the dog. Which reminded him – he still didn't know the cat's name. He usually referred to him as Cat and Oi Mate, but he should ask Eric what he was actually called.

In the living room Daniel looked at the empty deckchairs. There were no empty pizza boxes, beer cans or the lone trainer turned on its side on the floor. The sound of YouTube videos, Doc roaring a joke and drunken snores from Greg would be replaced by the leaky tap in the kitchen, the floor-board in an upstairs bedroom that groaned for no apparent reason and the hinge on the window in the bathroom that rattled in the slightest breeze.

A knock on the door made him jump.

Hazel, who was a lot more upright in her posture now, smiled up at him from under her sun visor. Her eyes disappeared into the soft folds of skin surrounding them and hid behind the plumpness of her round cheeks. In her free hand she had a brown paper bag.

'Good grief, Daniel, how terribly sad you look behind that smile,' she said. 'Is this a bad time?'

'No, no, not at all.' Daniel stepped back and allowed Hazel to come in. 'I just dropped Doc at the station.'

'Ah,' she said. 'And then there was one.'

Daniel led Hazel to the living room and helped her into a deckchair.

'That's better,' she said a sigh as she settled into the purple and white stripes of the chair. 'I saw your car pull up a short while ago. I had the kettle on so I thought I'd make a pot of tea and bring a flask over in case you fancied a cup.'

'Good timing, Hazel. I was just looking around at the empty kitchen. Eric's cat left the building in disgust.'

Hazel chuckled and held up the paper bag.

'There are a few supplies in here that might suit you then,' she said. Daniel took the bag and peered inside. 'Next to the flask is a pint of milk and some chocolate cake. Want to do the honours?'

Daniel smiled, a sincere smile this time. He nodded and went to the kitchen, returning with a tray containing two mugs of tea and slices of chocolate cake on side plates.

'You will have to give me the recipes of all these goodies you make,' said Daniel, taking a large, comforting bite out of his slice of cake.

'I certainly will,' said Hazel. 'I used to try to get my children in the kitchen, baking cakes and pies, but none of them could stand still long enough to pick anything up. They loved to eat the cakes and pies, mind you, even though they were very reluctant bakers.'

Hazel nibbled on her cake and sipped her tea with a smack of her lips.

'I used to like helping Gran in the kitchen,' said Daniel.

'That's right, you did.'

'Funny, when I first got back here, I remembered Gran as this strict authoritarian figure. But the memories of helping her in the garden and of baking are so vivid now that I've been here a while. I have to say that's thanks to you, Hazel, for filling in the gaps. You really helped me remember. I wish I'd visited Gran and Gramps when I was older. I'd have learned a lot more.'

'Perhaps you got out of the habit because your mother stopped going round to theirs when you and Annabelle were still only little.'

'Do you know what happened?' Daniel put his mug down. 'Annabelle said Mum told her we couldn't go round to visit them anymore but she refused to tell her why or what happened. They must have fallen out over something.'

Hazel leaned forward to place her mug and the side plate on the floor.

'Yes, they did fall out, Daniel. Actually, the trouble was between Molly and your mum. I suspect that's why she didn't talk about your gran to you.'

Daniel leaned back on his chair and looked hard at Hazel for her to continue.

'Your mum and your grandmother clashed an awful lot when your mum was younger,' said Hazel, her eyes flicking to the floor. 'In the first place Molly never wanted your mum to marry your father.'

'Why not?'

'Molly just didn't have a good feeling about him. She thought they were too different and . . . well, maybe you should ask your mum to tell you about this.'

'You're joking. Annabelle and I can never get a thing out of her. Something changed in her one day. She became distant. As if she'd left us. There in body but not in mind, Annabelle used to say. Then came the divorce and one day, after she'd been on her own for a while, she just took off. Packed her things, locked up the house and bolted. She sends cards and we both get the odd call but try to engage her in a conversation about our childhood and she freezes.'

Hazel nodded as if she knew this to be true.

'You can't just leave it there, Hazel. You've got to tell me what this is all about. I suspected there were family secrets and Mum was always weird when she brought us round to Gran's. Dad never came to visit Gran at all if I remember rightly. He certainly wasn't at her funeral. Did he fall out with Gran, too?'

'Oh, no. But he tended to keep his distance. Your mum told him that Molly wasn't in favour of their marriage, you see.'

'But why didn't Gran like him? I know Mum and Dad came from different backgrounds but it can't have been down to that. What did he do wrong?'

Hazel tapped her fingers together and bit on her bottom lip.

'It's okay, Hazel. Nothing you can say will change how I feel about my parents.'

'Well,' said Hazel, 'I don't think your dad treated your mum the way he should have done.'

'He had an affair, right?'

'Actually, they both did.' Hazel peeled off her sun visor. 'I don't think I should say any more.'

Daniel got up and walked to the window. He ran his hands over his hair, adding to the confusion it had already arranged itself into, and rested his palms on the back of his neck.

'Daniel,' said Hazel, turning towards him. 'Let's just leave this conversation for another time. Perhaps when things are looking better for you.'

He crash-landed into a deckchair and pursed his lips. 'Whenever that will be. I already miss Doc and Greg. Now everything seems so uncertain, and I still don't know what I'm doing.'

'You won't always feel like this,' said Hazel. 'You'll get your act together in your own time.'

Daniel shrugged. 'I feel as if I'm back to square one. I've been thinking about taking my personal training seriously and then there's the idea about training as a physiotherapist, but right now all I want to do is up sticks and get out of here.'

'We'd all miss you terribly.'

He puffed a loud sigh. 'You'd all get over it. A loser like me.'

'Don't you dare say that. And don't you dare sit there feeling sorry for yourself.' Hazel straightened her back and folded her arms. 'Remember I told you how remarkable a lady Molly was? How she had such an influence on the lives of many people? I also said she thought you were the most like her.'

Daniel nodded.

'Molly played piano at an old people's home for years before her death,' Hazel went on. 'It did the residents the power of good when she turned up there and played all the old songs. She'd visit some of the older folk in the village, make sure they were all right. People loved your gran. It was very easy for me to become friends with her. She was one of the most welcoming and kind people I'd ever met.'

Daniel smiled with sadness in his eyes.

'If you left, the folk around here would miss you, Daniel. You've changed my life for the better. I have found a good friend in you. And I don't need to tell you how highly the other walkers think of you.'

'Do they?' He wrinkled his nose.

'You have no idea what the friendships people have made in The Slow Lane have meant to them. And that's all because of you. Everyone looks forward to it. So you see how alike you are to your grandmother, Daniel? You would be missed an awful lot if you left, just because of your natural kindness. Now don't you let me hear you call yourself a loser again.'

'No pressure, then.' Daniel laughed and raised his hands.

'You might joke, but your gran never thought you were or would ever become a loser.' Hazel's face turned serious. 'Maybe I shouldn't say this, but did you ever wonder why it was your gran left this house to you and Annabelle?'

'You said she thought the world of us.'

'That she did, but most of all she didn't want it passed down to your mum.'

'Because Mum and Gran had fallen out?'

'Because she didn't think your mum was as responsible as you or your sister. Somehow Molly knew your parents' marriage wouldn't last. She wanted to know that her beloved grandchildren could have security. Molly said to me she thought you had a good head on your shoulders and she was happy to leave the house to you both. You see, no matter what you think of yourself, Molly didn't for one moment think you were a loser. She believed in you. And she was right.'

Daniel sat and pondered the idea that his grandmother had seen something in him as a young man. He remembered how pleased she was about him obtaining his degree and how she had high hopes for him. It wasn't too late to prove her right but he'd have to get his plans in order and stop being so half-hearted about his future and, as Hazel had so rightly put it, he'd have to stop feeling sorry for himself.

'So,' he said, 'Gran thought Mum was too much of a flake to take on the responsibility of two houses. And she didn't like the idea of her marrying Dad because she knew Dad would walk out on her one day. Turns out she was right about them.'

'Yes,' said Hazel. 'Molly also said that had they not married then she wouldn't have been blessed with two such amazing grandchildren. Only know that your gran had faith in you, Daniel. In you both. And whatever you go on to do I'm sure it'll be something that would make her proud.'

Daniel leaned forward in the chair and drew the skin down his cheeks with his fingers.

'One thing I didn't get from Gran was how good she was at judging people.'

'You mean people like Aria?'

He nodded.

'Well, just put Aria where she belongs,' said Hazel with a flick of her wrist. 'In the past.'

'I have. I'm over her and I'll get over Jess, too.'

'You might not have to get over her if you would only talk to her about what happened.'

'Oh, Hazel, I know you care but take it from me, Jess has moved way past the whole Aria thing. She's met someone. I saw them together last night and she's convinced we were never going anywhere and she's dropped me right slap bang into the friend zone.'

'I'm sorry, Daniel. Now I understand why you look so sad.'

Neither spoke for a long time.

'I should get going,' Hazel eventually said.

'Hold on, Hazel. Please.' Daniel looked at her imploringly. 'Okay, so I'm in a bad place at the moment, but I still want to know.'

'Know what?'

'There's more to your story about Mum, Dad and Gran than you've let on. What's the full story? Don't you think Annabelle and I have a right to know?'

Hazel shifted uncomfortably, a dark expression coming over her.

'You're right. Just promise me you'll speak to your mum after I've told you. I only know one side of this story and it would only be fair on your mother.' Hazel cleared her throat. 'It was a blazing argument that started it. Your mother and your gran had several of those as I understand it. Your gran was upset that your father dictated everything that happened in the house. She could see it was eating away at her, your mum. He was turning my daughter into a different person, Molly said. She described your mum as becoming lifeless, when she was always a joyful girl. Without direction when she used to have ambition and drive. She feared for you children, Molly did. Told me your mum defended him to the last, refused to see what Molly could see.

'This carried on for ages until one day both women snapped. I honestly don't know who said what but the upshot was that your mother told Molly she never wanted anything to do with her anymore and that she wouldn't be bringing the children over to see her or your grandfather. Of course that pleased your father but it broke your grandparents' hearts. She cried when she told me.'

Daniel remained quiet, looking sadly at Hazel, finding it hard to say anything because words became knotted in the tightness of his throat. He swallowed and took a deep breath.

'Looks like history repeated itself.' He looked to the floor.

'What do you mean?' Hazel's brow knotted.

'The reason I left Trevone, left the country, was because of my clashes with my father. I said more or less the same thing to him and Mum ten years ago when I packed a bag with no intention of coming back. Had it not been for Annabelle I probably never would have returned, not even for the odd visit over the years.'

'I'm sorry, Daniel. I never knew.'

He leaned back, stretched his neck up to the ceiling before turning to Hazel.

'Thank you for telling me. It helps me understand more about Mum. Annabelle and I never felt as if she was there for us. The distance that grew between us was always hard to move beyond.'

Hazel edged forward in her chair as if she wanted to reach for Daniel. He certainly felt as if a hug from Hazel would help him right now.

'You have to tell Annabelle what I've told you,' she said. 'You two need to talk to your mother and you must try to make amends with your father.'

Daniel pondered the idea. He wondered if his mother regretted not having made amends with Gran. Of course, for them it was too late. The fights he'd had with his father had driven him, and had kept him, away from home. If he could find an inch of the integrity Hazel had, he could be persuaded to make a phone call to his father – attempt a reconciliation. One day, perhaps.

'If you need to talk any of this through, I'm here for you,' Hazel said in a small voice. 'I should probably go. You have a lot to mull over.'

'Of course. Yes. Let me help you to the door,' said Daniel. 'I'll drop the flask round later.'

At the door Hazel put her sun visor back in place and turned to Daniel before she left.

'Don't worry,' she said. She wagged a finger at him. 'Life has a way of showing us our path. You won't always feel like this. Everything will fall into place for you and one day you'll wake up and be on the correct path for you.'

Daniel wasn't sure what to do with those words. He closed the door and knew for certain that the first thing he should do would be to stop feeling sorry for himself, especially as his sadness was rubbing off on someone he cared about. He thought about the members of the walking club and the idea that he had changed their lives in some way. They were a cheerful and happy group of people and he looked forward to Saturday as much as they did. For their sake, he had to be out of his slump, before the weekend.

46

Daniel spent a good five minutes chatting to a couple outside the café in the beach complex on Saturday, just before the walk was due to start. They seemed like nice people. The man was dressed in white shorts, a turquoise top and white baseball cap. The woman wore the same, only, instead of the baseball cap, she'd propped a large pair of sunglasses on top of her head. He introduced himself and the couple said they were called Ewan and Heather.

'You can start by telling me if you have any health concerns,' said Daniel. Heather seemed to take offence at this but Ewan happily piped up.

'Well, there's my back. Lower. Once slipped a disc and I still feel twinges every now and again. They say once you've had a back injury it never fully recovers and I think that's true. Then there are my knees,' he said. He bent one of them upwards and then bounced slightly on both legs. 'I do have trouble with my knees. Especially in the winter. I used to get hay fever. Terrible it was at one time. Took every anti-histamine tablet going until I found the right ones for me. Morrisons' own brand. But actually, I'm fully recovered from the hay fever now. I do snore occasionally and that drives the wife up the wall.'

'Daniel,' Hazel called him from a little way away in the car park. He turned and gave her a friendly wave to let her know he had this under control. It was about time he learned how to interact with the walkers the way Hazel did. He used to lead walkers for a living for goodness' sake.

'Right,' said Daniel. 'So anyway, we do take our time. Nice and easy and the people are so friendly.'

'Daniel?' called Hazel again in a light tone. He turned to her briefly and winked. It must be time to go.

'Do you have any questions for me?' asked Daniel.

'Yes,' said Ewan. 'Where can we get the most authentic Cornish pasties around here?'

Daniel frowned and scratched his head.

'To be honest, I'm not really sure.'

'No worries,' said Ewan. 'There's a farm shop close by, I believe. They're bound to know.'

'I'm sure they do.' Daniel smiled.

'Daniel,' called Hazel, more sharply.

'Excuse me,' Daniel said to Heather and Ewan. He trotted over to Hazel. 'What's up?' he said with a big grin on his face.

'What are you doing? You do realize they haven't come here for our walk, don't you?' Hazel shook her head.

'Really?' Daniel looked back to where the couple had been standing and saw them join a group of people who were about to board a coach. 'They could have said.' Ewan waved to him before climbing into the coach.

'You could have asked,' said Hazel. She turned to the rest of their group. 'Okay, everyone's here, let's head out.'

Annabelle slowly shook her head from side to side at Daniel, Mary rolled her eyes and the walkers joined the coast path.

The previous week had seen a rise in the number of people using the path and the walkers had found it difficult to maintain their slow steady pace while holding a group conversation. When they made a stop for refreshments they sat as far back from the path as possible to avoid the footfall. The path was not only busy with walkers but cyclists, runners and joggers, too. There was no sign of the Padstow Pace Masters who had either taken another route or had set out much earlier in the day, before the holiday makers and summer joggers showed up.

'Have you given any thought to changing our walking time, Daniel?' asked Hazel.

'Yes, and it's a good idea,' he said. 'Perhaps a walk after breakfast, say ten-thirty?'

Everyone was in agreement and so the new time was set for the following Saturday.

'You do remember it's your birthday next Saturday, don't you, Daniel?' Annabelle reminded him. The rest of the group were excited and Amanda started to make elaborate plans for a birthday party.

'We could have it at my house,' she said. 'I love to entertain and it would be an honour.'

'Please,' said Daniel. 'It really isn't a big deal. I didn't plan to have a party, but thanks all the same, Amanda.'

She flared her nostrils and turned to look at Oliver.

'What will you do to celebrate your birthday then?' asked Mary.

'Absolutely nothing.'

'You can't do nothing,' said Annabelle. 'Last year was your thirtieth, a big one, and I couldn't celebrate it with you. At least come to dinner. The children would love to share your birthday with you.'

'That's really kind of you, sis. I will,' said Daniel. 'Although it's not a big deal. I'm sure I won't feel any differently than I do now.'

'You might do,' said Hannah. As usual she had said very little during the walk, apart from to Curtis. They seemed to have an awful lot to whisper to each other about and it hadn't escaped anyone's notice that they occasionally held hands along the way.

'I felt differently when I turned thirty,' Hannah continued. 'A little bit more grown up and wanting to take risks. Risks I'd never taken before. That's when I left the hair salon I was working at and decided to become a mobile hairdresser. I haven't looked back.'

Daniel became thoughtful. Last year his thirtieth birthday was spent in Bar Casa Mia. It hadn't been special and he hadn't made any life-changing decisions as Hannah had, though one was slowly forming in his head.

'You did the right thing then, Hannah,' he said. 'I've been driving myself crazy trying to decide what I should do with my life. For work, that is. I've come to the decision that I'm going to train to become a physiotherapist.'

'This is a surprise,' Annabelle gasped. 'You never told me anything about this. But it's wonderful.'

'Since Hazel's accident, I've thought about retraining and I've done my research into courses.'

'And what about the personal training?' asked Annabelle.

'Oh, I'm going to continue with that, try to make a proper go of it because, depending on what we do with the house, I'm going to need something to pay for my training. I've thought about it a lot, especially in the last few weeks. I've backed out of the idea a lot but something always tells me it's the right thing to do.'

Hazel smiled at him, blinking tears from her eyes.

Hannah clapped her hands together.

'Marvellous, Daniel,' she said. 'And I'm sure you'll be wonderful.'

'Thanks, Hannah.'

Amanda and Mary were the loudest in their optimism and praise for his idea. He half listened to them as they planned his future, knowing in his heart that he had made the right decision.

Annabelle, eyes glassy, her cheeks pink, interrupted them by raising a hand.

'You're all missing the point,' she said, looking at her brother. 'Daniel says he knows what he'll do for work; he didn't say *where*, though.' She came and sat down next to her brother. 'But I know because I know you. You're going to try to find work in London, aren't you?'

'No,' he said. The group was still. He looked around at their eager eyes and at the tear escaping from Annabelle's. 'I've decided, at last, and finally, that I'm staying in Trevone. I once made a rash decision to run away from here and never come back. It was a crazy idea, something I decided on in anger and frustration. But I missed you, sis. Your children are extraordinary and I'd love to be a part of their lives. It's weird. I thought I knew all there was to know about this place but I never thought I'd come to love it the way I do now.' He looked directly at Hazel. 'Someone once told me a story about my grandmother. How she came to Cornwall to fulfil a desire and out of a sense of duty. But once she stayed here, she never wanted to leave. She fell in love with Cornwall and now that I've rediscovered it, I don't think I could ever leave here. My friends are here, my new best pal and my family.' He couldn't hold back the crack in his voice and laughed so that his lip would hold firm and not give in to a weepy moment. Though looking at his friends' faces he found it hard not to lose his composure.

Annabelle hugged her brother and sniffed.

'Welcome home, Daniel,' she said. 'You won't regret staying. And I know your business will do really well. Just don't ask me to do any posters.'

Daniel laughed and looked over at Hazel. She had just wiped her cheek and replaced her glasses. She gave him a warm smile and a deep nod of her head.

'Well, that's your working life sorted,' said Mary. 'Any romantic plans we need to know about?'

'None whatsoever,' Daniel said happily. 'I'm a confirmed male spinster for now and for the foreseeable. All I need is the scented candles. I've already got the cat. Well, sometimes at least. Even if I don't know his name.' He turned to Eric, who frowned.

'You've been feeding that cat the last few months and you don't know his name?' Eric scratched the top of his head and replaced his flat cap.

Daniel smiled and raised his shoulders. 'I seriously don't.'

At the same time, all the members of the group shouted, '*Bill!*' They looked at Daniel as if he'd lost the plot completely.

'But how did you all . . . Oh, never mind,' he said. 'Bill can keep me company when he's around.'

'I still think we should have some sort of celebration for Daniel,' said Amanda. 'How about after our walk next week we all do brunch on the beach? We'll each bring something and toast Daniel. We'll pretend it's your thirtieth again so it feels more special. Mine wasn't so long ago and it was special to me.' She paused and looked around at the blank faces. 'What are you all looking at? I'm telling you, my thirtieth was not that long ago.' She swung around to look at Oliver. 'You believe me, don't you?'

'I would have done, my dear, had you not shown me your passport photograph. There was some very telling evidence on the page there.'

They all began to laugh and as the laughter died down, Hazel spoke up.

'So next week, at ten-thirty then. A walk and then brunch. I suggest we meet on the actual beach for a change as close to the complex as possible so we won't miss each other. The car park is becoming too busy.'

As the group headed back to base, Daniel felt an easing of tension in the tops of his shoulders, tension he hadn't realized he had until he announced that he was staying in Trevone. He knew he had made a lot of people happy with his decision. Not only was the group pleased, Daniel felt happier in himself. Making the final decision had felt an awful lot like coming home. Hazel and Henry had had fond memories of their time in this part of the world, so much so that they finally settled here and, like him, Hazel couldn't tear herself away. He remembered what Hazel said about adventures. By staying in his hometown he was embarking on a new adventure and somehow he knew that it was going to be the biggest of his life.

47

The evening before The Slow Lane's first ever morning walk, there was a knock at Daniel's door. He was sitting on the kitchen floor, his back against the fridge watching the cat, hunched over his bowl of food. Daniel had tried calling the cat by his name, Bill. But for some reason he didn't respond, preferring instead to go by the names Cat or Oi Mate. He couldn't wait to tell Eric that he was now The Cat Formerly Known as Bill. Who calls a cat Bill, anyway? The knock on the door brought him back from a meandering mind in which he visualized the cat playing an electric guitar and singing 'Purple Rain'.

There was chatter from the other side of the front door. Daniel pictured the evening he was about to leave for the party Jess had invited him to but became derailed when his Italian guests turned up unexpectedly. He considered for a second that it could be one of the other walking guides from Mount Etna taking him up on his offer to visit him in Cornwall whenever they wanted.

When he opened the door Annabelle stood there with the children. Behind them was Hannah the hairdresser. He stepped aside to let them all in. Rasmus held up his arms so that Daniel could scoop him up for a hug. Hannah came in last carrying a small suitcase.

'Hannah? What are you doing here?' Daniel asked.

'I come to you, you don't come to me,' she said, following Annabelle who was beckoning to her from the kitchen doorway.

'What is this?' Daniel asked as he set Rasmus on his feet in the kitchen. The cat sat up. Ignoring his guests, he began to wash his face as he did after every meal.

'This,' said Annabelle, 'is a present from The Slow Lane. We're giving you a makeover for your birthday.'

'No offence, Hannah,' Daniel said, 'but I don't really need a makeover.'

Hannah blushed and looked at Annabelle.

'We considered,' Annabelle went on, 'that as you embark on your new career as the top personal trainer of Trevone – and beyond – that you ought to look the part.'

'But I haven't got going on the business yet,' he protested. He put his hands on his hair after seeing Hannah unzip her suitcase of hairdressing tools on the kitchen counter.

'You have to start as you mean to go on,' said Annabelle. 'You might have the physique of a personal trainer but you need the grooming, too. Once you look the part you will *be* the part and the phone won't stop ringing.'

'But no one knows my number.'

'Oh shut up, Dan,' Annabelle scoffed. The children giggled. 'Now run down to Hazel's for a kitchen chair. Hannah can't do her thing with no furniture in the house.'

Daniel did as he was told. Hazel was already expecting him and led him straight through to the kitchen.

'I don't know what I'm letting myself in for,' he said to Hazel once he'd carried the chair to the front door.

'Don't worry,' said Hazel as she waved him off. 'Hannah is a well-respected hairdresser and comes highly recommended.'

Daniel knew Amanda was a client of Hannah's and he hoped he wouldn't end up the same shade of red as Amanda at the end of his session.

Hannah whipped a towel around Daniel's shoulders once he was seated by the sink. She filled a bottle and squirted his hair wet.

'The good thing about this cut,' she said as she snipped and clipped, 'is that you don't have to go to any bother with it. I'll cut it tonight and after your shower tomorrow you just let it air dry and *Voilà*!'

'Really?' he asked.

Hannah nodded.

'And do I have any say in the style?'

'No,' said Annabelle and Mia.

'Fine,' sighed Daniel, sagging in the middle. 'Go for it, Hannah the hairdresser, my image is in your hands.'

He saw damp clumps of his hair fall to the floor. The cat sniffed around them and Rasmus ran through them once he'd revved up his engine.

'Better fly that plane in the garden, mate,' said Daniel.

Rasmus, Mia and the cat ran out to the garden to play and Annabelle sat on a deckchair as she watched Hannah at work.

A short while later, Hannah softly said, 'There,' and stood back.

'Can I see?' asked Daniel.

'I've got a mirror,' said Hannah. 'There you go.'

'Hey,' said Daniel with a definite look of approval on his face. 'It's not half bad. Thank you, Hannah, and thank you, Slow Lane.'

'I thought I'd film and take pictures tomorrow,' said Annabelle. 'Don't worry, it's not for the vlog. I thought that as we're on the beach you could do some poses and use the pictures for your website.'

'What website? I don't have a website.' Daniel pulled a face and looked at Hannah, bewildered. She smiled and began to pack her equipment away.

'You will have a website,' said Annabelle. 'I'll help you with it. And get you going on your own YouTube channel. Maybe TikTok.'

Daniel listened to Annabelle talking in the background about social media and a ring light for his videos. Once Hannah was all packed away Annabelle rounded up the children with a clap of her hands and bundled everyone out of the door.

'See you on the beach!' she called behind her.

Daniel smoothed a hand over his hair and hoped that in the morning he would have a *Voilà!* moment with his new style. The walkers would never forgive him if he didn't.

When Daniel woke up on the morning of his thirty-first birthday, he didn't feel any different to the day before, but he did have sticking-up hair.

'Damn it,' he said when he spied himself in the bathroom mirror. He turned on the shower to see if he could fix the damage a night's sleep had done to his new image.

Daniel knocked for Hazel later in the morning but found she had already left for the beach. He checked his watch and wondered why she had set off extra early. Of course, he thought, the walkers must have organized a surprise cake. Annabelle would have her camera at the ready and Hannah would have some tools handy to touch up his hair with. Surprisingly, none of them was on the beach when he arrived. Not even Hazel. Perhaps they'd planned to hide in the café, lighting candles for a massive cake, thinking they were going to give him the surprise of his life.

He sat on the sand waiting for the balloons and streamers. He practised his *Surprise!* face and wondered about making a speech. Feeling impatient now, he grabbed a handful of fine sand and let it cascade through the gaps in his fingers. He looked over his shoulder and still no one had shown up. There were a few surfers and swimmers out in the sea and groups of people on the beach, sunbathing, strolling, walking dogs and dipping their toes in the water.

Where was The Slow Lane? he wondered and got up to make his way to the café. Just as he dusted sand off his shorts he saw Jess walking towards him.

'Jess?' He blinked several times as if his eyes were playing tricks on him. He wondered for a split second why she wasn't cycling through to Harlyn. Surely the surf shop and school was open by now.

'Hey, Daniel,' said Jess. 'Happy Birthday.'

'How did you . . . Oh, I get it,' he said. 'It's a set up. They set me up.' He looked around for the walkers, expecting them to be disguised and poised around the beach, messaging each other with microphones on their cuffs, spy earpieces planted in their ear canals.

Jess nodded and laughed.

'I'm sorry about this,' said Daniel. 'I didn't know they were planning on getting you down here. I already told them you and I agreed to be friends. I imagine between Annabelle and Mary, you must have felt pressured to show up. It's okay. You can just stick around for the cake and get going afterwards.'

'Daniel, I chose to come.' She moved closer to him. Her skin had caught the sun, her face was relaxed. She smiled. She was clearly up for humouring his group. Maybe now if they knew he and Jess had talked, they would finally get off his case and stop bothering her.

'Well, thanks anyway,' he said with a quick bob of his head. 'I tried to put them off this whole matchmaking thing. Tried to tell them we'd moved on.'

'So you really have moved on, then?' Her brow creased.

'Well,' he turned his eyes from hers, 'let's just say, I'm trying.'

Jess bowed her head.

'You know, Daniel, when you came to the beach that day, the week after the party, I had an awful feeling in my stomach after telling you we should go our separate ways. I said it because I thought it would be an easy let out for you after we'd pledged not to get serious. Trouble was, I was already well into the idea of getting serious with you.'

'You . . . What?' he spluttered. 'Why didn't you tell me?'

'I'd seen you with that girl. It kind of confirmed that you only wanted something casual with me. I knew I wanted more and I was convinced you didn't, so I gave us a way out. No more pacts. Just nothing.'

'I hated the just nothing. I wanted to tell you about my ex.'

'Don't worry, I know all about Aria and what she did.'

'What? Really? How?' Daniel rolled his eyes. 'Of course. The walkers.'

'Actually, I bumped into, or should I say, your friend Hazel, strategically, bumped into me. I knew there was something odd about a little old lady with a walking stick coming into the shop to seek out surfing lessons.'

Both Daniel and Jess laughed. He scanned the beach again.

'I dread to think what she said about me to you,' said Daniel.

'Don't worry, Hazel is the best. She explained everything.

She told me about your plans to stay here in Trevone. Hazel seemed to be an authority on how you felt about me. She didn't spell it out exactly, but she hinted – in a big way.'

Daniel smiled and stepped in closer to Jess.

'I don't know what she hinted at but I know I don't want to just be friends, Jess.' He took a gulp of air. 'To see you in the distance, on your bike, to only get to wave to you and nothing more. You don't know how much I regret that no decisions, no drama pact. I wish we could have just gone for it. I wish I had just come to the party instead of bottling it. It was so immature of me.'

'I get it,' said Jess. 'You had to be sure about your feelings for Aria first.' Daniel lowered his gaze. 'The last thing I would have wanted was to be strung along while you made up your mind about her.'

'I wouldn't have strung you along. Aria was all over me, I didn't encourage it. I know how it must have looked and I don't blame you for being angry.'

'I'm not angry anymore. I told you that at the pub. Life is too short for that.'

'So what do I do now?' asked Daniel. 'Now that I know you have feelings for me and that you're seeing someone else.'

Jess laughed and touched Daniel's cheek.

'I'm not seeing anyone. That guy I was with is a friend of Noah's. He comes and works at the shop during the summer. They go back ages. Plus he's gay, so . . .'

'Really? I thought . . .'

'Well, you thought wrong.'

Daniel took another look around the beach.

'This is weird,' he said. 'I don't get why the others aren't all here observing my every move. They usually do.'

'Oh, they're here all right. Neatly hidden in various places. I believe your sister is filming the whole thing.'

'I guess we should give her something for the recording.'

'Absolutely.'

Daniel took Jess's hands and leaned down to kiss her lips. He brushed them very lightly with his.

'I was thinking something a bit more like this,' said Jess.

She wrapped her arms around his neck, pulled him close for a deeper kiss. His arms were tight around her body, not a fraction of daylight between them. They only broke away when they heard someone very close by clearing their throat.

'Now that we've got that out of the way,' said Hazel, 'maybe we should commence our walk? It's getting late.'

The walkers were not able to travel along bunched together on the path, ambling slowly in the casual way they always did. They weren't early enough to avoid other walkers using the path or the cyclists weaving around them. The Padstow Pace Masters had apparently decided on an earlier walk, too. They zoomed straight past The Slow Lane in what Daniel could only describe as a carefully crafted operation. Swift and silent, the Pace Masters were on the heels of The Slow Lane with military stealth and overtook them like a rush of wind.

Daniel led his walkers, his arm around Jess as she hugged his waist and held the hand he had over her shoulder. They walked slowly, the sun bathing their skin and spreading sparkles of light across the surface of the sea. Daniel pictured his grandmother at the beach in her old-fashioned bathing suit and wondered how many times she had walked along it with Gramps. He thought about Gran's adventures, how she'd left home to come to Cornwall and had fallen in love with the man she would marry and a part of the country he was truly in love with again himself. Silently he thanked her for believing in him, for leaving him a house that brought him back to somewhere special that led him to someone special.

Daniel turned back and watched his friends making their way along the path. Amanda and Oliver chatted together. Hannah and Curtis held hands. Annabelle was giggling about something with Margot, and Eric walked with Benny the dog just behind the sisters who were casually dressed for a summer walk in matching pink tracksuit bottoms and their Slow Lane T-shirts.

At the back of the group was Hazel. She smiled at Daniel and waved her stick from side to side in the air before giving him a gentle nod. He would have a lot to talk about with Hazel and a lot to thank her for. But maybe that could wait until they stopped for refreshments, a little further along the path.